GRUNT
TRAITOR

First published 2015 by Solaris
an imprint of Rebellion Publishing Ltd,
Riverside House, Osney Mead,
Oxford, OX2 0ES, UK

www.solarisbooks.com

ISBN: 978 1 78108 358 1

10 9 8 7 6 5 4 3 2 1

A CIP catalogue record for this book is available
from the British Library.

Designed & typeset by Rebellion Publishing

Printed in the US

WESTON OCHSE

GRUNT TRAITOR

A TASK FORCE OMBRA NOVEL

SOLARIS

To Martin Cochran,
Father-in-Law, Adventurer,
Race Car Driver, Alaska Traveler,
Solace Seeker and Korean War Veteran

We invaded ourselves first. Make no mistake about it, had the Cray not descended from the clear blue sky, we humans—as our own invasive species—would have killed ourselves off within two hundred years. Un-regulated population, pollution, water overuse, and our utter failure to shepherd intrinsically important flora and fauna would have been our crimes. Our punishment would have been starvation, suffocation, dehydration, and overpopulation. Maybe the invasion of the Cray was the best thing that could have happened to us. Maybe the advent of the Cray was our control-alt-delete. Regardless whether you believe this, we have an undeniable clean slate. What are we going to do with it? Are we going to change, or trot out the same old governments with the same old ideas?

Conspiracy Theory Talk Radio,
Night Stalker Monologue #1343

PART ONE

PART ONE

A hero can be anyone; even a man doing something as simple and reassuring as putting a coat around a young boy's shoulders to let him know the world hadn't ended.

The Dark Knight Rises,
Christopher Nolan

CHAPTER ONE

THE BATTLEFIELD WAS a disorganized collage of panic and desperation, where screams of human and alien mixed in a savage orchestration of unconstrained murder. We'd run out of ammo an hour ago and were locked in hand-to-hand combat with the multi-winged, jagged-clawed alien Cray. Orders still flew across the net, but I'd long ago ceased to follow them. I had another mission.

The jaw-clenched mantra *never leave a man behind* fueled my muscles as they powered the leg servos of my scratched, battered EXO across the dusty African earth. Airplane carcasses littered the landscape. A Cray hive split the sky like the devil's middle finger. Both man and Cray crunched sickeningly beneath my titanium-coated Kevlar feet. I ignored that and everything else. Let the others fight the Cray. Let them do the impossible. I had to find Michelle. I had to find Thompson. My eyes scoured the horizon, but all I saw were the humans and bug-like Cray locked in battle, the exoskeletal hands and the multi-limbed claws of the creatures who'd ruined Earth, each seeking the fastest way to do the other in.

Never leave a man behind.

Never leave a man behind.

My HUD flashed a warning as my heart rate soared with panic. Where the hell were they? A black hole began to grow in my chest, pulling hope into its abysmal maw.

"Romeo Three, prepare to evac," came Olivares's steady voice.

"Negative, Romeo Proper. We're missing Thompson and Aquinas." I spied an EXO trying to move and rushed towards it. The markings had worn away from a thousand Cray scratches.

"Mason, prepare to evac!"

I ignored the command, and reached the struggling figure. I helped it stand, then turned it. A grimy face, strong Irish features, wan smile: McKenzie.

"Thanks, pal. Thought I was done there for a second."

He pushed away, stumbled a few feet, then was jerked in the air by a pair of Cray. I watched as he was lifted higher and higher, then released. He slammed into the earth, crumpling like a beer can, servo fluid and blood seeping from the shattered mess of metal.

Wait. I'd seen this before.

"Mason, get your ass back here."

Olivares's command wrenched me free of my temporary paralysis. I broke into a run, ranging back across the battlefield. What had I missed? Where could they be? Then I saw it—a black box the size of a tractor trailer, sitting in the middle of an empty part of the battlefield. I headed towards it, but felt my legs slowing.

Checking my HUD, I saw my power was down to five percent.

Never leave a man behind.

I fought to move as fast as I could, but without power the EXOs were concrete suits. I was close enough now that I could see inside the black box. I slowed, then finally stopped a dozen feet away, my power at zero, my hope at zero, any chance of a future with the girl I loved at zero.

Michelle. Or what had once been Michelle.

"What have they done?" I wailed.

She hung from a pod affixed to the ceiling of the box, connected by tubes through which fluids moved in a slow soupy mix, presumably keeping her alive. She faced me, naked, the rivers of pain on her arms where she'd tried to commit suicide so long ago now stark white reminders of who she'd once been. If only that girl was still around. But she'd been turned into a horrific marionette. A hundred multicolored wires and cables ran from her shaved head to a computer terminal. I could only imagine her horror. Was she aware what had happened to her? What was it she'd said? *Can you imagine? Being taken over by another entity and not being able to control your own body?*

The aliens hadn't done this to her.

We had.

My rage corrected me.

Mr. Pink had done this to her.

Her body shook and trembled. She took a great breath and raised her head, and her gaze met my own. For one brief moment, we were those same two people, reclining behind the generators, interlocked, the end of the world not even mattering, living only in each other's eyes as we made each other laugh, cry and sing with pleasure. Then her face changed. She became sad, then angry, then enraged.

Killmekillmekillmekillmekillmekillmekillme.

The thought slammed into my head, devouring everything else. Kill her? Kill Michelle? I could never kill her. I'd rather die.

My suit powered up and I was once again able to move.

"Then why didn't you save her, asshole?"

I spun and saw McKenzie. "What'd you say?"

"You never saved her. She's out there now, and half machine because of you."

I beheld him as if he were flesh and blood, but I knew it couldn't be. I'd seen him die. We'd honored his body. I know this because it was the morning after she and I had—

Killmekillmekillmekillmekillmekillmekillme.

"Mason, get your ass over here."

"Then why didn't you save her, asshole?"

My eyes locked on another black box—five hundred meters away, according to my HUD. I pushed past the ghost of McKenzie and ran for it.

Killmekillmekillmekillmekillmekillmekillme.
Killmekillmekillmekillmekillmekillmekillme.

As each thought struck me, I stumbled, but I never went down.

The sound of drums began to come to me; a low heartbeat in the earth beneath my feet. At first it was on the very edge of my hearing, but gradually I began to make out the individual strokes. A drum like a drummer boy would play in a parade, like something that had been played for Washington's Army, or General Lee's, or General Patton's, or Mr. Pink's—the martial *rat-a-tat-tat* designed to bring everyone into patriotic lockstep.

"Mason, get your ass over here."

I ignored Olivares and began to sprint. Thompson was in there. He had to be. The drums... they'd saved me... he'd saved me. I owed it to the guy. I owed it to Michelle. Why did I ever leave them? Why did I—

"Mason, *get your ass over here.*"

I snapped my eyes open to a blistering desert sun lancing between breaks in the camouflage fabric above me.

"Mason? You sleeping?"

My mouth felt like cardboard. My lips felt like sandpaper. *Fuck.* I brought my hand to my face to wipe away the vestiges of the nightmare and sat up, putting my boots on the ground.

You're not in Africa, I reminded myself, shaking off the remnant of the nightmare. *You're in Death Valley, near Barstow, California. The battle is over and you're a survivor. You're also an asshole for leaving Michelle like that. You're a dick for not finding Thompson. You should fucking die for leaving those two behind, but instead you get three hots and a cot, you get promoted, you get to watch fucking videos of how great life used to be.*

Olivares came around the corner, dressed in desert fatigues, a maroon beret on his head, sunglasses covering his eyes. "There you are." He clapped his hands. "Come on, we got to go. This is last day of Phase I for the new recruits. They're going to be happy to get to the physical training."

I shook my head, not at him, but to get Michelle's image out of my mind.

"Listen, if you're not up for it—" Olivares began.

I stood. "Fuck that shit. I'm not a profile," I said. Profiles were soldiers who rode illness or injury to get out of work.

"Maybe you should be." His face was serious. He pointed to the side of his head. "You're not handling the mental shit well. I'm no psych, but you need to get over it."

I grunted. "You're right, you're no psych. You're also not in charge of me anymore."

We'd both been promoted to master sergeants when we'd arrived at old Fort Irwin in Death Valley. TF OMBRA required experienced non-coms to train new recruits, and had pinned the rose on us and a bunch of others from the other Cray kill sites. Ohirra had been bumped to lieutenant and was now working in intelligence. Of course Michelle was out there somewhere. I knew it because these dreams were her doing. She was making sure I felt like shit for not killing her. I'd aimed my rifle at her... I'd been ready to kill her for a moment, take her out of her misery... but I'd even failed in that. Then there was Thompson, our little drummer boy.

Never leave a man behind. I'd sure fucked that one up.

Olivares stepped in front of me. "Depression affects us all differently, Mason. Consider going to see the psych. Let them help you. Talk to someone. Just fucking deal with it."

I went to push past him, but he grabbed me by my collar. "You think you're so fucking tough."

I shook him off. "I'm not tough. I'm just unlucky enough to have survived."

He gave me a disgusted look. "You're a shit NCO, you know that?"

I nodded. "You always were better than me."

"It's not about that. It's about the recruits. If your shit isn't together, you're going to put their lives in danger next time."

Next time. That's all Mr. Pink could talk about. Next time. Where were the other aliens? What was going to happen next? Every surviving human on the planet was waiting for the other shoe to drop. Maybe they were here already. Maybe they were on their way. No one seemed to know the answer, but we needed to prepare the task force to combat it. How do you prepare a soldier to fight an enemy you know so little about? The same way TF OMBRA had trained me and all the others. We could only study the hypothetical. Like these recruits, we'd been locked in a cell for six months and forced to read novels and watch movies, then demonstrate our ability to critically think and understand the challenges posed by an alien invasion by completing a series of graded tasks.

We'd been given ninety-six manuscripts, forty-seven movies, and seven biographies.

The biographies included Julius Caesar, Chesty Puller, David Hackworth, and other soldiers.

Of the movies, I'd seen around half. They were the usual suspects: *Kelly's Heroes*, *A Bridge Too Far*, *The Guns of Navarone*, *Hamburger Hill*, *They Were Expendable*, *We Were Soldiers*, *The Dirty Dozen*, *Where Eagles Dare*, *Saving Private Ryan*, and *Platoon*. But there were also some foreign films I had never heard of, like *Ivan's Childhood*, *Kanał*, and *Gallipoli*. There were also some science fiction movies, such as *Starship Troopers*, the 2005 version of *War of the Worlds*, *Battleship*, *Battle: Los Angeles*, *Invasion of the Body Snatchers*, *The Puppet Masters*, *They Live*, and *Independence Day*; I'd seen all of them except *They Live* and *The Puppet Masters*.

I'd read many of the books already. Or *thought* I'd

read them; it was funny how being forced to answer questions changed the reading experience. They included *Armor*, *Starship Troopers*, *The Forever War*, *Old Man's War*, *Ender's Game*, *A Mote in God's Eye*, *Legion of the Damned*, *Hammer's Slammers*, and *Bolo*. But there were a lot I had never read, books by C. J. Cherryh, David Gerrold, Jerry Pournelle, and Robert Buettner, to name a few.

"Did you hear me?"

"Yeah, I heard you."

He turned to leave, then turned back. "Listen, Mason. That was some fucked-up shit that was done to her. But she helped us defeat the Cray. She saved us. Something in our fucked-up PTSD heads, some chemical change, has enabled us to do this. I know she wanted you to kill her, but without her, we'd all be dead."

"Which is why I owe it to her to do something."

"Don't go being a hero, Mason."

"I know you don't like heroes, Olivares, but sometimes you just got to be one."

"Wouldn't be necessary if everyone would do their fucking job."

I nodded. "What are the chances of that happening? It's why we've had to find heroes for as long as Christ was a corporal."

"That's not our job, now. We're not training them to be heroes. Our job is to train these recruits to be soldiers."

I snatched my beret from my pocket and adjusted it on my head. Then I snapped sunglasses out of my shirt pocket and put them on. "Come on, Olivares. Stop lollygagging. We got work to do."

He frowned, then smiled, and patted me on the back.

"There you go. There's the asshole Mason I know and love."

"You've never loved me."

"No, I haven't. I've never hated you either." And with that he left.

I stepped out from beneath the camouflage awning and followed in Olivares's steps. Staring at his back, I knew I couldn't say the same myself. I'd once hated him terribly. It had been Michelle who had reminded me how selfish it was to hate another human when there was a whole universe of Cray to hate.

THE EDGE, there is no honest way to explain it because the only people who really know where it is are the ones who have gone over.

Hunter S. Thompson

CHAPTER TWO

THERE WAS A time when Post Traumatic Stress Disorder was rare, something few soldiers had, invisible for the most part but as deadly as any wound. Not just confined to the military; first responders like police officers and fire fighters, nurses, doctors, paramedics were also put in situations that resulted in PTSD. Still, even they were few and far between. So trying to fill the ranks of Task Force OMBRA before the invasion had been a monumental task.

Take America, for example. Less than one percent of Americans served in the military, but it was documented that upwards of thirty percent of Vietnam War veterans, eleven percent of Gulf War veterans, and ten percent of the War in Afghanistan veterans had PTSD. Because of the peculiarities of the brain chemistry of those suffering the syndrome, Mr. Pink and the other TF OMBRA officers had sought us out and convinced us to join, often through coercion and trickeration.

But now?

Now *everyone* had PTSD. Not a single person on this

planet we call Earth was unscathed from the invasion. Not a single person was untouched. It was especially bad in the major cities where the Cray hives landed. The farther away from the hives, the less interaction civilians had with the alien monsters. But there were other monsters, human monsters, as deadly as the invading Cray.

We all shared in the realities of PTSD.

We're all fucked in the head.

So does that make it the new normal?

These were just some of the thoughts that ticked through my head as I stood in a row of five other master sergeants while a hundred recruits walked stiff-legged out of the old ammo bunker that had been revamped into a learning prison much like the one we'd had in the old Air Force base in Wyoming. Every race and creed was represented. There *were* no nations; that way of looking at people had no place in the new world. Blinking furiously at a sun they hadn't seen in six months, holding up their arms to block the light, every last one of them had shit-eating grins. They'd made it. They'd achieved Phase II. Now it was our turn to put them through their paces.

The wind whipped at their hair, swirling the Death Valley dust, stinging them. Tents flapped and snapped in the wilderness. Somewhere I heard an artillery shell fire. A tank went by, its treads squeaking and in much need of grease in this hot, arid piece of hell. Even in October, when the rest of the country was dusted with snow, Death Valley seethed with heat.

About halfway between Las Vegas and Los Angeles, Death Valley was home to Fort Irwin and America's 11th Cavalry Regiment. When the alien invasion began, the commanding general sent half of his force to Vegas, and the other half went to Los Angeles; both were decimated. Looking through the 20/20 lenses of hindsight, strategists believe that had they not split their force, they might have survived. Those the Cray hadn't destroyed died on the road trying to return. Ultimately it was TF OMBRA who found Fort Irwin and occupied it, their intention to bring down the twin Hollywood and Santa Monica hives. The Vegas hive still existed, but with nothing of value in a city once dedicated to the ideas of pleasure and greed, even OMBRA was hesitant to waste lives.

With the fort all but empty, TF OMBRA moved in and made it their home. They brought thousands into the empty barracks, using the mess halls and motor pools as if they'd been their own. The only hitch had been the families of the deceased soldiers. With no power and limited ability to feed themselves, many were already dead or dying by the time OMBRA arrived. They were greeted like saviors instead of invaders.

I spied someone familiar coming from the direction of HQ: Ohirra. Slender and Japanese, her implacable face showed several scars which she wore like badges of honor. She gestured for me to step out of line. Curious about what she wanted, I took a step back, turned smartly, than jogged over to her.

She wore the same patch on her left shoulder I had—Mount Kilimanjaro on a red field, with a slash through it. Survivors of TF OMBRA's first battle had taken an old tradition and revived it, sporting combat patches that inextricably linked them.

"What's up, Ohirra?"

She raised an eyebrow. "For the recruits."

I smirked as I saluted. "Sniper check, ma'am."

"That's better. How are you doing, Ben?"

"Good, Kimiko. And you?"

She gave me the same look she'd given me right before she'd made me tap out by getting my arm and head into a triangle as we wrestled. Her father had been a small circle jujitsu master and had trained her well. "Fibber."

I shrugged. "We're *all* fucked up."

"Olivares says that you—"

"Olivares should keep his mouth shut."

She frowned. "He's right. You need to see someone who can help you work it out."

I pinned her with my eyes. "You never saw her."

She bit her lip. "No, I didn't."

"Then you can't know. You'll never know."

"Listen, I didn't come here to fight."

"Then don't."

She sighed. "Listen, Mr. Pink wants to see you."

This stopped me cold. I hadn't spoken to the man since he'd taken Michelle away in a box. He'd been the one responsible for her transformation into a monstrous merging of human and machine—what they were now calling Human Machine Interface Devices, or HMIDs. I'd thought a hundred times what I'd say to him if I ever got the chance. Now, with the chance forthcoming, I didn't know. Since I'd come to Death Valley I'd seen him on several occasions. He'd even nodded to me once.

He was also the reason I wasn't floating face down in the water of the Port of Los Angeles, having given me the opportunity to live another day and capitalize on my skills. As affable as a piece of gristle, he was competent because he surrounded himself with the right people.

"Is there a problem?" Ohirra said.

I shook my head. "I just haven't talked to him since... you know."

She crossed her arms and smiled. "Is big bad tough Ben Mason scared of Mr. Pink?"

"No, no." I swallowed. "Of course not."

"Good, because for a second it looked like the Hero of the Mound wanted to find a rock and crawl under it."

I smiled weakly. *Hero of the Mound.* Although Kilimanjaro had been only six months ago, it seemed like years. Mr. Pink again—he'd made me a hero, because defeating the Cray had seemed so hopeless at the time. Everyone needed a hero to hang their hopes on. I just happened to be at the wrong place at the right time. "Haven't heard that bullshit in a long time."

She did the raised eyebrow thing again. "It wasn't bullshit. I owe my life to you. All of us who survived, we all owe our lives to you. Had you not made that mad run through the hive, we'd all be dead." Seeing the look on my face, she quickly added, "I've seen the debriefing report from you and Olivares. He gave you all the credit."

I shrugged. "Just did what I had to."

"You know, at first I thought you were a poser. No, really, I did. Back during Phase II, the way you acted, how you downplayed everything... I thought it was pretence. Then later I thought it was humility." She regarded me for a moment, gauging me. "But I came to realize it was neither. It's minimization, something a lot of us do without thinking. It allows you to not deal with the negative emotions of events, like the deaths of your eleven soldiers before the alien invasion and all those that came after. It's a form of depression, Ben, and it's not healthy."

Ten solidly flippant retorts perched, ready to launch.

But instead I said, "You're right. I know. It's my coping mechanism."

She grinned, the worry sliding from her eyes. "As long as you know. Ready to go?"

I began walking and she fell in beside me. We held a special bond, just like the one Olivares shared with us. It's funny. One could have a friend for life, go to weddings, funerals, football games, participate in every important event, bond like siblings, but those relationships still pale beside the friendship of combat veterans who'd fought, bled, and cried on the same piece of soil. It doesn't seem logical that one minute could so dominate an entire life, but it was true. Ohirra was my combat sister and I'd do anything for her, just as I'd do anything for Olivares, even though I hated the bastard.

We passed several groups of recruits who snapped to attention and saluted. Ohirra returned each one smartly, her face cold and professional. We finally reached the headquarters building, and I almost collapsed with joy as a wash of air conditioning flowed over me. The desk-bound REMFs always had the best accommodations.

"I bet you live in barracks, too," I grumbled.

"And eat our MREs on porcelain plates." She rolled her eyes. "Get over it."

Up two flights of stairs and down a hall took us to what had been the office of the base commander. A shouting match was going on inside—correction, a large man in a biker jacket, biker chains and a Mohawk was shouting; Mr. Pink stood stock still, inscrutable face, arms crossed. He was a study in black: black boots, black pants, and a black polo shirt with the OMBRA logo over the breast.

"You've got the room here. Why can't we stay?"

"This is a military base under the control of the OMBRA Corporation. It is not a sanctuary."

"Bullshit! This is Fort Irwin and it's owned by the American government."

"There is no American government."

"The hell there isn't. I hear their broadcasts every night."

I'd heard them too, but it seemed like too little, too late. It appeared that the Vice President had survived at a secure location and was attempting to re-establish control. The message that they were out there and ready to help seemed more one of desperation than necessity.

Mr. Pink grinned. I knew that grin. I hated that grin. "Feel free to contact your nearest representative... if you can find one."

The biker tried a new tactic and lowered his voice. "Listen, sir. The safety of my family is at stake. There are some terrible people out there, and there's only so much we can do to protect ourselves."

"While I appreciate your position, we can't be responsible." Mr. Pink nodded towards a soldier with a 9mm pistol in a side holster. "Sergeant Rust will escort you out."

The biker's face went through an evolution of anger, confusion, then acceptance. He left with his head down. I noted the patch on his jacket—*Semper Fi*, beneath the Marine Corps logo. He'd been a Marine and was probably still able to take care of himself. That he wanted someplace safe for his family indicated how dangerous it really was outside the fence. I'd heard stories, but had yet to witness it myself.

I watched him leave, knowing Mr. Pink might have very well given him a death sentence.

"How bad is it out there?" I whispered to Ohirra.

She remained silent, staring straight ahead.

"Mason, it's been a long time." Mr. Pink stuck out a hand.

I stared at it. I didn't want to take it. The moment stretched uncomfortably, yet he still held the hand out. I finally took it, pumped twice, and released.

He smiled, knowing he'd won. He turned and walked to his desk and sat. He adjusted a pile of paper, then gestured for me to take one of the two red leather chairs in front of the desk. I sat, deciding I might as well enjoy some comfort and air conditioning if I was going to have to deal with Mr. Pink and his bullshit.

Ohirra took the other seat. She put her hands on her lap and stared straight ahead. I knew her well enough to know how uncomfortable she was. I was intrigued to find out what was going on.

What Mr. Pink said threw me for a loop.

I'm the one who gave him his name; because of his similarity to the actor Steve Buscemi, who himself could wear ambivalence and evil as easily as he could a black suit and tie. Mr. Pink steepled his hands and asked, "Do you have anything you want to ask me?"

There it was. The elephant in the room. He was giving me an opening.

"Where's Michelle Aquinas?"

He smiled. "Classified."

I pushed aside my rising anger and asked, "Is she even alive?"

"Classified."

"Is she located here on Fort Irwin?"

"Classified."

I had to grit my teeth to keep from yelling like the man

who'd just left. "God damn it, if you weren't going to answer my questions, then why'd you get me to ask?"

"It was important for you to ask. And I did answer. Now you know what you are allowed to know."

I breathed deeply. "Is she in pain?"

Out of the corner of my eye I saw Ohirra's head move, slightly.

I turned to her. "What? Come on, Ohirra. You were her squad mate."

She made eye contact with Mr. Pink, who waved his fingers and sat back.

Ohirra turned towards me. "She's alive and doesn't feel any pain. They rewired her trigeminal nucleus caudalis and trigeminal motor nucleus—the brain's sensory relays. She feels no pain." She flicked her eyes to Mr. Pink, then hurriedly said, "She volunteered for this. She told me what she was going to do. At the time, she wanted—"

Mr. Pink cut her off. "All right, we've entertained Mason's questions, now to move on."

I turned to him and sat on the edge of my seat. "Wait a minute, what did Ohirra mean *at the time*? Did Aquinas change her mind? You can't hold her against her will."

"The status of Aquinas is not your concern."

"Bullshit she's not my concern." I wanted to tell him I loved her, but I wouldn't give him the satisfaction. "And what about Thompson?"

His eyes narrowed. "Who?"

"Tim Thompson, the other member of my squad you shanghaied."

Mr. Pink waived his hand. "Such dramatics." He looked to Ohirra. "What do we know about this Thompson?"

"Deceased. Buried at Kilimanjaro."

I watched their interaction carefully, but if it was all an act, then it was a real good one. So if Thompson was dead, what was it I kept hearing? Not for the first time, I wondered if I might be going crazy.

Mr. Pink sighed. "There you have it. Very sorry for your loss. Now, let's get to the point of this meeting. We need you for a mission."

"I'm not going on a mission for you."

"Might I remind you that you are in TF OMBRA, which is a military unit? When you are given an order you are expected to follow it."

I sat back and gave him the death stare. "Fuck that shit."

He smiled grimly. "If you want out of OMBRA, I can make that happen. We can put you on the other side of the fence with the rest of the unfortunates. Maybe you can help them live a day or two longer."

I was silent as I considered the offer.

After a moment, he added, "Listen, if you take this mission, then I'll arrange it for you to see HMID Aquinas."

This got my attention. "Why me? What makes me so special?"

"You seem to have the ability to do the impossible, Mr. Mason. Your ability to make something from nothing to complete the mission is uncanny. I'm sure there are others I could choose, others who have the same almost supernatural ability to land on their feet, but I don't have the time to seek them out."

"You'll let me see her?" I whispered.

"Ohirra here is my witness."

I glanced at her and she nodded, but didn't look at me.

"Fine, I'll do it."

"Good. Mission brief at 0600 tomorrow. You're dismissed."

I stood, adrenaline already surging through my system. My legs were a little shaky. I was going to get to see her. And she *was* alive. Elation quickened my steps as I was escorted out of the building, before heading to the tents on my own. It wasn't until I was halfway there that I began to slow, realizing that Mr. Pink had orchestrated the entire event perfectly. He'd even had a civilian present at the beginning to demonstrate to me how bad things were on the other side of the fence. Mr. Pink had known all along what I would say and do, and used it to his advantage. But while I hated the idea of being manipulated, I didn't really care. I was going to finish this mission so I could come back and see Michelle.

What we have done for ourselves alone
dies with us; what we have done for others
and the world remains and is forever.

Albert Pike

CHAPTER THREE

WHEN I TOLD Olivares that evening about Michelle and about what Ohirra almost told me before she was cut off, he stormed out of the tent in search of her. I hastened to follow and kept pace with him until we found her in the gym, putting a guy who looked like he could bench press a Buick through the paces. She'd let him up, he'd come in with a punch or a grappling move, then she'd lock onto his arm and bring him down and make him tap out again, from an arm bar, rear naked choke, guillotine, arm triangle, or finally the *gogoplata*. She leaped into the air, catching him on the neck with her shin. Instead of landing, she hung on, pulling his head into her leg with both arms, causing the blood to temporarily cease to flow to his brain. He fell like a bag of rocks. She landed easily, barely breathing hard, barely sweating.

She bent over and slapped the man's face gently a few times.

He sat up and grabbed for his head.

"You're going to have a headache," she said.

"What just hit me?"

"A hundred and ten pounds of Japanese jujitsu master," I said, stepping up and offering the man my hand.

He took it and stood.

She pointed to my feet. "Get your boots off the mat."

I looked down at my dusty combat boots and what had been a pristine blue mat. "Shit. Sorry." I stepped back, then got down on my hands and knees to try and wipe the dust away, but it was no use. I glanced up, ready to apologize again, but she'd grabbed her bag and was walking smartly away.

Olivares hurried after. He reached out and grabbed her shoulder, then found himself airborne as she grabbed his wrist, pulled him into her, bent, then straightened.

Everyone halted what they were doing, including me.

On the floor now, Olivares shook his head to clear it as she came over and stood next to him.

"Do not touch me. Never touch me," she said, then continued on her way.

I hurried over to Olivares and for the second time in as many minutes I helped up someone Ohirra had just dropped.

Olivares cursed under his breath, then hurried after Ohirra. We caught up with her about twenty feet outside the gym. At nine at night, the temperature had fallen to seventy, which actually felt chilly compared with the extreme day temperatures. Bugs dodged in and out of the generator-mounted portable lights interspersed around the camp. These same lights caught the sheen of her eyes as if she was trying hard to hold back tears.

"Ohirra, stop."

"I don't want to talk about this."

Olivares offered a hand. "She was your friend, too."

She blinked hard. Shaking her head, she said through gritted teeth, "I know that. Don't you know how hard this is because of that?"

"Then why let yourself be complicit?"

Only the sound of the generators served as an answer. I watched the emotions play on her face. I could tell she wanted to say something, but was holding back for some reason; I said as much.

When she turned to me, I said, "Trust us."

She exhaled as if she'd been holding her breath. "Even if I told you what I know, there's nothing we can do about it."

I shook my head. "I can't believe that."

"Believe it. She's not Michelle anymore. She'll never be Michelle again."

I was aware that Olivares was staring at me. I let the buzz of the generators fill a few moments as I fought to control my emotions. "But how do you know?"

"She's not the only one. She wasn't even the first. They've tried to unhook people, but they... they go insane. When they're hooked up they have access to the Sirens' broadcast feed—the communication feed between the aliens on Earth and those out there. They also have access to a lot of our minds. When you remove them from the technology, it's like losing all of your senses at once. They just can't take it."

Olivares jumped in. "Fine. We get that. But why?"

She shook her head and wiped a tear away. "You have no idea what the HMIDs can do... what they *have* done. OMBRA has them all over the planet. Without them, the human race as we know it would cease to exist."

"Come on. Aren't you exaggerating a little?"

"Not at all. We can trace the locus for virtually all

incoming and outgoing alien transmissions because of the HMIDs. We're still finding Sirens outside of hives who are providing reconnaissance information. We are now able to block their communications, forcing them to lose time and effort. The plan is to eventually learn their language so we can actually know what's being communicated. So yeah, the HMIDs are very important."

I'd held out so much hope, out of guilt and love.

I'd never thought I'd ever love someone again. I certainly hadn't been looking for it; I was a professional soldier, and not such a good one at that, and I'd been in so many wars. Iraq, Afghanistan, Mali, Kosovo... fucking Kosovo, with the field of dead. No wonder, really. I'd been submerged in a miasma of other people's hatred for too many years. And then she'd come. Then she'd wanted to be with me. Then she'd volunteered to leave me.

I asked a selfish question. "Why'd she volunteer?"

Ohirra sighed. "Her brain is wired better than most of us. Whether it's the neurosteroids affected by PTSD, or other chemical changes created by Dissociative Identity Disorder, or a combination of both, she... you didn't know about that, did you?"

"Dissociative Identity Disorder?"

"Multiple personalities. She's had the problem since she was thirteen. OMBRA recruited her because of it. It was under control with medication, but she was no longer on that medication. In fact, they've designed drugs to enhance it."

"They're making her more crazy? She didn't sign up for that."

Ohirra glanced at Olivares, who stood beside me with

his arms crossed. Then she nodded. "She did know. She was told it would be terrible. It was explained to her that there would be no going back."

"For the hundredth fucking time, then, *why did she do it?*"

"Because she loved you. She felt powerless to save you, except if she could change and become what she's become. She did it for you, Mason. Don't you get it? She made herself into an HMID for *you*."

I felt like I'd been hit by a truck. "For me?" The idea that someone would ruin their entire life, put their very existence in jeopardy, subject themselves to torture was absolutely beyond me.

But it wasn't, was it? It was the stuff of leaders, of heroes. We'd long been brainwashed into the idea of sacrifice. From John Wayne going against the bad guys alone to Clint Eastwood out to seek revenge. It was the essential message of the Western film genre, and of the old Kurisawa-style samurai films like *Yojimbo* and *Seven Samurai*, on which *A Fistful of Dollars* and *The Magnificent Seven* were based. Toshiro Mifune and John Wayne had idealized selfless heroism. Hell, I'd done it myself, racing ahead, going on secret missions, rushing into certain death in the hopes of saving the soldiers under my leadership. It was never something I thought of rationally, it was just something I did. Just as Michelle had done. Who thinks of the consequences when they want to save someone's life? I never have.

"And there's nothing we can do to get her out?" I asked.

"Not unless you want to kill her."

I leveled my gaze at her. "That's what she wants, you know."

"It's what *part* of her wants. She has so many personalities. They sometimes talk to each other. We have a speaker where we can listen in. I listened one day. She was a little girl, then she was a furious bitch, then she was herself, then she was a woman who sang *Oh! Susanna* over and over."

I tried to think through this out loud. "With so many personalities, how can she be useful?"

"They control her feed."

"So she's just a hooked-up guinea pig."

"Who's doing this so that we might live."

I stared into the night, emotionally empty.

"Tomorrow it's going to be your turn in the firing line."

Without looking at her I said, "What's the mission?"

"I can't get into details, but we've discovered a new alien."

My head snapped around.

"What am I supposed to do with it?"

"Bring it back."

Hell, there are no rules here—we're trying
to accomplish something.

Thomas A. Edison

CHAPTER FOUR

0600 CAME EARLIER than it should have. I'd slept in fits
and starts. Images of Michelle attached to her box, tubes
pumping glowing fluids in and out of her, ruled my
dreams, all to the soundtrack of her singing *Oh! Susanna*
in a cracked, off-key voice. It was almost like she wanted
me to see her. Her face was still beautiful—sculpted
cheekbones, dusky eyes, the same gaze that had held me
during the night behind the generators, the night before
she'd disappeared. But her skin was pale. Sores wept in
dozens of places. Then everything familiar was lost. Her
head had been shaved and she now wore a dark metal
cap from which an arm-thick cable extended into the
black box. Then there were the tubes. I wished I could rip
every one of them free and jam them up Mr. Pink's ass.

I sat at the regimental commander's conference table
along with Ohirra, two other intelligence officers, Mr.
Pink, a bald, thin man who stared daggers at everyone,
and a pudgy guy who looked like he could have been
a math teacher back when we had such things. I held
a Styrofoam cup of coffee and blew on it. As it cooled,
I glanced around the room. It had never been changed
after the alien invasion.

Fort Irwin had been the home of the National Training Center, a facility for brigade-on-brigade combat training. This could mean as many as eight thousand combatants maneuvering against each other, which required an incredible amount of space. The aptly named Death Valley was so hot and desolate that almost no one wanted to live there. With more than 900,000 square miles of training ground, NTC had more than enough space for armies to train effectively. The wall still held pictures of various battles, old commanders, and aerial views of the area. A flag of the storied 11th Armored Cavalry Regiment—a shield with a horse rampant across a diagonally-divided field of red and white— stood framed alongside them. To think that a unit that fought in the Philippine-American War, the Mexico Expedition of 1916, World War II, Vietnam, *and* Iraq, was decimated by the Cray and had ceased to exist; it would be staggering had I not also realized that the same could be said for each of the countries I'd mentioned. The world had forever changed, and like it or not, OMBRA was as much a country as it was a company.

A man wearing a lab coat and a NY Yankees baseball cap rushed into the room, setting a clipboard down at the other end of the table and taking a seat. "Sorry I'm late."

Mr. Pink nodded perfunctorily. "Okay, we're all here. Everyone introduce yourselves. My name is Wilson." He glanced at me. "I'm the OMBRA commander here at Special Operations Headquarters North America."

Ohirra introduced herself.

So did the two guys sitting next to her, who turned out to be Lieutenant Rosamilla and Lieutenant Reed—both intel types.

The bald guy's name was Drake; whether that was his first or last name, I had no idea. He was OMBRA's special security liaison and probably specialized in stabbing people in the back.

The guy who looked like a math teacher was Dr. Norman Dupree and was apparently an ethnobotanist. His voice and demeanor were more like a roughneck than a scientist, though. Could just be his southern drawl, but the way he held his shoulders and hands told me that he could probably hold his own in a fight.

Interesting.

Then came Mr. Malrimple. He was OMBRA Special Operations Chief of Science. He spoke fast, used few words, and was very New York in the abruptness of his actions.

Finally it was my turn. "We've all spoken about Master Sergeant Ben Mason. Most of you have seen his file. Although not everyone agrees with my decision," Mr. Pink said, glancing at Drake, "it's mine nonetheless. So now that everyone knows the players, let me explain the game." He turned to me. "This is all for you, Mason, so don't fall asleep."

I held up my coffee and smiled. *Jerk*.

"Lt. Ohirra, let's do big picture. Brief Mason on current Blue Force Order of Battle."

She nodded to Reed, who pulled out a map and spread it on the table. It was the world—Mercator projection—with annotated markings.

She pointed to our location to orient me. "This is where we are. OMBRA has a North American HQ in Buffalo, New York. The rest of the country is red."

Red meant enemy forces. Blue meant good. By the looks of it, we had a fingernail hold on the country.

"The good news is that we now know how to effectively use light against the Cray. NAHQ plans are to retake New England, then Pennsylvania, then New Jersey, then New York."

I nodded only because I couldn't yawn. "Sounds like a great plan."

"European command is in Bruges, Belgium. African command is at the Kilimanjaro Complex. Same place we fought, but you wouldn't believe the upgrades it has now. We have Mediterranean Special Operations HQ in the White Mountains of Crete."

She stood back and I noticed that most of Asia was purple, India was yellow, and Australia was gray. I asked about them.

"OMBRA has no visibility in these areas," Mr. Pink said. "Prior to the alien invasion, we warned the governments of every country we could what was going to happen. Most of the countries didn't believe us, but a few did. Sri Lanka has the Clarke Holding Company, named after famed science fiction writer Arthur C. Clarke. They're much like OMBRA, but one-tenth our size. Still, we passed information to them, in the hopes that they'll tell us what's going on in Australia."

"We have no information at all about them?"

"None. Asia is another thing all together. China has an organization three times the size of OMBRA called Shìjiè Xīn Zhìxù, which means 'New World Order.'" He shook his head. "At this point they are tight-lipped, unwilling to work with us, and evidentially don't want to be friends."

I grinned a little too maniacally. "That's a shame. You guys at OMBRA are such nice guys. Too bad no one is left to pay your extortion money."

Mr. Pink rolled his eyes.

Drake jumped in. "Politeness is next to Godliness, just as pain is next to my fist, young man."

I couldn't tell if he was kidding or not, but I was struck enough by the odd childish threat to shut up.

Mr. Pink gestured to Malrimple.

He glanced at me, but when he spoke, it was to his hands, clasped on the table. "Fauna. So far two distinct alien species have been identified—the Sirens and the Cray. These seem to be pre-invasion species designed to do what they did... reinvent the Dark Ages. There have been reports of something gigantic in the oceans, bigger than whales, purposes unknown. No further information. There are also reports of abnormal human activity in urban areas. Also NFI." He glanced at me to see if I was paying attention, then returned his gaze to his hands. "My climatologist has also indicated that in the last six months, the Earth has warmed by three degrees. Ham radio operators have reported sea rise by ten feet in Florida, Oregon, California, and South America, which suggests the ice caps are melting. There are also reports of fast growing flora in urban areas."

"Thank you, Malrimple."

"Am I done here?" he said, not bothering to look up.

I noted the man's impatience and wondered what his reluctance stemmed from. After all, he wasn't the one going out on a mission.

"Not yet. Wait for questions."

Malrimple sighed heavily.

Mr. Pink turned to me. "This is where you come in, Mason."

I could have left it alone. Maybe I should have left it alone. A good soldier would have behaved better. Then again, I never was much of a good soldier. So ignoring Mr. Pink, I spoke directly to Malrimple.

"Do you have a problem with me?" I figured blunt was the best method.

He looked up, his eyes wide at first, then narrowed. "No, not at all."

"I'm asking because you've barely made eye contact and your entire effort seems forced. You do realize I'm going out on the mission, Malrimple? You do know that it's going to be dangerous and your thumbnail sketch of the information is hardly adequate? I could have gotten this information in the mess hall just by talking to a few grunts."

Mr. Pink held up a hand. "Hold on now, Mason."

Malrimple squirmed like a bug at the end of a needle. "Can I go now?"

Mr. Pink nodded.

I rolled my eyes. Once Malrimple was out of the room, I leveled my gaze at Mr. Pink. "Seriously? Chief of Science?"

Mr. Pink hesitated, then said, "He has a lot on his mind. But that's okay. Mr. Dupree is going to brief you after this. Lt. Ohirra?"

"Okay, Ben. Here's your mission. We're going to infil you into Crestline via helicopter at 0200. We can't get you any closer to Los Angeles because of the twin hives. You'll be escorting Mr. Dupree. It's your responsibility to get him to where he's going and return him without harm."

I glanced at Dupree, who was smiling as if this was all a great adventure.

Ohirra added, "We're looking for the smallest possible footprint. There are too many unknowns out there at this time."

"Commo?"

"Prick-77."

I raised my eyebrows. The prick-77 was Vietnam era.

"It's okay. We have retransmitters in Crestline and Yermo with ground plane antennas. We've also attached an extender which will enable an additional fifteen miles."

"So that's twenty mile range. We're talking Rialto, which isn't anywhere near L.A."

She shrugged. "It's the best we can do."

Dupree spoke for the first time. "We might not have to get all the way into Los Angeles. There's a plant—a vine—that I need samples of. One of my counterparts in Argentina says that it is the locus for spores that may have deleterious effects."

I turned to Mr. Pink. "I'm on escort duty to get a *vine* using Vietnam-era equipment?"

Dupree sat forward. "You don't understand, Mr. Mason. This isn't a terrestrial vine. It grows impossibly fast. This is the next species. This could be a different form of attack, or it could be terraforming."

"Or both," Mr. Pink added.

The rise in temperature and the addition of alien flora definitely suggested something happening. This mission could mean a lot more than it seemed. But with only two of us—scratch that; *one* of us capable of using weapons—it was going to be sketchy at best. "What do we know about possible enemy forces in the area?"

"The twin hives of Los Angeles still hold a complement of Cray, but they don't stray far from their queens. Unless you get close, you won't have to worry about them. As far as civilians go, we've reports that more than half of the population was killed during the first attack and ensuing months. Of those who remain, I'd expect organized defenses, roving gangs, paramilitary groups." Ohirra smiled. "You know, the usual."

To Dupree I said, "Ever carry a gun?"

"I spent four years in the Marine Corps."

"Thank God. Then I expect you know your way around an M4."

"Make that an M16."

"Think of an M4 as an M16 that actually works."

He grinned. "Probably some scientist figured out what was wrong with it."

"Or enough grunts got killed for Congress to allocate the money for a new rifle."

Dupree kept smiling. "That's one thing we don't have to worry about anymore: Congress."

"You smile a lot, don't you?"

"Why not? This is a great time to be a scientist. I mean, aliens are invading and trying to take over our planet. What's not to love?"

I shook my head. "That's a whole lot of lemonade you're making."

He just kept smiling.

Once we have a war there is only one thing to do. It must be won. For defeat brings worse things than any that can ever happen in war.

Ernest Hemingway

CHAPTER FIVE

IT'D BEEN MORE than six months since I'd had to get ready for a mission. Back then, Olivares and I were preparing to climb down the mouth of an extinct volcano and the packing list was completely different. This was to be more of a reconnaissance. I was planning for three days max, then exfil, so I spent the rest of the day going over maps and checking my equipment. I chose to wear military fatigues, even though it would set me apart from the civilians I'd encounter; I figured they might see me as a friend rather than an immediate foe. I checked out two sets of Night Vision Devices, as well as two extra batteries for the AN\PRC-77, or prick-77 as we called it. For weapons I chose a P226, which I wore in a chest rig on my body armor. I selected a smaller P238, which I concealed in the small of my back. For my long rifle I was elated to find an HK416. It fired the same 5.56 mm rounds that the M4 fired, but was easier to clean and cold metal forged. I'd never fired one before. The closest I'd gotten to one was back in Africa when the infantry platoon used them in backing up my recon squad. But back then I'd worn an EXO suit and had little need for a mere rifle.

I also checked out a 416 and P226 for Dupree, along with 300 rounds of ammo for both of us. I'd have liked to have had more, but we could only carry so much. Then I packed a first aid kit with some quick clot gauze along with some super glue. Finally I found some MREs and broke them down. I prepared two canteens and had a two-quart shoulder sling canteen ready for Dupree.

Then I spent a few hours going over maps, planning several routes and concentrating on open spaces and safe areas in the event we were chased or had to go to ground, which I could almost guarantee was going to happen. Based on the desperation of the man I'd seen in Mr. Pink's office, it was a high probability that any encounter would be a violent one, which was why I intended to travel at night as much as possible.

I'd arranged for Dupree to come by at 1400 hours for a mission brief and weapons familiarization. Then I spent the rest of the day sitting in intel spaces beside the analysts keeping track of population movements outside the wire. Without satellite coverage, we were limited to UAVs for IMINT (imagery intelligence), which were used sparingly and always during the day. The only other int they were able to use was HUMINT (human-derived intelligence), which meant they had collectors both overtly speaking to refugees, and clandestinely embedded within groups.

Lt. Rosamilla briefed me. "God's New Army, or GNA, is the most organized of the groups operating in the greater L.A. area. Their HQ is West Covina Plaza, what used to be a mall."

"I've been there to see movies before."

Rosamilla made a face. "No such thing as movies anymore."

"Unless you count reruns."

"Fuck nostalgia."

I grinned as Bruce Willis, Clint Eastwood and Woody Harrelson rolled over in their Cray-made graves. I was starting to like Rosamilla. He said what he wanted and didn't hold back. I found that unique in a lieutenant. They were normally so tightly wound that even swearing in public would send them spinning into a panic.

"Back to GNA."

"Right. Their strength is about four thousand. They operate like a brigade, with four battalions of eight hundred people at remote stations and one battalion of eight hundred on site. Remote locations are Turnbull Canyon in Whittier, Chino Airport, Knott's Berry Farm in Buena Park, and Seal Beach."

Looking at a map, I noticed something. "So it looks like the 605 is their front. Are they actively fighting the Cray?"

"Negative. They stay away, and the Cray leave them alone."

"Then what's the problem?"

"The population west of the 605 is evidencing extraordinarily violent behavior. Reports are that they've become quite savage, attacking anything that moves."

"Jesus, you're talking like they're zombies."

"Perhaps their behavior is similar, but these people are alive. And we don't think it's behavioral. We believe its chemical."

I frowned. "So there's something in the water."

"Or in the air." Rosamilla shook his head. "We just don't know."

"Tell me about GNA. What's their mission?"

"They're led by none other than Paul Sebring."

"*The* Paul Sebring? The guy who hosted that amateur singing show called Sing America?"

"Same one. Turns out to be a pretty effective demagogue."

"I'd have expected it to be run by a general."

"The chief of staff is retired Major General Carlos Murphy, who once commanded the 4th Infantry Division."

"That would explain it. You know, I watched the show and wasn't aware that Sebring was religious."

"He's not. God is just a rallying point. He's built a core group, a cult of personality, which serves as his inner circle. We have a source inside, but given the challenges of distance and radio, our reports are weekly."

"Any thought of putting up some relay antennas?" I asked.

Rosamilla shrugged. "It's on our list of things to do, but it's a long fucking list."

"I hear ya," I said.

"Back to GNA. Right now they're doing what we can't. They're trying to establish a zone in which law and order is the rule, and are fighting back incursions from those west of the 605, as well as smaller groups in the area."

"What about these other groups? GNA doesn't sound so bad. There must be some that are more... how should I put it... like *The Road Warrior*?"

"There are. You'll have to pass through Fontana, which means you might come across Devil's Thunder. They were a biker gang, but after the alien invasion, they became a militia. They're your standard rape, pillage, and burn happy group of fellows. They control the I-15 corridor between Fontana and Victorville."

"Splendid. We're going to have to cross I-15. Why is it we can't land further west?" I sighed. "Oh, yeah. The Cray and their nasty EMPs. Speaking of, should there be any concern?"

"The Twin Hives give off a pulse of EMP with a coverage area between the 405 and 605 to the east and west and the 405 and Angeles National Forest to the north and south. It fires every seven hours like clockwork."

Over the next hour Rosamilla continued showing me the different players in the game.

Palm Springs was controlled by a battalion-sized element of Marines who had looted the supply depot-rail head at Yermo. Their policy was to shoot first and ask questions never. With the great windmills still running, they had a corner on the electricity market. If the Cray ever found them, their hedonistic, shoot-'em-up fuck-fest would forever change, but until then, they were a happy lot of Marines with enough booze and women to fuel them into the next century.

Rancho Cucamonga had a group called the Caspers. These white supremacists were trying to bring back the KKK and use the opportunity to ethnically cleanse their little suburban area.

Corona had the New Panthers, named after the local high school mascot. These guys seemed to be the only ones without an agenda. Just trying to keep families together and figure out a way to survive.

Then, of course, there were roaming bands of looters hitting houses and businesses. They were coming north from as far south as Anaheim. It was ridiculous, really. Rosamilla believed it was consumer habit. Now, with all the stores looted or destroyed, they were forced to push into the interior to achieve serotonin release.

On the walk back to my tent, I couldn't help wonder what we were fighting for. Back at Kilimanjaro we'd been fighting for those to our left and right. We gave it all so that they wouldn't die. But in the back of our minds we were also fighting for our families, our communities, our countries. We fought for the things with which we identified.

What was I fighting for now?

America was gone.

I had no family.

Our entire way of life was shattered.

Everyone was at war with each other.

Survival of the fittest was the theme of the day.

So what was it?

But I knew. I was fighting for Michelle. I was fighting for Thompson. I was even fighting for Olivares. I was fighting for every member of OMBRA Special Operations North America. I was fighting for them because they were my mates, my partners, my peers.

I knew what I was fighting for. So what was I fighting against? I'd never been a law and order guy. I didn't much care about anyone's belief systems or their private thoughts. Everyone had the right to believe in whatever stupid invented entity they wanted. They had the right to be wrong, too. But what I didn't like were bullies. I hated those who would take advantage of those who couldn't properly defend themselves.

Rapists and bullies.

Just like whatever alien race was orchestrating this attempt to end humanity.

Intergalactic rapists and bullies.

Never forget that no military leader has ever become great without audacity.

Carl von Clausewitz

CHAPTER SIX

WE FLEW NAP-OF-THE-EARTH through the clear full moon night, never more than thirty feet from the dirt to avoid hostile notice. Although Cray shouldn't be out this far, we didn't know what else might be watching. For all we knew, our every movement was being watched and recorded by spaceships in orbit.

The interior of the Blackhawk was dimmed. Her running lights had been turned off. There was no reason to announce our presence; the sound of the rotors would do that. I was able to convince flight control to divert to a secondary landing site instead of Twin Peaks. A ski resort on Mount Baldy was our target, not only because it was reported as abandoned and put us that much closer to our target area, but also because it allowed us to bypass any possible interaction with Devil's Thunder.

"Five minutes out," came the words through my headset.

I tapped Dupree on the shoulder.

He turned to me and nodded.

I noted the nervousness in his eyes. Good. I'd rather he be a little scared than overconfident. My plan was to find some mode of transport, perhaps a motorcycle or something similar, then hug the mountains and traverse west. I knew that anything in the vicinity of Interstate 10 was a target. It was just too major a corridor. Even 210 would be dangerous. I wouldn't be surprised to encounter armed groups on those roads, if not roadblocks... or both.

"One minute out."

I turned to check Dupree's pack, making sure all the pockets were closed and snapped and that it was secure. Then I turned so he could do the same for me. I tightened my AN\PVS-7 night vision goggles over my reversed baseball cap. Like enclosed goggles, the NVDs allowed both eyes to stare into a chamber in which a single telescoped lens gathered light so that I could see in the dark. The universe was green through the NVDs, and I watched as the ground came up to meet us. The helicopter sat down, the door slid open, and Dupree and I leaped out. We ran to the woodline as the helicopter rose and spun back the way it had come. When we reached the trees, we knelt, breathing heavily, searching for any hostile force who might have witnessed our infil.

"You good?"

Dupree was heaving beside me. "Could afford to lose a few pounds. Not in Marine shape anymore."

"Well, it's all downhill from here." It was literally true; Mount Baldy was about ten thousand feet above sea level and we were going to drop 8800 feet in the space of nine miles as we traveled south down the mountain to the city of Upland.

After we were certain that we hadn't been seen, we began the trek, hugging the edge of Mount Baldy Road. I kept my head on a swivel as we made the descent. I caught sight of several deer, as well as a startled coyote, but so far no humans. We were fifteen minutes into the journey when we turned a corner and the whole of Los Angeles was laid out before us. I halted, unable to move as I stared at a city that had once been a blaze of lights rolling all the way to the ocean. Now great swathes of darkness curled through intermittent lights. The largest area of light was a cluster in Covina which could only be the location of God's New Army. To the west lay a wall of darkness, which I knew had to be the 605. Not a single light flickered beyond the demarcation line the Cray called home. I hoped I'd get to see one. I hoped I'd get to kill one. Killing something might just fill the hole expanding in my chest.

We heard the sound of an engine. The hillside met the road to the left and to the right was a copse of trees.

I bailed off the road to the right.

Dupree took the left, absolutely the wrong way. Unable to get up the escarpment, he lay down in the ditch and hugged the ground. A motorcycle rumbled around the curve, lights off. The bike looked and sounded like a 650. The rider wore night vision goggles like mine. He geared down, then stopped about ten feet past our position.

I raised my rifle and put my sights center mass.

He turned the engine off, then pulled a pistol from a holster on his chest.

There was no doubt now that he'd seen Dupree. But had he seen me? I considered taking him out with my rifle, but I didn't know if there was anyone following him. I was also aware that the shot could be heard from a long distance. I made a decision and laid down my rifle.

His steps crunched on the gravel at the edge of the

road as he strode over to where Dupree lay ignobly in the ditch. The man stopped and raised his pistol.

"Get up or I'll shoot you dead."

I pulled my knife from its sheath and crept across the road.

He cocked the trigger.

"I said get up."

I didn't wait. I brought the knife around and sunk it into the man's ear. He grunted, then fell to the ground.

"Get up, Dupree."

He peeked from where his hands covered his head, then climbed unsteadily to his feet. I dragged the man across the road and into the trees. Then I got his bike and rolled it in the trees as well. All the while Dupree stood in the ditch, frozen. I grabbed him and walked him across the road.

When we were deep in the trees, I turned to him. His face was pale and slack in the green universe of my NVD. "Listen, Dupree. This is real. Snap out of it."

No reaction.

I slapped him. Then I slapped him again. I was about to slap him for a third time when he stopped my hand.

"Stop slapping me."

"Are you back?"

He nodded and licked dry lips.

I pulled a canteen free and gave it to him.

He opened it and took a tentative sip, then slung back some more. He closed and returned it, then made a disgusted face. "I froze back there."

"Yes. You did." I wasn't about to give him a break. "We can't have that."

He shook his head. "No, we can't. It just happened so fast."

"It always happens fast." I grabbed him by the collar. "Listen to me. From now on, if I do something, you copy it. Whenever something happens, look to see what I'm doing. Got it?"

He nodded.

I slapped him on the shoulder, then said, "Let's see what we have here." I knelt at the body. Caucasian, about forty years old. Plain features with a Fu Manchu mustache. Nose had been broken. He was bald beneath his do-rag. He still gripped the .357 Ruger Blackhawk. I removed the pistol and then took off the holster and put them in a pile. He carried a cell phone, which I found strange. It must have been out of habit. He had a ring of keys, which I also placed in the pile. He had a boot pistol; I didn't recognize the model, but it was a pearl-handled chrome derringer with two barrels filled with .22 long rounds. I rolled him over and saw the words *Devil's Thunder* wrapped around a stylized devil head with crossed lightning bolts behind it. I took the jacket as well.

I checked the bike next and noted its bulging saddlebags. On the left were foodstuffs. On the right were clothes and survival gear. He'd had enough food to last a week, as long as he could find a water source. Was he supposed to be a lookout? Was Devil's Thunder expanding their territory, or had they already?

I removed the saddlebags and tossed them deeper into the woods. I placed the pistols in my pack and shoved the biker's vest into Dupree's hands.

I glanced at the body. We'd been on the ground for less than fifteen minutes and we'd managed to kill someone. I couldn't help but smile. Things were looking up already.

It is easier to find men who will volunteer
to die, than to find those who are willing
to endure pain with patience.

Julius Caesar

CHAPTER SEVEN

THE MOTORCYCLE ALLOWED us to cover a lot more
distance than had we been on foot. Instead of leaving
the mountains, we took advantage of their cover. At the
end of Mount Baldy Road, we headed back up, taking
Cobal Canyon Mountainway. My goal had been to get
us to Marshall Canyon Golf Course before sunrise,
which would put us thirty miles from the 605—the
supposed infected zone. On the mountain roads we
passed several campfires, but never stopped to see who
was there. Once, we saw oncoming lights, and I was
able to slip the bike into some trees. Four motorcycles
and a truck roared by, heading back the way we came.
I wasn't able to see if any of them were wearing Devil's
Thunder vests. They could have been anyone. Still, we
didn't want any interaction. We just wanted to get in
and out as fast as we could.

We arrived at the course about 4 AM. We'd killed the
engine on the bike half a mile out and coasted the rest
of the way in. I didn't see any lights in the clubhouse
or hear any sound, except for the bubble of a brook
somewhere. I parked the bike about thirty meters away

from the clubhouse and had Dupree stand watch while I did recon.

Skirting around the outside I peered in the windows, listened for any sound, and continually sniffed the air, trying to get the scent of food, or cigarettes, or sweat. But there was nothing here. I'd hoped we'd have the place to ourselves, and it looked as if we would.

I returned to the bike, but I didn't see Dupree anywhere. I went to one knee and began to scan the area. I'd been gone fifteen minutes. A lot can happen in that time. I saw the bushes rustling and sighted in. They parted and Dupree walked out, zipping up his pants.

Seriously?

I stood and went over to the bike. For a brief moment, I thought about haranguing him for leaving his post, but then realized it would be wasted. I could see from his goofy smile that he was happy to see me and probably proud that he hadn't fucked up his job, even if he had.

We took the bike into the garage where forty golf carts sat, never to be used again. We checked inside the clubhouse. The kitchen had been ransacked. All the knives and food were gone. The store had also been gone through. Someone with a sense of humor had created a crazy tower of golf clubs. It seemed to sum it up. Not much to do with them otherwise. Who would play golf at the end of the world?

Once we were sure the place was empty, we found a spot near some windows with a view of the road over a couch and a pair of leather chairs. I left Dupree for a moment, took the radio up on the roof, and called in our position. Five minutes later I was downstairs. Dupree sat on the couch, staring at his pistol, which lay on the table in front of him.

He spoke without looking up. "I gotta tell you how sorry I am for what happened."

I shrugged. "It's behind us." I took off the rest of my gear until I was only in boots, pants and a t-shirt. I took the derringer and slid it into my own boot, then put my knife, a canteen of water, and my 9mm on the table in front of me. I leaned back and closed my eyes for a few moments. Finally, I opened them.

"Tell me about yourself, Dupree. What made you join the Marines and become a scientist?"

He grinned, a gesture that seemed more normal for his wide face than anything else. "My mom. We were living in Hixon, Tennessee. I didn't have a job and no place was hiring. I suppose I could have worked at a fast food restaurant, but I didn't want to be that guy, so I was applying for jobs like accountant and mechanic."

"Were you trained as an accountant or mechanic?"

"Hell, no. But that didn't stop me. I applied for all sorts of jobs I wasn't qualified for."

"Did you get any offers?"

"Hell, no. I wasn't qualified!"

I gave him a quizzical look.

"You see, I didn't realize that people had to be trained in these things. I just thought they went to a job and learned how to do it." Seeing my look, he shrugged. "I know, right? What rock was I hiding under during my childhood? Suffice to say I finally realized that I didn't have any training at all, so I needed to go to college. It was about that time my mom showed me where the military offered to pay for free college classes."

"Why the Marines?"

"Because when I went to the mall to sign up, the other offices were closed."

I snorted.

"I swear. So I became an oh-three-eleven. Know what that is?"

I nodded. "Infantry. Rifleman. It's what I am, except I'm an eleven bravo in the Army."

Now it was time for his eyes to narrow.

"What did I say?"

"You used present tense. You said *I'm an eleven bravo in the Army*."

"I did, didn't I? The Army... OMBRA. Not much difference I suppose. Back to your story."

"So I went to Iraq and ended up in the Kurdish region in support of Operation Provide Comfort."

That was before my time, but I remembered there had been a no-fly zone in place and the US had provided support to the Kurds shortly after the first Gulf War.

"When I was there I noted that several tribes refused to use medicine provided by UN doctors, instead insisting on local remedies. Bottom line, I was struck that they were so healthy. As it turned out, they'd discovered the medicinal values of the local flora, something that many indigenous groups used. Like how the American Indians discovered that willow bark produced a substance that could relieve pain and inflammation. What we now call aspirin.

"So when I got out, I got a veteran's loan and went to school. I might have been slow to find out what I wanted to do, but I figured it out eventually."

"And then the aliens invaded."

That grin again. "Know the difference between an ethnobotanist and a xenobotanist?"

I shook my head.

"Aliens. Now that there *are* actually card-carrying

aliens bringing their own flora, I can spend my time figuring out what the flora is, and what sort of relationship the flora has with the aliens, and what sort of relationship it will have with us."

"Relationship, huh?" I chuckled. "Whatever it is, it's a weapon."

"Why do you say that?"

"They're not going to import something just because it's pretty or it smells good. When we traveled to Afghanistan we had limited space on the aircraft. I imagine it's the same situation with the aliens. Limited space. They probably brought seeds and then dispersed them in urban environments. Mark my words, it was to do something bad to us."

That grin.

"You keep smiling. You do realize that this is the end of the world, right?"

He kept smiling even as he shook his head slowly. "Not the end, just the beginning of something new. Yeah, I'm smiling. It's a golden time. I'm at the pinnacle of my career. Everything I've ever dreamed of is within a thirty-mile reach. Yeah, it's fucked up what happened, but I'm about moving forward, not looking behind."

"Did you lose anyone?"

His grin tightened. "I told you, I'm not looking behind."

I suddenly got it. He *had* to be happy. He had to be positive. After all, the opposite was far worse. He approached happiness like it was a job, and to him it probably was. Who knew what his story was? Whatever had happened, he desperately didn't want to think about it. I'd respect his privacy. We were all a little broken. We all had something we didn't want to think about. We all had something to hide.

"We'll sleep in four-hour breaks. I'll take the first shift. I'll wake you at nine."

He nodded, rolled over so he faced the couch, then was still.

I turned to stare out the window and watched as the sun rose over my alien-infested planet.

Where today are the Pequot? Where are the Narragansett, the Mohican, the Pokanoket, and many other once powerful tribes of our people? They have vanished before the avarice and the oppression of the White Man, as snow before a summer sun. Will we let ourselves be destroyed in our turn without a struggle, give up our homes, our country bequeathed to us by the Great Spirit, the graves of our dead and everything that is dear and sacred to us? I know you will cry with me, Never! Never!

Tecumseh Shawnee

CHAPTER EIGHT

DRUMS BEAT IN a darkness so dense it held me in its cloying grasp. I couldn't turn. I couldn't blink. I wasn't even sure if my eyes were open. The drums grew louder and louder—

I awoke with a start.

Dupree stood unmoving at the window, staring out.

"What is it?" I uncurled myself from the chair, my back protesting.

"Golf," was all he said, but the word held a mystical quality it shouldn't have.

I jumped to my feet and went to the window. Sure

enough, three old men were out there playing golf. I pegged them to be in their seventies. They were all rail thin. One wore red paisley pants; another wore orange paisley. The third wore pants with neon green alligators on them. They all wore polo golf shirts, two-tone golf shoes and golf caps.

I rubbed my eyes to make sure I wasn't seeing things.

"How long have they been there?"

"Looks like they played all eighteen." He pointed. "This is the last hole."

The grass looked too long to play in, but as I thought that, my eyes began to pick up some details they'd missed before. Here and there were spaces where the grass was short, as if someone had come and cut it, or in this case, hit a ball from it.

"I bet they do this every day."

They were playing directly towards us. The green was beneath our window. The one with orange paisley pants selected a club and began to look our way and address the ball. *Oh, shit!* I grabbed Dupree and hit the deck. My hand slipped free and he remained standing.

"Get down. They'll see us."

He shook his head. "They can't. The window is mirrored."

I got slowly to my feet. "How do you know?"

He stood transfixed on the sight. "During my first shift, I decided to make a round of the building just to be sure."

The old man hit the ball.

We watched it sail through the air and land on the green, which I now noted had been cut. The ball hit, backspun, and ran towards the flag, only to stop three inches shy. This guy was no slacker. Then again, the threesome had probably played the game at this club every day, if not multiple times a day, since the invasion. I couldn't help smiling. I'd joked about it earlier, but to play golf at the end of the world was to laugh in the face of the invasion. I was reminded of the scene in *Apocalypse Now* where soldiers are surfing even though artillery rounds are raining down in the water near them. I never understood the scene until I went to war. I'd always thought that when Colonel Kilgore had his men surf it was an indulgence of the director. Now I knew better. What was it he'd said to Sheen's character? *"If I say it's safe to surf this beach, Captain, it's safe to surf this beach."* I'd always thought of it as a horrible demonstration of hubris, but now I knew, just as these three old men golfed in the face of the demise of the human race, it was motivation to continue. For these three old men, golf was their septuagenarian middle finger to the alien race trying to orchestrate not only their demise, but the end of the game forever.

I clapped in appreciation.

Dupree joined in and as two more balls hit the green and backpedaled to make a handsome triangle surrounding the cup, we continued clapping, an obtuse soundtrack to an ignoble event.

The man with alligator pants must have heard something. He pulled a compound bow from his golf bag and nocked an arrow. He turned, tracked something just out of our view, then shot.

A deer stumbled forward and face-planted. It was a doe—an illegal kill back when there were laws, but now, when the markets were closed, meat was at a premium.

The other two golfers patted the shooter on the back as he fist-pumped the air. The moment lasted exactly five seconds, then fear carjacked their happiness. They grabbed their bags and began to run in our direction.

We strained to see what they'd seen, but it soon became evident as two humans loped into view. Each held pieces of wood which they used to hit the deer over and over, splattering its head and crushing its ribs. Even when the head was unrecognizable, they didn't stop.

I ran to my bag and grabbed a Leupold Mark 4 CQ\T scope and centered in on them. They were average height. Both with brown hair. Their clothes were ripped and torn. One was naked except for a single shoe. As they bashed the dead deer over and over, it was as if they were mindless, like... zombies.

As soon as I thought the word, I hated it. To think that aliens would turn the end of the world into a bad *Walking Dead* rerun didn't wash. There had to be something else going on here.

I noticed their chests, shoulders, and necks. What I'd originally thought of as pieces of material looked like something else in the scope's magnification. Spots, maybe. Or growths.

Suddenly they stopped beating on the deer. Their attention jerked to the old man with alligators on his pants as he ran back to pick up a club he'd dropped. They took off after him. I took one look at their speed and knew the guy had no chance. I grabbed my rifle and ran for the side door. I heard Dupree following close behind. I shoved my scope into my pocket as I ran. When I hit the door to the outside, I turned right and jumped down the five stairs and onto the grass. I spun around the side of the building and brought up my rifle. I was too late. They'd caught the old guy and were drumming him with the wood just as they'd done the deer.

I shot one in the head.

The other turned to see where the sound had come from.

When we locked eyes, I knew I'd have to pull the trigger again. I made sure he went down.

Then I saw the other two old men, huddled near the far side of the building. I waved them over.

They came, giving the dead a wide stare.

"Where'd you come from?" asked the one in the orange paisley pants. Up close, I saw he wore a soiled gray polo shirt. He'd grown a beard that seemed as if it had never seen scissors.

The other one stared forlornly at the body. "Damn it, Gene. Why'd you have to go back for the club?"

Orange paisley apparently felt the need to explain. "It was his favorite."

"That killed him," I added.

Orange paisley nodded.

Meanwhile, Dupree had moved to the two dead men and knelt on the ground. "Now this is interesting."

I glanced over at the old man named Gene, his eyes staring wide to the sky.

"Careful of the fungees," orange paisley warned. The word sounded like *funjeez*.

"What's wrong with them?"

"We don't know. They come from the Hive Zone and kill everything they see."

Dupree whistled. "Fungees, huh? Not a bad name, I suppose." He turned to me. "Mason, let me show you something."

I kept my eyes on the two men. Neither looked as if they were armed. Approaching them, I noticed there were growths around their chests, shoulders and necks.

They looked like skin tags, but were too large.

"This has to be from the family *Ophiocordycipitaceae*. It's a family of parasitic fungi." He moved to the other body and began inspecting it, never touching it.

I took a broken piece of stick from the ground and prodded the flesh around these growths, then began poking the sacs. One of the sacs opened, releasing a barely perceptible whiff of spores.

Dupree saw what I'd done and backed quickly away. "Get away, Mason." He frowned as he pulled me away. "Never do that again."

I moved with him. "What's it going to do?"

"Your prodding released some spores. I think if we breathe them in, we'll end up like those two." He turned to the old men. "What do you call them? *Fungees*?"

They nodded.

Red paisley pointed to his neck. "They look like mushrooms."

Dupree nodded. "Very similar." To me, he said, "Let's get back inside."

"Are you two going to be okay?" I held my weapon in low ready, with the butt still next to my shoulder, but the barrel pointing towards the ground, so I could bring it up and pop off a few rounds if I had to... not that they seemed the type to want to overpower me. Still, better safe than dead.

They nodded.

"Then get out of here. If you want, you can come back for your friend tomorrow."

They started to back away.

"Wait a minute," Dupree said. "How many of these have you seen?"

They exchanged a look, and it was orange paisley who

finally spoke. "First one we saw was a few weeks ago. Then one or two every couple of days since."

"Have they shown the same behavior as these?"

"If you mean did they try and kill anything that moved, then the answer is yes. At first we thought they were zombies by the way they acted, but then zombies eat flesh, right? And since these things don't eat flesh, they can't be zombies, right?"

Dupree grinned. "Right. They are definitely not zombies. At least not like the ones we came to know and love in pre-invasion popular culture."

Respecting your opponent is the key to winning any bout. Hold your enemy in contempt and you may miss the strategy behind his moves.

David H. Hackworth

CHAPTER NINE

BACK INSIDE I asked, "What did you mean when you said not the kind of zombies we know?"

He sat on the couch, making notes in a small green notebook with a stubby pencil. "Ever heard of *Ophiocordyceps unilateralis*?"

"I can't even spell it."

Dupree glanced at me. Always that grin. "You're funny, Mason."

"Didn't that bother you, out there?"

"Oh, yeah. Sure did." He was drawing something.

"But you're smiling."

He paused in his drawing, but didn't look at me. "Know the difference between smiling and gritting your teeth?"

"No."

"Me neither, sometimes." He finished the drawing and showed it to me. "This is a badly drawn representation of *Ophiocordyceps unilateralis*."

It looked like an ant with a periscope, and I told him so.

He turned it sideways, then back again. "It does, doesn't it? But of course it's not. So here's what you're seeing. *Ophiocordyceps unilateralis* is an entomopathogenic fungus—a fungus that is parasitic in nature and can kill or seriously harm the host. It's also known as the zombie fungus. These fungi usually attach to the external body surface in the form of microscopic spores, like the ones you probably released from that sac." He shook his head and made a face. "The spores germinate and colonize the epidermis, eventually boring through it to reach the body cavity. Then the fungal cells proliferate in the host body cavity, usually as walled hyphae or in the form of wall-less protoplasts."

"What does all that mean?"

"This fungus enters the body of a specific ant in the Amazon. It takes root, then removes all motor control from the ant. Once the 'periscope,' as you call it, grows, the fungus then forces the ant to climb to a position so that the fungus can anchor it there. Then after a few days, the ant sprouts fruiting bodies that disperse the spores over a larger area, thanks to the height the ant reached before death."

I stared at the drawing, then at Dupree. "Are you fucking serious?"

This time he didn't smile. "Serious."

"Could these be terrestrial in origin?"

"We've never see it in humans, not that it isn't possible. There'd have to be some sort of genetic manipulation, though. What concerns me is the apparent territorial drive."

"The what?"

"Based solely on the pair we saw, it appears that the hosts attack those who aren't infected. This could be

Dupree nodded as he stared at the old men, then turned to me. "Why is it we're doing this, Mason?"

I knew where he was going. "Don't get sentimental on me. We all have to make sacrifices."

"He could be your grandfather. Would you do that to your grandfather?"

I remembered gnarled hands on mine as they taught me how to reel in a fish. One of my few truly perfect memories not sullied by the shit that had been my childhood. I lowered the barrel of my rifle in disgust.

"I'm going to need to check you out." Dupree pulled on some gloves, then a paper facemask. "What's your name?"

"Hen—Henry Maxwell."

"Okay, Henry Maxwell, tell me what happened." He walked over to Henry with a portable black light in his hands. He turned it on and held it over the face and shoulder area of the old man.

"We live less than five hundred feet west of here, in a resort home. We spent our days reading and playing games. Then every morning and evening we play a round of golf." He flashed a shaky grin. "You know I'm seventy-seven years old and a five handicap?"

"Is that good, Henry?"

I had to admit, Dupree had a charming bedside manner.

"Good, hell. It would almost put me on the PGA," he said. Then he gave a short bark of a laugh and beamed a plastic grin in my direction. "Do you believe people used to get paid to golf? What a world we had."

Dupree stepped back. "Yeah, what a world we had." He held up a hand. "Give me a moment, Henry, to confer with my colleague."

"Sure thing." Henry sat heavily in a chair, staring expectantly at us.

Dupree came over to me and directed me to follow him to his bag. I kept my weapon at low ready and one eye on the old man.

"What's up?"

He spoke in a hushed whisper. "You're right. He can't come with us. He has spores all over him. My guess is they got on him during the attack." He glanced back at Henry. "I'd love to take him back to evaluate the growth infection rates, but without a biohazard particulate suit, he'd be too infectious."

"What do you want to do with him, then?"

Dupree gave me a stern look. "I don't want to kill him."

"Okay, then. What happens if he infects someone else? You yourself said that this fungus has made humans the vector for its spread."

He nodded and frowned. "I know I said that. But what would you have me do?"

I turned to Henry.

When he saw my face he stood. "I'm not going with you," he said, his eyes searching mine for an answer.

"The same thing that infected the fungees that killed your friends has infected you. We don't know how long it will take, but Dupree believes that you'll become a fungee too."

Henry blinked rapidly as he took in the information. Then he looked to Dupree, who nodded in affirmation of my statement. Henry took a moment and closed his eyes. Then he opened then to stare out the window. The sun was setting over Los Angeles, sinking into the ocean. A golden light captured the flag on the eighteenth green, surrounding it with a nimbus of shifting gold.

Henry said the words slow and plain, "How do you know that will happen?"

"I'm a scientist here to learn about the epidemiology of the fungus."

"Is there a cure?"

"No." Dupree licked his lips.

Henry tried to speak twice, but each time his voice caught. He finally cleared his throat. "I was in Vietnam twice. Once fighting my way through Hue during the Tet Offensive in '68, then up in the highlands supporting special forces. I was just a grunt, you know. We were up on the Ho Chi Minh Trail, trying to stop Charlie from resupplying. One day my best bud, Vinnie Mafia, got stomach punched with a pungi stick."

Henry glanced my way, a sad look on his face.

"Know what that is, son?" Henry asked.

I nodded.

"I thought so. You look like you would." He returned to staring at the golden-hued green. "So Vinnie's bleeding all over God's creation. We're three days march from friendly forces. We can't call in air support because we're on the wrong side of the border. So Vinnie is basically fucked and he knows it." Henry chuckled now. "Know what that *mensch* said? *You gotta kill me, Hank. No, listen, I'm a gonner. I'll only slow you down so Charlie does the same thing to you. So kill me, already, why don't you?*"

That moment in Vietnam filled the room. I could almost hear Vinnie's words. God knows I'd heard them before. I'd had my own Vinnie. We'd called him Todd, but his full name had been Specialist Todd Chu. We'd taken fire from an enemy mortar and a piece of shrapnel had sliced his femoral. He'd begged me to kill him. I'd nodded and said I would, but in the end I didn't have to. He'd lost consciousness a few moments before he'd died. It had been quick.

Henry spoke again, but didn't turn this time. "Do you understand what I said, soldier?"

"Yes." My throat was dry. "Yes, I do."

Todd Chu had been a twenty-year-old kid whose parents had emigrated from Taiwan to San Francisco. He'd always felt their disappointment for not doing as well in school as they'd wanted him to. He'd loved watching his beloved 49ers and playing soccer. His favorite food had been BBQ chicken pizza, and his favorite beer was Anchor Steam. He was a true-blue American whose death was forever etched in the dirty sand of Al Kut, and he'd been my friend and fellow soldier.

Henry spoke for the last time. "So kill me already, why don't you?"

I raised my rifle and fired twice, the noise shocking in the silence that framed it.

Henry fell straight down, two holes in the side of his head.

I stared for a moment, then shouldered my rifle. I reached for my equipment. Then to Dupree, I said, "Come on. Let's get out of here."

My words seemed to shake him out of his shock. He stepped back and nodded, then hurriedly finished putting his kit away. A breeze brushed against us as we exited the clubhouse. It did nothing to cool me, but it did dry the wetness that had somehow found its way to my face.

Luck is where opportunity meets preparation.

Denzel Washington

CHAPTER TEN

WE LEFT THE motorcycle as a backup. I wanted to know that I had a quick way to evacuate, in the event we needed to or were on the run. We'd find another mode of transportation soon enough, I suspected. So we hung to the side of Golden Hills Road, which ran through an upscale housing community that was probably part of the golf course. Here and there we saw a light, but for the most part, the homes were completely dark. I only had about fifty percent power left in the batteries for my NVDs, so we didn't have that advantage. But with the wide open roads and few trees, we could see for quite a good distance.

We left Golden Hills and crossed a wide space that the map pegged as a gravel pit. On the other side was San Dimas Golf Canyon Course. This close to the mountain there seemed to be a lot of golf courses, which I didn't mind a bit. Urban warfare was my least favorite type of combat, especially patrolling streets with high-rise buildings. Every doorway, every window held the potential for death. In Iraq, I'd developed an ache in the center of my shoulders from the sheer stress of waiting to be shot in the back.

We walked side by side, carrying our rifles. I'd put my

Leupold scope on mine. We were about halfway across the gravel pit when I saw the coyotes—three of them, their eyes catching the sheen of the moon. I raised my scope and with enough moonlight, was able to pull in their image. Something was off about them. Coyotes normally avoided humans, unless they were rabid. These began loping towards us.

"Shit. Here they come." The last thing I wanted to do was announce our presence with gunfire. "I'll see if I can take them out, but if they get too close, open up on them."

I sighted in on the first and led it by about five feet as I pulled the trigger three times. The first two rounds caught it in the face and back, sending it tumbling to the ground. I fired twice at the one on the left as it juked and jived, and caught it. Must have broken its back; it was still alive, but couldn't move its back legs. Still, it tried to claw towards us.

Dupree caught the last one in a hail of full auto.

I pulled my pistol and strode to the one with the broken back. I put two in its head, then backed away as fast as I could.

"Hey, Dupree?"

"I see it. Better stay away."

"Those are ascocarps, aren't they?"

What looked to be a dozen knife-shaped outcroppings were sticking from the coyotes' chests and shoulders. The tips of each were dark, as if they'd been dipped in blood.

"Look at those *Cordyceps*. I've seen this type on a tarantula. Looks almost like antlers. Only this is a mammal."

I heard the high-pitched whine of a motorcycle off to the south.

I grabbed him. "Run!"

I took off at a dead sprint.

Dupree struggled to follow, his breath coming fast and furious. We made a rise in the gravel just as a motorbike skidded into the pit on the other side.

I shoved Dupree to the ground as I fell sideways, desperate to get below the pit's artificial horizon. Dupree landed face first and groaned as he slid another seven feet down the other side. I spun and put my aiming point on the bike rider's chest.

She was about twenty, thick in the waist and arms, and wore her hair in a Mohawk. She also had on night vision goggles and was surveying the area.

I jerked my head down when she looked in my direction. Two other motorcycles joined her.

I crabbed to where Dupree was struggling to roll over and helped him to his feet. We ran down an embankment, through several rows of trees, and onto the golf course. I sprinted across the fairway. Once I was in the opposite tree line, I found a low place and dropped my pack. I jerked the AN\PVS-7 free, turned it on, and slid it on my head, all before Dupree fell heavily beside me.

"Put your back to that tree," I said, pointing to where he wouldn't make a silhouette.

He scooted into position, then pulled out a rag, wetted it, and wiped blood from his face from where the gravel had lacerated him.

Meanwhile, I had my rifle ready as I scanned an artificially illuminated night. The sky, the ground, the trees were all different shades of green. I listened for the sound of a motorcycle, but didn't hear a thing.

Had they gone?

Had they decided to move on?

This was exactly the thing I didn't want—to be pinned down and lose time. I wanted us to be in and out, without interacting with the remnants of what had once been the Greater Los Angeles area.

Then I saw her.

She was on foot and sliding down the embankment we'd just come down. I saw her reach down to examine the gravel, probably noting where we'd disturbed it. Then she looked up... a hunter.

I glanced at Dupree and put my finger to my lips. When I looked back, she was gone.

Damn!

There was a trick an old sergeant had taught me when I was on guard duty one slick Fort Bragg evening. *If you look at a single thing, you tend to miss a lot of what's going on around you. Instead, look at nothing at all, and you'll have a better chance at seeing everything.* Now, fifteen years and an apocalypse away, I did just that. I stared at nothing, my gaze everywhere and nowhere at the same time.

One minute passed.

Then another.

Then I saw movement.

Miniscule, but it was unnatural, the round shape sliding around a tree near ground level. I snapped to the shape and made out the left side of a head. The ear. The chin. The nose. The singular optic from the NVGs pointing directly at me.

She had me, just as I had her.

How much time had passed? I suddenly became aware of our vulnerability. There'd been two others, right? So where were they? I know where I'd be if I were them.

"Dupree," I whispered. "Watch our six."

No response.

"Dupree."

Still no response.

I turned six inches and felt a barrel touch the back of my head. I didn't feel fear. I didn't feel despair. I felt *angry* that I'd let myself get into this mess. I let go of my rifle and slowly rolled onto my back. Someone ripped my NVDs free. The world went black for a moment until my eyes adjusted to the night gloom.

One man stood above me with an M16; another pointed an MAC-10 with a sound suppressor at Dupree.

The man above me whistled.

Fifteen seconds later Mohawk stood above me.

"Did you frisk them?"

"No, ma'am."

She squatted next to me. "Easy there, soldier. No funny stuff."

She moved me into a sitting position, then frisked me, removing all of my weapons and throwing my pack into a pile. When she was done, she flexicuffed my wrists and ankles. Then she did the same to Dupree. They went through our packs, separating the weapons into one pile, communications gear into another, and what was left into the final pile. When they came to the biker jacket, they stopped cold.

The one with the MAC-10 held it up for her to see.

She nodded, then turned to me. "Which one of you killed Lou?"

"Me," I said.

She appraised me with cold, unreadable eyes.

She had a nice three-inch scar on the right side of her face. A knife, maybe. Or shrapnel.

"Why'd you kill him?"

"So he wouldn't kill my partner," I said, telling the truth.

"What is he?" she asked.

I glanced at Dupree, who sat facing me, flexicuffed just like me. "He's a scientist. An ethnobotanist. We're here to figure out what's coming out of the area around the Twin Hives."

She exchanged looks with the other two.

"What do you know?"

I nodded towards Dupree.

He said, "You have animals exhibiting some alien strain of *Cordyceps ignota*. We saw humans with fungal growths much like those you'd find with *Ophiocordyceps unilateralis*, which seem to not only cause the host to serve as a vector, but to also create violent autonomous functions."

"The fungees," she said flatly.

He nodded. "Yes, the fungees."

She turned to me. "Who are you with?"

"OMBRA."

She raised an eyebrow. "For how long?"

"Since the beginning."

Her eyes widened. "I know you." She inhaled. "Hero of the Mound."

Now it was my turn to be surprised. The only way she could have known was if she was there. Mr. Pink needed a hero. We were being defeated at every turn and I just happened to be in the right place at the right time. I'd saved Thompson, who'd frozen, and fought off and killed dozens of Cray, all recorded through our EXO suit cams to be rebroadcast on the plasma TVs in the bunkers. "What unit were you with?"

"Romeo Six."

"You fought well. I remember when you brought back the remains of Romeo One Zero. I remember when you had our backs." I had another thought. "Where were you for Phase I?"

"Roswell."

"Where they kept the aliens?"

She snorted. "All they had was space junk. Now they have all the aliens they can handle. You up at Irwin, now?"

"Yep."

This was the moment. I could see it in her eyes. What to do with us? I knew that part of her wanted to let us go. We had a shared experience. We'd been in combat together and come out the other side.

"What now?" I asked, nudging.

She frowned. "Not sure. That you killed Lou puts a monkey wrench in things."

I regretted that we'd kept the jacket. "What was he to you?"

"He was in Romeo Six too."

I closed my eyes and shook my head. And I'd just killed him like it was nothing. "What was he doing with Devil's Thunder?" I asked, finally opening my eyes.

"He thought he'd have a better chance of survival. He wanted to get away from the 605 Wall."

"I hear Devil's Thunder likes to rape and pillage," I said evenly.

"There's no shortage of that anywhere nowadays." Her eyes hardened. "How'd you kill him?"

I could have lied, but I didn't. "I put a knife through his ear."

"From behind?"

I nodded.

"Did he even know you were there?"

I shook my head.

If she was going to kill me, she'd do it now. I could see my demise working through her eyes as she strained to find a solution that would be equitable to the memory of Lou, but also let me live.

Seconds passed.

"Who are you with? GNA?"

She grinned. "That shill? I didn't like him when he was on television. Why should I like him now?"

I shrugged. "He seems pretty popular."

"He just has good organization. I've known some who joined for the healthcare."

I snorted. "I knew people who joined the Army for that, back when there was health insurance."

"Lot of good that did them." She stared long and hard at me, then she stood. "Uncuff them," she said, pointing to the man with the M16.

He was tall, rail thin and bald except for tufts of hair clouding above each ear. "But he killed Lou."

"Lou knew what he was getting into when he left us." She shook her head. "Wrong place, wrong time. Now uncuff them."

"But Sandi!"

She whirled on him. "We talked about this when he left. What if he came against us? Would you give him your neck?"

He jerked his head towards me. "But he just stuck a knife in him."

"Steve! What would you have done if Lou had me in a corner? Wait for him to turn around?"

His shoulders sagged. "I liked Lou."

"Me too." She walked up to him and squeezed his

arm. "But he chose them over us. Phil, help them put their gear away. We're bringing them back to the farm."

Phil was about my height and I now noticed by the hang of the pants that he had a prosthetic left leg—something I'd become familiar with, after all the roadside bombs in Iraq and Afghanistan. His face was pocked with what I recognized as scars from embedded concrete. Another victim of an IED.

"Sure that's a good idea?" he asked evenly.

"I'm sure."

He nodded and began redistributing the gear they'd confiscated back to us. Once Dupree and I repacked everything, they gave us back our weapons and we were on our way. As we climbed back up the embankment to the gravel pit, I was completely aware that this was not how I thought this episode would end. Goes to show that life still had a few surprises left in it.

I'd like to share a revelation that I've had during my time here. It came to me when I tried to classify your species. I realized that you're not actually mammals. Every mammal on this planet instinctively develops a natural equilibrium with the surrounding environment, but you humans do not. You move to an area, and you multiply, and multiply, until every natural resource is consumed. The only way you can survive is to spread to another area. There is another organism on this planet that follows the same pattern: a virus. Human beings are a disease, a cancer of this planet. You are a plague, and we are the cure.

Agent Smith, *The Matrix*

CHAPTER ELEVEN

I RODE BEHIND Sandi, and Dupree behind Phil. We hugged the mountains as we headed west. Twice we saw groups of human scavengers, but they were going from house to house, filling wheelbarrows full of canned and boxed food. Eventually all of that would run out, and then what? If there was anyone left who wasn't a fungee, what would they eat? Remembering all of the movies they'd had us watch as a primer for our role at the end of the world, I found fault that they'd left out zombie films. At the very least *The Walking Dead* should have been something we were forced to watch and be tested on. I can just see some of the questions those silly scholars over at pre-invasion OMBRA would have come up with:

Did Rick shoot Shane because Shane had an affair with his wife, or because he was worried that Shane would ally the others against him and take over leadership of the group? What does this say about Rick's humanity? What does that say about his leadership?

Or:

Merle and Rick seem to be the antithesis of each other, but explain how they are really the same character assigned to different circumstances.

I almost laughed as I realized that I'd just done OMBRA's work for them. They'd never had to assign it to us. Those of us who had completed the training and survived were apparently capable of philosophy on the fly.

We eventually headed up Bonita towards Big Cienega Spring. At about a thousand feet, we turned down a lane and came to a wall of sandbags. A man came out with a headlamp and a shotgun. Another came out from the scrub to our left, carrying an AK-47. Once they saw who we were, we went in on foot, with Sandi and the others pushing their bikes through a break in the sandbags and around two switchbacks. Inside they had a motor pool consisting of nothing but motorcycles and a four-by-four, three sheds, a barn, and a two-story house of about twenty-five hundred square feet.

We were shown to one of the sheds, which looked like it had been set aside for guests or new recruits. We deposited our things, then went into the main house where a woman who looked eerily like the actress Kathy Bates awaited us in a very suburban-looking, shag-carpeted family room. She wore a housedress and sat in a La-Z-Boy rocking chair. A lamp rested on the table next to her. She drank tea from a blue mug that said 'I ♥ Cats.' She greeted us and asked us to sit.

"Sandi tells me you're a scientist," she said to Dupree without preamble.

"Doctor Norman Dupree, ethnobotanist at the University of Georgia." He glanced at me. "I'm now assigned to Task Force OMBRA at Fort Irwin."

"Who assigned you?"

"Acting Vice President Calhoun, Ma'am."

She arched an eyebrow. "I wasn't aware we had a government any longer."

"Most people aren't." He shrugged. "I'm not so sure it matters anyway. OMBRA seems to have the most resources, though, so it seems fair that I lend my efforts to theirs."

She glanced my way, then back at Dupree. "You're sure OMBRA has everyone's best interests at heart?"

Dupree nodded. "They want to survive, and they'll do everything in their power to do it. Sure, that includes being underhanded and unscrupulous, but then that's human nature, isn't it?"

She took a sip from her mug and examined us through the steam. I felt awkward standing in front of her. I thought we'd settled all of this outside, but then that had been with Sandi and her reconnaissance crew.

"Some would say that there's little chance to retain our humanity after this. What would you say to that?"

I stepped in. "We've been savage before. We'll be savage again. This is how we survive. We—"

"But at what cost? Should we survive if it means losing our humanity?"

I was about to answer, but I saw the subtle gesture from Dupree, so I let him.

"We have it in our very nature to survive," he said. "We can't *not* survive. Survival has been bred into us. Those of us who couldn't adapt to the savagery were eradicated from the gene pool eons ago."

"That doesn't answer my question." She smiled. "I asked if we *should* survive, if it means losing our humanity. What's your answer to that question, gentlemen?"

"Humanity as a word is merely the condition of being human. Humanity as a virtue," Dupree continued, "is associated with love, kindness, and social intelligence. You offering us a place to stay or sharing your tea is a sign of that virtue. So here we are at the end, and you're showing your humanity."

"Is that your answer?"

Dupree nodded.

"What if I was to say that I'm doing this out of selfish reasons... reasons wholly unknown to you that are completely my own? What if I was to say I was using you? Does that make me humane?"

Dupree nodded slowly as he spoke. "I think so. You *chose* these techniques to get your way. You could just as easily have *chosen* to torture us. This is the social intelligence aspect of the virtue."

"Interesting. What about you, Mr. Hero?" she said, addressing me. At my reaction to her choice of address, she added, "Sandi briefed me on your work in the shadow of Kilimanjaro. Very noteworthy. Are you aware of your juxtaposition in this tale with Hemingway's character Harry in *The Snows of Kilimanjaro*?"

"My juxtaposition?"

"Yes, how you and Hemingway's character both approached death."

"If I remember right, Harry died. I didn't."

"Is it as simple as that?"

Throughout Dupree's conversation, and now my own, I'd kept wondering what the point of this question-and-answer session was; whether, if we answered incorrectly, we'd end up killed. Sitting there in her lounger, drinking from her 'I ♥ Cats' mug, this woman could be a post-apocalyptic sphinx.

"Not quite that simple," I began slowly, recalling some of the conversations I'd both had and overheard in Phase I, back when we were locked up. "I approach death as an inevitability. I will die, therefore I'm not afraid of it. Hemingway's fascination with death is well-documented. Not only the way a man faced death in his fiction, but in his love for bullfighting. A friend of mine once said that *Death in the Afternoon* was Hemingway's love sonnet to bullfighting."

"And how did Harry approach death?"

"Selfishly."

"How so?"

"He cared only for what he was leaving behind and leaving undone. He had little concern for Helen, except to be contemptuous of her help." I shrugged. "I read the story several times and each time felt contempt for Harry. I didn't find him sympathetic at all."

"No compassion?"

"No. Not really."

She put her mug down, got up, and went to the kitchen. I noticed she wore pink furry slippers. I also noticed she carried a 9mm in a shoulder holster. Talk about juxtaposition. She came back with two plates and two warm diet sodas. She gave us each one. "Peanut butter and jelly. You two must be starving."

I grabbed mine and took several huge bites.

Dupree was a little less aggressive, but it was obvious he relished the extravagance. It was certainly better than our MREs.

She sat down heavily and watched us. When we were done she said, "Remember what you said about Harry?"

I nodded, washing the sticky peanut butter away from my teeth with soda.

"*The Snows of Kilimanjaro* could be a metaphor for our lives today."

"How so?"

"Harry is the population. Angry. Looking towards the past. Selfish. Grabbing for anything to survive. Not caring who they hurt. And you are Helen, Mr. Hero. You have to help them despite themselves. Remember in the story when Harry kept asking for things and she refused to give them?"

"Like the whiskey soda."

"Yes. *Tough love* is what we call it today. Social intelligence, as Dr. Dupree so eloquently provided, is your contract with saving them. It informs you on how you must interact with them. Sometimes to save something you have to cut away the dead or dying parts. Sometimes you have to let it figure its own way out. And then sometimes you have to step in to stop it from doing something terrible. Can you do that?"

"Sounds like an awful lot for one man."

She smiled quickly. "I mean the metaphorical you. I mean the heroes of the end days. People like you."

"I do that anyway." I shrugged again. "It's who I am."

"Yes, it is." She smiled and grabbed a remote control. She flipped it on and the television behind us came on, showing a documentary about Ancient Egypt. A DVD; for a second I thought that there might have been a live broadcast, but then I remembered how impossible that was.

Dupree and I glanced at each other quizzically. Then Sandi came into the room and beckoned us to follow her out. Once outside she turned to us, grinning so widely that her scar pulled at the corner of her mouth.

"Did she ask you a bunch of questions about humanity and the end times?" Sandi asked.

"I felt like I was part of a philosophy lecture," Dupree said, running a hand through his hair. "The peanut butter was scrumptious, though, so I guess it was all right."

I shook my head. "What was that all about?"

Dupree caught my eye. "You know who she looks like, right?"

"Kathy Bates, right? The one who sawed James Caan's feet off."

"That was a damn scary movie," he said.

"We get that a lot," Sandi said. "She definitely has that look, but she's not her." She shrugged. "Even if she was, it wouldn't matter. She's sort of our spiritual leader. This was her place. When we found it, she was being held by some thugs. We took it back from them and then fortified it. She only wants good people to stay here. Looks like you passed."

Me as a good person. Somehow I thought she might have made a mistake. No one who's killed as many people as I have, or done the things to others that I have, deserves to be called a good person.

As if she was reading my mind, Sandi squeezed my arm and said, "Trust in her. If she says you're good, then you are." She changed the subject. "We'll see you in the morning. I have to run a couple more patrols, then we'll talk about helping you get to the 605."

And she left us.

I turned to Dupree. "That was the strangest conversation I've ever fucking had."

"Wasn't so bad. Say, how'd you know so much about Hemingway?" He grinned. "Not to insult you, but I didn't know you were that well educated."

"Something Mr. Pink made us do."

He chuckled. "That Mr. Pink. He changes everything."

I agreed, but I'd be damned if I was going to say so out loud.

War is not an exercise of the will directed
at an inanimate matter.

Carl von Clausewitz

CHAPTER TWELVE

DREAMLAND FOUND ME soon after my head hit the pillow
on the military cot they'd provided.

The sound of drumming returned. In my dreams, I was
sitting in Point Fermin Park in San Pedro, overlooking the
green-and-blue Pacific Ocean as it crashed eternally into
the palisades. People moved around me and I should have
heard their conversation, but their words had no sound.
A terrier at the end of a leash barked silently. I couldn't
even hear the waves as six thousand miles of momentum
slammed them against the rocks at the base of the cliffs.
I couldn't hear the hoary rustle of the palms as the winds
shook them. The only sound was the *rat-a-tat-tat* of a
snare drum. I watched the horizon and listened for a time,
the martial insistence of the rhythm making me want to
march, to do *something*. I just didn't know what.

When I awoke, Dupree was standing over me, giving
me a sidelong look.

I stifled a yawn. I felt exhausted. "What is it?"

"You were having a conversation."

I pushed up on an elbow and tried to remember, even as
the wisps of the dream disappeared. "I remember the sea.
I remember the drumming. But that's all."

"Well, news flash. You were actually talking to someone."

"Are you sure?" I asked, searching his face. He nodded. "What was it I was saying?"

"You said that you'd come back for him. That you wouldn't leave him behind."

"Did I use a name?"

"You called him Thompson."

Cold shock lanced through me. "Are you sure you got the name right?"

"You used the name twice."

"What else did I say?"

"Your last words were, *What do you mean, you're nearby?*"

"You're certain I said that?"

"As certain as I am that we're having this conversation. Who is this guy Thompson?"

"We were in Romeo Three Recon together back at Kilimanjaro Base."

"I read the mission report. That was a rough battle."

"They all are." I ran my hand through my hair, trying to fully recall the dream, but it was no use.

Dupree cocked his head and seemed to want to say something. Then he turned away, evidently changing his mind.

I sat up fully. "What is it?"

"You called him a drummer boy. I think you said, *You're our little drummer boy*. Does that ring any bells?"

"He played in the Army band. He was undersized, too. I think there's an old Norman Rockwell painting of a young drummer leading an army. I can almost picture it. Whenever I saw Thompson, I'd think of that painting." I shook my head. "We left Africa without him. Mr. Pink said he was dead, but I knew better. I should have trusted my instincts."

"Do you often hear drums in your dreams?"

I jerked my head towards him, wondering how he knew. "Sometimes," I said carefully.

"Me too." He rubbed his forehead. "Ever since the mission started I've been hearing them."

What's worse than one person hallucinating? Everyone around him hallucinating the same thing. "What kind of drums do you hear?" I asked.

"Like the one you described."

And there it was. "You know, I always thought that was his way of communicating on a subconscious level. Several times during the Battle of Kilimanjaro I'd hear the drumming right before something bad happened. I got to where I'd trust it, believing without a doubt that Thompson somehow knew what was coming and was trying to warn me. Sounds crazy." I laughed. "I probably *am* crazy. Talking in my sleep. The sounds of a drum. What's next?"

"Don't doubt yourself too quickly. It could be true."

"That I'm crazy? No kidding."

"No, about him being nearby."

I stopped cold and turned to him slowly. "What are you talking about, Dupree?"

"It's not my specialty, but I know that the plan was to place an HMID near every active hive in order to interdict communications."

I shot to my feet and double-fisted his shirt. "How long have you known about this?"

"Weeks—months." He gulped. "I don't know."

"Did Mr. Pink tell you about Michelle, too? Did he

give you the whole story? Did he explain to you that I totally fucking failed her... that I couldn't pull the trigger? Was he laughing when he told you? I bet he was laughing, wasn't he?"

He struggled in my grasp, his eyes wide. I let go and backed away, my arms and hands shaking with adrenaline. What was I doing? Jesus.

I turned and balled my fists, watching them shake. I clasped my hands together and tried to ease my breathing. It'd been a long time since I'd had a PTSD episode. I flashed to the Mariachi band at Ports of Call in San Pedro and how I'd torn into them the day before I'd unsuccessfully tried to kill myself, foiled by the ubiquitous Mr. Pink. The three Mexicans in their over-the-top costumes hadn't deserved my anger. I can still remember grabbing one of their guitars and smashing it repeatedly over a table until it was nothing more than toothpicks, while yelling over and over *"I fucking hate Mariachis!"*

"No one ever told me about Michelle," Dupree said slowly from behind me. "I take it she was something special to you."

I didn't trust myself, so I didn't turn as I responded, "I loved her. She loved me. It's why she did what she did. Then when she asked me to set her free, I couldn't do it."

"It's a tragic irony. I think you'd feel this way regardless of what you did. Had you killed her when you had the chance, you might even feel worse."

I finally trusted myself to turn. "Sorry, Dupree."

He shrugged. "Had I known, I wouldn't have brought it up." He stuck his hand out to shake and I took it. Then he sat down.

I sat down on my cot as well.

We sat there facing each other.

I felt too awkward to speak. I'd fought people in the barracks before. Sometimes they'd deserved it. Sometimes they hadn't. It never really mattered. Soldiers had been fighting amongst themselves since Christ was a corporal. But Dupree wasn't a soldier. He was a civilian, a doctor. I felt uncomfortable around him. I guessed, when I looked at it, I was afraid of being judged by him. And now look at what I'd done. I'd given him the perfect opportunity to judge me as savage.

"My family survived the alien invasion," he said. He stared at his right hand in his lap. "A wife and two daughters. Gloria took care of us, feeding us, making sure we'd survive. I was sort of out of it. Stunned, really. It was like I was sleepwalking, those first two weeks. So I never realized that after the first week, our next door neighbor was systematically raping my wife every day. Martin had been a soldier and had more guns than I could count. He told my wife that he wouldn't kill us if she'd give herself to him. And the bastard was rough. She'd come home with black eyes and bruises on her arms. And you know what I did? Nothing. I really didn't notice."

He paused and as the silence widened, I felt the need to say something.

"Doctors call them the Four Fs of Post Traumatic Stress Disorder," I said. "Flight, Fight, Freeze and Fawn, the last being co-dependent. Freeze is a common option in the reptilian brain when neither flight nor fight is an option. With the alien invasion, we could neither run, nor could the average guy fight the Cray. We at OMBRA could only do it with our EXOs."

He began speaking as if I hadn't said a word, and when he did, it was with a voice so wretched it made me want to cry. "What I didn't know was that he was also threatening to rape my daughters. Jess and Chris were nine and eleven. They deserved a world better than what the Cray had given them. They deserved something better than what Martin represented. It all came to a head one evening when he broke into my house. I'd just begun to come out of my walking stupor when he burst in, a bottle of Jack in one hand, a pistol in the other. He told me what he'd been doing to Gloria, laughing the whole time. Then he told me what he was going to do to my daughters. My wife came at him with a kitchen knife and you know what he did?"

I was afraid that I did, so I didn't respond.

"He shot her point blank in the head. She fell like that guy Lou did. Straight to the ground. All the life gone from her. I stood there unable to move. Frozen. Fucking *frozen*. Then Martin laughed at me, grabbed Chris and took her in the other room. It wasn't her first scream, or her fifth, or her tenth that finally got me moving."

He looked up and caught me with a vicious stare. "It was her twenty-third scream. Know how I know that? Because I fucking counted them. I remember grabbing the knife from the floor and running into the other room only to find Chris naked and him trying to get his drunken penis into her."

He made a fist with the hand that had been resting on his lap as if it was around a knife handle. "I stabbed him twenty-three times, once for each of her screams. I killed him, then I threw up. I didn't hold my daughter. I didn't try and make her feel better. I didn't even apologize. Instead, I fell to the ground and cried, rocking myself like I was a five-year-old."

He blew out. "The next day I buried Gloria in the back yard. Then I took Chris and Jess to my sister's. She lived about ten miles away. Throughout the walk, no one said anything. When I got there, I turned them over to my sister, who was much more capable of taking care of them than I was. Then without saying a word, I left."

"You didn't say anything?" I couldn't help but ask.

"What was there to say? I'd completely let them down. I was a complete and utter failure as a man, a husband, and a father. Which is why I left. I might be a failure at those things, but by God I will *not* be a failure at being a scientist. Do you want to know why I smile all the time? Because it takes fewer muscles to smile, and I'm tired of my face fucking hurting all the time."

The land is sacred. These words are at the core of your being. The land is our mother, the rivers our blood. Take our land away and we die. That is, the Indian in us dies.

Mary Brave Bird, Lakota

CHAPTER THIRTEEN

WE ATE LATE and it wasn't until noon that we were dressed and ready to move out. Mother was definitely everyone's spiritual leader. The rough, the dirty, and the mean, they all melted in her presence, much like a dog would to its master, no matter how mean the cur. It worried me. Never one to let someone else's good ideas get in my way, I had no doubt that if she told them to kill us, they'd do it with a joyful alacrity.

Then, of course, there was Dupree. He was back to smiling again. Regret was perhaps the worst emotion one can have. Tie that with the shame of not lifting a finger as your wife was killed in front of you, and you're living in an abyss of self-hate. I frankly didn't see how he could live with himself. At least I'd tried to save the eleven men I'd lost in combat before the alien invasion, not to mention everything I'd done to try and save my recon mates at Kilimanjaro. I'd once heard a sergeant tell me, *The measure of a man is not how they react when times are good, but how they react in the face of an emergency*. It all comes down to fight, flight, or freeze, and I'd always chosen to fight.

The day was one of those Southern California fall days, with a bright blue sky that seemed to go on forever. It was somewhere near eighty degrees. The air was cleaner than I ever remembered it, probably because the four million residents weren't stuck in vehicular Sargasso Seas on the 10, 405, and 5. It was the sort of day that would find me kayaking the Port of L.A. Harbor or biking in Rancho Palos Verdes; maybe finish it off with a cold beer and a few slices of pizza while looking down at the ocean.

Then I turned to Los Angeles and beheld the change the aliens had already wrought. The Twin Hives rose like daggers thrown through the heart of the once great city. For all of its disparagers, Los Angeles had been the cultural and social heartbeat of the world. No other city had as much effect on the hearts and minds of the citizens of Earth as Los Angeles. And all down to the electronic successor of the Stone Age campfire.

My eyes were drawn to the southern extremes of the horizon. Somewhere over there was the Vincent Thomas Bridge, where my journey with OMBRA began. I'd chosen that bridge to jump from because my favorite movie director had jumped from it.

Movies.

Television.

Hollywood.

Just when 3D movies and surround sound were the norm, it was all ripped away, replaced by a reality far uglier than even Tony Scott could have produced with his directorial genius.

Back at the Twin Hives, a black blanket of growth

spread in all directions, all the way to El Monte and Montebello nearest the 605. The alien plant.

"What makes it black?" I mused.

"There are a couple of things that could contribute to that," Dupree told me. "Black plants are extremely rare in the natural environment. They've demonstrated lower maximum CO_2 assimilation rates, higher light saturation points, and higher quantum efficiencies of photosystem II than green plants—that's the first protein complex in the light-dependent reactions of oxygenic photosynthesis."

I think I almost understood what he said. Certainly enough to ask, "If they're more efficient, then why aren't there more black plants?"

"Black plants normally grow slower than green plants, which makes the rapid growth rate of this very interesting. I also wonder if it's using oxygenic photosynthesis, or something else."

"Whatever you said, it sounds bad."

"Oh, it is. It means that the plant isn't producing oxygen, but something else... something necessary for an alien species to exist... something that might be toxic to us."

I shook my head. "I'm used to seeing a problem, then shooting it or blowing it up. We can rebuild our electric grid. We can make new toasters. But now they're messing with the planet on a chemical level. How can we ever hope to deal with this—this terraforming?"

"I think once we find the interrelation between the various species being used to terraform, it will point to what we should expect from the master species that's coordinating this. Like the Sirens and the Cray, this fungus was either engineered or curated. The Sirens reported; the Cray ruined our defenses. Now the fungus is causing the human race to turn on themselves."

"And the plant?"

"It could have multiple functions, but the one that scares me the most is its ability to alter the oxygenation of the atmosphere." He shook his head. "I'm afraid we're going to have to go down there in order to find out."

"Mother figured that's what you'd want." Sandi joined us, with Phil close behind. She pointed to where the route cut south, through Los Angeles all the way to Seal Beach. "I know you've been traveling at night, but it's more dangerous then. We've gotten reports of infected animals, like those coyotes you killed last night, as well as infected persons."

"Interesting," Dupree said. "It could be caused by the pollination cycle of the plant. It could be nocturnal rather than diurnal."

I'd never heard of night blooming plants. "Why would it bloom at night?"

"It would depend on the relationship with the pollinator. I suspect that whatever pollinates the flowers does so only at night. If so, it would explain why there is more activity then."

"That's not why we're concerned about it being more dangerous at night," Sandi said. When we turned to her, she explained. "We just can't see the dangers at night. Between the fungees and the spikers, this fungus is spreading quickly. We've noted that they don't attack each other, but will attack the uninfected."

Dupree nodded. "That makes sense."

I turned to look at him. Of course, he was grinning. "No, it doesn't. It's fucked up."

He looked at me like one of my sergeants had when I'd said something stupid as a brand-new-doesn't-know-shit private. Then he spoke. "It could be a variance in light absorption. Fungi react to light in various ways. Light has long been known to be a source of information as well as illumination. Light causes adaptation in metabolic pathways, but it can also cause the onset of reproduction. If the fungi were to somehow affect the optical acuity of the host, it could possibly tell which biological organisms are infected by the nature of light absorption." He spread his hands. "Or not. Just a guess, I suppose."

He turned to me. "We're going to need environmental suits. We don't want to be anywhere near these plants without one. I don't know how far the fungus spores can travel."

Sandi tapped me on the shoulder. "We have a shipping container full of them we lifted from a dive shop. They're Viking HDS Dry Suits, which are hazmat rated. We also have oxygen tanks and an oxygen generator, so we can fill them if needed."

Dupree and I exchanged glances.

"You all seem to have thought of everything," I said.

"Mother gave us a list several weeks ago. She said we'd be needing them." Sandi paused to make sure I was paying attention. Then she added, "She knew you were coming."

"Of course she did." I made a mental note to watch our six. The best-meaning people followed David Koresh and Jim Jones right up until they went completely bat shit crazy. Mother might be no different. If she or her followers were going to construct their own version of the End Times, I didn't want to be anywhere near it.

Ever notice that these alien vines look a lot like kudzu? It used to be that alien vine was something that grew down South, covering anything that stayed in the same place for more than a minute. Now it looks like this alien version has been engineered to be something terrible. Stay away from the alien vines. Stay as far away as you can. For those who go in never come out.

Conspiracy Theory Talk Radio,
Night Stalker Monologue #1371

CHAPTER FOURTEEN

TWO HOURS LATER we were ready to go. But before we did, I took a moment to pull Dupree aside. I felt it was important to acknowledge his importance to the mission. I also felt it was my duty to make sure we had a connection. So while Phil, Steve and Sandi prepared the truck, I had a private moment with the smiling man who was busy readying his own equipment.

"This is it." I squeezed his shoulder. "Are you ready?"

"Like no one else. To think that in a few hours I'll be able to touch an alien organism."

"Well, let's not get ahead of ourselves. I imagine there's going to be forces at work to keep us from engaging."

The smile didn't budge. "I'm sure you'll figure something out. Not only do I need to take samples, but

I'm curious to see what the portable gas chromatograph detects beneath the canopy." He held up a nozzle, at the end of a small hose. "This is the sniffer here. That OMBRA has them already built is a nod to their dedication to the project. Something like this must have cost them billions."

I shrugged. "What's money when civilization ceases to exist?"

This made him laugh.

"Seriously, though, I want to thank you for opening up. We've all had it bad. Some of us have had it worse. But to have you here now, with me, on this mission, makes me feel like I have the absolute best and brightest with me."

His smile slipped. "You trying to give me a pep talk?"

"I'm a little out of practice. How'd it sound?"

"Contrived."

"Okay, then how's this." I put an arm on his shoulder and stared into his eyes. "Don't fucking get killed out there, because we need you."

I let go of his shoulder and stood back, raising my eyebrows as I gauged his reaction.

"Much better. I almost believed it that time." His smile slowly returned, like armor to be put on or taken off. "What do you think of Mother?"

I glanced over to where the other three were loading the oxygen tanks, to make sure they couldn't hear. "I didn't feel threatened and I didn't feel scared or worried, but that actually worries me. She has some sort of crazy charisma." I shook my head. "There's really no telling what she's capable of doing."

"Or willing to do. I've read about cult leaders before. What if she makes us drink some cyanide Kool-Aid?"

I nodded. "My thoughts exactly. But at least she

thought ahead enough to get hazmat suits. Last thing I want is to turn into one of the fungees. That stuff has made our world into one scary place."

"The problem is that you never knew how scary a place it was before. Parasitic species live all over the world. Ever hear of the *Leishmania* parasite spread through the bite of the *Phlebotominae* sand fly, which can affect the spleen, or liver, or even your bone marrow?"

I could swear his grin got wider as my frown deepened.

"And then there's Chagas Disease, and Granulomatous Amoebic Encephalitis, and the African Eye Worm, and the Tse Tse fly that spreads African sleeping sickness. Or worse, Nodding Disease, which kicks off ever increasing waves of epileptic seizures. Ever seen that? Parents have to chain their children to poles so they won't hurt themselves or someone else. Ever been into a village where children are chained to poles? Jesus, Mary and Joseph, it's a sight you can't unsee. Or even the simple botfly, which hatches and comes to term beneath human skin, climbing out of a rupture so it can find someone to do it all over again."

I was overwhelmed by information. I'd been happy to have been just a grunt, never having known any of this. "You. Have. Got. To. Stop."

He shrugged. "Just trying to let you know what you've been missing. Trust me, I can go on for days."

"Please, no."

We were interrupted by Sandi, who declared they were ready to go. They had loaded our gear into a black four-by-four pickup truck rigged for urban survival.

As we strode to the truck, I turned to see Mother standing on the front porch, smoking a corncob pipe, her eyes tracking us, her face blank. Smoke coiled in front of her face, but she made no move to blow it away. Her hair was set in old fashioned curlers. Finally she nodded imperceptibly towards me.

I returned her nod.

The truck looked like something out of *Mad Max*. Extra metal was welded everywhere to deter anyone trying to climb aboard, including a corrugated metal canopy with three inch holes. The holes, in turn, were covered with a fine screen mesh. The same metal and mesh covered the front and side windows. To enter, one had to either slide through the missing partition window or climb through a locked entrance at the tailgate.

"What's that for? Bird protection?" I asked in jest.

Phil stubbed out a cigarette and gave me a cold stare. "You really don't know what you're getting into, do you?"

I felt my grin tighten. "Why don't you tell me?"

Steve reached out to grab Phil's shoulder, but Phil shrugged it off. He glared at me. "I know you're a soldier," he said, "and you have all this great equipment and eat three squares a day and project outside the wire every now and then, but there are those of us who have been fighting every day since the invasion. While you've been in your mess halls and playing video games, we've been struggling to survive—street level, with the everyday promise of death."

He paused to light another cigarette.

I stood there, striving for patience I rarely had.

He sucked in smoke, then exhaled violently and gestured to the tire guards. "These are to protect us against the spiker plants, which can take out tires as easy as anything."

He pointed to the metal jutting from the sides of the truck at forty-five degree angles. "These are to stop fungees and spikers from getting close enough to the truck to grab hold."

He pointed to the mesh. "This is to keep birds and insects from getting in." He tapped his forehead with his forefinger. "Don't you get it, soldier? *Everything* out there is infected. The pigeons are as dangerous as a fucking tiger and attack anything they can."

Sandi came up and stood in front of him, her back to me. She placed both hands on his shoulders and said something I couldn't hear.

I'd encountered Phil's type of anger before. No one likes for someone to come in and take over their missions. It's happened to me, and I've done it to others. I'm sure Phil and Steve were as good as or better than anyone I'd ever served with. That they were still alive more than a year after the invasion was testament to their abilities. Still, if we were to succeed at the mission, it had to be as a team, rather than as a few pissed-off individuals.

Phil shook his head at something Sandi said, then stalked to the other side of the truck, where he began to slide into his kit.

Sandi turned to me and spread her hands. "So I see he gave you the guided tour."

Nicely played. "Is it really an issue with the birds?" The thought of being attacked by a flock of contagious birds seemed suddenly terrifying.

"Not so much anymore. Early on, as the black alien vine spread, birds were getting infected in droves. But they also attacked in flocks. Most of them have long since died. Now we get the occasional migratory bird that stumbles into the black alien vine footprint." She shook her head. "It's nothing as bad as it was."

"And the insects?" Dupree asked.

I remembered his description of the Amazonian ant. Of *course* insects could be carriers. Was I to be worried about ants and gnats and flies, as well? How could we hope to keep from being infected?

"As far as we can tell, the insects are infected, too. They're moving like a bow wave in front of the alien vine as it encroaches."

Dupree nodded. "There'd be a gray zone between the infected insects and the non-infected. Whether it's the deimatic behaviors exhibited by the infected or pheromones, non-infected insects would flee to the best of their ability. Of course different modes of locomotion would result in complete infection of some species before others as they are overrun."

I frowned. "You mean the faster bugs would win."

"Not just fast; flying bugs as well."

I stared at the mesh and shook my head. "So the butterfly is as deadly as a pterodactyl."

Steve came around the back of the truck in a hazmat suit without the mask and helmet. He looked like a black Michelin Man. "Thank God pterodactyls are extinct."

Sandi showed us to our suits and we wedged ourselves into them. The Viking HDS Dry Suits were made of vulcanized rubber. They were form-fitting and bulky. It was probably different in the water, but on land it was like I was wearing five layers of clothes. Still, it was better to wear this than to be exposed to infection.

We had our packs in the back of the vehicle just in case we needed them. I managed to rig a holster for my pistol on the right side of the suit. A bag clipped to the left held the flexible helmet. A rack of oxygen tanks which we'd use once we got closer to the action lay in the rear of the truck.

Phil got behind the wheel, and Steve sat beside him. Sandi rode in the back with us. She held a MAC-10 across her knees and wore black wraparound glasses.

"Let's hit it," she said through the back window opening.

The truck lurched forward and we headed down the mountain. Instead of following the 210, we turned north until we found Sierra Madre Avenue and took it west.

Several people stopped scavenging long enough to watch us pass. We didn't encounter much vehicular traffic.

During the first ten miles, we saw a lone motorcycle weaving through a line of wrecked cars. The rider wore a gas mask beneath a spiked black helmet, and had a sawed-off shotgun in a holster on his back and another holster affixed to the gas tank that held what looked like a semi-automatic pistol. He looked our way once, but made no move towards us.

We passed a side street where a pickup was idling at the curb. While a woman stood at the back of the truck with an AR-15, a man carried food from a home in a plastic laundry hamper. They just stared at us as we passed.

I guess we were the new normal.

Then things changed.

I felt the vehicle slow and I glanced out the windshield. A traffic circle lay ahead of us; across it was a school bus.

"Where'd that come from?" Sandi said. "Wasn't there yesterday."

Phil slowed to a stop about a hundred yards away.

"See what it says on the side?" Steve said.

We all saw it. On a white background beneath the windows, in sprayed red letters, were the words, *GOD'S NEW ARMY*. Beneath that in smaller letters it read, *NEW BELIEVERS WELCOME*.

Steve pointed to the left. "We could cross-country and then head south on North Dalton."

Dupree glanced in my direction. "What do they want?"

Sandi frowned. "Women, probably. Which makes you guys free to leave."

A man dressed in white, with a shock of shoulder-length blond hair, walked around the back of the barn. I aimed my 416 in his direction and zoomed in with my scope. White shoes, a white suit and a white tie, he looked every bit the southern preacher. I recognized his face. How could I not? He'd been a media darling for at least a decade. "Paul Sebring."

"Oh, hell." Sandi charged her submachine gun. "I was hoping to miss his reach. Phil, let's go four-wheeling."

"What do they want?" I asked.

"My guess? You."

"But can he know about our mission?"

"Must be someone up at Mother's."

I keyed in on movement from inside the bus. I zoomed in. Waited for the focus. Then—

"*Sniper! Everybody down!*"

I didn't wait for the other to shoot. I put two rounds into the sniper.

Sebring ducked as the glass exploded behind him. When he straightened, he was no longer smiling.

Phil threw the truck in gear and shot over the curb,

going south between a blue one-story cookie cutter home and a yellow two-story version of the same. The space along the side shrank to almost nothing as the metal on the truck's sides raked the wooden siding like the claws of some great animal against a gargantuan chalkboard. I held on and watched Dupree grit his teeth and close his eyes. Then, like a BB shot out the end of a straw, we were into the back yards.

Phil angled right to miss a shed, but it meant we hit a swing set square on, sending it up and over the truck in a clamoring of twisted metal.

We hit Desert Willow and swung left to the first intersection, and right onto Gardenia.

Sandi yelled to be heard. "You know we're heading square into GNA territory, right?"

Somehow Phil had managed to light another cigarette. As he took the next turn on two wheels, he said, "Not much choice." He jerked his head back the way we'd come. "With Big Ego behind us, I figured anything not in his direction was the right choice. I remember when they used to crucify members who tried to leave."

Steve pointed to a break in the trees to the right. "Through there."

Phil swerved into it. The truck bucked as it jumped the curb. Glancing towards Dupree, I think he'd decided it was best to keep his eyes closed through the entire chase. Probably a good idea on his part.

Sandi pointed to a pack of wild dogs, all with ascocarps protruding from their shoulders and heads. "Spikers!"

A mix of breeds from mutt to German shepherd to Chihuahua, they were already running to intersect us. The smaller dogs fell behind, but the larger ones, including the shepherd and a pair of Brittany Spaniels, were able to reach us before we passed, leaping towards us like kamikaze canines. All but one were stopped by the metal. A brindle greyhound hit the side of the mesh near where Dupree sat, clawed at it for a moment, then fell away.

"What was that?" Dupree said, his head whipping back and forth.

"Spiker dogs trying to eat you through the cage," I said.

He turned and stared, eyes wide. Then he scrambled to grab his helmet from the bag at his hip. With shaking hands, he put it on.

"What are you doing?"

He pointed to the spot the dog had hit. "Spores."

Sandi shook her head. "We're going too fast for that. You only have to worry about them once we stop, or if we get into the alien vine."

Phil shouted, "Hold on!"

I grabbed for the sides of the cage and watched with horror as we slammed into a corner of a Spanish-style stucco house. The impact shook me all the way to my teeth. The wheels were still spinning as they tried to find traction, grinding us against the side of the house.

Several of the spikers were still on our tail.

To the left came a shirtless woman whose head looked as if it had been burned: hair almost completely gone; black skin over bright red wounds. Fungal growths dotted her shoulders and neck, looking like distended nipples. She wore a pair of soiled panties and nothing else.

I raised my rifle, which put my aim just to the left of Dupree's head. He regarded me and I gestured him aside. As soon as he moved, I put a round through the rifle. It struck the metal around the mesh and ricocheted, causing me to jump. I aimed again, this time getting the round through the mesh. It struck her center mass in the chest, sending her rolling onto the ground.

I heard a buzzing sound about the same time Phil managed to get the truck free. It shot forward, throwing me off balance. I reached out and caught Sandi's breast, which earned me a punch in the sternum. I gave her an apologetic smile as I let go and transferred my grip to the truck.

Behind us came two motorcycles. Submachine guns were affixed to their fuel tanks. The riders wore full suits of racing armor with shin guards, knee guards, quad guards, articulated arm guards, and a full torso guard. They had red and white helmets that matched their armor. The prominent GNA on the front of their torsos said it all.

They opened fire as Phil jerked the wheel and punched the accelerator. We hit North Pasadena Avenue and slung south. The road was clogged with abandoned cars, so Phil was forced to careen onto several front lawns just to keep from crashing.

Sandi slid to the rear of the truck and fired her MAC-10 through the mesh, causing the riders to swerve to avoid getting hit.

Meanwhile the interior of Dupree's helmet was misted, the same sort of moisture you'd get on the inside of a car's windows if there wasn't any ventilation. *Oh Hell!* I clawed my way to him and fought to remove the helmet. He wasn't moving. The damned fool had put the helmet on and not the oxygen. What had he been thinking?

I found the connector and peeled the helmet from his head. As the truck bounced and jostled, I tried feeling for a breath. Nothing. I grabbed the back of his head and brought it to me just enough so I could make sure that he was breathing. I laid him down on the bed of the truck. That's when I noticed the blood coming from his left thigh. He'd been shot. I checked the wound and noted with relief that the femoral artery was undamaged. Had it been hit, poor Dupree would have already been dead. As it stood, the wound was barely bleeding.

Sandi fired off another burst of shots.

One of the bikers went down, ass over tea kettle.

The second biker fired twice more, then tore away, heading back the way he'd come. I guess without support from his partner, he wasn't willing to continue.

Hooray for our side.

Sandi pulled herself to the front of the back. "Let's get to Safehouse 3."

For the next twenty minutes, Phil drove the truck like an Indianapolis 500 professional race car driver. Twice fungees tried to block the way. Both times he swerved and clipped them, sending them tumbling like ragdolls into adjacent buildings. The number of spikers increased dramatically as we headed west.

We finally stopped at a small church wedged between Foothills Boulevard and the 210. The sign read *Indonesian Evangelical Church*. A gnarled Asian man held open a garage door. We roared inside, then he slammed it down and put several metal rods through the floor to secure it.

Dupree had come to a few minutes earlier, but he was deathly pale. I put a bandage over his leg wound. When they opened the rear of our cage, I helped him out. We soon found ourselves in the congregation hall, which had been set up with a meeting area near where the pulpit had once been, and cots where the congregation would have normally gathered.

While Sandi and the others secured the vehicle, I found a spare cot and got Dupree settled onto it. "What the hell were you thinking, putting the helmet on without checking for oxygen flow?"

He grinned weakly. "I forgot about the oxygen." He closed his eyes and winced. "Getting shot hurts, you know?"

"I know. It's why you try and avoid it at all costs."

"Where are we?"

"In some church. They called it a safehouse." I glanced around at the metal reinforced door and the barred windows and the men with rifles sitting round. "Looks pretty safe to me."

I turned back to Dupree, but his eyes were closed. His chest was rising and falling steadily, so that was a good sign. He might as well sleep while he could.

We've been cataloguing as many survival groups as we can. We have more than seven thousand in our database alone. Some are good but most are bad. If you can make it on your own, try to do that. Even the good groups have a bloody past which they could just as quickly return to if times got tough all of a sudden. Keep the information flowing, people. And remember, be careful out there.

Conspiracy Theory Talk Radio,
Night Stalker Monologue #1344

CHAPTER FIFTEEN

IT WAS MY bullet they found in his leg. Must have come from the ricochet. They were able to give him a unit of blood and had him on a drip just to bring back his fluids. As it turned out, the safehouse was run by Mother as one of her outstations. They were getting ready to abandon it to the creeping alien vine, much to the lamentations of Pastor Mercurio, the Indonesian leader of the long-gone congregation. Even now preparations were being made to move this part-forward operating base, part-MASH unit to somewhere in the foothills. Their only problem was trying to keep free of GNA.

"It's more than a cult to them," Sandi told me. "It's more than a religion. They're fanatics."

I kept my thoughts to myself. Mother and Sebring both had cults of personality and they both wanted for them and their members to survive. They seemed different sides of the same coin to me, although Mother occupied the definitely nicer side—or so it seemed, for now.

Now we sat around a table. Phil and Steve cleaned weapons. Mercurio wouldn't let them smoke in the church, so they were constantly going outside. I sat beside Sandi, and next to her was an ex-male stripper named Adam who had a face that looked somewhere between Richard Gere's in *American Gigolo* and a meth addict. He'd been showing Sandi a map of the infected areas that he was updating daily.

"It's crossed the 605," he said in a small voice. He pointed to several spots. "Right here it's all the way to Irwindale Road. We have no idea how it grew fast enough to reach there while the rest of it is still a mile back." He shrugged. "It's not like we even know how to stop it."

"See the Sante Fe Dam Nature Preserve?" Sandi said, pointing at the map. "The damned vines probably relished the soil. So much easier to grow in than concrete."

"I suppose so. That guy over there going to be able to tell us how to kill it?" he asked, his eyes darting towards where Dupree lay, softly snoring.

"We hope so. He's OMBRA's best and brightest." She flashed me a smile. "And this guy, the guy who shot him, is his bodyguard."

Adam sawed his jaws back and forth as he examined me. "Not much of a bodyguard, is he?"

I stared at him flatly. "No. Not much."

He jerked away as if I'd hit him. Good.

Sandi placed a hand over his. "How many more days?"

"Three, I think, maybe four." He licked his lips. "It's not just the alien vine, it's what comes out of it. There's some sort of bird that lives inside. We have yet to see one close up, but we think it's alien, as well."

"Maybe it's the pollinator," I murmured. Then when I saw them staring at me, I shared what Dupree had told me earlier.

"It's good that you came along when you did," Sandi said to me.

I shrugged. "Like Adam said, I'm just a bodyguard and not very good at that." I suddenly flashed to Michelle begging me to kill her. I shook my head and changed the subject. "You said Sebring was there for *us*."

She patted Adam on the shoulder and he simpered away to one of the cots. "He had to be. There's no reason for him to be so far away from his center of control. You must have something he wants."

"Not me. Must be Dupree. But even that's strange. Why would he need a scientist?"

"He's as desperate as any of us to stop the spread of the alien vine. It's going to kill us all eventually if we don't figure a way to stop it."

"So he tries to steal a scientist?"

"It makes a sort of sense."

I shook my head. I wasn't buying it. "We're missing something."

We were getting nowhere fast. Our plan was to leave at first light. I checked on Dupree, then worked with Steve to fix the hole the bullet had made in his hazmat suit. We spent a fruitless hour trying everything from melting rubber to applying a patch, but the suit's material withstood the best we could throw at it. Finally it was decided that Steve would stay back and give Dupree his suit. He wasn't happy about it, nor was Sandi happy about taking a weapon out of the expedition, but without Dupree, there would be no expedition to begin with.

By the time we were done and had the vehicle prepped and ready, it was going on ten PM. Dupree had woken once. He'd spent an hour jotting down notes, then we'd given him some food and sent him back to dreamland.

I soon found myself drifting through an ethereal landscape of Tony Scott movies. One minute I was Denzel Washington playing the redemptive Creasy in *Man on Fire*, and the next I was Maverick, the hotshot pilot in *Top Gun* who was brought to earth by the death of his best friend. Then, for what seemed like an eternity, I was stuck in Michael Rapaport's living room in *True Romance*, smoking joints with Brad Pitt and all he could talk about was about having sex with Angelina Jolie. It was the sort of thing where I knew it was a dream, but was unable to change it. I let it take me for a ride as Pitt droned on and on, getting increasingly more detailed and imaginative, until I was suddenly on a submarine, staring into the mad eyes of Gene Hackman. I knew that somewhere aboard ship Denzel was arguing with a crewman about the relevance of Jack Kirby's Silver Surfer over Stan Lee's version while he planned a mutiny to take the *Crimson Tide* away from Gene Hackman.

My fucking dreams were always like this. Was this what it meant to be a child of the 'nineties?

"Belay that order," Hackman said.

I turned to see who he was talking to. There was no

one behind me, so it was apparently me. I turned back only to have his face now an inch from my own, so close I could see the pores on his nose.

"I said to belay that order."

"Yes, sir," I began, then corrected myself. "Aye aye, Captain."

"You do know what to belay, right?"

The timbre of his voice changed from the deep baritone that loved arguing about the color of Lipizzaner stallions to something tenor and almost familiar.

"Belay! Belay! Belay!"

He screamed so loudly into my face that I jerked away and fell backwards, onto the deck. My head hit metal and I saw stars. Then came a sound like someone banging on the outside of the sub. At first I thought it was the sounds the metal made as the water pressure changed, but they were too regular; they sounded almost like drums.

I opened my eyes as I suddenly recognized the voice.

For a brief instant Gene Hackman's face was replaced by the boyish, button-nosed face of Tim Thompson.

Then I was underwater, arms flailing, breath exploding, chest bursting...

Drowning.

It doesn't take a hero to order men into battle. It takes a hero to be one of those men who goes into battle.

General Norman Schwarzkopf

CHAPTER SIXTEEN

WE LEFT ON foot the next morning, dressed in full hazmat suits with a four-hour supply of oxygen. I'd tried several times to radio in our position, but we were too far away from any of the re-trans stations. So instead of carrying a heavy doorstop, I left the radio at the safe house. I carried my HK416 in a sling, my Sig in a shoulder holster and a knife belted to my thigh. I could move well, although it felt awkward. The gloves limited my tactile sensitivity. The plastic viewport in the helmet both constrained my vision and caused it to warp as each step made the flexible helmet shift, sag or tighten, depending on how I moved my head, sometimes making the world seem like a moving acid trip. I couldn't help being reminded of the EXO I'd worn months ago, and wished I had it now. But it was going through some upgrades, specifically extending the battery power. As it stood, the EXO didn't have enough power for this mission. But still, where the EXO had heightened my abilities, this hobbled them. I needed to remember that. I couldn't count on my reactions to save us. I had to plan. I had to be careful.

Sandi wore her weapons the same way I did, although she carried a MAC-10 and a Beretta 9mm.

Dupree carried an HK416. If he had to use it, we were definitely in trouble. He walked with a limp, which made travel slower.

Phil was the happiest of us all. He carried a flame thrower and still wore the shit-eating-Merry-Christmas grin he'd had when Sandi first belted it onto him.

Dupree was in a decidedly good mood, especially considering I'd shot him the day before. Not that he knew that. He assumed he'd been shot by one of the GNA bikers. I certainly wasn't going to correct him.

Situated in a residential neighborhood, the safehouse stood between two east-west streets—Fifth and Sixth Avenues. These were broad affairs which still had occasional traffic. We wanted to avoid any interaction for as long as possible, so we left the safehouse by the back door and moved carefully between neighborhood homes. Phil was on point, the tip of the igniter nozzle already glowing with a small flame. Sandi brought up the rear. Dupree and I were in the middle.

I'd screwed a suppressor into the S4 barrel of my pistol. If we were going to need to fire, I wanted to make sure that we weren't heard right up until the point when it happened. I carried it at high ready, with the barrel pointed upwards and both hands on the grip.

We'd managed a block and a half before we startled a man sliding out of a window. He had the look of an animal. His face was dirty, his broken-nail-tipped hands were filthy, and grime coated every inch of visible skin. He regarded us for a moment, then bolted. We let him go. He was just hungry.

We reached North Vernon Avenue and paused at

the corner of a home. We'd heard engines for several minutes now and seemed to have discovered their locus. A GNA bus was parked down the block. Two armored men sat on motorcycles nearby. One of them could have been from yesterday, they looked so similar. Or it could just be their uniform. We could see through the metal-mesh windows that the bus was already half-full. As we watched, several men in full battle rattle and body armor were pushing people into the bus. I could see the rabbit that'd bolted from us earlier sitting uncomfortably in a seat. I watched as the last man was forcibly sat, and guessed as the guard did something out of sight that he must be handcuffing the man to something inside the bus.

True believers, my ass.

A vision of Charlton Heston yelling *"soylent green is people!"* played through my mind.

I felt my lips curl. I didn't like what was happening. These men were bullies and needed to be stopped. I fought the urge to do violent things but still couldn't stop myself from stepping forward.

Sandi pulled me back. "What are you doing?"

I gritted my teeth. "Nothing."

She saw the pained look in my eyes and nodded. "I don't like this anymore than you do, but we have to consider the mission."

She was right, of course.

Then she added, "Look at it this way. Maybe they're just getting them out of harm's way in the advance of the alien vine."

I nodded. It made sense.

We waited another ten minutes as they closed up shop and headed south, back towards GNA territory. We listened until we could no longer hear the sound of the motorcycles before crossing the street.

I caught movement out of the corner of my eye. I spun, but it was only three large black birds sitting on a wire. One must have moved its wing. I was about to turn away when all three took flight.

Directly towards us.

"Phil! Right!"

He turned and let out a roiling cloud of enflamed fuel, catching the birds ten feet out.

We stepped aside as they crashed to the street. Two were already dead and smoldering. The third flapped miserably in a circle, its wings half burned away.

I walked up to it, placed the heel of my boot on its neck, and put it out of its misery.

When it stilled, I turned towards Dupree. "This fungus is going to be the death of us."

He frowned. "Let's hope not, because that's their exact plan."

We reformed and crossed the street, now even more aware that threats could come from the sky. When I was about ten, I'd been in a field in Nebraska with my class. Our science teacher had been droning on and on about the life cycle of corn and how it was part of every stage of our lives when a flock of starlings suddenly appeared. They began to form complex, undulating shapes in the air. Mr. Kurtz—that was his name—called it a murmuration and said that it was a protective response. He pointed out a hawk on the outer edge of the swirling cloud of starlings. Like most of my classmates, I was mesmerized by the ever-twisting, constantly-changing avian ballet and couldn't tear my gaze away.

I remembered how in awe I'd been at that moment, as

nature revealed one of its hidden beauties to me. But now I was in fear of such a thing, re-imagining that moment, but with infected starlings murmurating in anticipation of an attack. Ten thousand beaks, rending, tearing, and ripping through hazmat suits, flesh, scraping bone, spores from their ascocarp spikes infecting us even as we lay dying.

Beautiful and deadly.

I hoped I'd never see such a horrendous thing.

"Look at that." Dupree rushed over to an animal corpse lying against the curb.

"Dupree!" I called, but there was no stopping him. I ran behind him, checking the ground and the sky for any threats.

He could barely contain his excitement. "Just like *Cordyceps ignota*. Remember the tarantula ascocarps I told you about? Look."

The dog had probably been an average mutt, one you would see playing with kids, or sitting on a porch, or rooting around in a neighbor's garden for moles. It had been brown and white with a smattering of black spots. Now the spots were pierced by long, cylindrical growths that branched out to look a little like antlers. These were even longer than the ones we'd seen on the dogs that had chased us earlier.

"They probably grew until the dog couldn't carry them anymore, their roots wrapping themselves around internal organs and squeezing." Dupree leaned in close to examine a particularly long, white-colored ascocarp. He glanced up at me with the look a million little boys had given their fathers. "Can we keep it?"

And just like a million dads, I shook my head. "We'll get one somewhere else."

He appeared to consider my response, then nodded. "Yeah. You're probably right." He stood. "Note the difference between the fungal growths on animals versus those on *Homo sapiens*. It's interesting that there's different infection vectors. I'd think it would be more efficient to have a single mode of infection."

"Maybe they don't work on everything."

He grinned. "That's exactly right. The difference in the mycelia could be because of the need to produce alternate actinobacteria. We'll make a scientist out of you yet, Lieutenant Mason. Good catch."

The idea of sitting behind a desk and staring into a microscope was right up there with scrubbing toilets or folding underwear. I shuddered internally, but knew I was safe from that fate, especially since I didn't understand half of what he'd said. "If you're done playing with dead things, we should be getting along."

We hit Bayless Street, a small east-west street, and decided to follow it to its end at Zachary Padilla Avenue. This was our cue to turn south. We had to cross the 210. But that was regularly patrolled. Zachary Padilla Avenue ran over the 210 with high side-walls originally designed to deter people from throwing things out of car windows onto the cars below, but which would now help screen them from sight. That is, unless the bridge was a chokepoint and there were people waiting for folks just like us to come haplessly across.

Phil stayed behind with Dupree while we checked the overpass.

Sandi took left.

I took right.

We both hugged the sidewalls as we combat crouched

quickly forward. Our pistols were out and in front of us at the ready.

The overpass rose to a crest, then descended back down on the other side of the 210. We couldn't see over the crest until we were halfway up the incline. Sure enough, two cars were pulled nose to nose to block our path. But I didn't see anyone as I swept my pistol barrel back and forth, seeking a target. I decided to double my speed. Running on my toes to reduce the noise, I made it to the car just in time to see two men glance in my direction.

They were making ramen on a portable propane stove. Both were Hispanic. One held a pair of chopsticks in his hand; the other held a .357. I noticed the body of a woman lying on a pile of purses, her pants removed, cigarette burns on her legs. I shot the one with the .357 in the head, then turned my gun on the second man. He dropped his chopsticks, sneered, and reached for his weapon as I double-tapped him in the face.

Both of them down, I slid over the hood of the car and onto the other side. I searched for a third man, but didn't see anyone.

Sandi vaulted over the hood of the other car. She swept the area with her pistol, then said, "Clear."

"Clear," I said.

Then we conducted a quick site exploitation. Besides various weapons and a food stash, we found a bag of rings, watches, and various jewelry. Like that shit meant anything anymore.

Dupree and Phil joined us. The scientist looked a little wide-eyed at the bodies, but didn't say anything. We were about to continue when I heard something. Muffled at first, it was someone pounding on the inside of the trunk of the car on the right. I told Dupree to pull the handle under the front dash.

When he did, we saw a middle-aged Asian woman, naked, bruised, and filthy. She regarded us with wide eyes. Yellow and blue bruises colored her face, telling of multiple beatings. The insides of her thighs and her breasts had the same mottling of old and new bruises.

I held out a hand, but she flinched away from it.

Sandi pushed me aside. "Come on. It'll be okay now." The woman hesitated for almost a full minute, before tentatively reaching out her hand, which I couldn't help but notice had broken and bleeding nails, probably from where she'd been trying to claw her way free of the trunk. Sandi helped her out of the car and leaned her a little unsteadily against a bumper.

Phil found a jacket in the backseat of the other car and gave it to Sandi, who then draped it over the shoulders of the woman.

Dupree stared at her, his mouth open, tears in his eyes.

I had no doubt he was reliving a part of his own past he never wanted to see again.

"What are we going to do with her?" I asked.

Sandi regarded me for a moment, then shook her head. "Nothing. She'll have to take care of herself."

"How—how can she?" Dupree's voice broke. "She needs... she needs..."

Sandi put a hand on his arm. "Those things don't exist anymore." Then she reached down, picked up the dead man's .357 and handed it to the woman.

She accepted the gun without looking, the weight of the pistol tugging her arm straight. I watched her eyes as they shifted from fear to determination.

"Come on," Sandi said. "Let's get out of here."

I took one last look at the woman, wondering briefly where she came from, where her family was, and if there was anyone she could go to. Then we left, Phil in front again as we descended the overpass. We'd gotten perhaps a block further when we heard a single gunshot.

No one turned around, not even Dupree.

Courage is rightly esteemed the first of human qualities, because, as has been said, 'it is the quality which guarantees all others.'

Sir Winston Churchill

CHAPTER SEVENTEEN

WE PASSED THE Northrop Grumman parking lot and reached a construction gravel pit at the end of the road. We looked across the pit and saw the black alien vine in person for the first time, a vegetative thickness on the horizon. Not so far off in the distance rose one of the Twin Hives. A few sentry Cray soared above it. There'd be more at night. Every step closer to the hives put the party in even greater danger. Fighting a Cray with an armored EXO was hard enough; they'd tear through the hazmat suits like they were made of paper. I checked my watch. We had six hours to get there and back. I didn't want to be anywhere near the alien vine in the dark.

The pit was clearly over a thousand feet wide. Skirting it would take too long, so we decided to go through it. Down below, in the center of the pit, rested two trailers, several pick-ups, and a large front loader. There was no sign of occupation, but we were wary.

I holstered my pistol and unslung my HK416. Distance was now more important than silence.

The uneven ground was tricky to traverse. I let Phil get well ahead of us; the last thing Dupree or I needed was for him to slip and fall and blow us all up. Even so, the grade was steep enough that we all fell at least once, Phil and me on our butts, Dupree on his side. Each time we checked the suits for rips or tears, but they remained sealed.

We made the bottom of the pit breathing heavily. My legs felt the stress of the descent. I couldn't imagine how Dupree felt. My face was hot and wet beneath the helmet. An itch had found a home at the base of my nose. I would've loved to scratch it away, but the suit wouldn't allow it. For a brief moment, I considered taking it off, but I'd seen enough of the fungees and the spikers to know that that's not how I wanted to end up. If it came to that, I'd do what that poor Asian women had done and end it myself.

Sandi and Phil decided they were going to clear the trailers, but I insisted on replacing Phil. Close Quarters Combat, or CQB, was a skill that required a lot of practice and trust between its practitioners. I knew that Sandi had that training from her association with OMBRA. Since we'd had much the same training, our level of trust in each other's ability would be greater.

The trailers were the same white single-wides I'd seen at construction sites the world over. Several of the mesh-covered windows had been broken. Doors hung ajar. They were arrayed in an L-shape, each with a set of faded wooden steps.

We were about thirty feet away when I held up my fist and we halted. There was no reason to rush. We needed to get a feel for the place. Observe it. Watch for motion.

I spoke low to pass the time. "So what's Phil's story?" I asked Sandi.

"He's Mother's nephew."

"So that's why he walks around like he has a stick up his butt."

"That and he's a piece of shit."

I glanced at her to see if she was joking, but there was no smile, no laugh. She was concentrating on the trailers.

"Well, at least he's our piece of shit," I said by way of a joke. After a moment I asked, "Why exactly is he a piece of shit?"

"He was a meth-head before the alien invasion. Lived in his parents' basement. Lit up one night and burned the whole place down. Killed his mother, father and little brother."

The alien invasion had leveled the playing field and given everyone a second chance. I'd met plenty of folks who'd done vile things. But when the fate of the Earth was at stake, they'd cast aside their selfishness and become brand new people.

There had to be something more here.

So I asked.

"Then what? Didn't he learn his lesson?"

Now she did turn to me. "He learned his lesson all right. Mother sent us after him. When we found him, he was at a convent up in the woods past Lake Arrowhead. He'd addicted fourteen women to meth and was exchanging the drug for sexual favors."

I turned to look at Phil. He could have been a grumpy neighbor. He could have been the guy who changes your oil. He could have been anybody.

She continued. "Two were grandmothers. Three were sisters. One was a double amputee from the Iraq War who'd gone to the convent pre-invasion to get her head straight. He tried to fight us, but we took him, tied him to a tree, and beat him for two days, then we took him back to Mother."

I realized that I'd been holding my breath. "What happened to the women? How are they?"

She shrugged. "I don't know. It wasn't my business."

"But they were addicted. They needed help."

"Didn't you hear me back there?" she snapped. "There is no more welfare. There are no more clinics. The world doesn't have those things anymore. The world as we knew it doesn't exist. We had nice things, but the aliens broke them."

I don't know what's worse. Knowing and doing nothing or not knowing at all. At least if you knew someone had a problem there was the opportunity to fix it. I stared at Sandi; her PTSD was front and center. Her method of dealing with stress was to push it away. How ironic that OMBRA's methods were to force everyone to deal with their stress, then help others deal with theirs. It was probably the reason she was no longer with the organization.

"Then why do you keep him around?"

"Because it's what Mother wants."

I got that eerie culty feeling again that I didn't like. It was time to get back to business.

"Which one do you want to take first? Left or right?"

"Let's do left."

The windows were too high to peek in, so our first look at the interior would have to be through the door. I didn't like the fact that the other door was so close and would be to our backs. It was a threat, and if this had been anywhere else, I would have thrown a grenade inside and be done with it. But this wasn't anyplace else.

There could be friendlies inside. And I didn't have a grenade anyway.

"Let's move in quick."

We stacked at the base of the stairs. Three wooden steps into the trailer.

"Ready. Steady. *Move*."

I surged up the steps, my rifle sunk into my right shoulder, grip tight, elbows in. I swung into the room, traversed from left to right.

Sandi came with me, dropping to a knee as she aimed her rifle on a lower level, traversing from right to left.

"Clear."

"Clear."

From our vantage we could see everything. The trailer was a large office with metal desks and chairs scattered around the room. The ground was covered with papers, maps and cardboard. At the far end was a bathroom.

I headed for it, taking small steps so I wouldn't slip on anything beneath my feet. Behind me, Sandi entered the trailer and put her back to the wall. She'd shoot anyone who came in the door. Towards the back I slowed. I thought I'd detected a sound coming from the bathroom, but the suit had a muffling effect and I couldn't be certain.

I brought the barrel low and curled it around the door frame. A black mass of hair stirred in the corner of the shower. Was it a dog? A cat? Then it shifted and I saw the white stripe.

I found myself in the awkward position of wishing it was a spiker.

Then it saw me.

Then it sprayed.

I realized that I was in a suit; not only could the vile liquid not get on me, but I couldn't smell it either.

It turned and glared at me with eyes colored red from my laser targeting light. No ascocarps. No fungus. It was just pissed that I'd barged into its barrow.

I turned and headed back towards the door. There were too many things dead out there to kill something for killing's sake. This one I'd let live.

As we exited the trailer we saw a pack of kids on top of the slope right above Dupree and Phil. They looked to be between five and fifteen. I counted roughly twenty of them. We were probably in their playground. With no construction workers and as out of sight as this place was, it would be the perfect place to do anything.

I was about to wave at them when something made me hesitate. I raised my sniper rifle to have a closer look and saw what I'd most feared: ascocarps.

They came bounding down the slope behind Phil and Dupree, who were oblivious to the threat. I began running towards them. Sandi opened fire behind me, which caused Phil to turn. As Dupree stared at me, still not knowing what was happening, Phil let loose with a great gout of flame that immediately engulfed a black-haired teenage boy and a red-headed girl who could have passed for Little Orphan Annie.

I cried out for them to stop, but knew they couldn't.

A fat kid fell, knocking two more kids off their feet. They rolled down the hill gathering speed, arms and legs flailing as gravity jerked them to its bosom.

Phil opened fire again, burning them even as they fell. But then he saw his mistake and he was too late. He scrambled to run, but the burning fat kid bounced and hit Phil in the face, carrying him ass over flame thrower.

The other burning kids came close to knocking Dupree down, but in the lucky drunken stumble I'd seen in professional winos, he somehow managed to come out unscathed as a burning kid rolled past on either side of him.

He saw me running for him and grinned his appreciation.

Then he went down.

A girl punched him in the groin and kept punching. As he hit back, another girl came and began to hit him in the head. He kicked the first girl away and tried to punch the girl hitting his head, but he couldn't find her. Somehow his helmet had gotten turned so the viewport wasn't near his eyes. So he did the only thing he could think of to protect himself, which was to roll into a ball like a giant pill bug.

All the while, Sandi had been firing. Most of the kids were down; if not dead, at least wounded.

I arrived at Dupree and butt-stroked the girl on top of him. Then I straddled him and began to fire.

Blam.

I killed a kid.

Blam.

I shot a girl through the head.

Blam.

I sent a bullet into the brain of a slender young man with a *Star Wars* T-shirt. Fucking *Star Wars*. Fucking Darth Vader. Fucking Princess Leia. If only we could have some civilized fucking aliens instead of the ones who wanted to terraform and destroy our children. Check that; to make the *survivors* kill the children.

They came at me and I took them out.

Sandi was doing the same near Phil.

Tears stung my eyes as I killed the last infected child. He was maybe five years old. The reason he was last was because his tiny legs couldn't keep up with the larger children. Blond hair and blue eyes—he should have been watching reruns of *Barney* or *Sesame Street* or whatever fucking shows kids watched before the alien invasion, not running at us infected with alien spores trying to spread the sickness. He got within five feet of me and I sent my final bullet into his head. I closed my eyes, not wanting to see. I heard him fall. I felt him roll at my feet. I pushed him away without even looking. Then I counted to ten, breathed deep, hitched up my big boy pants, and blinked the traitorous tears away.

I stepped aside and reached down for Dupree.

"Dupree! You okay?"

I turned him and saw that his viewport had been pierced by something sharp that had left a gaping hole four inches across.

He stared back at me more scared than I'd ever seen him. This was worse than a death sentence. Seeing the bodies of the children all around, some still smoldering, all I could think of was that if this was a movie, it certainly wasn't a science fiction movie. No, this was a horror film. All you had to see was the smoldering ruins of our future to prove it.

Extinction is the rule. Survival is the exception.

Carl Sagan

CHAPTER EIGHTEEN

I HELPED DUPREE to a sitting position. "It's going to be okay, man. We'll get this fixed and Charlie Mike," I said. *Continue mission*.

The scientist felt carefully around the lip of the broken plastic with his gloved hands. Dust had gathered inside and on his face. He pinched it between two fingers, then closed his eyes and sighed. He sat there for a moment, then looked at me. "Help me get out of this, will you?"

"Are you crazy? You need this."

"You don't understand. It's too late." He held up his black-gloved hands, covered in gray powder. "This is spore. It's already all over me."

My eyes widened. "But how? It's just a little break."

He gestured to a dead young girl lying not five feet away. Her face was dirty, but placid. Long red hair clung to her skin, partially covering the left side of her face. Dozens of round tuberous ascocarps covered her shoulders and neck. Each and every one had burst like a puff mushroom.

"It's all inside my mask." He got to a knee, then stood a little shakily as he began to fumble at the helmet.

I reached around behind him and pressed the locking

mechanism. Then I twisted and lifted. The helmet came away easily.

His dark brown hair lay flat against his head. Gray powder made a rectangular shape on his face. He concentrated as he removed his gloves, then peeled the suit down and stepped out of it. "Now I know where the term *monkey suit* comes from." He shook his head and *tsked*. "Last time I was this uncomfortable was at my senior prom."

"Because you took your mom?"

He glanced at me. "Because Rebecca said she'd let me into her pants that night and I'd gone out and bought my first condom. It was in my pocket the whole time and I could have sworn every teacher knew it was there."

He pulled a handkerchief from his back pocket and wiped his face as clean as he could. Then he sighed heavily. His shoulders sagged. His arms fell straight to his sides as he stared morosely at the ground.

"Do you want to go back?" I asked.

He took a moment to look at the dead children and shook his head. "They turned these children into vectors. If it's up to them, they'll turn the entire planet into a vector. No, let's Charlie Mike while I'm able. I was sent here to see the locus of the fungus, and by God I want to see it."

I grinned and squeezed his shoulder. "Okay, then."

I went over to where Sandi squatted by Phil. "How is he?"

"Dead. Neck's broken."

His head was turned at an impossible angle.

"I see you're broken up about it."

She stood. "Piece of shit should have suffered more."

Her eyes flicked in Dupree's direction. "What about him?"

"His helmet broke. He's a walking vector. Do we know how long he has?"

Sandi shrugged. "We're going to find out."

I glanced to where Dupree was taking inventory of his remaining equipment. "What about the flame thrower?"

"I'm not going to carry that heavy-ass thing." She pushed by me. "You want it, you carry it."

I watched her go and wondered what was going on inside her mind. I'd seen tough girls before. Some were authentically tough, a product of the streets. But others—most others, I'd found—used their toughness as a shield. It was far easier to hate things than it was to love things. Hatred required no nurturing. Hatred allowed no disappointment.

I followed and soon the three of us were heading up the other side of the pit, without Phil and without the flame thrower. I was better with my weapons than that monstrosity. Next time I had to fight something, I wanted to be able to do it with a weapon I was familiar with. I was first. Dupree walked in the middle, constantly scribbling in his notebook, and Sandi brought up the rear.

Over the lip of the pit it was only a few hundred feet of empty ground to Irwindale Avenue. There wasn't a soul in sight, which suited me just fine. We crossed the empty roadway and into the Santa Fe Dam Recreation Area. We could make out the encroaching alien vine over the tops of the trees. I guessed that the vine was topping out about a hundred feet off the ground. Where it wasn't clinging to something, it had trunks the size of hundred year old trees. We were less than a mile from the leading edge, which seemed to be seeking the water of the dammed lake.

Bodies of dead animals and a few people littered the ground. Fungal growths had sprouted from every one of them, creating an other-worldly terrain of skeletal alien bushes. After Dupree took a moment to inspect one coming out of what had once been a large raccoon, we avoided them.

A path rimmed the entirety of the lake. We took the northern arm. I was hyperaware, looking from the water to the sky to the ground. This close to the alien flora I didn't know what to expect.

Twice I saw something moving through the woods, but it wasn't letting us see it fully. The third time I saw it, I called our little party to a halt, then knelt and examined the forest through my scope. I took a full minute, then another. I was about to quit when I saw the slightest of movements. It turned out to be a tail. Long and tan, it was attached to the large body of a mountain lion, placidly staring back at me. I'd heard of them carrying hikers and bikers away, higher in the mountains. I guess with the population decline, they were getting bolder. With a touch of black on its face and an undercoating of white fur, it looked magnificent. I played my forefinger over the trigger, knowing I couldn't let this creature dog us. If we had to leave in a hurry, it could pick one of us off. It might just try and do the same as we approached the alien vine. Still, it broke my heart to kill something so imperious.

It growled, the sound reverberating over the water.

I watched as it leaped, not towards us, but away from something in the woods. It clawed and spat as it reared back and away from... a squirrel. Check that; not one squirrel, but dozens, and each marked with spiky fungal growths.

The mountain lion swatted one away, but another landed on its back and bit down. Still another was crushed by a paw, but two more latched onto its side. In a world without alien spore the mountain lion would've killed every one of them. But this wasn't that world. The infected squirrels had already done what the fungus had programmed them to do. It was only a matter of time before the mountain lion became a spiker, too. I couldn't let that happen. It seemed sacrilegious somehow, and I didn't want to have to face a mountain lion who wasn't capable of showing fear or running away because of the silent demands of an alien fungus.

So I fired, catching it in the side of the head, sending it hard to the earth. I watched the confused squirrels gather themselves, searching for a new source to attack, then climb once more into the tree. Had they seen us, I had no doubt they'd have come for us.

"You could do that to me, too," Dupree said. "I know you could."

"But I won't," I said, almost believing the lie.

He made a sad face. "Maybe you should."

I clasped him on the back. "Where's that happy guy who couldn't wait to see the aliens? Look." I pointed across the lake. "They're right there."

He sighed. "Might as well, I suppose," he said reluctantly. "We've come all this way."

We finally came to the leading edge of the alien vine. I'd seen pictures of it and seen the actual plant from afar, but this was the first time I was able to get a close-up look. The leaves were a deep black, even the undersides.

"Look there." Dupree pointed. "You can actually see the stolons moving."

I watched as an arm-thick length of vine snaked along the ground toward us. I glanced left and right and saw hundreds of the runners, slowly pushing forward along the ground. Here and there one would halt as it knotted, sending feelers into the ground. Then it would continue outward from the knot.

Additional runners hung from the vines overhead, grabbing trees, wrapping themselves around trunks. Further in I could see where they'd actually penetrated the sides of the trees and the foliage was already wilting and falling away.

Dupree stepped over the stolons and beneath the canopy.

Sandi followed him. Seeing I wasn't moving, she turned and raised her eyebrows.

"All right, all right." Slow as it moved, I was sure I could flee if needed. But the fact that I could see it moving at all left me ill at ease. I held my rifle at high ready, prepared to shoot if necessary—as if shooting the alien vine would do anything at all. Still, it made me feel better.

Once underneath the alien vine, I felt immediately cool. The canopy almost completely blocked out the light. I stepped carefully.

"What exactly are we looking for?" I asked, drawing even with Dupree. It was odd seeing him without the hazmat suit. He seemed just fine.

"Looking for?" His grin had returned full beam. "Anything. Everything." He knelt and touched one of the runners. "Realize that I'm touching something that was created on another planet." He held up the runner to show tiny hair-like filaments extending from it. "Look at these rhizomes. They're very active. I bet if I continued to hold this, they'd bore into my skin." When he put the runner down, the filaments sunk into the earth.

"This is a botanical wonder," he continued. "Our own alien vine, kudzu, is an invasive species. We used to say that the way you can tell where the American South began and ended was to look for the alien vine. That old *don't stand still* joke is for real with this stuff."

A shot went off.

I spun towards the sound.

Sandi stood, aiming down her rifle. A woman lay on the ground, but a man and a child continued to run our way.

Oh great. A family. Exactly the thing I'd wanted to kill when I woke up this morning. I raised my rifle and shot the man, while she shot the child.

Dupree acted as if we hadn't done anything. Killing mom, pop, and little Sally was the new norm, just like black was the new green. He kept moving forward until he spied a group of mushrooms growing on the side of an arm-thick vine like a group of warts. He ran to them, excitement bubbling out of him.

"Look here," he cried. "This is it." He grabbed a twig and pushed at them. "They're like lichen. This is the source of the spore. It grows in symbiosis on the vine and by the looks of it nowhere else."

"Except in the rotting corpses of the..." My voice trailed off.

"Yes, and there too," he said, grinning.

That grin.

He took several samples and then packed them away.

We moved on. Two more times we were forced to fire, but it was against individuals. We could handle the fungees in ones and twos. What I dreaded was a horde of them—like in *The Walking Dead*, but fast.

We came to a windowless concrete building, probably a shed. It had a metal door with a sturdy lock. That wasn't what interested Dupree. He ran up and examined the vines that festooned the concrete and seemed to be intent on covering it.

Dupree said something, but I missed it. I asked him to repeat it.

"I said *multitasking*. Not only does the alien vine host the fungus, but it's destructive. Look."

I leaned in and noted that the filaments had buried themselves in the concrete as easily as the dirt. In some places the concrete had already started to crumble.

"It might destroy the concrete," I said, "but I doubt it could do anything to the metal."

"Which would allow a suitably advanced alien race to get to the metal easier. Imagine finding an entire world covered with ore that's already been refined into metal and just sitting there to be taken. This is fascinating."

"Hurry up with your fascinating," Sandi said. "Just a reminder that your fungee clock is ticking. You're only good to us like you are now."

He never stopped grinning. "Noted." He circled the structure several times, then came back to me. "I want to get up there," he said, pointing to the flat roof.

I looked around.

Sandi merely shrugged.

I leaned the rifle against the side of the building, then made a sling with my hands. He put one hand on my shoulder, then a foot on my gloved hands, and I lifted.

He was heavier than I suspected, but I managed to get him to the point where he could reach the tip of the roof. He grasped it with both hands, then I centered beneath him so he could put both feet on my shoulders and heave himself upwards. He disappeared over the lip of the roof.

I grabbed my rifle and backed away so I could see him.

He pulled a specimen box from his pack and knelt out of sight.

My eyes were suddenly drawn to a set of leaves high above us that seemed to be moving independently. Then it happened in another place. Then another. Soon there were seven areas where the leaves were moving strangely. Then the leaves began falling.

Was the plant dying?

Could we be that lucky?

I flashed to that scene in *War of the Worlds* where the giant machines started to collapse as bacteria killed the aliens.

Then I saw the movement for what it was. They weren't leaves, but some sort of bird. Worse, they were all converging on the top of the building where Dupree was.

"Dupree! Look out!"

His head popped up. A look of surprise painted his face.

He held out his hand to stop one of the birds. It dodged his hand and landed on his outstretched arm. Through my scope it looked about the size of a parrot. Its black wings looked velvety.

Then another landed on him.

Then another.

"Are you okay?" I called up.

"They're moths."

I saw it now. Their wings weren't like a bird's, but rather an oversized butterfly, which had given them a leaf-like appearance. I also saw the needle-shaped beak, much like what I'd seen on hummingbirds, only much longer. As I watched, several more landed on his shoulders, another on the top of his head.

"What are they doing?" I asked.

"They seem to be observing. Interesting."

"What's interesting?"

"They presented themselves when I began to manipulate a flower, almost as if they were protecting it. I'm not touching the flower now, so they're not doing anything to me."

I knew what was coming. "Then whatever you do, don't touch the flower."

"What? Do we have time for experiments and clinical trials?" He disappeared from sight for a brief second.

He screamed. I could hear him fighting with something above. He rolled off the roof and onto the ground. The air left him in a *whoomf* and he remained still. Clutched in his right hand was long piece of vine with red flowers.

No sooner had he hit the ground than the moths came after him. The first one flew like a dart, embedding its beak into his stomach. A second impaled his hand.

I grabbed my knife and waded in, kicking and stabbing and stomping. The one on his stomach went flying, but the beak remained in his skin. I caught one in the air and stabbed it. Even as I stomped on one, another landed on my shoulder. I dropped my rifle and swatted after it, slamming my back into the wall of the building to crush it.

I stayed there to keep the creatures in front of me. My motions were more akin to "spiderweb kung fu"—the wild flailing I invented when coming in contact with a spiderweb—than anything I was trained in.

Dupree began to move. He shoved his hands against his stomach and rolled into a ball.

The moths were clearly trying to get at the flower still in his hand. By my count, I'd killed four of them. Two landed next to him and I left my position and hammered them into the ground with the butt of my rifle. I turned just in time to see the final moth. It sat on the roof. One of its wings was broken. In one smooth move, I sheathed my knife, leveled my rifle, and blew it to kingdom come.

I knelt beside Dupree and gently rolled him over.

He'd taken beaks in the face. One eye was swollen shut. One cheek had two spots that were already swollen and inflamed like a wasp sting. He was out of it.

I removed the flower from his hand and laid it aside. His breathing was rapid, but weak. He had all the symptoms of anaphylactic shock. Either he was allergic to whatever was in the beaks, or it was causing his body to send out more chemicals in response to it than he could handle.

His good eye fluttered open. It took a moment for him to focus, but he eventually found me. He tried to grin, but the swelling wouldn't let him. "Here," he whispered hoarsely. "Come here."

I leaned in close.

"Malrimple," he managed to say.

Why was he even bringing up the man's name? "What about him?"

"He knows."

"What does he know? Come on, Dupree. What does he know?"

"It's why he was an asshole to you. He's in charge... in charge of... Michelle."

I gaped at him. "What are you saying?"

"He knows... he knows. He feels..."

Dupree's body jerked several times. His breathing hitched.

I shook him gently. "What does he feel? What are you saying?"

His eye snapped into focus once more. "Guilty. He feels guilty." His body spasmed again. "They're not..." he started, but that's all there would ever be.

He'd stopped breathing. I immediately began pumping his chest. I couldn't breathe for him because of the suit, but I pumped for all I was worth. I worked for a feverish minute before I realized that it was futile. Whatever those damn moths were, they'd killed him.

I sat there and let my own adrenaline settle, my racing heart subside. In the stillness of that moment, I felt a breeze against my back, a breeze where none should exist.

Desolation is something we must fight against. I hear it from those who manage to communicate with me. I can see it in the way people behave. We must fight against this desolation. Don't give into the bleakness. And no, this isn't just about a glass half empty or half full. This is about survival. There are no halves in survival. We either survive or we don't, and the only way we're even going to have a chance at surviving is if the whole lot of us picks ourselves off the floor, dusts off our britches, and then commands us to go out there and survive. Desolation is nothing but a word to describe *I Quit!* It's a unit of measure for giving up. Don't give into it. Don't believe in it. Don't even pay attention to it. Let it rot in the corner feeling sorry for itself while you make a new life for yourself. Fuck desolation. That's right, here at the end of the world we can now say *fuck* on the radio and I'm joyful for it. Desolation my ass.

Conspiracy Theory Talk Radio,
Night Stalker Monologue #1366

PART TWO

Listen to the cry of a woman in labor at the hour of giving birth—look at the dying man's struggle at his last extremity—and then tell me whether something that begins and ends thus could be intended for enjoyment.

Soren Kierkegaard

CHAPTER NINETEEN

Fuck a duck!

Panic surged through me. My arms and hands began to shake. I couldn't catch my breath. I began to reason with myself, promising that everything would be okay, that I wasn't infected and that I wasn't going to go screaming into the night as I became one of the zombie-like fungees. Panic took over, shouting that all was lost, there was nothing I could do, and that I was royally and truly fucked.

Back and forth.

Hope and doom.

Doom and hope.

Everything was going to be all right.

Nothing would ever be all right.

I took a deep breath and squeezed my fists. I remembered one of my soldiers who'd been the victim of a roadside bomb north of Haditha Dam. I could still see Mike 1 laying in the field triage unit, third in line for emergency surgery, bleeding out, his legs disintegrated and the realization that he had no chance to survive dawning on him. I'd tried to console him, be there for him, but he'd shaken me off. His last words had been *Fuck Dylan Thomas*, and then the light had died in his eyes.

I hadn't known who Dylan Thomas was at the time, and I probably never would have cared except that the vehemence with which Mike 1 had said those final three words stuck with me. After rotation back to the Land of the Big PX, I looked up the old dead poet and it wasn't long before I'd figured out the reason why Mike 1 had been so upset.

Grave men, near death, who see with blinding sight
Blind eyes could blaze like meteors and be gay,
Rage, rage against the dying of the light.

Mike 1 hadn't wanted to rage. He hadn't wanted to fight the inevitability of his own death. He embraced the dying of his light. I felt the lure of that—the ability to fold into oneself and just give up was the easier road to take. In fact, to quote another poet, raging against the light *was* the road less traveled.

I inhaled deeply, feeling my entire body as if for the very first time. Every hair, every muscle, the roadmap of my skin, alive, alive, alive, yet on the icy downslope of death. Dylan Thomas's command to *do not go gentle into that good night* rung in my mind like the Liberty Bell that had sounded so long ago as a call for America's independence.

Be free, it demanded.

Don't go gentle, Dylan Thomas ordered.

Fuck Dylan Thomas, Mike 1 whined.

And then it was as if both Dylan Thomas and Mike 1 looked at me, their expectations clear in their eyes. Which road? What the fuck are you going to do, Mason? Seeing Mike 1's life dripping onto the floor and the pathetic acceptance of someone else's decision to end his life pissed me off. It was at that moment that I knew that I couldn't go skipping happily into the dying of my light, nor could I lay down and jam a thumb in my mouth, roll into a fetal position and whine until the last breath left me. Fuck no. If I was going to die, and it seemed absolutely certain that sometime within the next forty-eight hours that would happen, then I was going to do it with purpose.

I rifled through Dupree's pack and found several collection boxes. Three had already been used for the fungus; I put the flower in a fourth, and the moths in the others. Then I put the collection boxes back into the pack, along with Dupree's notebook. I grabbed my rifle and turned to go.

Sandi stood watching me.

There was too much I wanted to say to her, so I shook my head, pointed myself towards the way out, and began to put one foot in front of the other. I was aware of moth activity in the canopy, but they remained above us. Twice Sandi fired at something. I didn't know what it was, nor did I care. I just wanted to put distance between us and that damned vine.

Twenty minutes later we were back at the trailers. Dead children still littered the pit. I dropped the pack, lowered my rifle onto it, took off my holster and my knife sheath, and peeled myself out of the suit. Once out of it, I examined the back. Three holes, beside a five inch tear, probably the result of the moth that had landed on my back and which I'd crushed against the side of the concrete building. I had killed my killer.

My clothes stuck to my skin and my hair and face were covered in sweat. I pulled at my shirt to get air beneath it, then wiped my face and pushed my hair back. Then I turned to Sandi.

"What the fuck was that all about?"

"What do you mean?"

"When the moths attacked. You just stood there."

She shrugged. "They didn't attack me."

It took every ounce of control to keep me from closing the distance between us and slapping the smile off her face. "They didn't attack me either. They attacked Dupree. Our job was to keep him safe. Remember?"

She sighed and shifted her stance. "What would you have me do? Both of you were twirling and stabbing and firing. There was no room for me."

As she said it, I realized she was right. I'd swung blindly with my knife. I could have stabbed her as easily as not. My anger was misplaced.

"I saw your back and knew what had happened," she continued. "I wasn't sure how fast acting the spores were, so I was waiting to see how you were."

"I'm fucking mad."

"Then you're still human." She nodded to the pack. "Let me know when you're not mad anymore." She turned and began walking away.

"What will you do if I'm not?" I called after her as I grabbed the pack and the rifle and hustled to follow her.

"Shoot you," she said without turning around.

I thought about that for a second as I caught up to her. Then I said, "Just make sure you don't miss."

Whomever is careless with the truth in small matters cannot be trusted with important matters.

Albert Einstein

CHAPTER TWENTY

BY THE TIME we got back to the church, I was feeling twitchy. Sandi decided not to tell the others about me. She'd taken her own suit off three blocks from the church, so we both arrived looking the same.

Steve was pissed that Phil hadn't survived and didn't really care about Dupree. Why should he? We sat down and had a quick dinner of rice and ramen, all boiled from packets. I ate greedily, not realizing until that moment just how famished I'd been. Once done, I felt sluggish. My arms began to weigh so much I couldn't lift them off the table; my head grew heavy, as did my eyelids, and I gave in to it.

When I awoke I was in the back of the pickup, inside of a suit. My wrists had been ziptied together in front of me. It didn't take a rocket scientist to realize Sandi had drugged me. Even as I cursed her, I realized that I probably would have done the same thing. When I turned into a fungee, and there was no doubt in my mind that I would, I didn't want to infect anyone else.

I rolled to a sitting position, trying to keep my balance as the truck roared along a residential street.

"Pretty tricky back there," I said through the open back window.

Steve was driving. Sandi sat in the passenger seat. "I had to do what I had to do."

"Why didn't you just leave me?"

"I thought about it. But then I also knew that I owed you. What you did back there at Kilimanjaro saved us all, me included."

"What now?"

"I used your radio to contact Mother. She wants me to get you back to your rendezvous point. We've already put in a call to Fort Irwin. They're prepared to take you in. They definitely want Dupree's notes and his field samples."

I could just see the glee in Mr. Pink's eyes when he discovered that he had a live test subject to poke and prod. Being a guinea pig was the last thing I wanted. Then again, maybe I'd get a chance to take down Mr. Pink himself. Spread a little spore into him. I wonder how his Royal Smugness would appreciate being a fungee. Then they could test *him*.

"You know they're going to use me as a test subject, right?"

"Someone has to be the first. Might as well be the Hero of the Mound. Just think, if they find a way to cure you, then you can be the Hero of the Spore."

"Very funny. Being the Hero of the Mound was just propaganda. Enough people did enough great things fighting the Cray that day that it could have been anyone. And look at all the people we lost." I pictured McKenzie being carried into the air and dropped from hundreds of feet, his insides turned liquid by the impact. "If we ever figure out how to defeat the spore, there's the alien vine to consider, then the moths, then the hives, then the Cray, then whatever is controlling everything."

I turned around and stared back at Los Angeles. I could see the Hollywood hive far in the distance. What I'd give to take that sucker down. It was like a middle finger to everything we knew and loved.

We made it to the Marshall Canyon Golf Course with relatively little action, except for running down a group of fungees who tried to win a game of chicken against a metal-enhanced American-made pickup truck. Then it was the back roads to Mount Baldy. The problem was that by the time we hit the golf course I couldn't keep my hands and legs from twitching. I felt superheated in my suit and knew I was running a fever. Though I could no longer speak, my thoughts were working fine. My mind was clear.

When the helicopter was inbound and I couldn't get my body to stop spasming, Sandi said to me, "Fight this, Benjamin Carter Mason. Fight it like you've never fought anything in your life. It hasn't won yet."

I looked at her and tried to tell her to *fuck off,* but nothing happened.

Her face fell a moment, like she knew I couldn't respond. Seeing her reaction made it even worse. Still, she persevered. She reached through the rear window and grabbed my suited shoulder. "When next I see you, it's going to be so we can take down those fucking hives. Got it?"

Got it! I wanted to scream, but my body and brain were locked in a battle against the spore and clearly had no time for mere words.

The Blackhawk landed. Four soldiers in positive pressure suits exited the chopper. When Steve unlocked the back of the cage, they dragged me out. Then one of them put a black bag over my head. I felt myself being carried into the chopper, where they chained me to the deck, before it lifted off.

It wasn't that I let them do all of this. I had no choice. My body was no longer my own. I was effectively possessed. Michelle had been terribly afraid of possession; it had been her worst fear. Look at her now.

And then it struck me.

We'd argued about God. She believed in God and I didn't. She'd even spent time in a convent to try and deal with her own PTSD.

"Look at where we are," I'd said. *"The aliens attacked and took our planet. Do you think a God would allow that?"*

"Do not presume to know the will of God. For all you know, this could be the next Great Flood. It happened once. Why not again?"

"How can you believe in God after all this?"

"How can you not? Just because you can't fathom why this happened doesn't mean there isn't a God. It doesn't mean He *doesn't have a plan."*

I think I'd actually laughed at her. *"A plan. Fate. The idea that everything bad, everything good, everything* period *has been figured out ahead of time, is impossible to believe."* Even though I'd known I was making her angry, I hadn't been able to stop myself. *"That the Inquisition, the Black Plague, 9/11, pedophiles and the Cray are part of God's plan is ludicrous."*

I could still see her pitying expression as she'd said, *"I didn't say they were part of His plan, smartass. I said just because we don't know what's going on doesn't mean* He *doesn't have a plan. Is it all part of His plan?*

I don't think so. Maybe events happen, then His plan goes into effect." Then she'd stood. *"Here's what I've learned. Just because you don't believe in God, it doesn't mean He doesn't believe in you."*

Then she'd stepped quickly away. *"What does that even mean?"* I'd called after her.

She'd flipped me off.

"Not very God-like," I'd shouted.

Her single finger salute changed into a double-finger salute. Then she was gone.

I'd been so full of myself back then, at the base of Kilimanjaro, so sure I was right and everyone else was wrong; particularly someone who wanted to believe in God. Now, re-living the words we'd exchanged, I saw what a self-assured ass I'd been.

And I couldn't help but note that God had had the last word, for here I was, as possessed as Michelle, no chance to get away, and destined to become a monster.

I couldn't help but laugh at the irony of it all. So I did. I laughed loud, long and hard, even though the only audience I would ever have was me.

It is not in the stars to hold our destiny but in ourselves.

William Shakespeare

CHAPTER TWENTY-ONE

I AWOKE IN a cage in the center of a white room. My head turned, looking for what I didn't know. I had zero control. Four cameras faced me, mounted on tripods. Against one wall were two long tables supporting computers. Scientific equipment lined the other walls. The inside of my cage was Spartan, to say the least. In one corner they'd affixed a water dispenser that looked like a giant sized version of the ones you see in hamster cages. Beside this was a bowl. Both were affixed to a small door that could open only from the outside. The floor held no bed or furniture. I fleetingly noticed that I wasn't wearing any clothes. Only an adult diaper kept me from being on complete display. Awesome. I'd gone from being The Hero of the Mound to The Lieutenant Who Poops In His Pants.

I realized my head hurt. I wanted to reach up and feel it, but my arms refused to listen.

The door of the white room opened and a bald older man wearing a white laboratory jacket entered.

My body propelled itself forward toward the figure, until the cage stopped me, my head slamming into the bars.

Yep. That was it. *Ouch.*

I watched as my arms extended through the bars, fists wanting to bash.

The figure approached and stayed just out of arm's length. He held a clipboard and was making annotations. I tried to tell him I'd like a double cheeseburger with fries, but I couldn't speak. He jotted something down then walked across the room to the computers. His nametag said *Phillips.*

My head turned to follow him, and my arms shoved themselves through the cage towards him. This was going to get old real quick. I sure hoped they had a cure for this or had plans to kill me, because the sheer boredom of playing *Let's See What Mason Will Do Next* was already old.

Two assistants came in. One was a pretty blonde who reminded me of a girl I'd spent the night with in an off-limits area by Fort Bragg, and the other was a redhead.

On the off-limits list they'd had a notation that no one should go to 'the trailer at the end of Pike Ferry Road.' I'm not sure what they were thinking, but it was a menu for guys like me, and that was the first place I went. Turned out it was a low rent, soon-to-be-meth-den home for newly frocked hookers, only the girl who called herself Margret forgot to charge me. It had been fun and she'd been pretty hot, but I'd sweated the next few weeks, hoping that my pee wasn't going to burn and I'd have to go to the Smoke Bomb Hill clinic to get a silver bullet. I'd never gotten Margret's last name, but this fine young lady had a nametag which read *Westlake.*

For a while I reveled in my newfound skills at observation. I suppose when you aren't actively participating in what your body is doing, your mind compensates and allows you to notice more things. Like when Mr. Pink finally showed his ugly mug. I did my thing trying to get to him through the bars. He pointed at me and asked whether or not they'd found value in the specimens I'd brought back. I noted how tired he seemed.

Exhausted, even.

It's funny how I'd always painted him as the bad guy. It was a classic grunt move. If there's someone in charge of you making you do things you don't want to, then pillory them. After all, they were out to get you. They didn't know how awesome you were and refused to listen, so that's why you were made to do KP eight days in a row. In fact, very little you do is your fault; it's always the fault of the braniac who thought up your mission.

For a moment, as I watched Mr. Pink watching me, I felt empathy, but then he pointed at me. Someone said something I couldn't make out that made him chuckle.

Dude! Laughing at a guy when he's down? Fucking classy.

I wasn't sure what he was laughing at but in the ensuing ten seconds I experienced something absolutely terrible. As I stood staring at them and unable to do anything I felt myself fill my adult diaper in an awful back-bending butt-clenching exercise in adult poopage.

Just fucking great.

They ignored me for the most part. For a long time they worked at their stations. All the while I just stood there with a full diaper, unable to do anything but try and reach lamely through the bars. Then an MP came in with a rifle. He aimed it at my chest and fired.

I felt the impact and looked down. I saw the dart about two seconds before everything went black.

When I later woke, I realized that they'd changed me.

They'd turned off all the lights, so I gathered it was night. The only thing I could see were the blinking red lights of the video cameras. I stood there, doing nothing, my body waiting. Eventually it moved over and sucked down some water. Then my face shoved itself into the food. I couldn't see it but it tasted like a combination of cold noodles, lettuce and ground beef. It was both wonderful and disgusting at the same time.

Seconds, minutes, hours later, someone came in and turned the light on.

My body did what it always did and slammed into the bars as I reached for non-infected humans. The two women, Robinson and Westlake, turned on their computers and got to work. Phillips came in a time later. They spent all day doing something with blood samples.

Then I pooped my pants.

Then they shot me with a dart.

Then all was dark.

Awake, rinse, repeat.

I'm not sure how many days passed with this routine, but at some point during that time I began to notice a buzz in the back of my mind, almost like I was hearing someone talk but just couldn't make out the words. Then one day I began to understand.

Possessed Girl calling Infected Asshole, come in.

Possessed Girl calling Infected Asshole, come in.

She repeated the sentence over and over, as if she were talking on a radio and waiting for me to hear her missive on the other end. Sometimes she changed the words around, calling me *Infected Boy* or *Spore Man*, but the message was essentially the same. She wanted to talk. So after about the nine-hundreth time she said it, I concentrated on a single thought.

Infected Asshole calling Possessed Girl, I hear you Lima Charlie.

Inside the room, the scientist and his techs continued to work. My hands were waggling though the bars. There was no way to tell them I was somehow communicating with my long-lost girlfriend who'd become one of Mr. Pink's secret black box projects.

So they got you.

What could I say to that? What should I say? Of course they got me. Wait a minute... who was *they*?

I tracked you to Los Angeles, but then lost you.

Who is they?

What?

You said they got me. Who. Is. They?

They have a name for themselves that I can't translate. We're calling them Hypocrealiacs, named after the order of fungi to which Cordyceps belongs. Have the mycelia begun to grow? Sensing my confusion, she added, *The spikes?*

I can't see my body.

Then she was silent for a time. Later that night, after I'd been put to sleep, changed, then awoke, she returned as I stood waiting on something to capture my attention.

Do you want to see yourself?

How?

I've accessed the feeds to the cameras. This is from earlier today.

In the eerie quiet of the dark cell, I saw within my mind a hazy image of a man inside a cage. It was difficult to focus on the image in my mind and stare at the blinking red lights of the camera in front of me. The images bled into one other. Had I the ability, I would have closed my eyes to better concentrate. Still, I could see me in my diaper. My head had been shaved. Small mushrooms seemed to be growing out of my chest and neck. I looked pretty pathetic. I said as much.

As long as it doesn't go to your brain, you can live like this for quite some time.

I didn't need to ask what happened if it got to my brain. It seemed pretty obvious.

How do you know so much about them?

We've come a long way from just being able to interfere with the Sirens. Using the same frequency mapping, we can distinguish what frequency the Hypocrealiacs are using in their vectors.

Can you use small words? Remember, I'm just a dumb grunt.

There was a pause. She'd once responded to this by saying, *Yeah, but you're* my *dumb grunt.* But that was back when we'd actually owned our own bodies, before—

You still own your body. They're working to get you cleared and might just be close—

Did you just read my mind? How can you do that?

Only when we're talking. When you concentrate on what you want to say to me and then think something, you tend to do it the same way.

How is this possible?

Before when you thought I was messing with your dreams, remember?

Yes.

I was. The theta waves you use when you're waking

broadcast between four to seven hertz. I can tap into it because of what I am. But now that you're infected with Ophiocordyceps invasionalis, I can interact with you at 40 hertz, which is in the top end of your beta waves.

So it makes me like a UAV.

More like a manned-pedestrian vehicle, but that's the idea. We have a range issue though.

Is that why they have Thompson in West Covina? To do what you do here?

When she next spoke, it was the middle of the day and I was trying to kill Ohirra. Or at least I would have, had the bars not been in the way. Still, she stared at me just out of reach, pity in her eyes. It was the first time I'd seen her since before the mission. She mouthed the words, *I'm sorry.* Clearly she knew I was behind those crazy eyes and could see. I mouthed *it's okay* in return, only I didn't because I couldn't.

When she left, Michelle returned, as if she'd been politely waiting. I'd no doubt that she had.

How'd you know about Thompson?

He contacted me using my theta waves when I was on mission, only I thought it was just a dream. He's in Los Angeles, isn't he? Is he just like you?

He's the new model—Generation II. I need an electronic grid to emulate an antenna so I can receive and transmit super low frequencies. He can piggy back off other transmission devices like walkie talkies and FM radios and satellite receiver-transmitters.

Is he okay?

Is he okay? Am I okay? This is how we chose to fight. Only you asked me to kill you.

That I did. And you refused.

I should have done it.
You don't have it in you. You're a hero, not a killer.
I killed my own men.
You didn't kill them. The enemy killed them.
Isn't that the same?
Only if you're feeling sorry for yourself.

Funeral pomp is more for the vanity of the
living than for the honor of the dead.
Francois de La Rochefoucauld

CHAPTER TWENTY-TWO

DAYS PASSED, MAYBE weeks or months; I had no way
of knowing. The team had started wearing positive
pressure suits. I guess my fungal growths were getting
pretty gnarly.

One day they introduced me to one of my own. They
brought him up to the cage. I reached for them, but not
him. He had a red halo around his fungi. They shot me
with a dart.

When I awoke, he was in the cage with me. I ignored
him and he ignored me. Was this what it was like to
be in a zombie horde? I knew that two didn't make a
horde, but our total ambivalence towards each other
and our violent reactions towards living, non-infected
humans had to be similar.

We stood there.

We reacted to the non-infected.

We pooped our diapers.

Then they shot us with darts.

Oh the joys of my existence. At least Michelle and I
were talking. She was hopeful that they might find a
cure. They'd been exchanging notes with other OMBRA
locations. The black alien vine was evidently coming

out of every existing hive, as were the needle moths which were both pollinators and protectors. OMBRA was becoming aware of the dual nature of each of the alien species used in the invasion. Each invader had at least two abilities.

For the Sirens, it was to conduct reconnaissance and report back.

For the Cray it was to knock out the world's power grid and establish a foothold using their hives.

For the black alien vine it was to spread the fungus and destroy the cities.

For the needle moth it was to pollinate and protect the vine so it could continue destroying the cities and hosting the fungus.

And for alien fungus it was to infect every living thing and rid the planet of its hosts and... what? Then it dawned on me. When I next spoke with Michelle, I asked her.

The aliens... the Hypocrealiacs, they can use the infected too, can't they? They can be their eyes and ears.

You figured it out faster than OMBRA did.

It's why I'm in a room with no windows. It's why they put a black bag over my head.

We don't want them to know what we're planning.

But can't they hear us, like right now?

No, we don't think so. They seem to process things differently. I can key into their communications and it's more light and numbers than any recognizable language.

We talked about our lives in the Army before the Turn, when our enemies were merely people with different belief systems.

Days or weeks later, Mr. Pink finally showed himself

again. He had Malrimple in tow. They wore positive pressure suits much like the ones the others were wearing. I had the feeling something important was about to happen.

Mr. Pink didn't let me down. He spoke to me even as we tried to get him through the bars. "We think we have a possible cure. It's mostly worked on the dogs and cats we've tried it on, although I'm told that the morphology of the fungus that infects humans is slightly different from the fungus that infects animals."

I noted that he said *mostly*, which meant there was a margin of error. I wonder what happened then. Did the cure just not work, or did it kill? I guess I was about to find out.

Phillips jointed in the conversation, talking to me as though he believed I could understand him. "It's all in the streptomyces within the fungus. Pre-invasion streptomyces produced over two-thirds of the clinically useful antibiotics of natural origin, such as neomycin and streptomycin."

Okay, well, I knew what an antibiotic was, which made for one word in that sentence.

"But it's a totally different matter with this fungus. In *Ophiocordyceps invasionalis*, the streptomyces have the characteristics of *Parastreptomyces abscessus*, which was a novel organism not yet studied but almost always fatal. So instead of providing benefits, the streptomyces of the invading fungal agents bind with white blood cells by replicating phosphatidylserine-binding proteins found in the blood cells. By binding, they inhibit the white blood cell function, thus allowing the spores to grow unabated within the host."

Alright, I was pretty much lost in the Latin there,

but I knew what a white blood cell was, so I was more or less on top of the explanation. The fungus cripples white blood cells, so the white blood cells can't attack the fungus. I didn't even know white blood cells *worked* against fungus—I thought they were just for viruses and bacteria and stuff—but there you go.

"We've found a way to attack the streptomyces using a combination of invermectin, ZMAPP and broad spectrum antibiotics. If we can stop the immunosuppression, then your own body can fight the infection. So we're going to dart you up and get you into a medical suite we've created."

About damn time. Whatever all those things were.

But wait a moment. Did that mean that I'd lose my ability to communicate with Michelle?

Michelle, are you still there?

I am.

I never did tell you that I love you.

Don't get mushy on me, soldier.

Do you... can you still feel?

Yes. I can still feel.

And what do you feel?

That I've been robbed of a time when we could be together. But it wasn't Mr. Pink who robbed us. It was the Hypocrealiacs. She paused for a moment, and in the silence I could hear so much unspoken sentiment. *Listen, Ben. I have to tell you before they dart you. Sebring is creating more of us. No one knows but me and you. He's captured Sandi and he's looking to capture you. It's the PTSD. It's always been the PTSD. The chemistry in our brains makes being an HMID easier. Don't go back to Los Angeles. He'll know and he'll get you and make you into something like me.*

If it means we can be togeth—

Now you are being a stupid grunt. You fight your way, I'll fight mine. And Mason?

Yes.

I do—

I felt the dart hit me.

Fade to black.

The earth is attempting to rid itself of an infection by human parasite.

Richard Preston,
The Hot Zone: A Terrifying True Story

CHAPTER TWENTY-THREE

MY BODY SHUDDERED and fought. I'd wake for brief periods where pain ruled every haggard breath, then thankfully fall back into blissful, dreamless darkness. Cold and hot. Hot and cold. Twice I woke screaming, only to have arms push me down, voices speak to me as I fell a thousand miles into my fever. Then just as suddenly as the dart had put me out, I was awake, shivering on a narrow bed as light streamed through a high, barred window. When I reached down to pull up the sheets I'd kicked away, pain jabbed across my shoulders and neck. I craned my head and saw several sets of stitches on my left shoulder, probably where they'd removed the ascocarps.

It struck me that I could once again control my body. I held out my right hand and stared at it as I wiggled my fingers. Then I touched my shoulders and my neck, feeling stitches that even now hurt deliciously. I touched my face, feeling the stubble there.

"Hello," I said to no one at all, grinning as my voice filled the small space. Then I sang, "I'm a little tea pot, short and stout. This is my handle, this is my spout."

My voice was back.

I sat up in bed, wrapping the sheet around my midsection as I stared out the window. Never had the desert of Death Valley looked so good as at that moment. I tried to get up and sat down again as a sudden wave of dizziness gripped me. I let it subside, before standing more slowly this time, letting my legs and head come to a better understanding. I examined my room. It was a regular private hospital room, most likely in the base hospital. It had a bathroom and a locker. Beside the bed was a chair.

In the bathroom, I looked at myself in the mirror. I looked haggard and wan. I'd lost weight. My cheekbones stood out on a gaunt face. I could see my ribs. But contrary to my appearance, I felt healthy and hale. The stitches would heal. My hair would grow back. Was the infection truly over? Had they really cured me? It still seemed too good to be true.

I washed my face and hands, then brushed my teeth. From the locker I drew a set of MultiCams. I was busily lacing up my boots when there came a knock at the door.

"Come in."

Ohirra stuck her head tentatively into the room, then upon seeing me came in all the way. Her face glowed with pleasure. "They said you were awake. How do you feel?"

I stood and threw my arms around her. She accepted, a little surprised, then put her arms around me. I gave her a resounding hug, appreciating the feel of someone else. When I released her, she crossed her arms protectively. I laughed. I'd forgotten for a moment how reserved she was.

"I feel incredible. I—I thought I was a dead man."

"We all did."

"Then how?"

"Dupree. You have him to thank for this. Without his notes... he had it almost figured out. All Phillips and the others had to do was fill in the gaps."

"Dupree." I remembered how the needle moths had taken him down. "He was a good man. I should have been more careful with him."

"That's the Mason I know. Always taking the blame."

"No, really. I..." I sighed. "How long have I been out?"

"Since we brought you in when you were infected, or since we started the cure?"

"Uh... both?"

"Okay, but don't freak out, okay?"

"Why would I freak out?"

"We brought you in one-hundred and thirty-seven days ago."

"What? That's more than four months! Are you serious?"

She nodded. "The cure took three weeks."

"Three weeks," I whispered. "Four months."

"They've turned the basement morgue into a Level Four Containment Zone. Olivares sent out hunter teams to bring back more infected. They're figuring out how to speed up the cure. You and Ethridge were the first two on the planet to get cured."

Ethridge. He must have been the other one inside the cage with me. "Is he okay?"

"He's fine. Woke up two days ago. We've all been wondering when you'd be up and around."

I chuckled and sat on the side of my bed, feeling a little dizzy. "I guess I'm a slowpoke." I reached out to balance myself, feeling suddenly like I was going to keel over.

"Easy, Mason. You're weaker than you think. Your body has fought off an alien infection and you've been bedridden for twenty-one days."

"When can I get out of here?"

"Phillips wants to clear you, then you're on light duty for the next week. After that, we have a mission."

"Am I going back to L.A.?"

She nodded.

I remembered what Michelle had said about not going back, but I had to. Sandi had been taken by Sebring. I couldn't leave her.

"Can't we go any sooner?"

Now it was Ohirra's turn to laugh. "In your condition? You wouldn't make it a mile before you passed out. Give it a week, hero, then we'll see. This mission's too important for us to send you in before you're ready."

"So you waited for me?"

"This one's all about you. So take the rest of the day, then tomorrow we want you to come in for a mission debrief."

Now I was really intrigued. But Ohirra had been as forthcoming as she was going to be. I had to wait another hour and a half before Dr. Phillips saw me. Half an hour after that I was walking out of the hospital and into the bright, clear California air. All around me was the hustle and bustle of a busy military base. Trucks, soldiers, even a line of tanks. Overhead a Blackhawk buzzed in for a landing. So much life. So much activity. So much the opposite of my last four months. It still boggled me that I'd been in the grip of the infection for so long.

I stopped cold as a voice rang in my head.

Possessed Girl calling Dumb Grunt. Can you hear me, over.

I concentrated and tried not to smile. *Dumb Grunt to Possessed Girl, I read you Lima Charlie, over.*

There you are.

I couldn't help grinning. *I just woke up and I—wait a minute. Didn't you say that we were communicating using beta waves because of the infection?*

Turns out that your DNA has changed slightly. You're no longer strictly human.

What does that mean?

The infection... changed you.

What can I do? Leap tall buildings in a single bound? Fly?

Nothing like that. They think some of the effects reported might be permanent. For instance, Ethridge reported seeing red halos around the infected.

I saw those too.

We need to test and see whether or not you can still see them and whether or not the infected react to you in a similar way.

You mean by not attacking me?

Exactly.

Then I walked, and we talked. Even as I did and noted how weird our relationship was becoming, I realized that I didn't care. I'd wanted to be with Michelle from the first moment I saw her on the plane to Wyoming. I thought she'd been taken away from me forever. But now, at the end of the world as we knew it, we'd found each other again, and we were together...

Sort of.

A human being should be able to change
a diaper, plan an invasion, butcher a hog,
conn a ship, design a building, write a
sonnet, balance accounts, build a wall, set
a bone, comfort the dying, take orders,
give orders, cooperate, act alone, solve
equations, analyze a new problem, pitch
manure, program a computer, cook a tasty
meal, fight efficiently, die gallantly.

Robert Heinlein

CHAPTER TWENTY-FOUR

BACK IN MY hooch, I busied myself filling out a requisitions
form so I could replace my missing equipment. I'd hold
onto it until I knew the parameters of the upcoming
mission, but the very act of filling out the form helped
ground me in the comfortable bureaucracy of the
military. When I was done, I squared away my area,
before heading out to get a weapons issue. I wasn't
comfortable without them, even if I was surrounded
by several thousand armed OMBRA military men and
women. On the way back with my preferred P226 and
HK416, I finally realized that everyone was saluting me.
I'd noted that they were doing it before, but thought
it must be someone behind me. I'd been given a field
promotion to lieutenant before the last mission, but
this was really the first time I'd been in a garrison area

since that promotion. When I finally began to return the salutes, it felt like I was pretending at being something I wasn't. I told myself I'd get used to it. Part of me actually believed it.

When I got back, Olivares was sitting on the edge of his cot. He'd removed his shirt and was unlacing his boots.

He nodded to me. "'Sup, patient zero."

I nodded back. It was actually good to see him.

"I'd heard you recovered." He removed one boot, then started working on the other. "Glad to have you back in the land of the living."

"Glad to be back." I sat down on my cot and began unlacing my boots. "You going running?"

He nodded again. "What was it like?"

"About the most terrible fucking thing that's ever happened to me. I was trapped. The spores had complete control over me."

He looked up sharply. "You mean you knew what was happening but you couldn't stop yourself?"

"Yeah. Fucking horrendous."

He shook his head as he removed his other boot. Then he moved to change into shorts and a t-shirt. "Don't let any of the judies or joes hear that."

"Why not?"

"Right now the fungees are mindless zombies to them and no one hesitates to shoot. If they realize that there are actual human beings trapped inside the bodies, they might hesitate. And that could kill them."

I shucked off my boots and shrugged out of my uniform. He made a good point, one that I had better remember, especially since I was due to lead another team soon.

I put on my own PT uniform and we headed out into the cooling day. At six in the evening the temperature was down to a tolerable ninety degrees. I didn't know how far I'd be able to run, but I needed to get back in shape as fast as I could. Thankfully Olivares liked to run at a slow pace. Not so thankfully, he liked to do it for several miles.

"How was Vegas? Meet any hotties?"

He rolled his eyes. "It ain't your momma's Vegas anymore. Nothing but fungees and a hive."

"What'd you do?"

"That was months ago, you do know that, right?"

"For me it was yesterday."

"Pink had me escorting an HMID to a paramilitary team he has in place. Fucking nasty business. Since then, I've had to do it three more times."

"Did you know who it was... who they were?"

"The HMIDs? No. We never looked inside the black box."

"What about in your dreams? They can ride your theta waves."

He eyed me, then grunted an acknowledgement. "Maybe that's why we had nightmares every damn night."

We ran for a few minutes in silence.

"Where's the line, do you think?" I asked.

"What line?"

"The line we shouldn't cross. The line where we lose our humanity."

"You're talking about the HMIDs."

"I am. You called them *nasty business*."

"They are. If I didn't know they were helping, I'd crash the whole system. But it's one of the only things allowing us to fight what the Hypocrealiacs are doing to our planet."

I sidestepped a dead rattler that had been trying to cross the road; some dumb grunt had run it over rather than letting it live. "Is it fair, though?" I asked.

"They sign up for it."

"Brother, they sign up but they don't know what they're getting into." I remembered Michelle's command to *killmekillmekillmekillme*. She seemed to be of two minds now. When she couldn't communicate with me she wanted to die, but now that she could, all she wanted was to talk.

I stopped running.

My old friend Jon Carte had a saying when it came to girls. *They tell you what they think you want to hear. Listen to what they say and believe the opposite.*

It was a touch sexist, but could what Jon had said be true of Michelle? Was she telling me what I wanted to hear so I wouldn't come to her rescue? Do that terrible thing that she'd earlier begged me to do?

Olivares swung back by. "Come on, we've barely gone a mile."

I started running again. I ran the conversations Michelle and I had shared over and over in my mind. They'd been too happy, and in retrospect, almost forced. As my feet fell one after the other, I realized I'd been played. I ran another mile, then stopped again. I waved for Olivares to continue. He gave me a worried look, then continued on.

Hands on my hips, I waited for my breathing to return to normal. I wasn't sure how I was going to do it, but shouting her name out loud seemed over the top. So instead, I closed my eyes and just concentrated on

Michelle's name, throwing all my effort into it, blocking out everything else, making the sound of it my universe.

The result was instantaneous.

Whoa there, fella. You don't have to scream.

I wasn't sure how to get your attention.

That'll do it. I bet every HMID in a three state area could hear you.

About the HMIDs...

I received silence in return.

I remember when you begged me to kill you.

More silence.

What happened to that? Do you still want me to kill you?

A moment of silence then,

Why... are you offering?

What is it you want? I'm confused. Before you were invading my theta waves, telling me to kill you and giving me these God-awful nightmares. Now it's like we're two teenagers separated by a telephone.

If you mean do I like being an HMID, the answer is complicated. I want to be able to touch you. I'd love to taste food again or even walk. But I have so many connections, so many eyes from which to see, it's as if I'm the virtual version of the black vine, creeping out of the cities. I feel... I feel...

What do you feel?

I feel everything. I feel... useful.

Are you sure the word you're looking for isn't used?

Are you sure you just don't want someone to put your arms around?

There are plenty of young gals here in Death Valley. I'm sure one or two might want a piece of the Hero of the Mound. And yes, I'd like to wrap my arms around you again. But what I want to know is, do you want to be a woman or a machine?

Can't I be both?

I don't know. You tell me. Can you?

A long silence was finally followed by a single word. *No.*

Then which is it?

Why are you making me choose?

I'm not making you do anything. That's what this is about—our own humanity. It's about personal freedom. If we lose that, we lose everything. If we don't worry ourselves about it, then why in the hell are we fighting?

Don't you think that the needs of the many outweigh the needs of the few?

Of course I do, Mr. Spock, but if this wasn't something you signed up for and you want out, then you should be allowed to leave.

Even if by leaving I endanger lives?

So your argument is that it's okay to sacrifice yourself and do something that you don't want to do because it's the best thing you could do?

Yes. What's wrong with that?

I switched subjects. *Does it hurt?*

Emotionally? Physically?

Yes.

Emotionally I feel a sense of loss. There's a sense of longing I can't define. Physically, I don't feel any pain at all.

I channeled Jon Carte. *No pain at all? Come on, Michelle.*

It's nothing I can't handle.

What is it?

I was about to give up on any chance of a response

when she said, *Where the machine interfaces with my torso, there have been... infections. I was an early model. I'm told they've corrected the problem since me. I guess I'm the Model T of HMIDs.*

So what happened? What's that mean?

She laughed. *Let's just say I'm not going to win any beauty contests.*

I'm going to save you, Michelle. Just tell me where you are.

There's nothing left to save.

There's always something to save.

Not in this case.

Tell me where you are.

Silence.

Michelle, Goddamn it, tell me where you are.

Nothing.

I stood there for a moment, staring out at a landscape blurred by tears. I made the Herculean effort to move my feet and broke into a jog. It was a long two miles back to the hooch, long enough that I'd made a sound plan to free Michelle, even if it would mean the end of me.

The most terrible job in warfare is to be a second lieutenant leading a platoon when you are on the battlefield.

General Dwight David Eisenhower

CHAPTER TWENTY-FIVE

BEING A LIEUTENANT had its bennies. I was able to walk into Facilities Maintenance Division and get a map of Fort Irwin along with the generator tasking matrix. Without an electrical grid, everything we did was subject to support by generators. The more electricity needed, the more generators were required. So it was my thesis that I could locate the black box using the tasking matrix, and then align that with the base map.

I was hunched over these documents when Olivares returned from his run.

"How far'd you go?" I asked.

"Ten miles."

"Good for you."

"What happened to you?"

"I had a phone call to make."

His eyes narrowed and his brow furrowed.

"In a manner of speaking," I added.

He waved his hand at the map as he shed his wet PT clothes. "What's all that? Looks like a map of the fort."

"It is. By aligning the electrical needs on this document

with the locations of facilities on the map, I think I'll be able to figure out where they're keeping Michelle."

He stopped in mid-undress, one arm in the shirt, the other arm out. Then he laughed and continued undressing. "Good one. Did you forget that Mr. Pink said he'd let you see her?"

"If you think he's going to keep his bargain, then I have a Cray-Away spray to sell you that actually works."

"So all this is backup?"

I nodded.

"Why all this interest? I thought we'd dealt with that. Didn't Ohirra say it was Michelle's choice?"

"Not much of a choice," I mumbled.

"What's that mean?"

"She doesn't know what she wants. She's confused."

"Wait, how do you know what she wants?"

"We've been talking."

"You've been talking," he said in a disbelieving tone. "And how have you been doing that, Mr. Wizard?"

I explained to him what I'd been told about the changes in my DNA and how I could now communicate with her, and conceivably other HMIDs as long as they were in range. Then I summarized our conversations. Olivares went from incredulity to a sort of sadness. I called him on it.

"You don't believe me?"

"No, brother. I believe you. It's probably why they put the other ex-fungee Ethridge on my team. I just didn't know he had these abilities."

"Then what is it?"

"Did you forget about her dissociative identity disorder?"

"Her..." I *had* forgotten. Was that it? Was she flipping back and forth through her personalities? I let my pen flop onto the map and sat back. "Jesus, what do I do?"

"Maybe nothing." He leaned forward. "Listen, man. It was one night. One. Night."

I knew he was right. But it had been more than that. We'd made a connection. The rarity of two people actually seeing each other, feeling each other, on the same longitude and latitude, was something I'd experienced maybe three times in my entire life. It might have just been one night, but it made all the other nights that much more bearable, and unbearable at the same time.

I grabbed both sides of my head. When next I spoke, it was like I was a million miles away. "I know it was only one night and I can't explain it. But neither can the guy from World War II who had one night with an Italian girl right before he went to the front. Or stories we've all seen on TV about a man longing for the girl he dated in Saigon."

"Those were movies, man."

"I know they were, but they were a reflection of reality."

"You sound crazy, you know that, right?"

I sighed heavily. "I feel crazy." I gave him a look. "This shit has made me crazy."

"Rest easy. Listen, you almost died. You've been infected for the last four months. It's the end of the world. Fuck, dude. You have PTSD on top of PTSD. If I was a doctor, I'd say you were overcompensating and mirroring. It's a control issue. You had a total absence of control with the spores. Michelle has a total absence of control as an HMID. By trying to save her from her problem, you're trying to save yourself."

I stared at Olivares for a long minute. Then I said, "That's about the most sense you've ever made."

He grinned. "What about the time I said you were a better fighter than me?"

I grinned as well. "Okay, it's a tie for that time. But seriously, could it simply be that I'm mirroring? I know I'm being obsessive. I can feel it."

"I can see it too." Olivares stood. "Listen, get cleaned up and we'll go to the chow hall. You just need to let it leach out of you. Think about other things."

I stood. Glancing down at my plan for Operation Free Michelle, I couldn't help but wonder how crazy the whole thing sounded. "Give me ten and I'll be there."

"Sounds good."

I shed my smelly PT apparel and headed to the shower. Fifteen minutes later we were strolling across the compound to the mess hall. If I was lucky, they'd have chili mac. I'd never seen it in any restaurant, but it was a staple in the Army—the perfect merging of macaroni and chili, joined with a large amount of an unidentified government cheese.

And yes, I was lucky. They were serving great heaps of it.

Although our intellect always longs for clarity and certainty, our nature often finds uncertainty fascinating.

Carl von Clausewitz

CHAPTER TWENTY-SIX

A TEAM FROM the intel shop debriefed me for three hours the next morning. They were led by Ohirra, who appeared relieved that I'd managed to survive the mission and its effects. Afterwards, she made a call and Mr. Pink came in with Malrimple in tow. Mr. Pink appeared as self-assured as always, while the head scientist looked as if he'd just slid into someone else's skin. Remembering Dupree's last words, it could only mean that Malrimple felt guilty for managing the HMIDs. I'd love to be able to get him in a position where he could tell me what was really going on. I was pretty sure given the right circumstances I could convince him to cooperate.

Mr. Pink spread his arms. "You're a veritable miracle, Lieutenant Mason. How do you feel?"

"I feel good. Incredibly good, actually."

"Your body is producing increased endorphins. The changes in your DNA have triggered the pituitary gland to produce more than usual. It's like an afterexercise high."

That was the perfect description. "Yes. That's it."

Ohirra, always the worrier, asked, "Can he expect any problems with too much endorphin production?"

"Euphoria is common. Mr. Mason has to be careful that he doesn't disassociate with reality. A drop in production could cause depression, mood swings, and/or suicidal thoughts."

"What could bring it down?"

"Too much iron in the blood stream. Blood loss."

"So as long as I don't get shot and lose a lot of blood, I should be okay, right?"

Malrimple gave me a stony stare.

Mr. Pink looked to Ohirra. "Are you finished?"

She nodded. "I'll have a copy of the debrief on your desk by five."

Mr. Pink turned towards me. "What are your impressions?"

"Of L.A.?"

He smiled as if to say, *Of course*.

"It's nasty business," I said. "Survival groups are popping up all over the place. It's literally every man for himself. God's New Army could be the worst. They fired on us—chased us and tried to stop our mission. Do I understand it right that we're working with them?"

"We have to align ourselves with groups capable of protecting their people and territory, as well as establishing the rule of law."

"It's the old *we have to break a few eggs to make an omelet* excuse, right?"

Everyone in the room stopped cold. Even Mr. Pink seemed to have been startled by the remark. He laughed, immediately brightening the mood. "Glad to see that the best of you wasn't lost to your infection, Lieutenant."

"God's New Army and that madman Sebring don't have our best interests in mind." I could have added that he'd gone after Sandi and made her into his own version of an HMID, but I wanted to keep my ability to communicate with Michelle private for the time being.

"And what are our best interests, Lieutenant Mason?" Mr. Pink asked.

What was this, a trick question? "To win back our planet and get it back to where it was before the alien invasion."

"Malrimple, please tell our young idealist the projections."

Speaking as if each word cost a year of his life, Malrimple intoned, "The temperature has already risen by four degrees. We have reports that ocean levels have risen by seven feet and are still rising. The increased temperature has caused permafrost to begin melting, resulting in the release of massive amounts of methane. Even before the alien invasion, craters were forming in Siberia. Now the event is global. The earth as we knew it is gone forever. The climate, the weather, the temperatures all have yet to settle.

"If we happen to take back our planet, and if we are able to survive the new climate, it will still be more than seventy-five years before we can return to pre-invasion technology."

"And to do this," interjected Mr. Pink, "we need assistance." He held his arms out. "Do you believe that the men and women of OMBRA in Fort Irwin are capable of defeating all of the aliens west of the Mississippi, while also projecting worldwide without assistance? It's just not possible."

He put a hand on my shoulder, something he'd only done once before. "Listen, you're our moral compass. I'd rather not work with Sebring. He's mad as a hatter and an opportunist. But if we can make his desire for greatness meet our expectation for assistance, then we have an ugly partnership."

"Your *moral compass*," I repeated, not really knowing what to make of the comment.

"Your simple ideas of right and wrong, and that corporations and governments tend to manipulate the lives of its customers and citizens to their own ends, are absolutely correct. We think we know better. Often we manipulate ethics to the point that we redefine them. 'Right' becomes *acceptable*, or what we can afford. Some might see your candid comments as insubordination; I see them as reminders of what we should be doing."

It was several seconds before I realized he'd stopped talking. Even so, I didn't know what to say. I looked around the room and saw all eyes on me, so I felt I had to say something. "So your opinion is that GNA is a better option to partner with than the Cult of Mother because of their size and ability to defend themselves."

"That about sums it up," Mr. Pink said. "We're making tough decisions all over the planet. We don't always like who we're working with, but it becomes a necessity sometimes."

"Breaking a few eggs," I said.

Mr. Pink nodded and smiled.

"I understand that's where you've positioned HMID Thompson. Do you think it's smart, leaving them outside of your control?"

His smile fell. "I see HMID Aquinas has been talking a little too much."

I wasn't surprised he knew about my ability to communicate with the HMIDs. For all I knew, he'd planned it all along. I certainly wouldn't put it past him.

"I figured that out on my own. He's always been able to use theta waves." I gave him a stern look and a shake of my head. "And to think you told me he was killed in Africa."

He waved my comment away. "How does the communication work, between you and the HMIDs?"

"Peachy," I said. "Maybe ask Ethridge and he can give you a better explanation."

"We already have, but since you knew the HMIDs prior to transformation, I thought you might have some insight."

"You don't want to hear my insight. Speaking of HMID Aquinas, you told me I could see her upon mission completion."

I saw Malrimple glancing our way out of the corner of my eye, but I didn't turn my head. Instead I held Mr. Pink's gaze.

"Now wouldn't be a good time," he said evenly.

I concentrated and called Michelle the same way I had yesterday, but nothing happened. I tried again, closing my eyes and pouring every ounce of concentration I had into her. Nothing.

I opened my eyes. "What happened?"

Mr. Pink turned to Malrimple.

The scientist sighed. "She tried to take herself offline last night."

I'd noted that she'd been silent. I just figured she'd been on assignment or something. "What's that mean, *take herself offline*?"

"She's..." Malrimple glanced at Mr. Pink, who nodded. "She's injured herself."

I was stunned. She'd tried to commit suicide? One would think that in her new form, that wasn't possible, but she'd always showed the tendency. That's why she'd joined OMBRA. She'd thought it would be suicide by soldiering.

"Is she going to be all right?" I asked, controlling the emotion in my voice.

"We should have her rebooted and working within twenty-four hours," Malrimple said.

I stared at him, wanting nothing more than to wipe the condescending look off his face, retribution for his bald-faced dehumanizing of Michelle.

Mr. Pink must have noticed, because he put his hand on Malrimple's shoulder and turned him towards the door. To me he said, "I believe you have a medical appointment tomorrow morning, but in the afternoon we have a critical mission brief."

"I'll be there," I said without taking my cold gaze off Malrimple's back.

We make mistakes, we have our faults, and God knows some of us have more than our share, but when danger threatens and duty calls, we go smiling to our own funeral.

James Larkin

CHAPTER TWENTY-SEVEN

I SPENT THE rest of the day in my hooch. I'd made my plans. All I needed was to wait until nightfall. Occasionally I'd try and contact Michelle, but there was no reply. Olivares came and went. He tried to engage me in conversation, but when it became clear I didn't want to talk, he grabbed his things and left.

At dinner, I found a table and sat alone.

Ohirra came by, but I remained remote.

What I was about to do was permanent; something I couldn't come back from. I knew that if I told Olivares or Ohirra, two things would happen. First, they'd try and talk me out of it, providing solid arguments why I shouldn't do it. I'd listen, then tell them I was going through with it anyway. Then, after a fair bit of complaining and name calling, they'd join me. And I didn't want to put them in the jeopardy I was putting myself.

Ohirra knew I was planning something; before she left she whispered, "Be careful."

I didn't respond, nor did she expect me to. She took her tray to another table and was soon deep in conversation.

I finished my meal, dropped off my tray, then headed to the post library. It was crowded with lower enlisted, using the monitors and televisions to play the library's collection of DVDs. I found an empty chair and sat down, staring blankly at a disc of the sit-com *Friends*. I sat through five episodes, remembering where I was and who I'd been with when it had still been on television. The catchy intro tune was something we'd all danced to, waiting for the clapping parts. I allowed myself to take a short journey down the road of sentimentality as I wondered what Michelle and I could have had if we'd met all those years ago, before the alien invasion. Would we have become a couple, or would we have crashed and burned like so many?

At ten I rose and left the library. I found South Loop Road and headed south on it until I got to Inner Loop Road, which angled away from all the major activity to a cluster of buildings. I couldn't follow the road, so I continued another three hundred or so meters down South Loop, then angled into the brush. The desert terrain here was flat with the occasional scrub brush, and I kept my profile low as I moved.

I had the light of a quarter moon to guide me. I knew the field wouldn't be mined, but I wasn't sure if security was using ground surveillance radar. I kept my eyes out for the telltale signs, but there were too many shadows to be certain, so I crossed my fingers and continued until I got to the building's parking lot.

The building itself was in the shape of a large H. The side nearest the parking lot had windows; the other side, without, was where the most generators were allocated. The parking lot was lit by several portable light generators. Their sound would cover any sound I'd make.

I started to make my way into the parking lot when the side door to the building opened and two men came out. I ducked behind an old military Chevy Blazer and watched with increasing worry as they headed in my direction. Had I just chosen their car, out of two dozen, to hide behind?

But they stopped two cars down and got into a Dodge pickup. I waited until they backed out and drove away before I stood and quickly walked to the side of the building. Now I'd see how well security was working. I skirted the edge of the building, then sprinted across the middle space to the other side of the H. Once there, I went to the other end of the building until I could see the generator field.

Each generator had been sunk into a pit, leaving three quarters of the generator hidden, which also served as a sound dampener. I chose three generators, then quickly sabotaged them. I pulled a lead free from one, adjusted the fuel filter to starve another of air, and turned the third off completely. As they began to die, I ran to the side of the building, to a spot that would be hidden when the door opened.

With three generators offline, a response didn't take long. A man in a lab coat exited the building with a harried look on his face. He never saw me as I slid into the building. Now inside, I was greeted with white institutional walls. I was almost disappointed that there was no sign announcing that this was HMID headquarters. I reminded myself that this was one of three places that could be the home of the HMIDs, and it was only on a hunch that I chose this one. My hunch could be taking me to entirely the wrong place.

I heard footsteps and tried the nearest door. It was locked, so I tried the one next to it—thankfully unlocked—and quickly ducked inside. No lights were on, but I could smell cleaning chemicals. How clichéd! I was hiding in a supply closet.

I pressed my ear to the door and heard the footsteps go past. I counted to thirty, then opened the door to an empty hallway. From the hollow of my back, I drew my Sig Sauer P226 and held it at high ready. I went down a short hall, then peeked around a corner. Seeing it empty, I slipped down the hallway, keeping my back to the wall. Halfway down, a door opened right in front of me and out stepped Malrimple. We locked eyes right away. I saw his eyes go wide. When he opened his mouth to call out, I shoved the barrel of my pistol into his cheek, pressing the skin hard against his teeth.

"Don't make a fucking sound."

I could see the terror in his face. Part of me hated myself for relishing it.

"You're not going to get away with this," Malrimple whispered.

"I have no intention of getting away with this. Now take me to Michelle."

He stared at me, fear locking his legs.

"HMID Aquinas." I pushed the barrel harder against his skin. "Take me to her. *Now!*"

He turned to head down the hall.

I grabbed the back of his collar. "Don't fuck around. I don't like anything about you and wouldn't mind putting a round into your smug face."

He stiffened, then nodded.

I put the barrel of the pistol to the back of his neck and let him lead me down one hallway, then another.

A woman in uniform came out of an office holding a clipboard. She was looking down and might not have seen us, but when Malrimple stopped, she glanced over. She brought her clipboard to her chest and stared at me, trying to gauge what I was doing and what I should do.

I helped her out. "Go back into your office. If you think you need to call someone, then go ahead."

"What are you going to do?" she asked, her voice barely above a whisper.

"See my girlfriend," I said plainly.

Her eyes widened a moment, then she nodded and returned to her office. She closed the door and I heard the latch click into place.

We continued down the hall and came to a door with a keypad lock.

Malrimple hesitated.

"Punch it in," I said.

"This isn't the best time," he began.

"It's never going to be the best time. Now open the fucking door."

He sighed and keyed in an eight-digit number. The door clicked open and we pushed into an immense room. I recognized the black box immediately. But there wasn't just one—there were three of them. One stood at the end of the rectangular room, with the other two on either wall. Each had multiple cables exiting it. Some of the cables went through the wall to the generators outside, while others went to a row of computer servers squatting in racks against the walls. Here and there were tables with computer monitors and keyboards. At each one sat a worker. Another man in a lab coat stood at the servers, pressing lit buttons.

It took only a moment for me to take in all this, then my attention focused not on the visuals, but on the screams coming from the speakers. Michelle's voice.

"*Let me go. Please fucking let me go!*" she cried.

"What the hell is going on?" I demanded as she launched into another scream. But the moment I spoke, she fell silent.

The others in the room turned at my voice and upon seeing my gun, reacted. Most them stood and backed against a wall, but the man at the server pulled a pistol from his side.

"Drop the weapon, soldier," he said.

"Not a fucking chance."

"Doctor Malrimple, are you okay?"

"I'm fine, Doctor Cole. This is Lieutenant Mason. He wants to see HMID Aquinas."

Doctor Cole stared at me but didn't lower his pistol.

"You were with Norman."

I didn't know what he was talking about for a moment, then it clicked. Doctor Norman Dupree. I nodded. "I was there."

"How did he die?"

"Saving the rest of us," I said, realizing as I said it that it was absolutely true. "He died getting samples from the alien vine."

"You were there?"

"I was."

"You left him there?"

I licked my lips and nodded. "We had to. Listen, everything is going to be all right here." My eyes were mainly on the pistol, but I glanced at his face and could see him working through what he should do.

"You know they're going to arrest you," he said.

"I know."

Through the speakers came the words, "*You never should have come here, Ben.*"

"I know that. But I did."

She sighed, the sound like wind through the speakers. Doctor Cole locked eyes with Malrimple. "At least the screaming has stopped."

Malrimple nodded. "Go ahead and leave us, Doctor Cole. I'll be all right."

"Are you sure?"

"I don't think Lieutenant Mason wants to shoot anyone today."

Cole seemed to consider this for a moment, then holstered his gun and headed toward the door. I kept Malrimple between us, just in case he changed his mind. When he was out the door, I went over and slammed the pistol down on the internal keypad several times. I hoped it would be enough to bar the door.

When I turned, Malrimple was standing where I left him.

"Now, open that black box there," I said pointing to what had to be Michelle's.

"*No, Ben. Please don't. I don't want you to see me.*"

"But I've come all this way." I nodded for Malrimple to do whatever it was that had to be done. "They said you tried to take yourself offline. That you tried to kill yourself."

She was silent for a moment, then said, "*I'm a distraction. As long as I'm alive I'll be a distraction for you.*"

"I don't care. I love you."

"*You love the memory of us.*"

"Maybe I do, but you're as connected to that memory as I am. You can't tell me that you don't love me as well."

"*I do love you. It's just that now I'm... now...*"

"Now what?" I asked softly.

"*Now I'm a monster. How can anyone love a monster?*"

Malrimple had paused and was staring at me. If she was a monster, then he was her Frankenstein.

"What's her condition?" I asked him.

"She's ripped out most of her tubes. She's a Mod One and still has her arms. We removed them on the other modifications, for just this reason."

I gulped. "And why not remove hers?"

He shook his head. "It has to be her choice. She wanted to keep them."

I took that in and thought about what it would mean to have someone take off my arms. It was nothing more than another bit of dehumanization, and Malrimple clearly didn't think of Michelle as anything other than a machine, even if she did have to choose which body parts to throw away.

"Open the fucking box, Doctor Frankenstein," I growled.

He pressed a few buttons on his keyboard and the side of the black box opened. Gas escaped, obscuring what lay within for a moment. I made out cables, dangling wires, and a figure.

"Michelle?"

"*Please... please go away.*"

I stopped cold as the gas dispersed enough for me to see the body within the box. It was... wrong. It wasn't recognizable as human. It looked more like a log with attachments. Had Malrimple opened the wrong box?

"Michelle? Is that you?"

"*Ben,*" she gasped. "*Don't look at me!*"

Too late.

The gas faded away and I saw her in all of her miserable reality. She hung at chest level. They'd removed her legs. Why shouldn't they? She'd never walk again. Her body was ravaged with sores. Here and there the skin looked dead and rotting. Curious metal flanges spotted her body. Some had been capped; some ran out to transparent hoses, viscous red, yellow and blue mixtures traveling to and from her body. Still others dripped fluid, presumably ripped out by her thin, sticklike hands.

Her head was turned away from me, and her shoulders shook. Her head had been shaved, and the bald skin was gray and sickly.

Malrimple came up beside me. "We use her to assist new recruit HMIDs to assimilate. She has a way with the new ones that helps them better accept the drastic change in their reality." He sounded genuinely saddened as he continued. "She's in terrible shape. We've been trying desperately to keep her alive. She still has a use to us. She has value."

For a moment it almost seemed a human response, to the terrible toll being an HMID had wrought against Michelle's body, but I now realized he was lamenting the loss of an asset. To the scientist, she was no longer human. She was a thing to be studied, to be used. To be kept alive, regardless of the inhumanity of it.

I punched him hard in the gut, pushing my fist in as deep as I could while still holding the pistol. Then I brought my hand up and smashed it into his face, laying him out on the cold concrete floor.

I approached the black box and stepped inside. The floor was covered in viscous goo, but I ignored it. I holstered my pistol against the small of my back and took Michelle in my arms. She flinched at my touch and tried to push me away, but her arms had withered until they could barely support themselves. A slick cable descended from the top of the box to a flange at the base of her skull, I placed my hands lovingly around it and used it to turn her head.

Her eyes were the same, as was her nose and lips. If I could block out the rest, I could almost imagine we were still in the cave beneath Kilimanjaro, her face near mine as we made love on the cot behind the generators. But that was sentiment. This was now.

"Michelle," I murmured. "How I've missed you."

A tear fell from her left eye as she spoke. Her voice came both from the speakers and her mouth, creating an eerie chorus. "I saved your life in Africa, you know? It's the best thing I ever did."

I nodded and brushed her cheek. "They never knew we were coming. You didn't just save me, you saved everyone."

"I'm so tired of it now." Her voice was tiny and breathless.

"Even heroes need the chance to rest."

She smiled. "Is that what I am? A hero?"

"Of course you are."

"I'm not a monster?"

I shook my head as an ache grew in my throat, making it difficult to speak. "Never. You did what none of us would do. You're far braver than I ever was."

She smiled. "You're the Hero of the Mound."

I stroked her head. I felt a thin layer of fuzz beneath my hands. "And you are the hero of us all."

She closed her eyes and sighed, finally holding me.

I closed my eyes.

I'm not sure how long we held each other this way, but I became aware of a pounding behind me. I glanced over my shoulder and saw Malrimple working on the keypad, trying to fix it so that he could open the door. We didn't have much time.

"I'm really quite crazy," Michelle said suddenly.

I couldn't help laughing. "Yes, you are. But then so are we all."

"What now?" she asked.

I touched her chin. "I came to take you home."

Her eyes snapped open. "Thank you," she said. "Oh, thank you."

I reached down her body and pulled out each hose until the only thing that connected her to the infernal machine was the cable attached to her neck. I folded her into my arms, so that her hips were over one arm and the other held the back of her neck. I leaned down and kissed her once. She opened her eyes and we had a final kiss, even as her fluids drained away.

She looked me in the eyes. She tried to speak but she couldn't, but I heard her words in my mind.

"I love you too," I said aloud. Then I pulled the main cable out of the back of her neck.

Her eyes snapped shut.

Her breathing hitched.

And sometime in the next few seconds she died.

I began to sob. I sat like this until they came and took me away. I barely felt it as they threw me to the floor.

I barely felt their kicks. In my mind I lingered with Michelle, with the memory of us, locked in the tight, forever grip of my soul.

> Each of you will fail, but you will fail in
> your own unique way, and therefore I will
> dislike each of you on an individual basis.
>   John Scalzi, *Old Man's War*

CHAPTER TWENTY-EIGHT

THE WALLS OF my cell were covered with colorful words and phrases. I especially loved the limerick about the woman from Venus with the curious body shape. I found myself concentrating on the words, because not to do so would mean remembering what happened two days ago. Like the name *Renate*, scratched into the wall on its own near the corner. Was Renate someone's wife? A long-lost girlfriend? A gal he'd met at one of the many bars in Barstow? *SNAFU* turned up a lot, which didn't surprise me. *Situation Normal, All Fucked Up* could explain half of my existence on this planet.

That afternoon, a guard came and had me put my hands behind me and through a rectangular gap in the cell bars so that he could ziptie my wrists together. Once that was done, he grabbed the back of my collar and led me out of my cell, down a set of hallways, and into a small but brightly-lit conference room.

I'd wondered when they were going to lower the boom. I'd known they'd be madder than hell at what I'd done, and I hadn't cared; to let things continue as they were would have been immoral and impossible. I'd done what had to be done, and I'd do it again tomorrow. Of course, now that they were going to lock me up and throw away the key, I wouldn't get the chance.

Still, I was curious to see how the cast of characters would react. First I saw Ohirra and Olivares sitting in the cheap seats against the wall, along with a dozen other young officers I vaguely recognized. A conference table had been set up with a single empty metal folding chair facing it. Centered behind the table sat Mr. Pink, and to either side of him were a bruised and battered Malrimple, Doctor Cole, Lieutenant Colonel Hendrix, and Colonel Wade. Drake sat in a chair by the window, a submachine gun across his lap. He had an unpleasant smile on his face.

At the very end of the table on the left side was a stocky, red-haired stranger wearing a US military uniform, with a patch I'd never seen on his shoulder: the stars and bars of the US flag, inside the cameo of what could only be George Washington, giving America's first president a red, white, and blue face.

The guard led me to the chair and placed me in front of it. I tried to get his attention to remove the zip-ties, but he ignored me. I sighed as I stood like a pet monkey in a kangaroo court. I let my flat gaze fall on Mr. Pink and waited for the theatrics to begin.

After five minutes, he made me sit, introduced himself and the men at the table. The man at the end was introduced as Major Vincent Dewhurst of the New United States of North America. I let my gaze linger on him, wondering why he was here.

"Mr. Mason, we have brought you before this panel to determine the punishment for the murder of HMID Aquinas. We have a complete audio and video record of the event. All the members of this panel have reviewed the record several times and concur with the chair's assertion that you deliberately broke into the Fort Irwin HMID lab, assaulted Doctor Malrimple, and killed HMID Aquinas. There will be no trial. The determination has been made. Do you have anything to say for yourself?"

I said my words slowly. "It looks like you have everything you need."

"Is that all you have to say?"

It was. But I wanted to throw eggs at them. And I didn't want it on record that I murdered my girlfriend. Far from it; I did what had to be done. "After watching the audio and video evidence, do you really think it was murder? Seriously?"

"What would you call your role in the death of HMID Aquinas, then?"

"Assisted suicide."

Malrimple snorted.

Cole shook his head.

Fuck them both.

Only the stranger, Dewhurst, showed any sort of positive emotion, smiling slyly.

Mr. Pink turned to Malrimple. "Doctor, do you have anything to say to this?"

Malrimple's eyes widened, then he sighed dramatically. "I thought this was settled."

Mr. Pink nodded. "It is. But Mr. Mason gave a fair response. What do you say to his assertion that it was assisted suicide?"

"Pure nonsense. We were bringing her back online so that she could assist in the integration of a new HMID." Malrimple pointed at me. "It was through his efforts that she died."

I grinned as I said, "Ask him why they had to bring her back online."

Malrimple began slowly, as if every word was a great effort and he couldn't believe he had to explain this to us. "HMID Aquinas removed several of her transfusion tubes, necessitating immediate critical emergency care. She lost sixty percent of her fluids and was unconscious for several hours. But through the heroic efforts of Doctor Cole and his technicians, we were able to bring her back into operation." Malrimple clasped his hands together and leaned forward. "It doesn't matter. It cannot be assisted suicide; HMID Aquinas was classified a machine, not an individual."

Mr. Pink frowned and glanced at Lt. Ohirra. "Oh, dear. This could be a problem."

As if on cue, Ohirra stood and came to my side. She stood at attention as she addressed the panel. "Gentlemen, the verdict of murder must be repealed. A human can't murder a machine."

Malrimple and Cole exchanged frowns.

"Now wait a moment," Doctor Cole began.

But Ohirra wouldn't let him speak. "Either Aquinas was a machine and it is nothing more than destruction of OMBRA company property, or she was a person and it was assisted suicide. It's clear that the reason she had to be brought back online was because she ripped out her own tubes, as detailed in Doctor Cole's reports."

I wanted to smile at Ohirra's performance, but I couldn't find the right muscles to make it work.

"Wait a minute," Malrimple said. "You said we were going to vote on a punishment."

"I did. But Lt. Ohirra has brought a compelling

argument to our attention, based on your own comments to the panel."

Malrimple sat back and pointed at Ohirra. "But she works for you."

Mr. Pink grinned, something not pleasant to see. "As do you, Doctor Malrimple."

The scientist appeared to be about to say something when Mr. Pink addressed the stranger. "Major Dewhurst, what's your take on the situation at hand?"

"You know our stance on these HMIDs," he said in a clear New England accent. "We neither use them, nor do we promote their use."

"We understand your aversion to the Human Machine Interface Devices. What do you think—are the HMIDs human or machine?"

"Seems to me that you should have figured that one out when you first devised these terrible things. Doctor Malrimple, if I may ask you a question, how do you differentiate between a human and a machine?"

Malrimple was wary. He knew something was going on, but his ego wouldn't allow him to remain silent. "What do you mean?"

"Does a machine have free will?"

"Of course not," Malrimple said frostily.

"Then a machine couldn't try to kill itself, could it?"

Silence.

We all waited for a response, but none was coming.

Major Dewhurst spread his hands. "There you have it. And unless OMBRA has a law against assisted suicide, Lieutenant Mason is free to go."

"Wait a minute!" Malrimple shot to his feet.

Mr. Pink glanced at the scientist. "Sit down." Then he turned to Dewhurst. "Does the New United States of North America have any laws on the books covering this?"

Dewhurst smiled. "Are you granting us jurisdiction here?"

"Not exactly," Mr. Pink said. "We just want to know where you stand."

He shrugged. "Federal law has never prohibited assisted suicide; it was always a matter for state law. And since all state and local laws have been superseded by Rex 84 and the military is now in command, no laws prohibiting assisted suicide are in existence."

Mr. Pink turned to me. "Lieutenant Mason, you are free to go."

I sat in my chair, watching Malrimple. He looked ready to foam at the mouth. He began to whisper urgently into Mr. Pink's ear, but he was done. Mr. Pink ignored him and stood, shook hands with the men on the board, and left the room. I was left with Ohirra, who brought out a knife and cut my zipties. I rubbed my wrists.

Once Malrimple and Cole had stormed out of the room, I said, "You planned that pretty well."

"Mr. Pink made us practice," she said.

"What if I hadn't said *assisted suicide*?"

"I would have brought it up."

"Why the farce?"

"There's been an ongoing argument between Malrimple and OMBRA since the program started. Mr. Pink has had to remain a fair arbiter. He felt it was time to get things out in the open. New policies are going to be put in place to protect the HMIDs and treat them as humans."

At least there was a silver lining in this shitty cloud.

"And Dewhurst? Who is he?"

"Your new boss."

I stared at her.

"Come on. I'll explain on the way. We're two days late on the mission brief."

She started out of the room, and I followed. "I had something I had to do first."

Without turning she said, "Yes. Yes, you did."

Isn't it funny that the first thing to go were the laws of the land? Isn't it funny how much we hated some of the laws, how they separated us into competing groups. Laws about gun control or abortion or speeding seemed so important to us before everything changed... before the aliens came and bitch-slapped us into the Dark Ages. How important are those laws to us now? Our version of an apocalypse happened. Governments fell. Humanity almost ceased to exist. Everything we knew is gone. Now we're living in a post-apocalyptic world. It's inevitable that laws return as we transition through our current landscape into a post-post-apocalyptic world, which I define as a return to normalcy. As we defeat the aliens, as we gather into small groups, as we try and recover, we'll begin creating rules. These rules will become laws which will once again separate us. Some are eager to reinstate some of the laws if only to protect their own brand of law and order. Perhaps this time we should pay more attention to how we do it, to what laws we choose to enforce. After all, I think those of us who've survived have figured out what's important to us. Look around. Look at the people around you and the things you've been able to scrounge. What's important to you? What laws do you think should be necessary to protect it?

Conspiracy Theory Talk Radio,
Night Stalker Monologue #1381

PART THREE

PART THREE

These are the times that try men's souls. The summer soldier and the sunshine patriot will, in this crisis, shrink from the service of their county; but he that stands it now, deserves the love and thanks of man and woman. Tyranny like hell is not easily conquered yet we have this consolation with us, the harder the conflict, the more glorious the triumph. What we obtain too cheap, we esteem too lightly; it is dearness only that gives everything its value.

Thomas Paine, after the
Declaration of Independence

CHAPTER TWENTY-NINE

MAJOR DEWHURST STOOD at the front of the room addressing me, Olivares, Ohirra, and seven enlisted soldiers I didn't recognize. He'd spent the last twenty minutes talking about the recent past and the effects of the invasion on different areas of the country. They'd been able to contact every region and begin organizing military forces, with the exception of Alaska, the northern Yukon Territory, and Texas.

"Rex 84 was originally a readiness exercise developed to suspend the US constitution, declare martial law, place military commanders in place of local and state officials, and detain those believed to be an immediate security threat to the sovereignty of the United States, in the event the President declared a national emergency. The New United States of North America adopted Rex 84 as its blueprint for a way forward. As the special liaison to OMBRA Special Operations, I will guide you in the execution of our missions."

I felt the stirring of patriotism as he spoke. I'd had my share of gung-ho hoorah moments throughout my career, especially when I was younger. Watching movies like *Rambo II* or *Rocky III* filled me with a comfortable shared warmth, charging us, preparing us to face an enemy who wanted nothing more than our deaths. Since the creation of the first army, it's been a hard thing to take a civilized young man or woman off the street and make them eager to fight for an invisible ideal. Yet it happens all the time. Indoctrination, a little propaganda, and a lot of imagery served to turn my younger self into that Army private who wanted to fight for God and country. Then I did, and my friends died around me. I got promoted and they got body bags. So I started to fight for them alone. I'd forgotten—no, I'd ignored—that there was perhaps an ideal to follow other than to keep my men and friends safe. The ideological appeal to my warrior spirit had gone AWOL...

Until now.

As I listened I was conscious of my reawakening patriotism. *The New United States of North America.* I liked the sound of that. It rolled off the tongue much better than OMBRA.

"Power to govern and change had been taken from the people of the United States," continued Dewhurst. "The richest one percent and the corporations controlled those who would represent you. Not that the politicians didn't *want* to support your local needs, but in order to have a chance to vote for you, they had to accept the handshakes of those who were opposed to you. Ironic democracy, isn't it?

"Then came the era of the contractor, especially the defense contractor. Do you know how much money the former American public paid to prosecute the wars in Iraq and Afghanistan? There are those who called them proxy wars, who said the tail was wagging the dog. And the number one company that benefited from the wars was none other than our friends at OMBRA."

We all looked at each other, wondering why he was going down this path on an OMBRA compound in front of a bunch of OMBRA soldiers.

"I know what you're thinking. Here we are on OMBRA's doorstep. Why are you talking about OMBRA?"

I liked this guy.

"First of all, this isn't OMBRA's compound. This is Fort Irwin and belongs to the New United States of North America."

Olivares raised his hand.

Dewhurst nodded for him to speak.

"Did you tell Mr. Pink about that?"

Dewhurst looked confused for a moment, then said, "Oh, you mean Mr. Wilson. He's well aware of our philosophical differences. But at the end of the day, OMBRA is a defense contractor. They like to argue that they're a nation in their own right, but realistically they're still the same old contractor they were before the invasion."

"Then why are you working with them?" I asked.

"In North America we've come to an agreement with them to assist us in the reclamation of the continent."

"What are you going to pay them with?" Olivares asked.

"That hasn't been decided." Dewhurst stepped forward and pointed at us. "For the record, your service is duly noted. Your government appreciates that you stepped forward, some of you before the alien invasion," he said, looking at Olivares and myself. "Such dedication is what makes a country strong. Like America, that had at its foundation the heroics and sacrifices of our founding fathers. Phrases such as *I've not yet begun to fight* and *I only regret that I have but one life to lose for my country* ring through history, and are as relevant today as they were two hundred and fifty years ago."

My thoughts flipped back and forth as Dewhurst continued to talk. Could it be true? Was there going to be a re-establishing of the government? A creation of services for the people? If we could stop the spread of the alien vine and find a way to mass produce the cure, perhaps we could create some semblance of a society. I hadn't thought of anything but war for so long, it was difficult to fathom anything else.

I tried to remember when I'd last been a civilian, unconcerned with survival. I could almost say high school, but San Pedro had been thick with gangs, longshoreman, and union thugs. You had to belong to something to survive, and I'd never belonged to anything before, making me an instant target. I'd joined the military as much to save myself from the streets as to find somewhere to belong.

When my mother passed shortly after I completed infantry training, there was nothing left to tie me to civilian society. I didn't watch sports; I didn't want much television. In fact, even the movies I loved had more to do with the military than anything else. Tony Scott's *Man on Fire* was the perfect example, a story of a broken ex-soldier at odds with society. I think I liked that movie because it resonated with who I thought I'd become. Before the alien invasion, broken soldiers had become broken ex-soldiers. Now, the only thing a broken soldier becomes is dead. Because until the aliens were kicked off our planet permanently, we were *all* soldiers, like it or not.

Dewhurst wrapped up his introduction, then kicked everyone out except Olivares and me.

He pulled up a chair and sat cowboy style.

"So what'd you think?"

Olivares gave him a level stare. "Patriotic mumbo jumbo."

Dewhurst didn't flinch. This close I could see a scar running from his jaw all the way to his hairline near his right ear. "Not much for patriotism, huh? Company man?"

"Patriotism was a tool to get people to do something they wouldn't ordinarily do. *Rah, rah, sis-boom-bah. Kill a commie for your mommie. Nuke 'em till they glow*. It's all part of our indoc as soldiers."

Dewhurst nodded. "So you're the pragmatist. That makes sense." He looked at me. "That would make you the idealist."

I shook my head. "I'm not so much for patriotism either. I fight for those around me. I don't fight for a symbol."

"Sometimes people need a symbol to remember what they're fighting for."

"Like that patch on your shoulder?" I nodded at the red white and blue cameo of George Washington.

"Exactly. The union jack. The stars and bars. These are all symbols to rally around. You two have been the tip of the spear since this started. But remember, the greater part of the world's population were the shaft of the spear. They weren't close to the action, but by God they were affected by it. I'd like to think that I'm fighting for their future, so they can rebuild what was lost."

I grinned. "Now look who the idealist is."

"Oh, I make no bones about being an idealist. I was talking about you."

Shaking my head, I said, "I'm no idealist."

"You're certainly no pragmatist. A pragmatist wouldn't have put his fellow soldiers in jeopardy to become the Hero of the Mound."

I felt the blood rise to my face. "I did what I did to save Thompson."

"Did you give any thought to how your actions might affect the group? Were you concerned that they might do the same for you that you did for Thompson?"

I held back the first seventeen words I had for Dewhurst. When I unclenched my jaw, I said instead, "We fight for each other. I saw a man down. I saved him. End of story."

"Do you see yourself as a hero?"

"*Hero* is a label someone else gives you for something they were incapable of doing themselves, based on time, ability or distance. I'm just a grunt."

"What do you think, Olivares?"

His olive-skinned face remained impassive as he stared at Dewhurst. Finally he tore his gaze away and looked toward me. "He and I have had this conversation. Mason is a grunt first. Has he been a hero? Yes. Is he a hero? That's situationally dependent."

I nodded at Olivares. He ignored me as he focused on Dewhurst. "My question is, why are you coming in here and laying turds all over our yard? First you badmouth OMBRA. Where was the United States when OMBRA came to their door warning them? Where were you when the shit hit the fan? And coming in after the fact to try and measure the viability of one man's heroism against the threat of annihilation is something I'd expect from a sophomoric congressional aide, not from a military officer."

Dewhurst took it all in, nodding through it all, as if this was what he expected. When Olivares was done, the Army major smiled slightly. "I guess you're both an idealist and a pragmatist, Lieutenant. Like Mason, you believe in right and wrong. You believe that humans are good and aliens are evil. You believe that I'm an asshole and you're in the right. But the pragmatist in you says that all humans aren't good, that I'm probably not a complete asshole, and that you are sometimes fallible."

Dewhurst looked at me. "Soldiers by their very nature are pragmatists *and* idealists. It's a sliding scale, but all soldiers demonstrate both of these attributes. Some have more of one, some less. You, Olivares, are more pragmatic, while Mason here is more an idealist. This is good. This is what I want in grunts to lead my mission."

"I've never really thought of myself as an idealist," I argued.

"Then why'd you join? Why'd you continue to re-enlist? I've seen your records."

Olivares's eyes narrowed. "You've seen our records?" He glanced at me.

I wondered why the concern. I sure as hell didn't care if Dewhurst saw my records. They were what they were. "Why'd I join? Because I had nothing else to do. I joined because I needed a bigger gang than the 8th Street Angels to have my back. Why'd I stay? Definitely for the chow."

Dewhurst grinned and pushed himself to a standing position. "Okay, boys. That'll be all for now. I just wanted to get to know you. Each of you has your own team. They should be in your team rooms, waiting."

He started to leave and I said, "We don't even know what the mission is going to be."

He paused. "Didn't I tell you?"

I shook my head.

"We're going to strap you into EXOs, air-drop you over L.A., and you're going to blow up the hives the same way you did at Kilimanjaro." Then he left.

Olivares and I stared at each other.

"But they don't have volcanoes in Los Angeles," I finally said.

Grunts on the line, where the enemy wants them dead, still goof off—even knowing that by letting their guard down they might die.

David Hackworth

CHAPTER THIRTY

"YOU DON'T LIKE him, do you?" I said.

"He's a little too full of himself."

"He reminds me of Mr. Pink," I said.

"He certainly has the manipulation down." Olivares stood to go.

I couldn't help but put my nose squarely into his business. "What is it in your records that you don't want anyone to see?"

"None of your fucking business."

I laughed, and his face shifted to anger.

"Glad to see you're still the same old asshole," I said.

"Glad to see you're the same old nosy fucker."

I sighed heavily.

"What?" he yelled. Clearly the issue about his records was a big deal.

"I knew the honeymoon wouldn't last."

He sneered. "It never does."

I let him go first, then got up and followed. His team room was down the hall on the left; mine was down and on the right. I headed to my room, opened the door, and went inside.

Right away I saw Ohirra as she sat talking with three enlisted soldiers.

"Afternoon," I said, taking a chair and sitting with them. "Ohirra, you on the team?"

"I'm to be your intelligence liaison."

I watched her face for any sign of emotion. Technically she outranked me, if you considered time in grade. She could take the team if she wanted.

"I was just telling them about your time in Africa," she added.

"Don't believe that Hero of the Mound crap. It was pure propaganda." To the new three, I said, "I'm Lieutenant Benjamin Carter Mason. You can call me LT, or you can call me Mason. Just never ever fucking ever call me the Hero of the Mound. Got it?"

I watched as the nervousness was replaced with wary humor. Ohirra had probably been talking me up; I wanted them to realize I was as human as the next jerk lieutenant, just maybe a little luckier.

"So introduce yourselves."

The first guy reminded me of Thompson, so much so that he could have been his older, bigger brother. Blond hair and blue eyes, he was the farmer-linebacker version of our little drummer boy. His hair was cut in a flat top. He had the hard sculptured cheekbones.

"I'm Stranz," he said. "Been looking forward to getting some work off the compound."

Both Ohirra and I waited for more, but Stranz leaned back and thought he'd said enough.

"What's your background?" I finally asked.

"75th Ranger Regiment. Then part of a QRF with

SOCOM." He grinned and nodded like he was fucking Billy Badass and we'd already realized it.

There was this thing every soldier, Marine, airman, or seaman did whenever they encountered each other for the first time. They racked and stacked themselves by duty assignments, operational deployments, and trips to various warzones. It wasn't long before everyone knew who'd done what. But I was the lieutenant and I wasn't playing that game.

"This isn't an interrogation, Stranz," I said, leaning forward, my voice filled with razor blades. "This is an interview. You're not on my team until I say you're on my team. So if you want to sit back and act like the king of assholes, feel free, but it will probably mean you're never getting off compound."

Now it was my turn to sit back and appraise him openly as he slack-jawed stared at me. "Do you want to begin again?" I asked.

I could see him almost get mad as he snapped his mouth shut, then caught himself. He nodded, took a deep breath, and said, "I'm Corporal Rennie Stranz, sir. I was with 75th Rangers in Afghanistan and was assigned to a SOCOM QRF. My specialty is infantry and heavy weapons. I was assigned as OPFOR here at National Training Center when the world shit the bed."

I nodded as he finished. "What were your QRF missions?"

"We didn't have any, but I spent a lot of time preparing."

"I spent a lot of time in the motor pool, corporal, but that doesn't make me a mechanic."

"Yes, sir," he stuttered.

"If you're going to brag about being part of a Quick Reaction Force, it better be fucking relevant. Got it?"

He nodded quickly.

"Why are you on my team?"

"I'm a certified EXO mechanic and have logged over a thousand hours in the remodel."

Finally, a good reason. "You should have led with that." I turned to the other two. "Next?"

A young black kid with chiseled features, curious gray eyes, and a head shaved bald sat forward in his seat. "Sir, I'm Private First Class Malcom Macabre," he said with a West Indies lilt. "They call me Mal, sir. I was assigned to the 1st Battalion, 508th Parachute Infantry Regiment, 4th Brigade Combat Team, 82nd Airborne Division in Operation Enduring Freedom in 2012. I was in Maiwand manning heavy weapons."

"Is that your only experience?"

He nodded.

"Then why am I being assigned you and not someone with more experience?"

Ohirra chimed in. "PFC Macabre was awarded two Soldier's Medals for saving the lives of his fellow soldiers in non-combat situations at Fort Bragg."

"Two?" I asked. In my entire career I'd only heard of one being given away. A Soldier's Medal was the highest medal in the peacetime Army and awarded only to those who'd saved someone's life.

Ohirra nodded. "Two. In a six-month period."

One Soldier's Medal would tell me he was conscientious of his fellow soldiers. I wasn't sure what two meant. I reminded myself to ask Mal what he'd done.

"You weren't assigned to Fort Irwin. How is it you came to be here?" I asked.

"Yes, sir. I was on leave in Colorado skiing with some of my mates when the alien invasion happened. Fort Carson was hive central, so we headed here."

And finally, "What about you?" I asked the third soldier.

She looked a little stunned, but quickly recovered. She was clearly Middle Eastern. She had a scar across her nose like it had almost been cut off. She wore a flattop just like Stranz, only hers was jet black. Only concern I had was she was five feet tall if she was an inch.

"I'm Corporal Sula Ali, Sir. I spent three tours in Afghanistan assigned to Psychological Operations."

I ignored the suppressed smiles from both Stranz and Macabre and asked, "What does PSYOP do in the field?" Because I didn't actually know.

"Sir, we go into each village and embed ourselves so that the populace understands our message and is comfortable with our presence."

I stared at the other two and said, "So you don't work from an FOB?" The other two would have projected from a forward operating base, returning to it so they could sleep snugly behind high security fencing.

"No, sir. We lived with the indigs."

"Did you feel the danger?"

"Every damned second."

"Then why'd you do it?" I asked, knowing the answer but wanting to hear it said aloud.

"It was important that they knew we were all in like they were all in. They were used to people rushing out from FOB and then back to FOB and leaving them alone. We stayed with them. We became part of the village."

"You made them part of the team," I said.

"And they made us part of their family," she added.

I observed the soldiers. I had these three, Ohirra, and then Dewhurst, who was leading the overall mission. Six grunts on my team. Six grunts to take down one hive, while Olivares took down the other hive with six of his own.

> Tonight we're going to show you eight silent ways to kill a man.
>
> Joe Haldeman, *The Forever War*

CHAPTER THIRTY-ONE

WE STOOD INSIDE a hangar-sized building in an old OPFOR motor pool. Insignia and dates told the tale of who'd been the opposing forces from the 1970s on, including a special section for the Tarantulas, a small, special elite force designed to capture and kill the enemy's senior leaders. The crest was of a black tarantula with knives at the end of every hand. The same crest was on the chests of the twelve EXOs that stood before us in two lines of six.

I remember back when the Faraday Suit was revealed. Its invention had been a logical response to the threat of the Cray. We'd all read Scalzi and Steakley and knew how they'd portrayed power armor and powered exoskeletons. Borrowed from Heinlein's *Starship Troopers*, which were in turn borrowed from E. E. Doc Smith's Lensman novels; it wasn't as if there was a copyright on the idea. When mere humans were forced to fight creatures so much larger than themselves, they needed mechanical assistance to survive, which was why the Electromagnetic Faraday Xeno-combat suit, or EXO, was invented by OMBRA technicians. To keep us alive, and to foil the Cray's inherent EMP capability.

The problem was that EMP hardening caused immense problems with communications. Fortunately, OMBRA devised a method using Extremely Low Frequencies (ELF) with a ground dipole antenna established through the soles of the EXO's feet. Since the majority of EMP energy is seen in the microwave frequencies, the system was capable of operating on a battlefield in which EMPs had been brought into play. Advanced digital modulation techniques allowed them to compress data on the signal, allowing real-time feeds between team members and back to base. A backup, transmit-only communications system resided in an armored blister atop the helmet. Called the Rotating Burst Transmission Module (RBTM), it was comprised of a one-inch rotating sphere inside of the blister with its own battery power. One side of the sphere was able to pick up a packet of data when rotated 'inside' the Faraday cage of the EXO; when rotated 'outside' this protection, it transmitted the packet as a burst.

The EXO itself was an armored and EMP-hardened powered exoskeleton suit that stood about nine feet tall and had about double the bulk of a strong human. The outer covering alternated layers of Kevlar and titanium, bonded together to protect both the wearer and the grounding web. Internally the suit had hardened electronics for video feeds, voice communication, targeting, night vision, sound amplification/dampening and vital sign monitoring, along with heating, cooling and an air rebreather system with CO_2 scrubbers, all powered by extremely light, high-energy rechargeable batteries. All systems were controlled by eye movements, through an internal HUD system with Gaze technology, or remotely from base as a backup.

The techs had succeeded in improving the HUD system from the previous generation and had also been able to improve on the batteries. I could remember when an entire EXO had seized, leaving me locked inside and dying. That was a wonderful moment in my personal history.

Each Recon EXO had three primary weapon systems.

The integral rocket launcher (IRL) was mounted over the left shoulder on rails, so as to rotate it back out of the way or bring it forward to firing position when needed. The standard payload was thirty Hydra rockets with air-burst warheads set to detonate at a range determined before launch by the suit's internal targeting system. Missiles were free-flight after launch, with a hardened internal timer for detonation. This system was designed to engage alien drones at maximum to medium targeting range.

Pulled out of mothballs at Aberdeen Proving Ground before the invasion, the XM214 was the EXO's primary attack armament, a six-barreled rotating minigun fed from a backpack ammo supply through an ammo feed arm. OMBRA modified the original 1970s General Electric design, giving the system three backpack-mounted 500-round ammo boxes linked together, for a total of 1500 rounds. The original 1970s electronic controls, which could modify the rate of fire on the fly, were micronized, hardened against EMP, and incorporated into the ammo boxes. The servo that spun the barrels only engaged when the automatic harness system that pulled the weapon back out of the way was released.

When all else failed, a grunt needed a blade. A meter long and sixteen centimeters wide, TF OMBRA's harmonic blade vibrated at ultrasonic frequencies, making it thousands of times more effective at slicing through armored opponents than a normal blade. The weapon was made from Stellite to help withstand the vibrational forces as well as any environmental extremes an OMBRA grunt might encounter, and the vibration was generated in the hilt by an electrically isolated system powered by a high energy battery.

We reviewed the improvements to the new model against the model I'd previously worn. Most of the advancements were in electronics, shielding, and battery power. OMBRA technicians had raided an abandoned Siemens plant outside of Munich and found the plans for the next generation batteries. Those plans had been incorporated into the new EXOs, extending the range from ninety minutes of activity to a startling twenty-four hours.

Wearing the EXOs sure beat returning to L.A. in an environmental suit. Not only would we be secure from spores, but we'd be able to rip through any fungees who'd go against us. Even as I thought this, it gave me pause. I remembered that while my body was controlled by the spore, I was a mute, helpless audience to what it was doing. Part of me wanted to explain this to my soldiers, but another part of me, that pragmatic part which needed them to survive, promised that telling them would do absolutely no good, and could get them killed. There was no way to get a cure to the infected prior to our mission. If they came at us, we'd have to take them down, pure and simple. I let the reality of that wash over me and knew it was a responsibility I was going to have to bear all by myself. Then with utter horror, I remembered the children who'd attacked

Dupree, Sandi and me in the gravel pit. We'd taken them down like mindless zombies. It was only now that I realized that they were probably crying in their own minds, wondering what the world had done to them, screaming for us not to hurt them. I frowned. Not what the *world* had done to them, but what the Hypocrealiacs had done. I was suddenly grimly determined to take a version of hell to the aliens that they'd never imagined.

They finally released us to our own EXOs. Everyone had been rated to wear them. EXO practice had been a general part of their training. Sula's had to be retrofitted for her small stature: a sort of booster seat was created for her legs and the internal arm actuators were extended for her hands. We climbed inside and began the process of getting to know our battlesuits. We were going to have a day to practice in the mock village of Ertebat Shar, then we'd go into L.A.. Our mission timeline was to hit our target in ninety-six hours. Not a large window.

We were designated Tarantula One, because Dewhurst was with us. He was in charge of the overall mission, which we'd still not been briefed on. He'd promised to let me and Olivares in on the secret this evening. All hush-hush; it wasn't as if the enemy had anyone nearby to steal the plans. In the meantime, I was designated the battle captain for combat operations, making Dewhurst one of the members of Team One.

I called them to form behind me. When the great doors of the hangar opened, I began jogging and watched in my HUD as each of them fell in line behind me. We exited as a disorganized mob and stayed that way for a good while. I ordered us into single file and yelled at the team for not keeping distance between each other.

They tried to get it by sight and couldn't do it. After I told them to use their front and rear laser targeting nodes, they were able to calibrate their machines to stay within parameters. I was trying to teach them that it was less about what they could make the EXO do and more about what the EXO could do for them.

When they got to the point where they could keep an equal distance, I had them flow into a V formation. At first they were all over the place. Again I advised them how to use the EXOs, and they were soon programming the machines to do the work for them. After switching from a single file to a V and back several dozen times, we then worked on overwatch and bounding overwatch.

Twice Stranz complained about the drills, wanting instead to shoot something, and twice Sula shut him down.

Dewhurst was silent throughout the exercise, as were Ohirra and Macabre. And for good reason. By the time we were done, we were huffing and puffing with exertion. The suits took on much of the effort for us, but we were still using our muscles and bones to actuate the movement. I drove them hard and wanted them to feel the effort. So as we stood in a circle and faced each other, gasping for breath, I checked everyone's life signs. Dewhurst's were the worst. His heart rate was at ninety percent of his max, while everyone else's was at seventy percent.

"This was nothing, ladies and gents," I said to one and all. "If you're breathing hard, it's because you've gotten soft."

"We're not soft. It's just we've never been in combat with these before," Macabre said.

"Felt more like band practice," Stranz said, laughing.

"I think we made some hearts, maybe stars."

"Funny," I said. "Going to be even funnier when you fail to move into the correct formation and you find yourself all alone as Craybait. We looked like shit out there, but at least we got better. You need to learn to trust your suits. Use them, don't force them. Like any tool, they're only as good as the operator. We're going to practice again in four hours. Meanwhile, I want you to find a tech and get them to show you how to field strip the ammo accelerators. I want you to know the parts inside and out. If you need to, make that tech your best friend. Stranz, help them out."

Sula and Mal groaned, but didn't argue.

They needed to know how close to death they were. "I'm going to break it down for you, Barney-style. Back at Kilimanjaro, we didn't know what we didn't know. We went out and fought and were picked apart. We were *lucky* to win. That's right. You heard me. Lucky. Since then we've improved our TTPs. When we go into L.A., we're not going to go in as a group of individuals. We're going in as a team, with interlocking fields of fire. My goal, and yours as well, is to assure that we all survive whatever shenanigans Major Dewhurst has up his sleeve."

As if on cue, Dewhurst, whose heart rate was lowering slower than the rest, said, "After this evening's exercise, I'll be able to brief everyone. The final pieces are being put in place. I just want to make sure everything is safe and secure."

"You heard the man," I said. "Park your EXOs and get them ready. You have four hours."

Friends may come and go, but enemies accumulate.

Thomas Jones

CHAPTER THIRTY-TWO

DEWHURST HAD QUARTERS near ours. He took a shower, then came into our hooch and sat down on one of the chairs. He looked his age, which was the problem. He sucked down one bottle of water, then another. I clocked him at about forty. He shouldn't be in as bad a shape as he was.

"You were a reservist," I said, rather than asked.

He nodded. "I was. My day job was as a GS14 civilian at the Department of Energy Research Lab. I was assigned to National Falls, Idaho."

"Long way away from here," Olivares said.

"Long way away from anywhere, now." Dewhurst leaned back and took a deep breath. Then he looked at me with his penetrating eyes. "I audited your feed and saw you watching me."

I wasn't aware that a feed could be audited. I knew now. "What'd you come up with?"

"That I'm in questionable shape."

"I concur," I said. "What are we going to do about it?"

"Nothing. I'm going on the mission."

I raised an eyebrow.

He glanced at me and shook his head. "Seriously. I'm in charge of the mission."

I glanced at Olivares, who nodded imperceptibly.

"You'll be in charge of nothing if you don't take this seriously."

"I am."

Sighing, I said, "You're not. You're too invested. I've seen too many grunts die and I'll be damned if I lead some of them just so you can get your rocks off on a suicide mission."

Dewhurst stared at me, then looked to Olivares for support. He gave him a cold blank stare; there would be no help there. Dewhurst returned his gaze to me. I saw a sadness there, but then this was the end of the world, and sadness was on all of our faces.

He started to speak, hesitated, then lowered his head so I couldn't see his eyes. "I have a stent."

"What's that mean?" I asked.

"My heart is at about seventy percent."

"Then what the hell are you doing out here with my grunts?"

He closed his eyes, fighting against himself. "I was TDY to Washington D.C. for a conference when they attacked. They put a hive down on Idaho Falls and wiped everyone out within hours. My wife, my son, my two daughters. Everyone. You want to know why they put a hive on such a backwater place as Idaho Falls? Because almost our entire inventory of W84s are contained there. Seven hundred and fifty-two backpack-sized nuclear warheads, each capable of delivering a fifteen-kiloton nuclear explosion."

I blinked twice. "Backpack nukes? Do we have nuclear hand grenades, too?"

Olivares laughed. "Problem with a nuclear hand grenade is you can't throw it far enough."

But Dewhurst wasn't laughing.

"We seriously had backpack nukes?"

He nodded but kept staring at his hands. "What's worse is that the Cray were evidently worried about them. Why else spare a hive on them?"

"You said almost," I said.

He looked up. "That's right. Forty-eight were secreted around the U.S. at different military bases. Had the public known, they would have been in an uproar. But it's been that way ever since the creation of the W54 during the Cold War, and it's remained so during the transition through the newer models."

"How many are here?" Olivares asked.

"Seven."

"And we're going to deliver them to the hives," I added.

"Not all of them." He held up two fingers. "Only two."

"Will that be enough?" Olivares asked.

"It should be. They're almost as strong as the bombs we dropped on Hiroshima and Nagasaki."

Olivares's eyes shot wide. "Shit. Those things leveled cities. We'll kill everyone and everything, us included."

"So it *is* a suicide mission." I snapped my fingers. "Damn, I was getting used to the chow hall food."

"It's not a suicide mission," Dewhurst said.

"Then how are we going to get out of the blast range?" I asked.

Olivares rolled his eyes. "It's what I said earlier: nuclear hand grenade. Throw it as far as you can, you're still in the kill range."

Dewhurst shook his head. "An urban surface detonation would create a seventy-five foot deep crater and carry debris and radiation twenty-two thousand feet in the air. The fall out plume would reach twenty kilometers in the first thirty minutes. Prior to that, wind from the explosion and over-pressure would turn people and objects into missiles, if they didn't disintegrate first, hurling them outwards at hundreds of miles per hour. Radiation levels within five kilometers would be instantly lethal for anyone surviving the explosion over-pressure. Lethality would decrease up to fifty kilometers. Everything in the first mile radius would be turned to dust. Within five miles damage would be complete, radiating outward at lesser and lesser rates."

Both Olivares and I were silent for a long minute.

Finally, I asked, "And how is this not a suicide mission?"

"The hive is made of an impenetrable substance. As you noted at Kilimanjaro, all attempts to penetrate it failed."

I remembered and saw again in my mind's eye the airplanes that kamikazied over and over into the sides of the hive. Passenger jets had taken down our World Trade Center, but had zero effect on the hive.

"The Chinese launched eleven DongHai-10 missiles against the hives in Beijing and Shanghai, believed to be carrying payloads of ten to twenty kilotons. Reports are that they leveled both cities, killing hundreds of thousands, turning once-impressive urban settings into deserts."

"What happened to the hives?" I asked, then held up a hand. "Let me guess. Nothing."

"Exactly. At least one DongHai-10 was a direct hit and it barely left a scorch mark."

"What about the Cray?" Olivares asked.

"The Cray outside the hive were decimated. Two days later Cray were seen exiting the hive."

Remembering the giant, wormlike entity that created the creatures, those Cray were probably newly minted, which meant that the radiation had probably affected the soldiers inside the hive, but not the mother. I shared my thoughts and Dewhurst agreed.

"Our thoughts exactly."

Olivares sat down on the cot beside me. "How did you get all this information? How was it transmitted?"

"Our government is in cooperation with the former Chinese government, along with dozens of other governments, I might add. Like us, they've been using UAVs to obtain information. Not only are they tiny and almost invisible thanks to their size, but they're highly maneuverable. And they have the added benefit of being cheap and easy to produce."

"But that still doesn't explain how you got the information." Olivares leaned forward. "It's not as if you can pick up a phone and call. All we have are old radios."

Dewhurst looked as if he was about to say something, then changed his mind. After a second, he said, "We've been bouncing AM radio signals off the ionosphere for decades. Ham radios are the new telephone system. We have a single ham operator in Alaska who is our re-transmitter, call sign KL3DBS, so yes, it is almost like a telephone."

Olivares waggled a finger. "Nice try, but I think you have a satellite."

Dewhurst didn't respond other than to glance at me, then back to Olivares.

Olivares leaped to his feet. "I knew it! We do have satellites. What else do we have?"

Dewhurst gave a stone-faced stare. "We don't have satellites."

"Whatever, man."

I waved for Olivares to shut up. "The reason you want us is because we've done this before, right?"

Dewhurst nodded.

"We're going to smuggle the nukes into the hives."

He nodded again.

"How the fuck are we going to get out?"

"I'm still working on that."

"You're still working on that," I repeated slowly and without hope. "Sounds like a suicide mission to me."

Dewhurst leveled his gaze on us. "I once had a sergeant major who told me that every military mission is a suicide mission until everyone gets back alive."

"Well, we better figure it out before we do it," I said, realizing that I really didn't give a shit if I died, but I did care about the lives of soldiers in my care, including, it appeared, Dewhurst himself. "Listen. You want to get out there and get back at the aliens for killing your family. I get that. And I'll let you be part of the team. You just ask yourself one question. Do you think that by coming you're putting someone's life in danger? Because these people—these young men and women you've selected to be part of these teams—*they're* your family now."

Dewhurst regarded me with wounded eyes. "I'm not going to put..." He had to stop. He choked up and fought to swallow.

Olivares, with uncharacteristic compassion, tried to put his hand on Dewhurst's shoulder, but the major shrugged him off.

"Do you—do you know how when a dog knows it's going to die it tries to find a place to hide?" He searched our eyes for some connection. "I know I'll make the mission. I know I'll be there for our grunts." He sniffed. "But if I get to the point where I can't make it—if I find my body unable to do what I need to—I'll put no one in jeopardy. I'll find some place to go. You won't even know what happened. I won't be that guy you have to come back for."

I shook my head slowly.

"Come on," he said in a shaky voice. "Don't make me beg."

"You don't have to beg, Major," I said, "You had me at the dog."

He stared at me for a time, then nodded, got up, and walked out.

Leadership is a potent combination of strategy and character. But if you must be without one, be without the strategy.

General Norman Schwarzkopf

CHAPTER THIRTY-THREE

I LEFT Olivares and headed back to the hangar. I wanted to make sure our teams' EXOs checked out. I would have hoped Mr. Pink had arranged for us to have the very best, but I had to be sure for myself. About halfway across the compound a young corporal ran up to me: Hoby Ethridge. We'd shared something no one else did. We'd survived the spore.

"How you doing, Ethridge?" I asked, continuing on my way.

He fell in beside me. "Going crazy, sir."

I slowed and gave him a sideways glance. "Crazy is a state of mind, corporal. One *could* say that we're all crazy."

"It's the voice in my head. He won't stop talking to me."

This stopped me. I hadn't had a voice in my head since Michelle died in my arms. The memory slammed into me like a freight train. I'd done a terrific job compartmentalizing... until now.

"Whose voice is it?" It couldn't be Thompson's. We were too far out.

"He calls himself Peter. He knew Michelle." Ethridge glanced around. "I think he's a little crazy. He keeps singing this song that doesn't make any sense."

"When's the last time he spoke with you?"

"He's in here now," he said, poking at his head.

"And you can't understand him?"

"Not at all. It's like he's singing in a foreign language."

I saw a jeep passing by and waved for it to stop. Two privates on their way to offload some trash. Both saluted sitting down. I ordered both of them out of the vehicle, then had Ethridge climb into the passenger seat. This was something we needed to get to the bottom of.

I drove to the HMID facility. Last I'd been here it had been night and Michelle had been in her death throes. This time, instead of sneaking inside, I parked the jeep, got out, and knocked on the door. It took a minute, but eventually a tech answered. Seeing me through the window, the young woman backed away and almost ran back into the main room. I could have told her that if I'd wanted to sneak inside, I probably wouldn't have knocked.

A few moments later my favorite person in the world appeared. He glowered as he came to the door. He didn't bother to open it, instead just stood inside staring at me through the glass.

"Open the door, Malrimple."

"Or what? You going to shoot me?"

"I never took you for a drama queen."

The aging scientist shook his head and started to turn.

"Peter won't get out of this guy's head, Malrimple. Something's wrong with the HMID."

This stopped him. He stared at Ethridge for a moment, then returned his gaze to me. "We can't get him to stop," he finally admitted.

"Do you know what he's broadcasting?"

"It's hexadecimal code, recited in a looping series of seventeen languages."

"Do you know what he's saying?"

"It's the results of a data mine we had him do during an alien transmission download two days ago. Something in Los Angeles is communicating with an orbiting ship. We've been monitoring the activity and trying to decode it ever since we first created the HMIDs. Peter is our attempt to try something different."

"What do you mean, different?" I asked warily.

"He's a savant. His math is off the chart, but he's on the spectrum."

I stared at him. It must have been obvious that I had no idea what he was saying, so he added, "He's autistic. Ever seen the movie *Rain Man*? That's Peter. We were hoping he'd be better able to decode the transmissions, but it seems to be backfiring." Malrimple opened the door. "Might as well come inside."

"Why is Peter talking to Ethridge and not me?"

"That's a good question." He waved for us to follow, then glanced back. "Let's see if we can figure this out. I expect you still know your way."

I smiled. "Like the back of my hand."

Malrimple led us through the halls and into the HMID chamber. Michelle's machine stood open and empty against the wall. The machine on the left appeared dark. But the one on the right was the center of attention. Five techs worked around it, inputting data from several portable devices. Doctor Cole, who stood in the center of the room at the server tower, finally noticed that we'd entered. He immediately drew a 9mm pistol and double-handed it towards me.

"Not again, Lieutenant Mason."

"It's all right, Dr. Cole. I invited him in."

"But Dr. Malrimple—"

The head scientist waved the other man silent. Cole snapped his mouth shut but gave me a look that promised violence if he'd only get the chance.

We approached the team of techs.

"Sutter, where are we?" Malrimple asked.

A sweaty, middle-aged black man turned and shook his head. "Not sure what's happening. All the servers are maxed. HMID Salinas has tapped into a fire hose. There's nowhere else to put the information."

Malrimple nodded. "He's accessing Corporal Ethridge's brain as well. It's as if he's looking for more space."

"Has he tried to access Lt. Mason?"

"No. And we need to know why."

Sutter stared at me as he thought about what to do. Then he grabbed one of the techs. "Joub, take a look at the root code. I want to make sure nothing's been rewritten."

The young Arab woman nodded and began to type into her pad. It took about thirty seconds for her to find something. "I found it. Someone wrote code putting Mason off-limits for HMID communication."

"Who'd do that?" I asked.

Malrimple turned back to the center of the room. "Dr. Cole, do you know anything about this?"

Cole shook his head.

"Joub?"

She shook her head as she punched at her pad. "This doesn't make sense. I haven't seen this before."

"What do you have?" Malrimple looked over her shoulder.

"See here," she said, pointing at a line of code. "I haven't seen anything this pure. It's almost as if a machine created it. But then look here." She pointed at another line of code. "This isn't the logical flow. This is intuitive."

Malrimple nodded slowly. "This is HMID Aquinas's work."

"What? How could it write code?"

"It didn't write it. It thought it and made it happen."

I didn't know what they were talking about, but talking about my dead girlfriend as an *it* wasn't going to happen. "She. Call her a fucking *she*."

Both Malrimple and Joub stared at me. Malrimple's eyes softened as he nodded. "All right, Lt. Mason. We'll do that. Won't we, Joub?"

"Uh, yes, sir."

"So what is it that *she* did?" I asked.

"*She* wrote code that made it so that you were invisible to HMID Salinas," Joub said.

"Why would she do that?"

"I don't think we'll ever know." Malrimple pointed to the data. "I want to save this and look at it later. Let's bypass this line and open it up for contact between HMID Salinas and Lt. Mason." He eyed me. "You ready?"

"If it'll help."

"I think it will," Malrimple said. "All of this is new to us. We're not sure what's going on, but HMID Salinas was onto something, and I want to make sure we find out what it is before we lose it."

I glanced at Ethridge, who looked as if his head were about to explode. I didn't want to invite pain on myself, but part of the battlefield was in the mind. Michelle had fought there. If I could help out by letting them use me, then I would.

I nodded.

Malrimple gave Joub the thumbs up.

She typed on her pad.

A flood of ants invaded my brain, ticking, clicking, moving in and out of my thoughts. I felt my jaw fall open and my eyes slammed shut. There was no pain, but I couldn't think of anything else except my brain filling with a million, billion trickling points of thought—ideas skittering at the speed of light. I was being filled and filled and filled, beyond capacity. I fell to my knees. My mind was a hurricane of ideas, numbers, people, places, things both human and alien and strange. I felt myself forget to breathe.

Then a wash of nothing.

"Mason, are you okay?"

I breathed.

My heart beat.

I was alive.

"Mason, are you okay?"

"Lieutenant, it's gone. It's over."

I opened my eyes. My throat was raw, as if I'd been screaming. I must have been.

"Lieutenant—thank God."

"I thought you were dying."

I cleared my throat. "I thought I did." I sat up with the help of two of the techs. "What happened?"

"It's gone," Ethridge said.

"What's... where'd all the information go?"

Peter spoke, both through the speakers and inside the wide-open expanse of my mind. "I can now translate the Hypocrealiac language."

After a moment, Malrimple put his hand to his head. "Oh, my God."

Sutter shook his head. "Computational space. He needed your brain so he could work his algorithms." Seeing my confusion, he added, "One pre-invasion study estimated that the brain has around a hundred billion neurons, each with a thousand synapses capable of making connections—think of synapses as doing the work of data storage. That's a hundred trillion data points, or one hundred terabytes of info. Another study estimated the brain's capacity at closer to 2.5 petabytes, or twenty-five hundred terabytes of binary data. Before the invasion, we stored petabytes in the cloud and had literally an endless capacity for storage. Since then, in this time of austerity, we have been forced to use whatever servers weren't fried. It looks as if HMID Salinas required more space. He found it with you and Corporal Ethridge."

"Theta waves," I said.

Malrimple nodded.

I stood, a little wobbly on my feet. "Glad I could be of help." Then I turned a little too fast. Everything went fuzzy and I fell to the floor.

Today the guns are silent. A great tragedy has ended. A great victory has been won. The skies no longer rain with death— the seas bear only commerce—men everywhere walk upright in the sunlight. The entire world lies quietly at peace. The holy mission has been completed. And in reporting this to you, the people, I speak for the thousands of silent lips, forever stilled among the jungles and the beaches and in the deep waters of the Pacific which marked the way.

Douglas MacArthur

CHAPTER THIRTY-FOUR

A NEW EXCITEMENT filled the compound as news of the breakthrough made it through the ranks. I would have thought that the information would have been classified at the highest levels, but Mr. Pink, ever the social manipulator, was using it to inspire confidence, much as he'd done with me, televising my Hero of the Mound stand over Thompson's fallen EXO. Our mission had been postponed by at least twenty-four hours so they could discuss the ramifications of the newfound ability to translate what the aliens were saying to each other.

The night before, my brain had felt like a sponge with all the water squeezed out. I'd spent most of the time in a daze, missing night practice with the team. But when I awoke that morning, I felt refreshed, eager. I spoke with Dewhurst right after I got up, but he brushed me off as he made his way to a high-level meeting. I tried to contact Mr. Pink, but he was busy. Frankly, I wanted to know what going on. After all, I was now a lieutenant. But while a lieutenant outranked a sergeant major, that same lieutenant was the lowest level of the officer ranks—still essentially a grunt.

The more things change... I thought. So here I was again, training with the soldiers while others decided our fate. I was a mushroom—fed shit and kept in the dark.

I'd paired Stranz with Sula, and Ohirra with Macabre. We'd moved past the wide, flat Dust Bowl to a narrow valley marked on the map as the Devil's Spit. I stood on top of a hill and watched as they moved first one way, then the other, practicing bounding overwatch. Normally one team would provide fire protection while the other would rush forward, establishing a position. Then they'd switch. But where individual soldiers would normally limit their rush to three-to-five seconds, while in the EXOs I'd commanded them to make ten-second rushes. Their servo-assisted legs could carry them twice as fast and far. Combined with the armor-plating and the ability to deliver damage faster, I wanted to make sure we pushed the EXOs to their limits.

I'd always thought that our strategy against the hive in Africa had been flat. Part of that came from never having used the EXOs in combat before, and having to feel our way through the fight. And we hadn't been entirely aware of the abilities of the Cray, or known what was in the hive.

Now all that had changed.

We now knew how the interior was structured. We understood the Cray and their reaction to intense light. We knew how they attacked. We also knew we were going to deliver a thermonuclear device right into their midst. So it was up to Olivares and me to come up with a plan that would ensure mission completion and survival.

"Tarantula One, this is Tarantula Chief, inbound to your location."

I checked my HUD and watched as Dewhurst's EXO made good time through the Dust Bowl and to my location. He arrived a moment later, and I told the team to take ten.

"What's up, boss?" I asked.

"Switch to private channel one."

I switched. "Okay, what's up?"

"They kicked me out."

"Kicked you out? What does that mean?"

"Arguably the biggest discovery—the most important breakthrough in the history of mankind—and they want to monetize it."

Monetize it? "I don't get it."

"Your clowns at OMBRA had the audacity to ask me to contact our new government and invite them to pay for the right to have access to the translation data. OMBRA will provide real-time translation services for a fee."

"Watch your blood pressure."

"Fuck my blood pressure. Remember Iraq? We spent one hundred and thirty-eight billion dollars on contractors in Iraq, and what did we get for that? A country worse off than when the war began—a broken country that only an alien invasion saved from being overrun by third-rate terrorists."

"How do they expect you to pay for it?"

Dewhurst sighed heavily. "In land. As a sign of good faith, we allowed OMBRA to own whatever land they were occupying. I know I said earlier that Fort Irwin was ours, but I didn't want to confuse anyone with the complexities of our relationship. After all, for all of their greed, they were hammering the aliens better than anyone else. Out of appreciation, we gave them some land. And now they want more."

"Did they say what they wanted?"

Dewhurst's EXO nodded.

"And?"

"Colorado, Utah and Wyoming."

"The *states*?"

"All three of them."

Audacity was the word. OMBRA wanted to own a fair chunk of what used to be America. "What are they going to do with them?"

"Whatever they want? Hell, I don't know. Turn the whole area into one big fucking amusement park."

I thought about that for a moment. "Why don't you just withhold your support? Use the nuclear bombs as leverage."

"Because we're not like them. Although it handcuffs us to an ideal, we think it's the best way for our fledgling country to begin. We consider OMBRA, whether they like it or not, part of our new nation. They are citizens, pure and simple, and it is the federal government's responsibility to protect its people."

And there it was. That ideal I so much loved. Protect the innocent from bullies—in this case, the Hypocrealiacs.

"What are we going to do?" I asked.

"What's this *we*, Lieutenant? You've been part of OMBRA from the beginning."

"I joined OMBRA because I thought it would be a far more entertaining way to die than jumping off a bridge."

"How has that worked out for you?"

"I seem to be an abject failure at dying."

"You know what they say, if at first you don't succeed..."

"Yeah, I've been living that one all my life. So what are we going to do?"

"I'm not sure. I'll have to think about it." He gestured toward the canyon floor. "How are they doing?"

"Coming together as a team. Are we still doing the mission?"

"OMBRA's abject greed aside, we still need to retake our planet."

"So we're going through with it?"

"Absolutely, Lieutenant."

I held out my hand. "Then let's join the others. You have a lot of practice to make up for."

He grunted. "That's right. I'm a regular slacker."

We jogged down the incline to join the others. Soon, I'd broken us down into three teams, conducting bounding overwatch up and down the canyon. We kept at it until noon, then headed back to the Dust Bowl. Tomorrow would be a live fire exercise, and if we were lucky, the day after that we'd be in mission.

No bastard ever won a war by dying for his country. He won it by making the other poor dumb bastard die for his country.

General George S. Patton

CHAPTER THIRTY-FIVE

THAT AFTERNOON I was summoned into Mr. Pink's office. I didn't know what it was about, but I felt like I had back in school, being summoned by the principal. I was asked to go right in.

Mr. Pink rose from his desk and gestured for me to sit down. I didn't like that at all. Politeness from him terrified me. He wore the same black pants and black OMBRA polo that he usually wore.

"I haven't spoken to you since the hearing. How are you doing?"

That he was asking me meant he wanted something. "I'm doing fine," I said.

"And the team? They coming together?"

I nodded. "I'll have them ready for the mission."

"I'm sure you will." He stared at me for a long moment. "We go way back, don't we, Lieutenant Mason?"

I grinned. "We're regular best buds. BFFs even." My eyes narrowed. "What's this all about, Mr. Pink?"

"Do you know that even my generals call me Mr. Pink? I stopped correcting them a long time ago. It's gotten to where I like it."

I remained silent. He'd get to the point eventually. After all, we had a mission in two days, so he had to let me go by then.

He stood and paced to the window, where he stopped and stared out at the hot Death Valley afternoon. His hands were clasped behind his back as he contemplated something. Finally, he turned back to me.

"We're worried about your loyalty to OMBRA."

And there it was.

"What about it?"

"We're concerned that Major Dewhurst is actively trying to compromise you."

"You're mistaken."

He sighed. "We have a record of your conversation with Major Dewhurst this morning."

I felt myself getting mad. "You listened in on our private conversation?"

Mr. Pink shrugged. "We were concerned."

"Fuck your concern. That was private."

"Not as long as you're in an OMBRA EXO, it's not."

I thought of a dozen things to say, including some ideas he could try out with his own mother, but kept my mouth shut. Instead, there was something I wanted to make perfectly clear. "You're still mistaken."

"Didn't you hear me? We know what you said. We have a transcript, if you want to read it."

"Not about that. You said you were worried about my loyalty to OMBRA. I've never been loyal to OMBRA." I let that sink in for a moment, then added, "I'm loyal to the men and women around me. I'm loyal to the grunts."

"But we assumed..." He shook his head.

"You're a company looking to make a profit at the expense of the world. That you're forcing Dewhurst's hand and asking for three states in exchange for this breakthrough sickens me. It's embarrassing to wear the OMBRA logo."

"That's a little dramatic, now, isn't it?"

"Is it? That farce of a hearing we had the other day established that HMIDs were human. When Peter Salinas broke the code, was he doing it as a human or an HMID?"

"I see where you're going, Mason. It's always been the right of companies to own the intellectual property of its employees when created during paid hours."

I paused for a second at the legal mumbo jumbo, then changed courses. "Regardless, OMBRA is a means to an end. It has the biggest and best military and gives me the greatest ability to kill as many aliens as I can."

"But you're not loyal."

"Hell, no! Do you want to know who I'm loyal to? Ohirra, for one. I'm loyal to her because she had my back. Want to know who else? Thompson. That's right. HMID Thompson, who you've parked with Sebring's God's New Army."

I realized I was standing and shouting when the door opened and the secretary asked, "Is everything all right in here?"

Mr. Pink waved her away. "You can have your seat back, now, Lieutenant."

I sat slowly, aware that my blood pressure was through the roof. Even so, I wasn't about to apologize for my beliefs.

Mr. Pink brought his thumb to his mouth and chewed on the nail for a moment. "It's good to see that you're loyal to *someone*. This New United States of North America is something you could be loyal to."

"It could be. I don't know enough about it. My country ceased to exist. Even if it didn't, I was never really fighting for a flag, or a bald eagle, or a president. I was fighting for grunts."

"We're concerned that Major Dewhurst might do something he can't recover from."

"I'm not worried about that at all. We have a mission to take down two hives, and by God we're going to complete that mission."

Mr. Pink regarded me for a time, then nodded. "That will be all, lieutenant."

I was clearly dismissed. I stood but didn't move. Finally, Mr. Pink looked up at me.

"Is there something else, lieutenant?"

"You mentioned that we go way back. We do, indeed. I want to tell you that I appreciate you saving my life. I'm thankful you locked me up in that Godforsaken cell to help me learn how to better fight the aliens, and to make me realize that there's something good about my PTSD-fueled existence. I want to thank you for letting me fight, when all I wanted was to die."

He blinked at me, clearly unprepared for my words.

"I also want you to know that I'm loyal to *you*, as a person. Not to OMBRA, not to a company, but to Mr. Wilson. The man who I call Mr. Pink just to fuck with him. In a way, you're a grunt just like the rest of us. Just like Thompson, Ohirra, and my new team. I fight for you as well."

Then I turned and strode out of the room.

Let him chew on that for awhile.

Hell is empty and all the devils are here.
William Shakespeare

CHAPTER THIRTY-SIX

THE NEXT MORNING we waited outside of the mock village Ertebat Shar, ready to attack. Originally built to represent an Afghan village, it was all my team had to allow us to practice moving and shooting in an urban environment. OMBRA didn't have any mock-up Cray, but they did have the ability to program images into our HUDs, so the targets we were going to fire on were completely digital. The challenge of simultaneously representing an attacking alien to six different HUD feeds turned out to be easy enough for HMID Salinas. His assistance allowed the OMBRA techs to create realistic independently operating three-dimensional representations of the winged aliens. Even so, we were still using live fire, just to get the hang of the noise, reloading, and recoil.

There was little doubt that we were going to destroy the village, so Tarantula Team Two was standing by the other mock-up village, ready to go in and do the same thing when their turn came.

I checked everyone's vitals and flipped through their feeds. We were full ammo and ready to rock and roll.

As I waited, I couldn't help but replay the conversation I'd had last night with Dewhurst. He'd spent several hours communicating with the new government through AM channels. When he was done, he found me where I was conducting last minute checks on my team's EXOs.

"I heard Mr. Pink called you in," he'd said.

I'd decided not to tell Dewhurst that not only were they were listening in on our private channels, they'd also heard us talking about walking away from OMBRA. I said, "He just wants to make sure I'm one hundred percent ready for the mission. My body and mind have been through a lot."

"Have you thought about what we discussed? I spoke with my representatives. We need heroes like you and Olivares in the new government."

"They need me here, too."

"Being here and being part of the New United States of North America aren't mutually exclusive."

"So you'd want me to spy for you?"

He laughed. "Nothing like that. But as a government we operate on behalf of the people. As a military we ensure the safety of the people. We'd be concerned if OMBRA were doing anything that could harm the safety of our citizenry."

"I'm not really a joiner," I'd said.

"Do you realize why they took Fort Irwin? This backwater, Godforsaken military post on the ass-end of the Mojave Desert? China Lake Weapons Center, that's why. Where the nukes are kept and the Goldstone Deep Space Communication Complex is located. As of now, OMBRA owns all of seven of our W84s, as well as several prototype missiles and associated technologies, as well as all of our deep space radio antennas. How do you think they're able to tap into the aliens' communications so easily? They own Goldstone. They also own the one in Madrid. The only one we don't know anything about is Australia, because absolutely no one knows what's going on Down Under.

"So they have our best offensive capabilities, along with our best way to communicate and track the invading force, and are holding them over our heads like the fucking sword of Damocles if we don't cough up enough land to pay for it. Do you think that's fair?"

"Fair hasn't been a part of our universe since the planet was taken from us."

And then he'd walked away.

He'd been largely silent this morning, except for the occasional glare. He might as well get used to it. I wasn't the sort to be forced to join. I normally did things because I wanted to, and right now I didn't want to do anything other than this mission.

"Tarantula One, this is control. Prepare for telemetry to snap in. On my count: five, four, three, two, *one*."

Our HUDs suddenly lit up with fake telemetry of several hundred Cray swirling in a mass above the village. I spent the first several seconds agog at the seamless integration of the real and the digital. Had I not known that they didn't exist, I wouldn't have believed it.

Across the top of my HUD were five small boxes representing each of my team. From left to right they were Dewhurst, Ohirra, Stranz, Mal, and Sula. I quickly selected and flipped through each one to check their vitals, their weapons and ammo status, and their view through their own HUDs. Everything checked out.

Our goal from this exercise, other than to throw a shit-ton of ammo into the sky, was to converge on the village center and hold it. I snapped my minigun in place, comforted by the weight and heft of it in my Kevlar-gloved hands, even though most of it was held by the support arm. I depressed the firing lever and let the barrels spin several cycles as I began to scan the village and the sky, marveling at the realism of the digital Cray.

"Listen, grunts," I said, "this is an exercise. I know it, you know it. But don't be fucking around. I need to evaluate your ability to shoot, move, and communicate, as well as to follow orders. I say something once, I expect it done. If I repeat myself, you'll answer for it. Are there any questions?"

Silence said it all.

"If you let enough of the Cray get close enough to do damage, your suit will shut down and you'll fall over. That will mean you're dead. None of you better end up dead. Tarantula One-Two and One-Three, move out."

Ohirra and Stranz ran full speed towards the center of the village,

"Tarantula One-Four and One-Five, move out."

Mal and Sula moved out behind them. When Ohirra and Stranz got to the first buildings on the edge of the village, they put their backs to the walls and opened fire, bullets zipping into the sky from their miniguns. I watched as Cray winked out of the HUD.

"Tarantula One-Six, move with me."

Dewhurst and I ran full speed towards Ohirra and Stranz's position.

Mal and Sula ran right by them, moving an additional thirty yards into the village. When they stopped, they put their backs to a building and opened fire as well.

Both Dewhurst and I fired several rockets from our shoulder-mounted Hydra units. As I passed Ohirra and Stranz, I saw the missiles seek and find non-existent

Cray and explode. Then we passed Mal and Sula, penetrating thirty more yards into the village. When we stopped, we switched to miniguns and laid out a line of rounds into the descending Cray.

As soon as we stopped, Ohirra and Stranz moved.

I kept one eye on everyone's vitals.

As Ohirra ran by, the number of Cray in the air tripled and they all dove for our location at once. I fired through an entire magazine and spent a precious five seconds with the auto-loader rearming.

Dewhurst took twice as long, after failing to realize he was no longer firing.

Once Ohirra and Stranz found their position, Sula and Mal moved out.

Cray were falling at a great rate. Our rate of fire was working well, as were our interlocking fields of fire. In real life the battlefield would be filled with Cray corpses.

I watched as Mal tripped and stumbled into Sula. She lost her balance and fell, her minigun still firing in our direction.

I dove to the ground.

Dewhurst hadn't even seen what happened. He took sixteen rounds across the front of his EXO and promptly fell over.

"Cease fire!" I screamed across the net. "Cease fire!"

As I got to my feet and ran over to Dewhurst, I checked his vitals. His heart rate was still high, but there was nothing else wrong. I fell to my knees beside him and checked his armor. Luckily for him, it didn't look like any of the bullets had pierced it.

"Tarantula One-Six, how do you feel?"

"None penetrated," he said, his breathing quick.

"Then why did you fall?"

"Seemed like the best thing to do at the time."

I was relieved that he wasn't actually hurt. I wasn't really upset at Mal or Sula either. This was why we practiced, to get through things like this. Then I noticed that my HUD was blinking red all over. Ohirra, Sula, Stranz, Mal, and now me. We were all dying. Correct that. We were at zero power. My suit was breached. I was dead.

I tried to move and couldn't. My suit was locked. In my rush to see if Dewhurst was actually hurt, I forgot to tell Exercise Control to stop the exercise. The Cray had kept coming. In our first foray into Ertebat Shar I'd gotten everyone killed. On the bright side, there was nowhere to go but up.

The water is rising. Constant tremors have been reported from ham operators in Chile and other areas of South America. Streaks of light litter the night skies at the bottom of the world. If the aliens are trying to put us underwater, then they have a grand plan. Scientists believe that if the Antarctica Ice Sheet melts, it would result in about a two-hundred-and-thirty-foot rise in sea level worldwide, surely swamping most of the world's cities. How could they do that, we ask? Some say they're bombarding us with small comets spread over a large area to do the most damage. Two years ago I never would have believed it. But now...

Conspiracy Theory Talk Radio,
Night Stalker Monologue #1713

CHAPTER THIRTY-SEVEN

AFTER SEVENTEEN FORAYS into Ertebat Shar, expending eleven thousand rounds and three hundred and thirty missiles, I was finally satisfied that my team wouldn't get themselves killed within the first five minutes of the mission. Each of us had had our moments. Of particular interest had been when Stranz and Ohirra decided to remove a building with missiles to improve their fields of fire. That single event triggered something in the rest of the team and by the end of the morning, there wasn't a single building left standing. Exercise Control was going to have to get to work constructing a new Ertebat Shar if they wanted to train for any future missions.

Both the exercises and the venting were important. My grunts needed to be able to work together. I think we'd accomplished this.

When we finished, Dewhurst limped off to a meeting, which Ohirra attended as well in her capacity as a senior intelligence officer. I took the rest of my grunts back to the barracks, where we showered, changed clothes, then headed to a private officer's lounge where I'd arranged for a little party. Before them was a spread of food unlike they'd seen in one place since before the alien invasion. Inspired by the spread that Mr. Pink had provided when he'd recruited me, I'd arranged for burgers and pasta, and whatever vegetables and sweets the cooks could come up with. Fort Irwin was limited in what it had to provide, relying on the vast warehouses of canned goods and MREs stored here to support all the training units. The logisticians had established relationships with many of the outlying ranches still operating and were able to get a trickle of dairy and meat. What the chow hall had provided to my grunts represented more real meat than they'd had in the last six months.

I'd also arranged for a case of beer, which had been iced in a cooler. When I opened it, my grunts stared lovingly at it, unable to move. For a moment I wasn't even sure they were breathing.

"Is this all for us?" Mal asked.

I grinned widely. "Thought you all might want something good before we go into the shit."

Stranz gave me a look. "Like a condemned man's last dinner," he said.

"If that's what you want to call it." I shrugged. "I could have blown this off and made it so that tomorrow was no big deal. I probably would have done it that way, before the alien invasion. But I figured we ought to be reminded about how great we had it, about how awesome it was before the Cray attacked and took everything from us. I thought a full stomach might motivate you."

Sula held up a burger with a huge bite taken out. "Um all forit," she said around a huge mouthful.

"Dig in, guys."

I watched as they loaded their plates and found a table. I grabbed a burger, fries and a cold beer and joined them. We just sat and ate in silence for awhile. It wasn't until I was on my last French fry, scooping up a red swirl of ketchup, that anyone said anything.

"I could get used to this," Mal said. He held up a hand to stifle a belch. Stranz got up to get another plate, while Sula was still working on her pasta.

There was something I'd been wanting to ask Mal. "Ohirra said you were awarded two Soldier's Medals. Can you share what happened?"

He glanced at me, his face suddenly solemn. "There was a house fire. I was driving to work back when I was stationed at Fort Bragg and came across this house on Sycamore Dairy Road. Fully engaged, is what the firemen later said. I pulled over and got out, which is when I heard the screams. I was able to run inside and get the mother out, but no matter how many times I tried to go back in, I just couldn't make it to the rest of the family. I heard their screams until they cut off. Then I knew it was over."

"How old were they?"

"Five and seven." Mal frowned. "The firemen later said that it had been a short circuit in the kids' bedroom."

"But you were able to save the mother."

"Lot of good that did. She killed herself a year later. The day after they gave me the medal, in fact. She was at the ceremony and decided she just couldn't take it." Mal looked at me. "Promise me you'll never give me a medal. Will you promise me that?"

I nodded slowly. "We don't do medals anymore. The appreciations we show for duty are meals like this." I went over and grabbed two beers. Opening them both, I put one before Mal and sipped the other one. "What about the other medal?"

"Yeah, Debbie Downer, tell us another sad story," Stranz said.

Empathy-challenged for sure. Was it PTSD or was he just an ass?

Mal rolled his eyes. "I saved a dog."

I snorted beer. "You what?"

"He saved a dog and it bit him," laughed Sula. "Show him the scar, Mal."

I looked from Sula back to Mal. "Yeah, show me the scar."

Mal got up and unceremoniously pulled down his pants. I was about to say something when both Dewhurst and Ohirra entered the room. They both stopped and stared, then looked at each other and shook their heads.

"Didn't know this was *that* sort of party," Dewhurst said.

Stranz, Sula and I burst into laughter.

I waved at Mal. "Continue, please."

He pointed to a diamond-shaped scar on his left calf, then pulled his pants back up. He also showed me where his left hand had a bunch of smaller scars.

"So how did saving a dog get you a Soldier's Medal?"

"It was a military dog," Mal said, sitting back down and picking up his beer. "It had been hit by a car and left beside the road."

Dewhurst joined us at the table, three burgers on his plate and nothing else. "Did you know that a military working dog holds the rank of sergeant on the battlefield?"

Sula laughed at that. "See, Stranz? Even the dog would outrank you."

Stranz scowled and stared daggers at Sula.

"He was supposed to be promoted to sergeant on the day the aliens attacked. He's never let us forget it, either."

"Is that true, Stranz?" I asked.

"I'd worked hard. My father was a sergeant, my grandfather was a sergeant, and his father was a sergeant. It was just something I wanted to achieve, is all." He looked at Sula, who was smirking. "You wouldn't understand."

"Of course I wouldn't understand," she said, rolling her eyes. "I've never wanted to achieve anything. I didn't even *have* parents. I was a miracle birth, born from the union of a plant and a stop sign."

Mal and Dewhurst chuckled.

I smiled, and noticed something going on with Ohirra. To Stranz I said, "Do you want to be a sergeant?"

"Yes, sir."

"Fine. Then you're a sergeant."

He blinked at me. "Just like that?"

"Just like that. If I can go from master sergeant to lieutenant, then you can be a sergeant." I glanced at Ohirra and under my breath, asked, "I can do that, right?"

She nodded slightly.

"There you have it." I turned to the rest of the group. "May I present Sergeant Stranz."

Everyone clapped. After a few moments of Stranz smiling happily and uncomfortably, I turned back to Mal.

"So the dog bit you."

"Yeah. It bit me, but it was bleeding pretty badly. I just let it chew on my hand while I carried it to the trunk of my car and put it in. Then I took it to the Fort Bragg vet."

"And they gave you a Soldier's Medal for that?"

He nodded. "I told them I didn't want one, but they insisted."

"Medals aren't really for those they award them to," Dewhurst said. "They're for everyone else, to see the achievement and to dare them to match it." He nodded to Mal. "Congrats, kid."

"Thank you, sir."

"What's your story, Sula?" I asked. "Where are you from?"

"Los Angeles," she said. "Westwood."

I nodded slowly. "I'm from Pedro. Were you in Westwood during the invasion?"

She shook her head. "We were in Vegas to celebrate my birthday. They were killed there."

I shook my head. "You've got to wonder why Vegas, of all places. Why waste a hive there?"

Dewhurst answered around a mouthful of burger.

"Nellis Air Force Base and the Nevada Test and Training Range, where Area 51 is located."

I glanced at him. Area 51. With all the rumors, one had to wonder if they weren't true. "Did they really keep aliens there?" I asked.

Dewhurst shrugged. "Maybe. Who knows? Does it really matter now?"

I stared at him for a moment. I supposed he was right. What did it matter now?

"What if the aliens invaded us because we captured some of their people—er—aliens back in the day?" Mal asked softly. "What if the problem started with Area 51?"

"Or Roswell?" Sula added.

"Or what if we could go to the aliens we have in custody, free them, and get us to help them fight the Cray?" Mal said.

I would have laughed, but it made a sort of obnoxious sense.

Just then Ohirra threw her fork down. "Will you shut up? Stupid, stupid, *stupid*." Then she froze. Realizing what she'd done, she got up and hurried out of the room.

I glanced once at my grunts, then hurried after her. I caught up with her halfway down the hall. I was smart enough not to touch her. "Hey, what's going on?"

She kept walking, head down.

I scooted past her and placed myself in front of her. "Seriously, Ohirra. What is it?"

She tried twice to go around, then said, "Move."

"I'm talking to you not only as your friend, but as your mission commander. You're obligated to answer me."

She seemed as though she might argue, then she sagged against the wall and leaned there, one hand on her face.

"What's wrong?" I asked softly.

She sighed. "We just came from a meeting where they briefed us on the initial results of the translations." She looked at me and shook her head. "You're not going to believe this."

I leaned against the other wall and crossed my arms. "Try me."

She looked down, then back at me. "As it turns out, there *are* no invading aliens."

"What? How can that be? What about the Cray?"

She shook her head in frustration. "I said it wrong. Remember what we postulated back in Africa? It's true. The species we've encountered so far have specific tasks. The Cray, the Sirens, the needlers, the alien vine, even the spore; purpose-made, purpose-sent. But the master alien race, the ones controlling them, they have no intention of coming here."

I gulped as a hollowness filled me. "Then *why?*"

"They want to mine us."

"Mine us?"

"They want our iron. They want our sodium. They want our silicon. They want our water. They're in the middle of a war and we're just a convenient planet to harvest."

"What about us? What about humans?"

"They don't care about us. They don't want us and they don't want to live here. They're just trying to get rid of us, like a colony of ants in your garden."

I thought that a cockroach analogy might be better than ants. They're far harder to kill. But it was the master aliens' dismissal of us that pissed me off. Like we didn't count. Like we didn't *rate*. Their hubris slayed me. "Do you know what this means?" I finally asked.

"That we have no target, no way to kill them," she said. "No way to convince them to stop. As soon as we figure out how to wipe out the Cray, they'll just send something else."

"We don't know that," I said. "They might just as well not send another alien species. Hell, there might not be any more alien species to send." I held up a finger. "And consider this. It also means that we can operate a little easier."

The idea apparently startled her. She looked at me quizzically.

"If they don't want us or care about us, it means that they've underestimated us. Just look at what we can do. One, we can defeat the Cray on their own terms. Two, we're about to defeat them without all that loss of life we had in Kilimanjaro. Three, we have a cure for their zombie plague. Four, we've figured out a way to translate their language into something understandable."

She'd nodded as I ticked off each thing, then added to it. "Five, they picked on the wrong planet."

I grinned. "Absolutely. They saw our planet as someone might see you, walking down the street. A pretty girl, easy on the eye, even easier to take and maybe bend to your will."

She'd raised her eyebrows and grinned as I was speaking. "Then *BOOM*," she said, making her hands explode. She grinned and nodded. "Do you really think I'm hot?"

Now it was my turn to raise an eyebrow. "Easy there, Lieutenant. Keep it in your pants."

She punched me lightly in the chest and laughed.

"Seriously, though. Think about this. If we can beat back the Cray, and if we can find a way to destroy the alien vine, these master aliens, whoever they are, will be forced to come."

"Or send in the next wave."

"There's got to be a limit to their resources. All we have to do is outlast them."

She nodded, smiling, all trace of disappointment gone.

"Ready to go back inside?" I asked.

She leaned forward and kissed me on the cheek, then followed me back in.

Every man gotta right to decide his own
destiny.

Bob Marley

CHAPTER THIRTY-EIGHT

WE WERE ALL a little hungover the following day, and
six in the morning felt earlier than it should have. We'd
ended up drinking the beer, then Dewhurst brought out
a twelve-year-old bottle of Macallan. We all exchanged
our origin stories, because like all superheroes and
supervillains, everyone had a tale. Nothing was a big
surprise, but it was in the sharing that we became closer.
Towards the end of the night, after we'd become experts
in word slurring, Dewhurst told me that he was glad to
have me along. I remember telling him the same thing,
then we hugged. Probably why we had trouble looking
at each other this morning.

While the technicians were preparing our EXOs for
action, we had one final mission brief, prepared by
Malrimple and Mr. Pink. So it was with bleary eyes and
alcohol-soaked organs that we sat in a conference room,
sucking down coffee and water at astonishing rates.

My grunts sat on one side of the table, while Olivares
and his team sat on the other. Their heads were held high
and their eyes were bright as they stared in judgment at
us. Olivares raised his eyebrows when I gave him a *fuck
you* look, but neither that nor my single finger salute

caused any reaction. Going into a life-or-death mission with all your wits about you was a simpler matter and a reasonable expectation. I reminded myself to consider that, the next time a case of beer and a bottle of twelve-year-old scotch inserted themselves between me and the next day's mission.

Mr. Pink, Malrimple and Lt. Reed came in and took seats at the end of the table. Mr. Pink glanced at us, then had to look once more. If something crossed his mind, he didn't share it with us. Instead, he brought the meeting to order.

"We'll keep this short so team leaders can make any last minute mission adjustments they need. We're still on track for a fourteen-hundred-hours mission start. Dewhurst has arranged for two AN-42s to carry you to your drop points. Team One, you'll be dropped to a location just north of Mother. They are available for assistance if needed. Team Two, you'll be dropped to a point near Seal Beach where GNA can link up with you."

I'd rather there have been on-site support from OMBRA proper. But Mr. Pink wanted this to be an in-and-out special operations mission. He didn't want to have too many grunts on the ground once the detonations occurred. He also wanted to enhance his relationships with the civilian groups in the area.

He glanced around to see if there were any questions, then continued. "Plan for an oh-three-hundred-hours detonation. If you can manage to make them simultaneous, it improves the element of surprise. If not, do the best you can. If there are any changes to the mission, I will have HMID Thompson relay messages to both Ethridge and Mason. Questions?"

Again, there were none, so he turned the briefing over to Lt. Reed. "Things have been moving fast since we've been able to translate the enemy's transmissions. It reads like a machine language, which is one of the reasons HMID Salinas was able to make this breakthrough. Olivares and Mason were the first to infiltrate a hive from below ground. Their TTPs are the standard. We've uploaded a tactical map package to each of your EXOs. Team One, you have schematics of the L.A. Metro as well as the storm drain system. Team Two, you're in a better position. That the hive settled on Disneyland was extraordinarily helpful. There are more than two thousand miles of tunnels beneath the amusement park, and the map provided should allow you to get to your destination easier.

"Regarding detonation, both W84s have the capacity for a ten-minute delay. That's not long, but if you can get out of the shadow of the hive and put some buildings between you and the blast, you have a more than respectable chance. Your EXOs have minimal radiation protection, so use them. Our projections are that if the nukes are positioned underground and beneath the hives, the hives should absorb most of the blast and soak up most of the radiation. Since they are so impenetrable from the outside, they're likely just as impenetrable from the inside. Dr. Malrimple?"

The chief of science wiped his brow and leaned forward. "Expect more fungees, spikers, and needlers, although they shouldn't present a problem in your EXOs."

I flashed to the kids in the pit. Even without the EXOs, they'd been easy to kill. But of course then you had to live with yourself.

"We have a new report, this one delivered via ham operator from Marseille. It appears that some of the behaviors of the fungees have changed. While we're still cataloging reports of them attacking and infecting the uninfected, there's a new behavior which appears to be more static in nature." Seeing our confusion, he held up a hand. "Let me explain. We believe there's possibly an additional pathogen. Using what we now know about *ophiocordyceps unilateralis* and *Ophiocordyceps invasionalis,* we realize that the Hypocrealics have the ability to modify and weaponize fungi. By extrapolation, they might also have the ability to control the motor functions of the afflicted."

Dewhurst held up a hand. He looked like he wanted to be anywhere but in the conference room. "What exactly are you talking about? Can you just cut to the chase?"

"Two days ago, several hundred fungees surrounded the Marseille hive. They didn't move. They didn't fall down. They stood there until the attack."

"Wait a minute," I said, looking around. "What attack? Who attacked whom?"

"We had an OMBRA special operations team, much like your own, trying out a pesticide called Vanderbilt University Allosteric Agonist Number One, or VUAA1, which essentially renders the user invisible to certain species of insects and needlers—what we're calling those moth-like creatures who attacked Dupree—because it causes sensory overload. When an insect senses a certain odor, blood or the sodium in human sweat, it vectors towards the target. What Vanderbilt scientists were able to do before—"

"Doctor Malrimple," I said more loudly than I

wanted to, "about the attack. You said this happened two days ago?"

He nodded.

I turned to Olivares. "Thinking what I'm thinking?"

He frowned. "They knew."

"That's right," I said, turning to Mr. Pink. "They fucking *know*."

Lt. Rosamilla, Ohirra's counterpart on Olivares's team, asked, "Who knew what about what?"

"The Cray knew about the attack before it happened."

Mr. Pink shook his head. "They couldn't have. There were no radio communications twelve hours prior as per SOP. Once on the ground, tactical coms were limited in range." He shook his head again. "No way."

I sighed. "Not radios. HMIDs."

Mr. Pink looked to Malrimple. "I disagree. We've seen no evidence of them knowing we can break their communications, nor have we seen evidence that they can communicate with our HMIDs."

I couldn't help but laugh. "Seriously? That's pretty much what every scientist and world leader said right up until the point the Earth was invaded. *We've seen no evidence.*" I turned to Mr. Pink. "Seriously?"

Mr. Pink stared at us for a long moment, then rubbed his face. "Doctor Malrimple, we need to look at this. If they can communicate with or have access to our HMIDs, this creates new challenges, especially if our HMIDs don't realize it's occurring."

"I think we should abandon the mission," Olivares said. "I can't see the immediate benefit of putting these soldiers in danger."

I nodded. "What he said. We could be walking into a trap."

"Now, wait a minute," Dewhurst said. "We can't—we shouldn't abandon the mission just because the Hypocrealics might be able to listen in on the HMIDs. It's pure supposition. And frankly"—he turned to me—"I'm disappointed at this rush to judgment."

I started to say something, but Dewhurst had a question for Malrimple. "What is it these fungees did? Did they attack the special-ops team? Did they fire laser beams from their eyes and fart thunderbolts?"

One of Olivares's men snickered, as did Sula and Mal.

"Major Dewhurst," Malrimple said, shaking his head.

"I just want to know. What did the fungees do?"

"Nothing."

"Nothing?" Dewhurst leaned forward. "I'm sorry. I'm not sure I heard you correctly."

"I said that they did nothing."

"What's the significance of that, do you think?" Dewhurst asked. "I mean, you're proposing that we shut down a mission because these fungees did nothing. To use your own word, Mason, *seriously?*"

Malrimple sighed. "What I was trying to get across is that I believe that there's another vector out there that delivers a yet-to-be-determined organism that then—"

"Causes people to do nothing," Dewhurst finished.

"The vector could be an endoparasitoid much like *Dinocampus coccinellae*, or they could just be manipulating the autonomy of the fungees through manipulation of the same receptors."

"How will these fungees be any more of a threat than any other fungee?" Dewhurst asked.

Malrimple stared at the major with hate in his eyes. "They won't."

Dewhurst spun to Mr. Pink. "All this science is good, but we need to concentrate our efforts. This double mission represents our best chance at giving the Hypocrealics a one-two punch. If we do this and it works, it will resonate on every ham radio throughout the world. It will be the Hero of the Mound written large, because it's not just one hive, but two. Combine that with Malrimple's VUAA1 bug spray and his fungee cure, and suddenly we have some hope that humanity might just survive this mess."

Olivares eyed Dewhurst, then said, "I still say that we should stop the mission and put the HMIDs on radio silence until we have this thing figured out."

All eyes were on Mr. Pink as he thought through his options, so no one was looking at Mal when he said, "Or you can talk to them."

He blanched under our sudden attention.

"What do you mean, Private?" I asked, wishing he hadn't said anything.

"Sir, what I mean to say, sir, is that if the aliens can communicate with our HMIDs, then doesn't it mean we can talk to them?"

"What, and ask them to leave?" Stranz asked.

"Is that such a bad idea?" Mal countered.

I held up my hand to both of them, then looked at Mr. Pink. "Clearly there's a lot we don't know. My guess is that Doctor Malrimple's staff is going to be even busier than they already are. But that really doesn't affect my mission. We put our teams of EXOs on the objective, deliver the nukes, and exfil. Nothing said here seems capable of changing that."

Mr. Pink considered for a full minute, the ticking of the wall clock the only sound in the room. Finally, he stood. "The missions are on. Malrimple, assemble a team to work on this HMID issue and report back to me ASAP." Then he left.

Ohirra was staring at me.

"What?" I asked.

"It's just that you sounded like a lieutenant just then."

I grinned. "Not that old nasty monosyllabic master sergeant?"

"Did you just say *monosyllabic*?" she asked.

"I did."

"Then you're definitely a lieutenant."

Olivares got up, giving me a frosty glare. "More like a lieutenant who's going to get us all killed." He headed for the door. "Come on, squad, to me."

I watched as his team filed out and hoped he wasn't reading our future.

> I suspected skydiving was dangerous when they asked me to sign a waiver. They confirmed my suspicions when they asked me to pay in advance.
>
> Anonymous

CHAPTER THIRTY-NINE

SUNLIGHT STREAMED THROUGH the windows as the aircraft banked over San Bernardino. Hooked up to a static line and about to jump from a military aircraft, I could almost imagine I was back at Fort Bragg, about to parachute with twenty-two others, as our stick tumbled from an airplane above Sicily, Normandy, or Salerno drop zones. The static line would ensure that our chutes deployed; all we had to do was stay out of the trees. If the pathfinder hadn't done his job, we'd soon be hanging from the long leaf pines like human Christmas ornaments. But more often than not, we'd hit the drop zone, do a parachute landing fall—tucking the chin, bending the knees, falling to the side—then leap up, shred our chutes, stuff them in our D-Bags, and head toward the detail trucks.

Ah, to have those days back.

As much as it had sucked at Fort Bragg, those were halcyon days, as much a part of my magical, mythical memory as the summer fields of a Ray Bradbury novel.

Instead of that reality, here we were, six humans

locked inside EXOs, with two Chinese cargo chutes attached to each of us and about to leap out the back of a former Soviet cargo aircraft and into an alien-infested city. Of course, no one had ever jumped from an aircraft in an EXO before. It took a lot of faith to trust our lives to a few techs who did some math and gave us a thumbs-up because they believed two Chinese-made parachutes would keep us from slamming into the ground. And if we had to do a PLF, we'd probably take out whole buildings. I was hoping we might be able to perform standup landings, but realistically I just wanted not to die, especially since I was carrying the suitcase nuke on my back. Although it was protected in a Kevlar case, I was afraid to so much as bump it.

"Tarantula One-One, this is Tarantula One-Six." Dewhurst was calling me on a private secure line.

"Two, what's up?"

"Just got a change of mission message. We're adjusting our drop zone."

Why did Dewhurst get a message and not me? Fucking rookies.

"Where are we going?"

"We're to link up with a different group for support. Dropping in ninety seconds."

As he said the words, the red light at the back of the aircraft began to blink.

"Sharing drop zone location now to all Tarantula elements," Dewhurst said, switching to a team feed. "Import new drop zone data and prepare to jump."

I toggled the location information, observed the drop zone, and checked for visual landmarks I could use to mark our drift. We'd have to rely on sight; without GPS and with the distractions of falling out of a perfectly good airplane, it was going to be tricky. Seeing the location, I immediately wondered what was going on. The plan had been set to land north of Big Cienega Spring and link up with Mother's crew. Landing in West Covina was the last thing I wanted. No, correct that. Landing at God's New Army headquarters at the West Covina Mall was the last thing I wanted.

"Dewhurst, what's going on?" This was what happened when the person in charge of the overall mission wasn't one of the tactical commanders. How could I expect to lead him into combat if he was going to keep me in the dark?

"Classified for now. Charlie Mike. Dewhurst out."

Continue mission, my ass. I was about to say something when the red light in the back of the plane switched to yellow. The sound of the ramp unlatching was followed by a rush of air as the ramp lowered, revealing a keyhole of gray-blue sky.

"Thirty seconds to jump point," Dewhurst said over the net.

Instead of arguing, I tapped into each soldier's HUD and JMPIed the person in front of them in turn. I couldn't get the last man, Stranz, but this would have to do. Everyone checked out visually. Now all we had to do was hope that two Chinese cargo chutes would hold the weight of a human and an EXO.

We were about to find out.

Digits counted down from ten in my HUD. When they hit one, we all surged forward, nut to butt. I stepped out first, tumbling slightly forward to better allow the static line to deploy the low-hanging Chinese chutes. I was aware of the movement, but was blocked by the suit from the feeling of air rushing past me or the 360-degree whirling-out-of-control feeling I always had those first few seconds of a jump. If I wasn't feeling the onrushing tug of gravity, it could have almost been a video game.

Then I was jerked backwards as both chutes filled with air.

Nope, I thought grimacing inside my EXO, *not a video game at all.*

My chutes were holding. I didn't see any EXOs plummeting by me, so that was a good sign for the others. I quickly toggled through each of their HUDs. Everyone seemed fine, if not experiencing skyrocketing heart rates. I couldn't access Dewhurst's data, however. He'd cut my access. I couldn't figure out why, but we'd be sure to have a face-to-face once we landed.

Keying in on the drop zone and careful of my enhanced EXO strength, I pulled my left risers, well aware of my need to tack into the wind. It gusted, pushing me off course, and I went with it, circling back around. The drop zone was a wide green space beside what might have once been a school. Trucks were aligned alongside one end of the DZ. It looked like several hundred people were arrayed around the area in what only could be an ambush.

Suddenly smoke flared from a grenade, marking the center of the DZ. I noted the way the wind took the dark gray smoke, adjusted, then came in for a landing, wanting it to be like baby feet on cotton with the weapon of mass destruction attached to my back. The landing was both lighter than I expected and harder than I wanted. I felt the impact in my bones as the momentum of the EXO abruptly stopped. My mouth began to bleed a little. I think I might have bit my lip. But that hardly mattered.

I ripped my chutes free, then got on one knee and

brought my weapons to bear. The Hydra aimed at one edge of the ambush while my minigun tracked back and forth on the other edge.

"All Tarantulas, deploy in defense formation upon landing. Interlocking fields of fire."

"Belay that order," Dewhurst said, grunting as he hit the ground. His wasn't a standup; he want sprawling several feet, taking grass with him.

"Bullshit. Tarantulas, defend!"

Sula, Mal, and Ohirra hit the ground standing. They took up formation beside me.

Stranz came in last, skidding to a stop while ripping free his chute. I noted that he'd painted sergeant's chevrons on the arms of his EXO. He glanced at Dewhurst, hesitated for a moment, then joined us.

Which left Dewhurst standing in the middle like a private who didn't know what to do.

"Mason, stand down," he yelled through the coms.

"Explain yourself, Dewhurst. My grunts aren't doing anything until I tell them." I wasn't sure what deal he'd made with the devil, but I wasn't about to let my grunts get hurt.

"I said, *stand down*."

I could hear the fury in his voice, but didn't give a shit. "Never!" I kept my gaze focused on the forces arrayed before us. My HUD counted one hundred and forty-seven targets. Three groups held RPGs trained on us. A group at each end of the ambush had heavy machine guns—M2 50-calibers. I created aiming points over each spot and shared them with my grunts. "Lock Hydras on locations and prepare to fire."

"Jesus Christ, Mason. Do you want to start World War III?" Dehurst demanded.

"I'm not going to let you get my grunts killed." To the team, I said, "Prepare to fire on my mark."

"Mason, get your head out of your fourth point of contact. We have a change of mission."

I was tired of the bullshit. "Here's what I know. We were briefed to link up with Mother but here we are in the heart of GNA territory with one hundred and forty-seven targets pointing their weapons at us. This isn't exactly a friendly welcome, Dewhurst. And it makes me wonder why you haven't joined us yet."

I keyed a secure line back to headquarters at Fort Irwin, hoping I was close enough to a retransmission site to get my coms leapfrogged in, but got nothing but static. Then I keyed a secure line to Ohirra. "Do you know what's going on?"

"I don't, and I don't like it." I could hear her breathing. "Wait, who's that?"

A figure separated from the center of the ambush and began walking towards us. Only one celebrity asshole would wear a white suit at the end of the world during an armed confrontation—Sebring. I zoomed onto him. He was unarmed other than his smarm and smile.

"Keep steady," I said over the team net. "Fire only on my command."

I stood, but kept my weapons trained on the GNA.

"Okay, Dewhurst, explain."

"Nothing to explain. I got a message to change mission to link up with GNA. It could be anything. Mother is closer to the 605. Perhaps the fungees overran her. Goddamn it, Mason, I'm just following orders. Same thing you should be doing."

Was I being over careful? Was I letting my prejudices against GNA color my leadership?

"Then tell Sebring to have his people stand down. If I so much as detect a laser designator on our position I'll have my grunts open fire. So unless they want to see how much violence and lead we can throw at them, *they* stand down."

"Got it," Dewhurst said.

On a secure channel, Ohirra said, "You know we don't have lead rounds, right?"

"It sounds better than saying depleted uranium. Be on alert, Ohirra. Something's rotten in Denmark. And yes, I know we aren't in Denmark."

"Just trying to keep you straight, Mason."

"Right. Thanks."

Sebring walked right by us, smiling beatifically like he'd done so often on his show, when the telephone audience voted a singer off. He was always so sorry, but I just knew there were different thoughts behind that professional smile. *So sorry you sucked. So sorry they didn't like you, but thank you very much for the ratings, my slick new car, my house in Malibu and the sweet ass of this model I've been banging. Now if you would shuffle back to your Walmart job, knowing that you've just burned through your fifteen minutes of fame, wondering why it couldn't have been you, sliding into that dark place where you know you suck and you can't stop sucking except to shoot yourself to end your hopeless existence, I'd sincerely appreciate it.*

Yeah, that was the real Sebring.

"Major Dewhurst, I got the message from OMBRA and brought together as many of God's New Army as I could in such short time," Sebring said.

As he passed me, he actually winked at me.

Asshole.

"The GNA is pleased to be at OMBRA's disposal," he continued. "What is it we can do for you?"

"You can start by telling your men to lower their weapons. My team leader here has a hair-trigger and says that if any of them even points a laser designator, he'll have the team open fire."

Sebring looked at me. Instead of worry, he showed disappointment, as if I was a bad child. "Why would he do that?"

"Better to ask why I wouldn't," I said.

And there it was. A flash of worry. Just a hint of it, but enough for me to feel a moment of elation.

Sebring pulled a walkie-talkie from the small of his back and spoke into it. "Everyone lower your weapons. No laser designators. These are our friends and we should treat them that way." He turned to us, his smile wide once more. "I always thought the golden rule was one of God's best rules."

I watched the GNA lower their weapons and power down their equipment, my HUD zooming in and out on different locations.

On the team net, Sula asked, "What's the golden rule?"

"Do unto others as you would have them do unto you," said Stranz. "My mother said it all the time."

"It was Jesus who said it," Mal said. "Actually, in the New Testament it says, *Do to others as you would have them to do to you.*"

"That's just a translation difference," Stranz said. "Its roots are really in the Old Testament. Leviticus 19:18. *Forget about the wrong things people do to you, and do not try to get even. Love your neighbor as you love yourself.*"

"Let's keep God out of it for now," I snapped. "If He wants to be a part of this, He can come down and kick the shit out of the Hypercrealiacs." Then I added, "How about the Tarantula rule. *Be prepared to fuck up thy neighbor before he fucks you up.*"

Ohirra chuckled uncharacteristically.

Sula and Mal gave an *aye-aye.*

Stranz and Dewhurst remained silent, which gave me a start. I checked their coms and noted that they were both in a secure conversation. What was Dewhurst up to now?

> Trust is hard to come by. That's why my
> circle is small and tight. I'm kind of funny
> about making new friends.
>
> Eminem

CHAPTER FORTY

WE'D LANDED AT Cameron Elementary School. Instead of heading towards GNA headquarters at West Covina Mall, we headed southwest. Sebring sat in the passenger seat of a convertible Cadillac with three of his men, all heavily armored and armed with automatic rifles. We followed behind. Ohirra had the rear and Stranz had the front. The rest of us marched two abreast, with me and Dewhurst side by side and Sula and Mal right behind us. I had everyone on high alert. Not that we were worried about any fungees, but we didn't want GNA to have any surprises for us.

It did surprise me, however, that we'd left the one hundred and forty-seven GNA members behind and that Sebring apparently trusted us with his life.

I was also worried about the lack of contact I had with Thompson. He should be able to communicate with me as easily as Michelle or Salinas had, but there was nothing. I tried several times to blast out a call, but again... nothing. I decided to try something different.

"Olivares, this is Mason, can you hear me?"

Nothing but static. I tried twice more and was about

to give up when I heard a thin voice on the edge of hearing. "Mason, this is Olivares. What's wrong?"

That was my friend. Always assuming I'd fucked up. "Nothing's wrong. Permission to speak to Ethridge." While I could have called Ethridge myself, etiquette demanded that I do it through his mission leader. Something that Dewhurst didn't seem to understand.

There was a pause long enough for me to wonder if I'd lost coms, then, "Permission granted."

I sent a secure ping to Ethridge and waited. After about ten seconds, he pinged back and we went secure. "Ethridge, this is Mason. Are you in contact with HMIDs?"

"Affirmative," he said, his voice even thinner and laced with more static than Olivares's. "HMID Thompson has been assisting."

"Please tell Thompson that I am with Sebring and ask him why he hasn't contacted me."

"Affir—ve."

Damn it. He was breaking up. We kept walking. I continually cycled through everyone's status and my HUD's active movement tracker, out of habit rather than necessity.

A few seconds later I heard, "HMID—tethered to—can't—Sandi—" Then nothing. I tried several more times to reconnect, but we must've been too far apart and I had no luck.

What had he meant? Why was he talking about Sandi? Assuming, of course, that it was the same Sandi I knew?

We suddenly changed direction and turned west down East Vine. I wasn't familiar with the area. I used our pre-loaded digitized map and found the cross streets; we were heading towards South Glendora Avenue. I scanned my map for any hint at our destination, but couldn't find anything obvious.

We were seven miles from the 605 and twenty-five miles to the hive, and had used less than one percent of our power. The batteries were truly a miracle. If I'd been wearing a Generation I suit, we'd have spent at least twenty-five percent power by now, if not more.

We left a subdivision and found an empty strip mall to our right. I picked out several major chain stores. Two men wrestled over a shopping cart beneath the sign for a paint store. Could there really be huffers in this day and age? I also saw a man with a rifle standing on top of a building across Glendora. My HUD tracked four more soldiers on adjacent buildings.

"Dewhurst, are you seeing this?"

"I see. They belong to GNA; just providing overwatch for the civilians in the area in the event of a fungee sighting."

"Mmm-hmm. Still, Tarantulas, be on alert."

We rounded the corner and headed into a U-shaped plaza. A sign read *Hong Kong Plaza*. All the cars had been removed, revealing a large flat surface.

Sebring had his car parked on the far side, and Stranz was the first of us in the lot.

"Stranz, what do you see?"

"It's empty down here. I'm tracking five men on the roof, but no other movement." Then he said, "Strange."

My spider sense tickled at the back of my neck. "What's strange?"

"Well, everywhere we've been windows have been busted out and doors bashed in. But this place is different. All the mirrored windows look like new. All the doors look new, too."

"Did you say mirrored?"

We kept moving into the lot and I saw what he meant. Every window had been replaced with mirrored glass. Why would someone put in new mirrored windows? Then it hit me. "Tarantulas, form on me!" Mirrored windows are for hiding behind.

I opened fire at the windows, aiming high, near the roofline; I didn't necessarily want to kill anyone, I just wanted to see behind the glass. Sula, Ohirra, and Mal saw what I was doing and did the same. I noted that Dewhurst and Stranz had drifted over towards Sebring. What was going on?

As the glass fell and the dust settled, I saw.

Each store held a two-man squad standing behind armor plates, with an M134 tripod-mounted minigun. The center store, a big-box toy store that had once sold Power Rangers and Barbies, now held a no-shit M60A3 Vietnam-era tank with a 105mm main gun. Only one store front held something other than a weapons system, and that was the one nearest Sebring, who'd been protected from stray bullets from our miniguns by Dewhurst and Stranz standing in front of him. A long black HMID box rested in this one.

"LT, see the mines beneath all the windows?" Mal whispered.

I'd missed them. Sure enough, attached to the wall and painted the same color as the rest of the building were claymores. I counted seventy-two of them. I didn't see any wires, so someone must have hardwired them into the building, probably so they could be activated from a single main switch. Each one could fire seven hundred one-eighth-inch steel balls out to fifty meters in a sixty degree arc, killing anyone in their wake. Minimal damage would occur behind them. Probably blow out some of the bricks and cement.

I turned to Dewhurst. "What's in this for you?"

"Your government wants an HMID, Mason. OMBRA refuses to sell us one, but Sebring has one to sell me."

"Why not just trade a state for one, Utah, maybe."

"Let me rephrase that. OMBRA's price is too high and we can get a better deal with GNA."

"What's in it for Sebring?" I asked, jerking my head towards the guy.

"He wants an EXO so he can reverse engineer it."

"So you're going to trade your EXO for an HMID?"

"Not mine; Sergeant Stranz's. Your government wants a copy as well."

I stared at him for a moment, equal parts pleased that the shoe had dropped, and pissed that I hadn't seen it coming. "You keep saying *my* government, but I don't really have a government. America's democracy was murdered by the Cray."

"Republic," said Stranz. "We had a republic, a representational democracy. In the end, people didn't have very much say."

"And you, Stranz? What the hell are you doing?"

Dewhurst spoke first. "Let's be civil about this. He wants to rejoin his country. Don't you think everyone has that right? Like Mal and Sula; they have that right, too. Do you want to rejoin your country? We need some help rebuilding and could use your expertise."

I could have said something. I could have argued against it, but I kept my mouth shut. Dewhurst was right. If they wanted to go, then fine, let them.

"I'm with the LT," Mal said.

"So am I," Sula said.

"And you knew better than to ask me," Ohirra finished.

"You heard them," I said, pleased with my grunts. Now it was my turn. "Stranz, you can always change your mind. I don't know what he's promised you, but I've always been above board. I've always treated you with respect and honor. Where's the honor in this? Why all the trickery? The thievery? One of the principles of our founding fathers was that *the only reliable basis for sound government and just human relations is Natural Law.* Weren't we just talking about the Golden Rule? Do you want to be treated the way he's treating us? It's only a matter of time, Sergeant Stranz."

Dewhurst laughed. "All right, all right. You had your say. Let me conclude this transaction and I'll be on my way."

"Wait a moment," I said, eyeing the weaponry arrayed against us. "What's going to happen to us?"

"Mr. Sebring assures me that he'll let you continue your mission. It's your government's assertion that your mission is critical and he understands that."

"Stop calling it *my* government. Any government I'll have doesn't lie, cheat, and steal."

He laughed again. "If you're naïve enough to believe that, then you'll never have a government. Then of course, OMBRA is your de facto government now, isn't it? How have they treated you lately? Locked you up any?" He turned to Sebring. "Let's conclude this. My transportation is inbound in six minutes and I want to be out of here before there are any snags."

I decided that I didn't want to waste any more time arguing. I toggled Dewhurst's status in my HUD and gave the command for his suit to shut down, but nothing happened. I went through the sequence again, thinking maybe I'd done something wrong, but still nothing happened. Damn!

Sebring nodded, then looked at me. "Lieutenant Mason, if you and your men would please just stand aside, I'd appreciate it. We'll get you on your way in no time at all. Of course, to ensure your cooperation, I've prepared several things that should dissuade you from interfering, as I'm sure you've noticed."

Dewhurst had been one step ahead of me all along. Had he ever intended to do the mission?

"Did you hear me, Lieutenant Mason?" Sebring pressed.

"I heard you. Yes, I've noticed."

"Excellent." He turned back to Dewhurst. "Now, the suit, please."

Dewhurst turned to Stranz and ordered him to give Sebring the suit.

I noted that Stranz and Ohirra were on a secure private line. I watched as Stranz looked down at the sergeant's chevrons painted on the arms of his EXO. I could almost hear his thoughts. I hurriedly contacted Sula and gave her a set of orders, which she immediately followed. I felt her slide in behind me, but kept my attention on Stranz instead of alerting anyone to her movement.

Dewhurst must've noticed the private conversation as well. "Ohirra, stop whatever you're doing."

"You're not in my chain of command," she said.

"The hell I'm not. This land you're standing on belongs to the New United States of North America."

"Actually it belongs to God's New Army," Sebring said with a smile. "But we'll discuss that later. So am I getting my suit or not?"

Dewhurst put an EXO hand on Stranz's arm, the gesture covering the sergeant's chevron painted there. "Come on, son. Don't listen to her. Your country needs you. It's depending on you. She's only in it for a profit. We're in it for a future."

If my eyes had rolled any harder, everyone would have heard them. Still, I wanted to see how Stranz would respond.

"First let's get the HMID out here," he said. "Moving it with the EXOs will be much easier."

Sebring nodded. "Indeed, it will."

Dewhurst and Stranz entered the store front, got behind the HMID, then pushed it through the broken window. The glass piled in front of the composite metal box as it was pushed into the parking lot. What would have taken a dozen men and rollers took the two EXOs hardly a minute.

Stranz walked up to Sebring, who was beaming at the feat. "What do you think?"

"I can't wait to try it on. A suit like that—"

His last words were choked off as Stranz put a hand around his neck.

Ohirra shouted, her voice magnified through the speakers on her suit. "No-one move or he'll crack Sebring's neck."

My HUD was flashing as laser indicators bloomed from more than a dozen weapons, but no one opened fire.

Stranz adjusted his grip so the man was facing forward, his back to the EXO, Stranz's arm around his throat.

Dewhurst took a few steps back. "What's going on?"

"Your plan worked, Major. Mr. Pink will be pleased," Ohirra said.

Sebring fought to speak. Finally, "Your plan?"

Dewhurst shook his head. "I don't know what they're talking about. This isn't any plan of mine."

Somehow Ohirra had orchestrated something right under my nose. While I admired her, I wished she would have brought me in on it. I reminded myself to have a conversation with her later.

My HUD began tracking an inbound aircraft and identified it as a Chinook helicopter. A few seconds later, we could hear it.

"You're not going to get away with this," Sebring managed to say.

"No, he's not," I said. I directed Sula to perform her task.

She removed the nuke from my back, then took off, running first out of the kill zone, then down the street. One of the men on the roof took a pot shot at her. Whatever. Even if it had hit, it wouldn't have done any damage.

"What are you going to do?" Dewhurst said. "Stop me?"

That was exactly what I was going to do. I went from standing still to full run in two seconds, barreling into him and bowling him over. He tried to bring his minigun up, but I grabbed it with both hands and wrenched it back and forth. He hit me with his free hand, trying to dislodge me where I was straddling him. With a final yank, the minigun came free, in a shower of sparks and pops. With my left arm, I managed to grab the wrist of the hand that was hitting me. My right arm came down, using the minigun like a hammer, striking him over and over. I saw his faceplate crack, and his helmet start to collapse.

Then a white burning sound surged through my brain, evaporating everything else. I fell back, losing track of my hands, my weapon, the universe. My world was white noise, layers of static on static on static. I barely felt myself being struck by something.

Images began to flash through my mind—Mother, the aged Hollywood actress turned cultish survivor group leader. Was it her doing this? Was she psychic, somehow, and assaulting my senses? The images sped up—men, women, children, animals, Mother, men, women, children, animals, Mother, men, women— before crystallizing into a single image: a high school photo of Sandi. Last I'd seen of her, she'd been helping me out of the black alien vine. Could it be her?

Sandi?

The noise somehow got louder. More pain. I could barely think the words, *Turn down the noise. Sandi, is that you?*

The blow that hit me felt like a Volkswagen had been dropped on me. I opened my eyes and saw that Dewhurst was now on top of me, bringing his minigun around for another hit. I managed to catch it with both hands. We strained against each other.

Help me, like a lance through my brain.

I brought my left knee up and simultaneously threw my might into my right arm, jerking him forward. He flew past me and I struggled to my feet, noting that Sebring was still in Stranz's clutches beside the box. Mal standing off to my left, Sebring's men in front of the car with their weapons trained on us, and the automatic weapons and claymore mines arrayed against us. The sound of the helicopter was closer: here to take away the box.

Help me!

Sandi, softer. For the love of God, softer.

Help me! A shotgun firing against my nerves.

I turned too late and felt Dewhurst crash into my back, sending me skidding across the parking lot until my chin rested against one of the mines. The words *FRONT TOWARDS ENEMY* were my entire universe until I managed to stand.

"Sandi," I said aloud, my focus not on Dewhurst but on Sebring. "You took her. You made her into one of them."

"Soldiers are easier. It takes less time. Makes less mess. Will you just let me go? I'm sure we can sort this out."

Help me, Mason, like I helped you. Gone was the pain, replaced instead by a deep fear... her fear.

Sandi, what can I do?

Killmekillmekillmekillmekillmekillmekillme...

And there it was again. Just like Michelle.

Dewhurst came after me. I waited until he was almost on me and kicked out, catching him on his hip. He spun and fell, his torso resting inside a storefront.

I backed out into the center of the parking lot.

"Sandi, where's Thompson?" I said aloud.

He's here. He can't talk to you. They wrote code to block you.

I nodded. Just as they had with Michelle. Of course. For the plan to work, Thompson couldn't be able to talk to me. Sandi either, for that matter. *Did he erase your code?* I blasted.

Yes, but he can't do his own.

Sandi, can you?

I don't know how yet.

How did you get here? I asked.

GNA captured me after we dropped you off. They were waiting for me; they wanted to turn me into...

I tuned her out as Dewhurst picked himself up off the ground. I was tired of this. It was time to end it. I already had yellow status warnings on my hydraulics. I probably had a leak somewhere.

To Mal and Ohirra I said, "Get ready."

I stalked over to Dewhurst, still shaking the butterflies from his head. I reared back and punched his face as hard as I could, shattering the glass. I reared back and punched again, sending my fist through the soft tissue of his face. His nose collapsed, his cheekbones and jaw shattered. He could barely breathe. I stepped back, to let him suffer for a while.

"You want an EXO, you can have this one," I said to Sebring. Then to Stranz I said, "Kill him."

Stranz hesitated a moment.

Sebring's eyes shot wide just before a dozen rounds hit Stranz's faceplate. Although they hardly did any damage, Stranz brought up his hands in reflex, releasing Sebring, who immediately ran towards his men.

Son of a bitch.

As much as I wanted to chase him down, we needed to get out of the kill zone. I dove into a storefront and ran around behind the tank. The hatch was open so the tank commander could watch our battle. Stupid. He dropped down when he saw what I was about to do, and managed to snap the hatch in place just before I leaped atop the tank from the rear. So instead of firing into the tank, I began looking for something to rip or break. But other than an antenna, the only thing available was the 105mm barrel.

Meanwhile Mal, Stranz and Ohirra dove into the storefronts nearest them, taking out surprised machine gun crews and destroying their guns. As I watched this unfold on their HUD feeds, I decided to try it with the tank. I climbed onto the front of the tank and grabbed the barrel with both hands. I don't think anyone had taken the EXOs to their limits, but I was about to try. I put my feet on the turret, wrapped both hands around the barrel, and heaved backwards.

Thompson told me to tell you something, Sandi said, like a machine gun rattling across the inside of my head.

I grunted with exertion. *Do you want to go ahead or am I supposed to guess?* My arm servo indicators were flashing red. I dove into the diagnostics and saw that I'd breached and was losing fluid. Still, I kept hauling upward, using my legs to push away, even as I kept pulling.

There's a new kind of alien in the hive. Thompson's calling it a Master, because it gives orders. He says you need to capture it.

Was that a little give I just felt in the massive barrel, or had it been my imagination? My HUD was now screaming at me. I felt the turret begin to rotate and yanked with every ounce of power I had remaining. I was rewarded with the metal beneath my fingers bending four inches. If they fired, the round would never make it through. I tried to dive off the tank, but I never made it. The barrel exploded just as I launched myself. The force of the explosion hurled me through the air and through the drywall separating two stores. My arms dangled uselessly. Destroying the tank's barrel had only succeeded in decimating my arm servos. It was pretty hopeless.

"Did you blow the tank?" came Ohirra's voice.

"That I did."

I tracked the others through their feeds as I climbed to my feet. I needed to find the central control for the claymore mines. I wasn't sure if one or two could hurt an EXO, but all of them going off at once sure could. My guess was on the roof, where the operator would be safe. I could either order one of them onto the roof, or we could un-ass this AO.

Ohirra found me. According to my feeds, any members of GNA at ground level were either dead or dying.

"Why are you standing that way?" she asked. "Are you hurt?"

"Arm servos busted."

"We're a long way from tech support," she said.

"I'd shrug if I could."

"What's the plan?"

"Mal and Stranz, to me," I said across the net. To Ohirra I said, "Let's punch through the back and get out of here."

"What about GNA?"

"Fuck 'em if they can't take a joke."

She tilted her head. "They'll be pissed."

Stranz arrived, his EXO scarred with bullet trails.

"That was a neat little trick," I said to him.

He grinned sheepishly. "Sorry about that, sir. The LT here thought it would be best if we kept it quiet until later."

"Yeah, about that." I frowned as I glared at Ohirra.

"You can dress me down later. Right now, let's get out of here. Stranz, help Mal, will you?"

I turned and saw that Mal had grabbed the EXO containing Dewhurst's body.

"What's that good for?" I asked Ohirra.

"Servos. Maybe we can fix your EXO."

Why hadn't I thought of that?

Ohirra deployed her minigun and opened a hole through the back wall into the alley behind it.

"Do me a favor and destroy the HMID," I said. It was really mine to do, but without the ability to move my arms, I couldn't do what Sandi wanted.

"You're right, we don't want it falling into the wrong hands."

"Yeah." That would do for a reason. Sandi should have been out here with us instead of inside, butchered around a hundred cables. I wasn't about to make the mistake of not killing one of them when they begged me to. I always paid.

One more reason to hate Sebring and his GNA.

One more reason to hate *any* organization.

One more reason to love the idea of having these grunts by my side.

I stepped through the hole and broke into an odd, loping run, my arms dangling uselessly. I heard the Hydra fire and watched in the feed as the HMID box blew. The explosion set off the claymores, creating a cacophony of fire and flying metal.

Ohirra ran beside me.

Mal and Stranz were behind her, carrying Dewhurst's EXO between them.

Everything was just fine. We made three blocks before my HUD tracked an incoming RPG round. Mal dropped his side of the EXO and ran to intercept it. The round struck his head at 295 meters per second and exploded, sending shrapnel flying in all directions. Mal's chest and head were completely gone.

Stranz found the source and sent Hydra missiles to the location.

Then Ohirra picked up the other side of Dewhurst's EXO and we ran on.

Charlie Mike.

Fucking Charlie Mike.

Award Mal another fucking Soldier's Medal.

What you leave behind is not what is engraved on stone monuments, but what is woven into the lives of others.

Pericles

CHAPTER FORTY-ONE

WE CAUGHT UP with Sula and found a tire warehouse three miles east of the conflagration, where we went to ground. Someone had made a fort of tires inside. Against what, we couldn't tell, but by the musty smell, it was evident that no one had been there for some time.

Sula and Stranz took post while I clambered out of my suit. I was happy to do so. Running like an ostrich was surprisingly hard; I kept overbalancing. I wore nothing but a pair of toe shoes and Kevlar skivvies.

Ohirra removed her EXO as well, revealing her hard physique. She pulled out a breathing mask from the compartment on the side of the EXO to keep her from breathing spore.

We immediately went to task, reaching inside Dewhurst's helmet to pull it free. I'd unlocked his system from my command module before I'd removed my suit, or it would have been impossible to get into it without gear we didn't have.

I sat back and gazed at the features I'd ruined with my fist while I queried my conscience. We'd broken bread together. We'd had drinks together. We'd been officers together, albeit he was a major and I a mere lieutenant. We'd survived an alien invasion. We'd both lost things and people we'd loved. We arguably had more in common than we hadn't.

So why didn't I feel any emotion about his death at my hands?

Because he'd been trying to force me to make a choice I would never make. He wanted me to ally myself with him over his fellow grunts. As much as I despised OMBRA and all it stood for, people like Mr. Pink understood about grunts and about what we do and how we do it. Dewhurst never really got that. He thought that some high ideal and far away government was more important than the people around him. Someone had sold him a load of faulty goods and he'd fallen for it.

If there was one thing I knew—and I'd said it over and over—we might start out fighting for a cause, but in the end I'm fighting for the men and women to my right and left. I fight for them because they will fight for me. Dewhurst had made a decision not to fight for us, and in this new world of ours, that made him our enemy.

I stood and helped Ohirra remove his body from the suit. We took it to the back of the warehouse and laid it out. No sense being disrespectful.

"Do you think you can fix my servos?" I asked as we walked back. Both of us were feeling the cold and had goosebumps on our skin. We were aching to get back into the warmth and protection of the suits.

"Not sure. Going to go scrounge some tools, then I'll let you know." With that, she left and began rifling through boxes and containers.

I went to where Sula and Stranz were standing guard. Standing next to them in my skivvies made me feel extraordinarily small.

Stranz was glowering at the world, while Sula was staring at the ground.

"How are you holding up?" I asked Sula.

She'd almost lost it over Mal's death. Evidently, they'd been as close as brother and sister.

"I'm holding."

I could see through her faceplate she'd been crying. "It happened so fast," Stranz said.

"It always does," I said.

"Why do you think he did it?" Stranz asked. "Giving his life like that?"

Sula sighed. "It's who he was. He never put himself first."

"Any one of us would have done the same thing," I said.

Stranz looked at me sharply.

"Yes, Stranz, even you. I know beneath that knucklehead of yours that you'd do it. It's in our DNA. We just can't help it."

"What about Dewhurst?"

"He wasn't like us. He wasn't a grunt. He was too much a dreamer."

Stranz lowered his head. "So you're saying that it's not okay to dream?"

"Not at all. Dreaming is fine as long as it doesn't interfere with the wellbeing of your fellow grunts. We can all dream of a better world, but then we'll work together to achieve it. He dreamed of something in spite of us." I clapped Stranz on the back. "You'll be fine. And by the way, that was an Oscar-worthy performance back there."

Sula brightened momentarily. "It even fooled me."

Stranz's wan smile fell as he shook his head. "I'm sorry I didn't kill Sebring."

I shrugged.

"He's still out there. He's going to want to kill us for what we did."

"He's going to have to take a number, then."

I left them and went back to where mine and Dewhurst's EXOs lay. Staring at them, I wondered what the next hours would entail. I had a nuke to deliver and an alien to capture, if Thompson were to be believed. Oh, to be able to talk to that little troublemaker. To think that he volunteered, as well. Did he regret it, like Michelle? Would he ask me to kill him, too?

Ohirra returned with a rusty hammer, three screwdrivers, and a pair of pliers. She held them up and gave me a sad look.

"Is that it?" I asked.

She nodded. "I'm not going to be fixing any servos with these."

"Can we fit my helmet onto his suit?"

She stared for a moment, then her eyes brightened. "I can't believe I missed that. The only problem is that you ripped the minigun off. You won't have any weapons except the Hydra and your blade."

"Can't be helped," I said. "I'll redistribute the rounds to the other EXOs. I'm sure you'll have my back."

Nothing like wearing the suit of a man you'd just killed to brighten your spirits.

To me, the thing that is worse than death is
betrayal. You see, I could conceive death,
but I could not conceive betrayal.

Malcolm X

CHAPTER FORTY-TWO

THE INSIDE OF Dewhurst's suit smelled like onions.
It took me fifteen minutes to recalibrate the Gaze to
my optics. Ohirra had removed my command module
from my suit and replaced the one on Dewhurst's so all
of my settings were saved. Five icons lined the top of
my command window. I toggled through the statuses
for Sula, Stranz, and Ohirra, noting that they were at
seventy-five percent power. Two black icons represented
Mal and Dewhurst. I deleted both of them, but made a
mental note to hold a ceremony for Mal if I was ever
able.

I shook my head. Fighting and funerals. There were
some who felt that funerals were a waste of time. I'd
heard arguments that the entire world needed a funeral
after what had happened. Perhaps it did. Such ideas
were beyond my ken. All I was concerned about were
my men and women, my friends, and those with whom
I'd served. The funeral rite, whether formal or quick,
gave me a moment to breathe, to remember them, to
perhaps take a piece of them and make it mine. I'd been
to far too many funerals and I was destined to attend

many more. For as long as there were grunts willing to put themselves in harm's way, there would be funerals.

I glanced around the warehouse. My suit lay in pieces, hacked apart by our harmonic blades. We couldn't bring it with us and we didn't want Sebring or his men to get their hands on any more EXOs. I had no doubt that they'd rounded up Mal's suit, but with the command module destroyed along with the HUD, it was pretty useless.

Ohirra decided we should keep Dewhurst's command module. As small as it was, it was the closest thing to a supercomputer we had and she felt it might come in handy. In areas of science, I deferred to her, so it now rested in my EXO's internal pouch.

I strode to where Stranz and Sula stood. "Status report," I said.

Stranz stepped aside so I could look out the window. "I'm tracking some UAVs in the vicinity. They know we've gone to ground; they just don't know where."

My HUD said the same thing. Some sort of micro-unmanned aerial vehicles, probably homemade, using lithium batteries and circuits that hadn't been fried by the Cray. As long as they were this side of the 605, they could fly them without fear. But once inside, they had to be aware of the seven-hour pulse.

"Where are we on the EMP pulse?" I asked Ohirra.

"The hive will next pulse in two hours, twenty-seven minutes, and thirty-six seconds."

I didn't want to lay low that long. We needed to get into the hive as quickly as possible. Optimum was an 0300 detonation and it was already 1745. With twenty miles to go and an untold amount of fungees to wade through, we needed to get moving.

I pulled up a map and showed them my plan. We were in a warehouse off East Temple Avenue. If we took Temple northwest, we'd be across the 605 and the 10 before anyone knew it. I arbitrarily picked the Jack in the Box in El Monte on Ramona Avenue for a rendezvous point if we got separated.

When everyone was ready, we slipped out the back door, past Dewhurst's body.

"Should we take out the UAVs with missiles?" Sula asked.

"Negative. Let's save our ammo for the Cray."

I counted down from ten, then we booked it, moving as fast as our servos would allow. It took six point seven seconds for the first UAV to track us. We kept moving, Sula and me on the right side of Temple and Ohirra and Stranz on the left. Warehouses and strip malls rose on either side of us. Here and there we could see a dead body with spikey ascocarps growing from it.

"Watch your interval," I said over the net.

Getting too close to the person in front of or behind us would provide a larger footprint and a more seductive target. As it was, if we could maintain our spacing and our speed, we'd be able to evade anything they threw at us short of an intercontinental ballistic missile.

Temple was turning south, but we were heading straight. We left the pavement and crossed a frontage road. An immense three-story warehouse stood before us. We ran to the left and were about to race around the building when my spider sense went through the roof, a mere second before my telemetry indicated an incoming RPG round.

"Evasive move three!" I screamed across the net.

We dove to our left and completed two somersaults, then dove forward and completed another somersault.

An RPG round struck the ground where Sula had been standing.

I traced the trajectory; it had come from atop the building. I wasn't about to climb up. I'd be too large a target.

"We have motorcycles coming from the east," Ohirra said.

I had to make a snap decision.

"Stranz, defend our rear. Sula, deploy your Hydra and take out whatever is on the roof when you get a lock." I ran to the corner of the building where Ohirra stood. "Report."

"Not good. They have forty pax arrayed in defensive formation."

"Weapons?"

"Heavy machine guns and RPGs."

Our EXOs could take small arms fire, but would most likely breach against a sustained rate of fire from larger rounds.

"Can we go around?"

"Not until we know what's on the roof. For all we know, they might have a platoon of RPG gunners."

I smacked the side of the building. "Where'd they get them all?"

"Army national guard depots. They're all over L.A. Being underground probably kept them safe from the EMPs."

Suddenly Sula fired three rockets. I saw them hit targets, followed by secondary explosions as RPG rockets cooked off.

"Are there more?" I asked.

"Can't be sure, sir."

"Motorcycles are getting closer."

Two blocks away.

Fuck it. "Everyone up!" I leaped and caught the bottom of the fire escape. A few seconds later it was tumbling around me, pulled from its housing by my EXO's weight.

"This way." Ohirra was scurrying up an immense water pipe, using the steel brackets attaching it to the building as hand and footholds. By using the brackets, she wasn't putting all of her weight on the pipe.

I ordered Sula to go next. She slipped a few feet halfway up, but caught herself.

I heard the minigun rip from above, then spin to silence.

"Roof is clear," came Ohirra a little breathlessly.

I sent Stranz up next and watched for a moment as he scuttled up the pipe, then turned when my HUD flashed a warning as a pair of motorcycles came within range. I selected heat-seeking and sent four missiles their way. For a second I was able to see the RPG gunners behind each driver before both bikes exploded.

Stranz reached the roof.

I leaped and started to pull myself up. I felt several shots strike my rear. My HUD told me that several Tangos had come around the building to try and keep me from climbing out of their reach. I sincerely hoped none had an RPG. I was almost to the top when I heard a ripping sound from above as Sula fired her minigun at the Tangos targeting me.

Ohirra and Stranz pulled me the rest of the way up.

Just then a small UAV with four rotors and a camera

rose into our eye line. I gave it the middle finger with the EXO glove on my right hand, then Stranz cut it in two with his harmonic blade.

The roof was a sea of ventilation pipes and air conditioners. We all rushed to the center and crouched. From our locus, there was no way anyone could target us, even if they were able to keep eyes on. I glanced at Ohirra, who now had the nuke strapped to her back.

"You do know if that gets hit everyone's dead within several miles."

"Charming," she said. "Way to brighten my day. But if that happens, then we won't have any problems, right?"

"Yeah, you could say that."

"What now, sir?" Stranz asked, worry seeping into his voice.

"What's wrong, sergeant? Think we're sitting ducks?"

He gulped. "We are if they have mortars."

"What's the chance they'd have mortars?" I asked. And as soon as I did, Murphy's Law laughed at me. The sound came from several hundred meters to our west and was a dull *whuumpf*.

"Incoming," Ohirra yelled.

Seriously? Mortars? GNA was better supplied than some of my units in Iraq. I tracked the incoming round and watched it take out the southwest corner of the building.

Shit! We were going to have to move.

"Ohirra, track us a way out of here. Everyone, I'm taking control of your targeting control in a few moments. We need our ammo, but it's not going to do anyone any good if we're dead."

They glanced at each other, worried.

"Listen, I'll get you out of here," I said, almost believing it. Olivares had once told me I was a killer and not a leader—that I got my men killed because I didn't know how to lead. It might have been true then, but I'd be damned if it was true now. "For now, I want any UAV with eyes on us destroyed. I don't want anyone helping correct their mortar team's lousy aim."

I left them and went to Ohirra just as another *whuumpf* sounded. I paused as I tracked the incoming round, then ignored it as it landed almost in the same place as the last one.

I crouched beside Ohirra behind a giant air conditioning unit. "What have you got?"

"Look there," she said, pointing.

I followed her gesture and saw a mass of civilians moving our way from the other side of the 605.

"Who are they—oh, shit, fungees."

I counted more than two hundred inbound vectors heading towards the GNA forces, who were so intent on destroying us that they'd forgotten to guard their flank. Even as I watched, I saw a wave of fungeed men, women and children sweep into the rear rank of GNA. For a moment, I couldn't separate the two groups. All firing had stopped. All we heard were screams. Then GNA opened fire on their new attackers, turning their backs to us.

Sula fired on a UAV with a missile. She missed with the first, but scored with a second.

"Find a way clear, Ohirra?"

I saw a line appear on my HUD, detailing our escape route, which seemed to take us directly through a large section of GNA. "Are you certain?"

"Their backs are turned, and even if they weren't,

everyone has dropped their RPGs in favor of close combat weapons. If we can make a mad dash along this path in the next sixty seconds, I think we can make it through."

I shrugged. "Why not?

"You go first. Sula, you're next. Stranz, you're next after Sula, and make sure no-one attacks her six or we'll all get blown up. I'm coming last. Don't worry about controlling your weapons. I have master control, starting now."

"How are we doing this, Ohirra?" I asked as we all got in line. I began tagging targets along our route of travel and assigning them to our EXOs. I was moving so fast my head was spinning.

"We're going to lower ourselves, then full out run. I'm not sure that the three-story fall would be good for the servos, so better waste a few seconds than do something we can't undo."

"Not like we have any more spare suits." I gritted my teeth and concentrated on my HUD, counting on my body to get me where it needed to.

I could hear Ohirra take a deep breath before she said, "Ready, steady, go!"

And she was loping across the roof. We fell in line behind her with five-meter intervals between us. She slid over the edge, lowering herself before letting go, then Sula, then Stranz, then me. I paused for a moment from attending my HUD to make sure I didn't land wrong, but once I began sprinting across the parking lot in front of the warehouse, I returned to my targeting plan.

My grunts' Hydras were all out and ready to fire. I waited until Ohirra was within twenty meters of the first group of GNA engaging with fungees before I let twelve missiles loose, three from each EXO.

Every one found a target as we ran towards the battle lines, exploding almost simultaneously.

A pair of motorcycles went up, the shockwave and shrapnel sending combatants tumbling into the air. Ohirra ran under an exploding SUV as it rocketed into the sky, Sula close on her heels. As the vehicle crashed back to earth, Stranz vaulted the ruined hood. I was so integrated into my display that I almost fell over the wreckage, managing to inelegantly stumble around it.

I'd sent two rounds into the hastily constructed mortar pit and couldn't help smile when their stash of 40mm rounds cooked off.

I felt hands grabbing at my EXO and I jerked my harmonic blade free. I swung blindly in all directions as I continued targeting. A laser indicator found Sula. I tracked and targeted the device to the edge of the warehouse and sent three missiles into it, smiling as a plume of fire and smoke rose from the area.

Then we were across, no longer in the GNA lines. I kept running, no longer targeting, instead checking the status of each of my grunts. Everything was green. No one seemed to be hurt.

We ran under the 605, ignoring the occasional fungee that hurtled towards us. Sometimes they'd come at me, then turn away, battering their hands and fists on the others. They recognized me as one of their own, just as I recognized them from their red halos. We ran away from them rather than engaging with them. After all, there was no reason to kill them unless we had to.

We were now beneath the black alien vine canopy. No longer did we have the wide open vistas of Greater Los

Angeles with views of the ever-present mountains. Now all we saw was the black roof of our new world, with things moving in the shadows, needlers flitting through the leaves, and death everywhere we looked. Even the buildings looked murdered, the alien vines breaking them open and turning them to dust.

We are not retreating. We are advancing in another direction.

> General Douglas MacArthur

CHAPTER FORTY-THREE

WE WERE FORCED to go to ground at the El Monte shopping center. Ohirra was dehydrated and had begun to stumble the last mile. The suits enabled us to wade through hell, but inside them we were very human. When we stopped, I had Sula and Stranz help Ohirra, giving her water slowly so it wouldn't make her feel worse. We had little onboard water and food. We'd expended a tremendous amount of energy and needed to get it back.

We'd stopped at what had been a women's clothing store. Someone had pulled off all the clothes and placed all the mannequins in the middle of the store, where they'd painted them in an impossible variety of garish colors. The greens, blues and yellows were brilliant in the gloom. I both kept watch and checked our time to detonation. It was taking too long to get to our target. We had no idea what was waiting for us at the hive and had to reserve as much time as we could to deal with that unknown. Every second we stopped, every moment we were forced to slow, put the entire mission in jeopardy. Of course, the fault lay with Dewhurst. Had we connected with Mother and her forces, we would have begun much closer to our objective. I knew one thing for certain: whatever we were doing, it had to change.

After twenty minutes, I had Stranz switch places with me and checked on Ohirra.

"How is it?" I asked, eyeing her as she climbed back into her EXO.

She shook her head. "Stupid, stupid. I shouldn't have let myself get like that."

"It is what it is. You ready to go?" I knew the answer from her stats, but wanted to give her the chance to reply.

Instead she said, "This is untenable, isn't it?"

"It is what it is," I said again. "Right now we just need to move. Every second is a second we can't get back."

She frowned. "Then let's go."

I shook my head. "Let's give it twenty more minutes. I need your firepower and your advice. I don't need you falling out."

She started to argue, but I held up a hand.

We waited the twenty minutes and I was pleased that her CO2 max had increased to an acceptable level. No sooner did I say it was okay than we were in file out the door, heading down the alien-vine-shadowed street. The vine had ignored the cars and anything made purely of metal, instead seeking those things it could smash and crumble. Here and there the wooden homes were already giving in to the alien vine. Concrete was going too, albeit to a lesser degree. I had no doubt that the deeper we went into the vine, the worse things would be.

Two hours later I was rewarded with visions of almost complete destruction. Rows of homes lay fallen and crumbled, not even a shadow of what they once were.

Traveling through the waste of what had once been the pinnacle of consumer culture was in and of itself a memorial to how great we'd had it. It was also a reminder of how quickly it could be taken away.

We were coming up on Almansur Men's Golf Club when our HUDs flashed a warning, tracking an unidentified aircraft above the alien vine.

An aircraft? This close to the hive? I'd lost track of the EMP bursts, but it was suicide to get this close. At first I thought it might be a UAV, perhaps even belonging to GNA. But it was much larger. My targeting resolved it as a Chinook. Could it be the Chinook that had come for Dewhurst and HMID Sandi? If so, what was it up to now? It was certain to draw the attention of the Cray, which was something I wanted to postpone for as long as possible.

I'd had everyone form on me to prepare for possible assault when a spasm of PTSD rocked me. The world dissolved into a mélange of Michelle, scarred and crying in my arms, while I saw men with saws and knives and pliers cutting, ripping, attaching hoses and cables to Sandi, who screamed my name over and over. I gritted my teeth so hard my jaws ached.

"Mason?" Ohirra's voice came from somewhere past Saturn.

I wanted to scream. I wanted to run away from the image. What I was witnessing was the rape of a person, on a fundamental level. They wanted all of her and took it. Seeing it, even if it was my fucking crazy mind's version of what had actually happened, made me want to track down every single member of GNA and OMBRA and rip them apart with my own hands.

"Mason!" Ohirra shouted over the coms.

The image dissolved in a rain of electronic confetti and I was once again in the alien vine gloom of the new Los Angeles.

"Sorry," I whispered hoarsely. "I'm back."

"What happened?"

Fucking PTSD, I wanted to say, but some questions were better left unanswered. I searched for the Chinook, but it was no longer there. What had happened to it?

As if sensing my confusion, Ohirra said, "It traveled west. We lost it through the vine."

"What do you think it was doing?" I asked.

"I think they were searching for us."

"Yeah, me too. Let's get going. We need to be careful."

We traveled ever westward. The hive wasn't visible but we knew where it was. I'd thought about traversing Burbank, then trying to sneak up on the Cray by way of Laurel Canyon or Coldwater Canyon, but time was flying away from me and we had to make as direct a route as possible. In a strange way, the black alien vine canopy was going to be our most useful tactical asset. Just as it concealed the denizens of the sky from us, it would also block the Cray's view, which should enable us to get closer to the hive without raising contact sooner than we would want to deal with it.

We hit the L.A. river as night fell on the city. Climbing up the embankment and onto the reclaimed ground of Piggyback Yard, we spied several hundred fungees. They stood still, facing in all directions, the trunks of their bodies moving together in an invisible breeze, as if they were all weeds in a wide, fallow field. I saw a red halo around each of their necks.

"I don't like this," Sula said.

What's the worst that could happen? I wanted to ask, but knew better. The only question was whether to go around or through them. There looked to be thousands of them.

I drew my harmonic blade. "We're going through."

"We're just going to kill them?" Sula said.

"They're not human. They won't ever be human again," I said, knowing that wasn't exactly the truth.

"But let's not kill unless we have to."

"Ohirra, I have lead, you have rear. Stranz, you're behind me, then Sula. Let's move."

I strode forward. When I encountered the first fungee—a young man who could have been, should have been, in high school learning algebra or staring at the girls and their budding beauty—I pushed gently past him. He stood next to a woman who reminded me of a cashier I used to see at a grocery store in San Pedro.

I worked straight through the infected masses, moving as steadily but as lightly as I could. Ohirra had been right. This wasn't a field to be harvested. They were people. I'd use my blade only if I felt it necessary.

We were perhaps halfway through when Sula started to cry.

"Maintain composure," I growled. I could understand her feeling. The sheer number of the fungees was something else. The question was, why had they been placed here?

"They're moving. They're getting closer together, but slowly."

"They're closing in?"

"Projection says we'll all be tightly packed in less than thirty seconds."

Was this pocket of infected humanity an early warning device for the hive, or had I blindly led the team into a living minefield?

"Bring about your blades," I said. "I'm cutting a path through."

Suddenly the entire field was alive with hands searching for purchase on our EXOs. They gripped and grabbed the others, but left me alone. It was as if a command had been given, something was *directing* them. Then I remembered what Michelle had said, that the Hypocrealiacs were using the fungees to watch us. I grabbed one of the fungees in my EXO hands and stared into its mad eyes, concentrating, trying to make a connection, trying to open a doorway so I could somehow communicate with it or with what was behind it. Was a Hypocrealiac staring back at me through this poor man? Was it studying me, watching me, trying to figure out what I was doing? The fungee's hands scrabbled at my face plate, nails breaking and fingers leaving bloody trails as it tried to push away from me and get at the others. Its mouth moved silently.

There was just no way. Even if the Hypocrealiacs were using the fungees to conduct their own reconnaissance or as early warning devices I couldn't bring myself to do them harm. I hurled myself away from the creature, sheathed my blade, and pushed through. I couldn't cut them. I couldn't kill them. I'd *been* one of them.

I made it to the other side of Piggyback Yard and into the street. When the others joined me, we stared back at the figures. None followed, but they watched us as we moved on.

We were in Chinatown. The dragon gate had been ripped down and all the colorful signs had been used to board up doors and windows on the lower floors, while the upper floor windows had been covered in plastic. Most of the cars had been pushed to the sides of the street. We felt eyes on us as we strode down vine-shadowed Hill Street. My HUD detected heat signatures on the second and third floors of the buildings lining the street.

"Ohirra," I began.

"I see them."

"Be on the watch, Tarantulas," I warned.

"Look at the windows covered in plastic," Stranz said. "Notice the people behind them?"

It looked as if the residents of Chinatown had created their own hermetically-sealed environments, creating their own barrier to the spore, which would allow them to survive it until the next threat emerged. The problem for them was that *we* were that next threat. They were well within the destruction radius of the bomb. If what OMBRA techs said was true, Chinatown would be hit with a blast of radiation so severe that nothing would survive.

"Should we tell them?" Ohirra asked.

I nodded. "We owe it to them. Ohirra, why don't you go knock on a door and see if someone answers? The rest of you, to me."

Sula, Stranz and I went back to back. They brought their miniguns to bear and I readied my Hydra in the event there was an attack. Not that I thought the people in the buildings meant any harm, but I wasn't about to put my people in danger if I could help it.

Meanwhile Ohirra went to first one door, then another. I toggled her feed so I could see what she saw. Finally one of the doors opened, revealing an elderly Chinese man standing in a hazmat suit.

"Please leave," he said. "We don't want any trouble."

My HUD detected movement at virtually all the windows surrounding us. I had no doubt that we had more than a dozen weapons trained on us.

"You don't understand," Ohirra said. "We're here to help."

"We don't need your help," the man said, trying to push the door closed.

But Ohirra wouldn't let him close it. "Listen. In less than seven hours we're going to detonate a nuclear bomb at the hive. This area is too close. The radiation will kill you."

The man stared at her through his plastic faceplate. I'd seen a movie once with John Wayne, or Robert Mitchum, or one of the other old movie stars. The movie took place on the Great Plains, and I remembered a scene where a family of settlers were told that the Indians were going to come and wipe them out. The settlers didn't seem to care. They insisted on staying, believing that they would figure out how to get along.

"Thank you for the information," the man said, and started to close the door.

"You do understand that you're going to die?" Ohirra said. "There's nothing you can do except escape."

"We understand," the man said. He offered her a serene smile.

"There's a group of fungees near Piggyback Yard. I'd be careful of them when you evacuate," she said.

"We're not leaving. This is our home."

"But don't you get it? If you stay, you'll die."

"We've been told that before. This is our home. We're staying here."

And with that he shut the door.

Ohirra stood, staring at it for several seconds.

"Come on back," I said.

"But they need to know..."

"They know. You told them. If they want to stay, then let them."

"But they're all going to die."

"It's their choice." I turned to continue down the street. "Stranz, take point."

He ran forward fifty meters.

Ohirra rejoined us and I had her take the rear.

The 110 had once carried drivers from the Valley into the city, and city folks into the Valley. We met the 101 just south of our position near Chavez Ravine, which had once been a great L.A. meeting place called Dodger Stadium. The tall, elevated highway was already crumbling beneath the insistent knots of black vine. We were forced to climb over the larger chunks of rubble.

We eventually crossed under the 110 and were skirting Dodger Stadium when our telemetry began to scream as a rocket streaked from the upper deck of the stadium. I shouted for Stranz to get out of the way. A moment later, he was thrown through the air, slamming into the side of the buttress holding up the freeway.

I got a word of warning for all you would-be warriors. When you join my command, you take on a debt. A debt you owe me personally. Each and every man under my command owes me one hundred Nazi scalps. And I *want* my scalps. And all y'all will git me one hundred Nazi scalps, taken from the heads of one hundred dead Nazis. Or you will die tryin'.

Lt. Aldo Raine, *Inglourious Basterds*

CHAPTER FORTY-FOUR

"OHIRRA! FIND THAT sniper!" I yelled, running to Stranz.

Sula took shelter behind a giant concrete slab that had fallen from the highway. Her Hydra was up and waiting for telemetry to give her a target.

I got to Stranz just in time to pull him ten meters out of the kill zone before another RPG impacted. I staggered from the force of the explosion. Concrete rained down on us.

Sula fired two missiles at the same time Ohirra unzipped the sky, sending a hundred rounds in five seconds into the upper deck of the stadium.

My telemetry was for shit under the ensuing cloud of concrete dust, but I'd let them sort it out. I checked Stranz's vitals and they were all over the place. His eyes were closed, but he was breathing... probably just unconscious from the impact. He hadn't taken a direct hit, but even in an EXO, shrapnel could be a deadly thing if it was big enough and hit just right. I checked the integrity of his suit and didn't see any broken seals or rips.

"Sula, with me," Ohirra said over the net.

I watched for a moment as they moved in sprinting overwatch up an embankment, then across an immense parking lot toward the stadium. The black alien vine had yet to overtake the stadium, which sat high on a hill. I'd noted that the vine seemed to want to maintain its own level and tended not to climb higher. Even the Hollywood Sign was free from its clutches... for now.

"Wait for me," I ordered.

"I can take him," Ohirra said.

"Negative. *Wait*."

Using my command switch, I powered down Stranz's suit, then powered it back up. As advanced as the technology was, I was using the same methods I would have used on an old desktop PC. After thirty seconds, his vitals returned to normal.

I shook him until his eyes fluttered open.

"Eggs and bacy, time to wakey! Rise and shine, sleepyhead."

He brought a hand to his head. "What hit me?"

"Close call," I said, standing, then offering a hand. "RPG just missed."

He accepted my hand and I helped him up. Then I turned and ran towards the stadium. It was nothing more than a giant hunching shadow of darkness in the overcast night, but my EXO was capable of rendering it in perfect clarity with Starlight technology.

Another RPG round arced toward me, but without any seeking technology, it was easy to avoid. By the time Stranz and I had joined the others, Ohirra was virtually dancing with impatience to take down the sniper.

"What's our plan?" I asked.

"Go in there and fuck them up," Sula said.

"Nice. But I was looking for something a little more detailed, because the minute one of us goes through that entrance to the field," I said, pointing, "we're going to be a target."

I could see Ohirra working through the problem, then her shoulders sagged. "You're right. It's a trap."

"Either that or some wannabe sniper taking potshots at us from extreme range. Here's what we do. Let's stick together and go up internally. I've been to a hundred games at the park; I know this place inside and out."

We moved two-by-two through the ground floor, past kiosks that once sold souvenirs and food stalls. An elote cart had been all but demolished. I paused before it and gave a silent eulogy for what had been my childhood treat during the seventh-inning stretch.

We kept moving around the inside of the stadium until we were even with the center field wall. We climbed a staircase, which got us to the mezzanine level. The blue and red Dodgers symbol was everywhere, as a reminder of what fifty-six thousand people once did two hundred days out of the year. The silence, followed by the crack of the bat, then the roar of the crowd used to electrify me.

We passed a kiosk that used to serve Doyer Dogs. I could still make out the menu, which showed a picture of the hot dog smothered in nacho cheese, chili, jalapeños and pico de gallo. As I'd gotten older, these gut bombs had replaced the elote as my cuisine of choice. I remember polishing off seven of them one fall Saturday afternoon, only to pay for it later, lying crumpled on the bathroom floor with my stomach a hurricane of *what the hell did you put in me!*

I sent Ohirra and Sula towards the first base foul ball seats.

Stranz and I went to the third-base foul ball seats.

When both teams were in place, we climbed up one more level and headed towards the seating areas through a tall, wide tunnel. After seeing the first hint of green on the field, I spied the blades of the helicopter.

"Careful," I said. "Now we know where the Chinook landed." I thought for a moment. "Let me pop my head out first and draw their attention. When they fire, both of you take them out."

I motioned Stranz to hang back, then I took three steps forward and peeked around the corner. My HUD went crazy as it counted targets in five locations, including directly above me. I spun just in time to see a man in a hazmat suit and body armor putting an old fashioned LAW rocket launcher to his shoulder. He was close enough to the opening that I was able to jump and grab his leg. I jerked it, the ankle breaking as his leg folded towards me. The rocket launcher clattered to the ground at about the same time three RPGs shot toward me. Instead of diving back in the tunnel, I ran to my right, towards the seats behind home plate and the press boxes from where most of the fire was coming.

The RPGs hit, obliterating the entrance to my rear.

I ordered Stranz to mirror my movements from the inside and shortly saw his ammo numbers tick down as he opened fire.

I brought out my harmonic blade and swung it over my head as I screamed, "*Take me out to the ball game...*"

Sula and Ohirra's rockets found homes in three of the ten press boxes, blowing them to smithereens.

"*Take me out with the crowd...*"

Another hazmat-suited target swung around, aimed his RPG at me and fired.

"*Give me some peanuts and apple jacks...*"

I saw the round coming towards me in slow motion and twisted my body to let it fly harmlessly past.

"*I don't care if I never get back...*"

I was on him as he tried to reload. I separated his upper and lower halves with one great swing of the blade. I spied another man behind him and started to swing, until a great explosion blew me clear out of the press area. I tumbled backwards, leaving a trail of broken seats in my path, coming to a halt upside down against the cage behind home plate.

"What was that?" Ohirra said over the net.

I righted myself, exchanging my dizzy upside-down view of the universe for a dizzy right-side-up. My vitals said I was fine, except that my heart rate was through the roof. Stranz's vitals, on the other hand, were black—which could only mean two things: either his suit was offline or he was dead.

"Ohirra..." My torso felt like Mike Tyson had done a round on it. I lumbered forward and pulled myself up, retracing my path of destruction. "You and Sula, to me."

She ran toward what was once the press box. We'd destroyed three of the boxes; now they all ten were nothing but a black smoking hole. We met at the start of the rubble. Ohirra wasn't even breathing hard. She'd left Sula back to cover us, which was a better idea than my command. I arrived huffing and puffing like I'd just run a marathon after smoking a carton of Pall Malls.

"What was that?" she asked.

I shook my head as much to clear the ringing as in answer. "And where's Stranz?"

I waded into the wreckage, pulling aside wood and concrete. I found one hazmat-suited body which had been blown in half. Deeper in I found three more, all in various states of dismemberment. A fourth was lying beneath a collapsed desk. He was still alive... until I planted an EXO foot on his face and pushed. I didn't care for these men at all. They'd earned their fate when they'd tried to kill us. I was more concerned for Stranz.

I found him at the back of the press area, in what would have been the access tunnel; it had partially collapsed on top of him. His suit was dark. It looked as if Thor, Loki and every Frost Giant in the pantheon had hammered on it until it was as dimpled as a bowling ball. His hands were claws at his neck and he wasn't moving.

I fell on my knees beside him and leaned down so I could peer into his faceplate. His eyes were bulging. His tongue was turning blue. As I came into view, he stared at me, dying.

Fucking OMBRA techs had made a flawed design. Maybe if I put one of them in a powered-down suit, they'd see the need to fix their error. I reached around the back of the helmet and twisted, trying to remove it so he could get air. It was caught on something, or dented, or both. I cried for Ohirra. It took the two of us to rip the helmet free from its connector. When we got it free, Stranz gulped gratefully for air.

"Okay, kid. You're going to be all right." I unlatched his suit. "Are you injured anywhere else?"

He was still gasping for air, but managed to shake his head.

I stood and began removing my EXO.

"What are you doing?" Ohirra asked.

"I'm immune to the spore. Chucklehead here isn't. He needs to—"

"We've got incoming Cray!" Sula shouted.

I stopped what I was doing, re-attached my EXO and began tracking six of the incoming creatures. It was long past sunset; they were about due.

"Let them come to us. Everyone on my mark. Ready, Ohirra?"

"Ready."

"Sula?"

Nothing.

"Sula?"

"Sebring is here and says he'll blow the nuke on my back if we don't give up."

Sebring. Of course. He wanted a suit and he wanted the nuke. He was the reason for the helicopter.

"Well, then tell him he's going to have to wait until we take care of the Cray." I checked my weapons and realized I didn't have my harmonic blade. I'd dropped it during the explosion and it was somewhere down there in the dark. I grabbed Stranz's and unsheathed it. "Take it easy, kid," I said to him.

The Cray were half a click away when I got another idea.

I brought up my Hydras and targeted them. Once locked, I fired all six missiles. Five of them found a home, but the sixth missed as the Cray juked. Ohirra hit it with one of her missiles and it exploded in the sky. Now to ensure there wouldn't be any more.

Ohirra began to speak, "I thought you wanted to—"

I cut her off. "Make sure there's no incoming. I'm going to take care of this."

I marched over to where Sula was standing. Sebring stood behind her, tiny next to the EXO. He wore a yellow hazmat suit a little nicer than the ones his cronies had worn. Question was, how had he gotten the better of Sula?

"Sula, report."

Her eyes were wide and glassy. Her lips trembled as she spoke. Gone was the sure woman grunt I'd come to know. This was someone else entirely. "I was watching the battle and he came up on me. He says he has a claymore attached to the nuke and that if he presses the switch, it will kill us all." She paused as she struggled to speak. "Do you think it's true?"

"Probably. I see you hiding there, Sebring. Why don't you come out so I can see you?"

"So you can shoot me? No way."

"It takes a worm to assume everyone is a worm."

"You can call me whatever you want, tough guy in the superhuman suit, but I'm a survivor. Now give me your suit."

"This old thing?" I toggled a secure line to Ohirra. "Can you get a shot on this guy?"

"Negative. He's too close to Sula."

"Any inbound?"

"There's activity above the hive, but nothing moving this way."

"Keep monitoring." Back to the public address system. "I don't know if this is your size."

Sebring laughed. "You're one of the funny ones. Dewhurst already told me that it's pretty much one size fits all."

"Ahh, that Dewhurst. Always full of surprises." I held out a hand. "I don't suppose you'll let us continue our mission to save L.A., would you?"

He laughed. "What makes you think I want L.A. saved?"

I had no answer to that.

"I had power on television. I could make or break a new act. I resurrected careers and became bigger than Casey Kasem. Then the world changed and left me with the only thing I have of value—my ability to convince others of the value in something... in this case, *me*. I require chaos. I curate strife. I need something to point my finger at and to tell my people that it's the reason for all of their hunger, pain, and misery. I need that, like I need your suit and this nuke. Now, give me the damn suit."

I began to unlatch my helmet. "Well, if you put it that way..."

"Two more incoming," Ohirra said.

"Mind taking care of them, dear? I'm a little busy right now."

"Lieutenant, you don't have to do this," Sula began.

I gave her a smile that stopped her from saying anything else. I climbed out of the remainder of the suit and stood in the cool fall evening, wearing only a pair of toe shoes and Kevlar skivvies.

"Now what, Mr. Sebring?"

He glanced from the suit to me. It was obvious that he'd never thought past his threat. He had a Claymore detonator in his right hand and now he could have my EXO. But how was he going to get into it without putting himself in harm's way?

Finally, he gestured behind him, towards the dark entrance to the stadium's kiosk.

"You want me to carry these there?"

"That's right," he said.

I picked up the EXO with two hands and managed to drag it towards him. I got two feet before I had to adjust my grip and turn around and pull it. The EXO with ammo weighed well over three hundred pounds. It took everything in me to move it.

"Easy," said Sebring.

"Suit's too heavy for me to do anything," I grunted as I passed him, pulling the EXO behind me. I craned to see his left hand. I paused, wiped my brow, then glanced again. I could just make it out in the shadow between the rear of Sula's EXO and the wall. He carried a pistol. It looked like a pocket 9mm, like a P238. Just big enough to fit in his palm while retaining the stopping power of a 9mm, using .380 ACP ammo.

I resumed heaving and pulling the EXO into the darkness.

"Hey," Sebring called. "You went in too far."

"Sorry man."

"Bring it back out. To where I can see it."

I walked to the edge of the darkness, my hands on my knees, feigning exhaustion. "Can't do it. It's too heavy."

I could see him peering into the darkness. Finally he said, "Just don't move. Get it?"

"Got it." Just come a little closer, asshole.

He moved towards me, squinting into the darkness.

He took another step and as he moved away from Sula, I could see the wire running from the firing device to the claymore. He'd looped it; it could have been ten meters long. I could shout for Sula to cut it, but it might be too late. Better to work through my own solution.

Another step. He waggled the pistol towards me. "Don't move."

"Not even thinking of it," I said as if each word weighed a thousand pounds. Every nerve fired in preparation.

He took another step. I could see the space between the lever on the firing device and the device itself and knew what to do.

One more step and I lunged forward. I shoved my left hand into that space, then gripped the firing device, trapping his fingers, the skin between my thumb and forefinger blocking the contacts. He let out an angry croak, then brought his pistol around. He was so eager to kill me that he'd fired before he realized it. The round passed harmlessly between us. The sound of the round and the kick of the pistol shocked him, and in that microsecond's hesitation, I jammed my thumb under his and twisted my hand counterclockwise. If he didn't release the weapon, I'd break his thumb.

The pistol skittered into the darkness.

His eyes went wide.

I headbutted him once, twice, three times.

Fucking rookie-wanna-be-terrorist-cult-leader.

He fell to his knees, dazed.

I stood over him, a vulture, the Angel of Death, an eagle prepared to deliver the final blow. Breathing heavily at the release of my dammed up adrenaline, I was prepared to kill him right there.

Blood tricked in my left eye and I wiped it away.

I yanked the clacker from his hand, flipped the bail

to put it on safe, then went to the mine. It was attached with hundred-mile-an-hour tape. I ripped it free, then shoved the mine down the back of Sebring's pants. Finally I gave the firing device to Sula.

"Use it if you need to."

She stared at it for a moment, then her tight lips slid into a dark little smile.

I ran to Stranz, who was almost recovered. I helped him out of his suit and to his feet. He stood shakily. I steadied him. There was a danger in him being outside the suit, but there were no fungees or alien vines near the stadium. He couldn't continue in his suit, so he'd have to take mine.

He started to protest, but I shook my head to cut him off.

"I'm immune to the spores. Whatever they did changed my DNA."

We heard a scream, then the sound of metal pounding concrete, over and over and over.

Both Stranz and I ran to where Sula was stomping on Sebring's dead body. She'd started on his chest and moved to his head, using the full might of the servos to slam into the flesh and bone of what had once been a man.

"Dear God," Stranz said.

"Sula," I whispered.

She whirled. "What? I can't kill him? He would have certainly killed us."

I shook my head at the savagery. "Is this what we've become?"

"Nothing more than what you did with Dewhurst," Stranz noted. He stepped over a pool of flesh and blood to grab the claymore. He removed the blasting cap, rendering it inert, then tossed the mine aside.

"But he was a traitor. He put us in jeopardy. We trusted him." Even as I said it, I realized how pointless the argument was; in the end, they were both still dead.

Stranz did something then that I'd thought beyond him. He put both his hands on Sula's EXO's torso and spoke quietly to her. I couldn't hear everything he said, but I heard enough to know that he was calming her down. I nodded in appreciation. He'd only ever wanted to be a sergeant, and I'd made him one almost out of pity. Now it looked as if he'd truly earned it.

A fool thinks himself to be wise, but a wise man knows himself to be a fool.

William Shakespeare

CHAPTER FORTY-FIVE

THE HELICOPTER PILOT had been hiding in the shadow of the infield. Ohirra leaped down the stadium and caught up to him just as he was trying to turn the engine over. She jerked him out of the seat and waited for me. I spent several minutes stripping dead men, scrounging clothes. I didn't for a second want to continue the mission in nothing but my underwear. Luckily, between those who'd been shot and those who'd been tossed by the explosions, I was able to find boots and a pair of fatigues to wear.

I also found two 9mm pistols and eight full magazines.

Stranz came up beside me, wearing my EXO. Fresh sergeant stripes had been painted on his arms—I'd done it myself, with Sebring's blood. He handed me a sheathed harmonic blade, scrounged from his old EXO. He'd fashioned a rope around it so I could carry it across my back. Not that I thought I had any chance of winning against the Cray in melee combat, but it might keep me alive long enough to continue the mission.

Down on the field, I spoke to the pilot. It turned out that they had more than enough fuel for us to escape if need be. I took him in the back of the Chinook, then hog tied him.

I hoped we'd be able to use the helicopter to get back in time after the nuke had been planted.

Now with just Sula, Ohirra and Stranz still in EXOs, we headed towards the 101 Freeway. We had a little over six miles to go before we reached our next decision point—the Metro station at Hollywood and Highland. That would put us just north and less than a mile away from the hive.

The trick would be to get there without me getting killed. If I found that I was at all a distraction or detriment to the mission, then I'd find a way to solve the problem, even if it meant my death, and I told them so. None of them tried to argue, which was a mark of their dedication to the mission. They knew and understood, simple as that. A lesser version of me would have been hurt, but I knew better. This was it. Whether I set the detonator or one of them did, it had to be done. My dying had absolutely nothing to do with it.

The order of march was Stranz, Sula, and Ohirra. Sula carried me in her arms like an awkward, giant ugly baby, as all three EXOs jogged through the snarled mass of cars that now made up the 101. I kept my eyes to the canopy above us and watched as the needlers flew back and forth, doing their business of pollination. Twice one flew towards me in an aggressive manner, but when it came near, it merely hovered, inspected me, then flew away.

We passed the exit to Filipino Town and Echo Park. What had once been home to drifters, half-price hookers, and dealers was now a deadman's land of fungees. I spied a mass of them surrounding the water of Echo Park Lake in four deep rows, swaying in unison to an unfelt wind. We kept to the freeway, but I wondered if I'd experience strange memories if we got closer to them. What had that been about? Then I remembered how HMID Salinas had used my brain for computational space. What had they said? Each human brain had a capacity to hold 2.5 petabytes of binary data. Were these groups of fungees the same as neurons in the human body? Were they being used by the Hypocrealiacs as external brain space, or storage space for something important? I remembered the reports of groups of fungees surrounding a hive. They weren't there to protect anything. They were there for their brains.

This new information seemed incredibly important, but I had no way to send it. We were too far for FM transmissions, and nothing could have survived the constant EMP pulses this side of the 605. I sent out a thought to Ethridge but got nothing in return. Either he wasn't in range or I just didn't have the knack for this.

You could try and use the fungees as a conduit for your transmission.

Where had that come from? Was it Thompson? *Thompson, is that you?* No response.

Could it be true? Could I tap into their brains and use it to slingshot, much like FM retransmission stations were used to boost the feed?

I realized we were slowing.

Ahead of us was the off ramp to Melrose. A mass of fungees six rows deep stood across both north and southbound lanes of the 101.

To Sula I said, "Tell Stranz to stop and wait for further orders."

We stopped, and I closed my eyes to concentrate better. The voice had recommended I use the fungees. It only made sense. I reached out to them with my mind. My DNA had been changed so I was more like them than not. If only I could—

I was hit with an avalanche of memories—colors, smells, feelings filled me to bursting. I was laughing and crying, yelling and babbling. Christmas dinner and dog shit and burned marshmallows filled my nostrils. I felt love and despondency, as titanic mountains of emotion collided into me, reducing me to the sum of my parts. I felt myself slipping away, falling, losing myself, forgetting who I was. I drifted in a sea of everyone's sorrow, life a half-remembered dream.

Drifting.

Drifting.

Then the feeling began to wane. It slowly came back to me. Tony Scott. My name was Tony Scott. No, that wasn't right. Mason. My name was Mason. My first name was Ben. Tony Scott was a movie director. He'd killed himself.

I became aware of a new noise. It grew louder and louder until it became my universe.

"Mason!"

The word rang like thunder.

"Mason!"

The sound of worlds colliding.

"Mason, wake up!"

My eyes snapped open. "What's..." My mouth felt like raw hamburger. It hurt to speak.

"Dear God, you're back," Ohirra said. "We thought we'd lost you for good."

"What happened?" I managed.

"You lost your mind," she said, her eyes narrowed through the faceplate of her mask.

"You were screaming and laughing," Sula said.

I turned to her. She'd been crying.

I looked around. We weren't on the 101 anymore. We were inside a building, what had once been a store. Part of the roof had collapsed from the intrusion of torso-thick alien vines.

"Where's Stranz?"

Ohirra nodded towards the door. "Standing guard."

I licked my lips. "Full report."

Ohirra stared at me as if I might explode. "You made us stop at Melrose. Then you went into a fugue. You remained like that for about five minutes, then you started to scream and yell and cry. I didn't know you spoke Japanese. Or Russian."

"I don't."

"Well, you did then."

"What'd I say?"

"You said, 'Don't go, Hitomi. Stay with me.'"

I shook my head. "How long?"

"Two hours."

I struggled to sit up. "Two hours? What time is it? Why didn't you Charlie Mike?"

Ohirra sighed. "There's the Mason I know. Frankly, we were about to leave you. It's midnight and we have three hours to detonation."

"You should have left." I ran my hand over my head and mopped the sweat away. I was aware how parched I was, probably from all the screaming. "Water?"

She held out a bottle. "We found this in the back."

I uncapped it and drank the whole thing down, the warm liquid luxurious as it entered my system.

"What happened?" Ohirra asked.

I told her, working it out as I spoke.

She took it all in, then asked the most important question. "Who was it who told you to connect?"

"I thought it was Thompson."

"But you said he didn't respond."

"He didn't, but I assumed..." I shook my head. "Right. Never assume."

"Do you know who I think it was?" she asked, her voice suddenly tight and on the edge of anger.

"It's one of the Masters. It was a Hypercrealiac."

"And you just gave it access to your brain. Mason, how could you? It lured you. It tried to capture you. It probably read your thoughts."

"I didn't mean—"

"Dammit, Mason, this was what Olivares talked to you about. You're our leader. You can't just go off doing things on your own. You can never tell when they'll affect us."

Fucking hell. First Olivares and now Ohirra, and they were both right. "You're totally right. I felt a sort of assimilation happening. I was becoming part of a larger whole. I think the Master is using the fungees for their brain capacity."

"But you said it spoke to you."

"Remember, when I was a fungee I still had full brain function. All of my autonomous functions were still my own, including thinking. Do you think maybe the purpose of the fungees isn't only to infect, but to gather so that they—*we*—could be used later by the Masters?"

"The real question is, did it get the mission parameters?"

I thought about it for a moment. "I don't think it works that way. I don't think it got anything useful."

"How can you be sure?"

"It stands to reason that if it knew, then it would also know my location and send Cray to stop us." I got to my feet. "Stranz, any movement?"

"Nothing, sir," he said, without turning. "Glad you're back, sir."

I walked over and slapped the back of his EXO. "Me too, Sergeant." I spun to Ohirra. "I can hear your thoughts. Maybe it's lying in wait. Maybe it knows our mission but not our location. All good ideas and all valid. But unless we're going to hang out here to discuss them further, we need to Charlie Mike. Is that good for you?"

Ohirra nodded, clearly unhappy. She approached me in her EXO, making me aware of how much larger she was in her suit. "If you want to lead, then lead. That means don't go anywhere we can't follow."

"You're right. I got it. Now, are you ready?"

"Ready."

"Good," I said, clapping my hands together. "So where are we?"

Sula gave a report. "In a 99 Cent Store off Sunset, east of the 101. We're a mile and a half away from the Metro entrance. All three of us are at or around thirty-five percent power, and we have half of our ammunition left." She reached down and picked a harmonic blade off the ground. "And here's your sword."

I found the sheath, slid the blade into it, and slung it across my back.

"Then let's go."

When I saw Sula hold out her arms for me to climb on, I shook my head.

"I'm on foot the rest of the way. This close to the hive, we need everyone ready." I glanced at Ohirra. "Especially if the enemy knows we're coming."

Our land is everything to us... I will tell
you one of the things we remember on our
land. We remember that our grandfathers
paid for it—with their lives.

John Wooden Leg, Cheyenne

CHAPTER FORTY-SIX

IT WAS AS dark as I'd ever seen it outside. The moon was
hidden by clouds. Except for the illuminated displays
inside the EXO helmets, there wasn't a single man-
made light for miles. I turned back to the team. Even
though they towered over me, I was still the boss, and
as such, I felt the need to say a few words before the
final push.

"So this is my Saint Crispin's Day speech," I began,
gazing at each one in turn.

I opened my mouth to speak, but before I could utter
a word, Stranz asked, "Who's St. Crispin?"

I paused; I actually had no idea. I just remembered the
speech. I looked plaintively at Ohirra, who thankfully
spoke up.

"Who St. Crispin was isn't as important as the speech,"
she said. I nodded for her to continue as she glanced at
me. "King Henry V gave his men a speech on the eve of
the Battle of Agincourt. England was outnumbered five
to one. The French had thirty-six thousand troops while
the English only numbered about eight thousand."

"Jesus," Stranz said. "Talk about walking into a slaughter."

"*Into the Valley of Death rode the six hundred*," Sula murmured.

"Kipling," I noted.

But Sula corrected me. "Tennyson," she said.

Ohirra nodded. "'The Charge of the Light Brigade.' England didn't fare so well there. Six hundred light cavalry were sent against more than twenty thousand Russians during the Crimean War."

"So far this is a sucky speech," Stranz said. "We know we're outnumbered. You don't have to rub it in."

I couldn't help a grin. Stranz was right. I needed to see if I could save it. "Shakespeare commemorated the speech in the play *Henry V*," I said. "I saw the movie version and every time I see it again, the speech gives me chills. Sure, it talks about being outnumbered, but it also talks about pride. What was it the King said, Ohirra—*the fewer the men, the greater the share of honor*?"

She nodded. "It was the idea that the English didn't need as many men as the French because they were intrinsically better. Don't forget this was the first large-scale battle in which the English longbow was used. The French didn't know what to do. The arrows crippled them."

"The French lost something like ten thousand men while the English lost less than two hundred," I added.

"Seriously?" Stranz seemed stunned.

Sula let out a low whistle.

"They had better weapons, just like we do," I said.

"So what does St. Crispin's Day have to do with it?" Stranz asked.

"It was used as a touch point, a date to mark their destined victory. I actually memorized this one stanza: *He that shall live this day and see old age, will yearly on the vigil say to his neighbors that 'To-morrow is Saint Crispin.' Then he will strip his sleeve and show his scars, And say 'These wounds I had on Crispin's day.'* It's the idea that they'd survive, and that everyone who wasn't part of the battle would wish they had been."

"And it worked?" Stranz asked.

"The English won pretty convincingly," Ohirra commented.

"Then again, it could be the more advanced weapons they were using," I said.

"How many Cray do you think there are?" Sula asked.

I shrugged. "Hundreds. Maybe thousands."

"How do we know this isn't more like the Charge of the Light Brigade?" Stranz asked.

I looked to Ohirra to answer that one and she immediately jumped in. "The Charge was against several battalions of artillery, and many thousands of rifles. It was really a hopeless gesture."

Sula closed her eyes and spoke. "*Cannon to right of them. Cannon to left of them. Cannon behind them. Volleyed and thundered. Stormed at with shot and shell. While horse and hero fell. They that had fought so well.*" When she opened her eyes again, she saw we were all staring at her. "One of the poems we had to memorize in English Lit. I also had to memorize 'The Raven.' Want to hear that?"

I chuckled. "No thanks. I just didn't know I was in the midst of so many literary grunts." I glanced at Stranz.

"Don't look at me. I peaked at *Green Eggs and Ham*."

"I will not eat them with the Cray. I will not eat them any day. I do not like green eggs and ham. I do not like them, Sam I am."

Stranz grinned. "Hey, that's good."

Sula nodded and added, "Quoth the Raven, 'Nevermore.'"

Stranz shook his head. "I've always thought that's a stupid name for a raven. Never understood why there had to be a poem about it either."

I stared at Stranz for a long moment, then broke into laughter. Sula joined. Stranz did too, even though he didn't know why. Even Ohirra joined in. When I was done, I wiped tears from my eyes.

I surveyed my team of grunts. I couldn't have been more proud. "You ready to go kill some Cray?"

All three grunts shouted, "Huah!"

I turned to head out the door and heard Stranz say, "Turned out to be a pretty good speech after all."

I grinned as I slipped into the Los Angeles night.

The suicide bomber's imagination leads him to believe in a brilliant act of heroism, when in fact he is simply blowing himself up pointlessly and taking other people's lives.

Salman Rushdie

CHAPTER FORTY-SEVEN

STRANZ AND OHIRRA hugged the buildings on either side of the street about thirty meters forward of where Sula walked with me down the center of the road. Silence was a must. I'd ordered harmonic blades drawn. This close to the hive, we'd have every Cray in the area on us if we so much as capped off a single round.

I missed being able to check everyone's status and observe what they were seeing through their feeds. This was old-school leadership—like being back in Iraq or Afghanistan, but with aliens instead of IEDs.

One thing was for sure. Whatever had taken over my brain hadn't been able to divine the nature of our mission. I'm certain if it had, it would have sent the Cray to attack us. For all I knew, the Master didn't even see us as intelligent, or any different from a dog or cat, or any other animal running around on Earth.

At Normandie, we turned north until we hit Hollywood Boulevard. We paused in the lee of a liquor store where they promised *Checks cashed for free and a sale on six-packs of Corona!* while Stranz scouted the area ahead. We only had a few blocks to go before we could enter the nearest Red Line station where Western crossed Hollywood. Although I didn't relish going underground, it could possibly get us where we needed without us having to encounter the enemy.

Stranz had been gone five minutes when Ohirra came to me.

"We've got to go. Now!"

"What is it?"

"The Cray. They know we're here. They're headed our way." How did they know? Then it hit me: they'd tracked us all the way through the eyes of the fungees. "How many?"

"Stranz said all of them."

Sula was already running down the street towards the Metro station six blocks away.

Ohirra wanted to carry me, but I wouldn't have it. I ordered her to run on ahead and get Sula inside with the nuke. If I didn't make it, then I didn't make it.

I poured on the speed, deciding to leave the blade sheathed on my back. The old running with scissors adage came to mind, except the blade was far worse than any pair of scissors I could imagine.

Far ahead, I saw Sula stop and bring her minigun to bear. She sawed the air with bullets, ripping back and forth.

Even further ahead, Stranz fired a phalanx of rockets.

Suddenly it was raining Cray. They fell, dead and dying, through the alien vine; some fell on cars, exploding what glass remained. Some fell on the pavement, cracking it where the vines hadn't already broken it apart, their arms curled, wings torn.

I went temporarily blind as images flashed through my brain like shotgun blasts: Kilimanjaro where the Cray attacked and tore through our ranks, all claws and slashing; where they rose from the ground, pulling us into their clutches; where they tore through our encampment, even though I wasn't there. Then Iraq, where pieces of my men fell around me after the roadside bomb went up, then Afghanistan where a group of children died when a man wearing an explosive vest ran up to an American officer.

I crashed into the side of a wrecked truck and sprawled painfully across the asphalt. I struggled back to my feet, slipped once, then kept running.

My grunts were pouring rounds and rockets into the sky, standing in a small circle at the top of the Metro station opening.

My face felt swollen and bloody from where I'd hit the ground. It figured I'd find a way to injure myself before enemy contact. I kept willing my grunts to head down into the station, but they remained in place.

I caught movement out of the corner of my eye and was able to dive for cover just as a Cray launched itself onto the hood of a car in front of me. Spikes jutted out from the knobs of its knees and elbows. It regarded me with a cluster of spider eyes in the center of its mantis-shaped head.

I came up against a man-thick alien vine and pulled myself behind it.

The Cray came at me, wings flared, four sets of claws reaching for me.

With the vine between me and the enemy, I pulled the blade from my back. I could feel it vibrating slightly in my two-handed grip.

The Cray had to circle around me, but I kept the thick vine between myself and it. It was obvious that it didn't want to rip through the vine even though it could have done so easily. Maybe that was something it had been programmed not to do.

The Cray lunged right.

I swung sideways and felt the blade bite. The Cray fell back as ichor bled from the meter-wide wound, pieces of its stomach slipping to the ground.

I spun on my heel and ran. I only had a block to go. I could see more Cray coming through the canopy and landing on the roofs of buildings to either side of the street. I was down to a half-block when I saw Stranz and Sula head down into the Metro. The pile of Cray in front of them was twice as tall as they were.

Ohirra stayed and began to fire at the Cray nearest me.

I was fifty feet away when I saw a Cray descend and grab her. It started into the air, but let her go when she struck it in the face with a hammer blow from her EXO fist.

She pointed down the stairs, as if I needed to know where to go, then fired a burst into the Cray.

I passed her just as it fell.

She tried to sidestep, but it caught her and knocked her to the ground.

I was halfway down the stairs when I glanced back and saw another Cray land by Ohirra. It began to claw at her faceplate and chest. She didn't move; either dead or knocked out. Without getting closer, I couldn't tell. I dropped my sword, grabbed my 9mm pistols and fired both of them, sending rounds into the Cray's side. Eighteen rounds later it fell out of view.

Suddenly Stranz was bounding past me. He grabbed Ohirra and pulled her from beneath the weight of the dead Cray. I snatched my blade from the ground and ran in front of him, down three flights of stairs into the darkness. I stumbled once, then found my balance at the bottom where Sula stood, her suit lighting up the vicinity.

While I waited for the others, I reloaded my pistol. I was almost done when an incredible explosion rocked me. Concrete dust fell, temporarily blinding me.

Stranz and Ohirra came clattering down the stairs. He had one of her arms around his neck and he was supporting her as best he could. Once they hit the floor, he let her go. I watched as she fell to her knees, but no farther.

"Is everyone all right?" I asked.

"Got the wind... knocked out of me," Ohirra said.

"What was that explosion?"

"I had to close the front door," Stranz said, "Or else we'd have Cray at our backs."

"Stranz, check out everyone's vitals and ammo status."

"What are you going to do?"

I snapped on the flashlight I'd taken from the Chinook. "Going to check the tracks and see if they're clear or not. I don't know how much damage the alien vine has done below ground. For all I know, it's as bad down here as it is up there. I'm hoping for otherwise, of course."

I jumped down onto the tracks and headed west, saw where vines had penetrated the ceiling and walls and, even as I watched, were growing and moving like a thousand cilia in a long, dark throat.

I stared into the alien foliage, the world-eater, consumer of humanity. I heard it speak to me and I turned and marched back to the others.

Just because you're paranoid doesn't mean they aren't after you.

Joseph Heller, *Catch-22*

CHAPTER FORTY-EIGHT

STRANZ, SULA AND Ohirra stood on the platform, conversing, and I stood in the darkness, my light off, watching them. I wondered what they'd think of me standing there. Would they know the truth of it? Would they appreciate the need to change our mission?

I stepped out of the darkness and strode to the platform. Stranz reached down and helped me up.

I went to Sula and began to unstrap the nuke.

"What are you doing?" Ohirra asked.

"Removing the nuke." I spoke as calmly as I could. I didn't want to give anyone cause for concern. "There's been a change in mission."

I saw Ohirra glance at Stranz. The ensuing silence told me they were conspiring against me, probably devising some sort of treason. I'd seen their kind in Kosovo. Someone gives an order and they try and find ways to not do it, poking holes in the reason, thinking of alternatives. Didn't they understand? An order is just that—an order. It's not open for interpretation or conversation.

"I wasn't aware you had communication, Mason," Ohirra said.

I finished unstrapping the nuke, then set it on the platform. The mini-Faraday cage the OMBRA techs had designed doubled the nuke's bulk, and once we got it out, it would be far easier to carry.

"Understandable," I said.

I went to remove the access panel from the W84. It had four recessed pins. I knelt before it, unscrewed each one, then pulled it free and set it on the cold concrete. The display was dark, except for a single blinking red light that indicated that the power source was still functioning.

Ohirra touched my shoulder. "Mason, we shouldn't take it out. There could be Cray in the area. One EMP and we lose the weapon."

"I understand what you're saying," I said. What I really wanted to do was put my gun to her head and pull the fucking trigger, but I needed to remain calm. The voice had explained everything to me with irrefutable logic. All I needed to do was follow it and then everything would be right with the world.

I kept working, even as I felt their eyes on me. Both Dewhurst and I had gone through several hours of training prior to the start of mission. I, in turn, had provided Ohirra and Mal training as my backups. Mal wasn't with us any longer, but Ohirra could surely see what I was doing.

"Why are you disarming the nuke?"

I sighed, wishing for the love of God that she'd have something more useful to add than her inane fucking questions.

I felt her hand on my shoulder. I tried to shrug it away but couldn't. Instead, she pulled me backwards and turned me.

"Lieutenant Benjamin Mason, are you under the control of an alien entity?" Her face was dead serious.

"I can assuredly tell you that I am not under control," I said.

"How do we know he's not lying?" Stranz asked.

I turned to him, but didn't say anything.

"Maybe he's doing what he's supposed to do," Sula offered.

"Are you done now?" I asked Ohirra. "I need to finish."

"And what is it you're finishing, Mason?" she asked.

I thought for a moment, then pulled free my pistols. I shot her in the faceplate eight times, then spun and shot Sula in the face eight more times.

The others were too stunned to move as I drew my harmonic blade. Stranz was bringing out his minigun. I swung with all my power and hewed down through it with the blade. Then I brought the blade back up, severing Stranz's right arm just above the elbow, bisecting his sergeant's stripes.

He screamed.

I screamed.

Sula screamed.

Ohirra kicked out with her leg, catching the side of the blade near the handle. The kick was so strong that I had to let go of the blade or break my wrist trying to hold it.

My bullets hadn't done any serious damage to their faceplates, other than to crack and pit them. Stranz, on the other hand, was down on the ground trying to keep his blood from gushing out of his arm.

I dove for the blade and grabbed it just as Ohirra lunged for me. I was on my back, the coldness of the concrete seeping through me, chilling my bones, freezing my soul. I held the blade up using two hands, ready to skewer anyone who came near.

Ohirra backed away from me.

I stood unsteadily, the blade suddenly incredibly heavy. I felt my vision dim, then constrict until all I could see were my enemies down a long, thin tunnel. I heard the blade crash to the ground. Then everything turned white—white universe, white noise, white light spearing through me until I became part of the whiteness, the essence of me forever lost. Just when I thought it would never end, a metronomic noise began to leak through the whiteness. A steady, even beat.

Boom. Boom. Boom. Boom.

It came faster and faster and faster.

Tat-Tat-Tat-Tat

Then faster still.

Rattltat-Rattltat-Rattltat

Then finally it was a full on drum roll. *Rattlrattlrattlrattlrattl.*

What was it?

Who was it?

Could it be?

Sorry if I'm late to the fight. I had a line of code I had to deal with.

Softer. Softer, please.

Mason, this is Thompson. Can you hear me? His voice boomed in my head.

Softer, I begged, my brain mush.

Mason, this is Thompson.

I can't... wait, what have I done? I attacked—oh, my God!

You were under the control of the Master. You still are.

Then how?

I've managed to partition off an area of your brain. What goes on here is for you and I only.

Ohirra, Stranz, are they—

They're hurting, but I think they'll understand.

Understand that I tried to kill them? Understand that I was a shit leader who tried to make them dead? How the hell could you understand something like that?

They do, Mason. They understand. They know you wouldn't do something like that of your own free will. It's not in your nature.

What do you know about my nature?

That you're tougher on yourself than anyone could ever be to you. That you're a born leader and that we'd all follow you into the mouth of Hell.

I let that sink in for a moment, then asked, *You say I'm still under control?*

Yes. It wants to study the nuke. It saw in your mind what it could do and wants it rendered inert.

How the hell am I going to get out of this?

I have a plan.

An image began to materialize in front of me. It was Thompson, standing smartly in his Task Force OMBRA uniform, beret canted rakishly.

That's not how you really are.

No. They've removed my arms and legs. I'm bald and wearing a skullcap connected to wires and cables.

Lovely, I said, seeing Michelle in my mind's eye.

I regretted that she wanted to die, but it was her choice, Mason. You did the right thing.

And you? Do you want to die, Thompson?

Absolutely not. This was... is... the best thing to happen to me. I've always wanted to be a hero. I've always wanted to make a difference. At first I was too small, but when I froze in Africa, I discovered I was too scared for combat.

You ended up making it work.

Only because I didn't want to disappoint you, Mason. My fear of you not liking me was greater than my fear of dying.

And now?

Now I'm where I'm supposed to be. I'm a modified Gen I, with the capacity of a Gen II. This stuff comes natural to me. And now that you've been changed by the spores, we can communicate, as I can with any of the Cray or fungees.

Wait... you can communicate with the aliens?

I can communicate with the Sirens and the Cray as well as each and every fungee. You should remember, inside the fungees they're perfectly normal.

We ran through several groups of them. We thought the master might be using them for processing power.

Almost right. They're my doing. I brought those fungees together. Think of each group as a remote server, or even a static IP address. Moving from one to the other keeps the Master from finding my location. I've been communicating with the other HMIDs, and we're starting to work together.

So what are we going to do?

You're going to deliver the nuke to the Master.

I can't possibly get past all the Cray by myself. And now my team is in no shape to help.

On the contrary, we're going to walk right up to the Master, say hi, then poke him in the eye.

We?

Yep. I'm going with you.

But how?

Think of me as a hitchhiker of the mind.

As easy as that?

Oh, you have no idea how hard I've worked for this moment.

Now what?

Now you say a few last words to your team.

The white faded, returning me once more to the Metro station platform. EXO lights formed a glow around the area, and the ground was an awful red.

Blood.

Too much blood.

Oh, hell.

Victory at all costs, victory in spite of all terror, victory however long and hard the road may be; for without victory, there is no survival.

Sir Winston Churchill

CHAPTER FORTY-NINE

STRANZ WAS DEATHLY pale as he lay on the platform, his suit discarded, his eyes shadowed. Ohirra was out of her suit, checking the tourniquet. Any concern for the spores had gone by the wayside as she needed to attend to Stranz's wounds. I smelled burned flesh and noted that smoke was drifting slightly from Stranz's stump. Sula stood a few feet away, her minigun still spinning. They must have used the heat from the gun to seal the blood vessels. God, how that must have hurt.

I stood facing them.

Part of me wanted to still shoot them, to kill them. I recognized the Master's will. But another part of me, the part controlled by Thompson, wanted to run to them.

Choose your words carefully, came Thompson's voice. *I don't know how much it can understand, and I have limited control.*

Ohirra turned towards me, fury and worry doing battle on her face.

Sula regarded me with fear.

The Master was keeping me from feeling the guilt I

knew I should have been experiencing. Knowing that it should have been there was enough to keep me grounded and realize what a terrible thing I'd done. I was the worst sort of grunt: a traitor. First I was a traitor to OMBRA, then to Dupree, then to the New United States of North America, and finally to my own grunts.

The punishment for being a traitor used to be hanging.

I vowed then and there that I would discover a way to pay for what I'd done. Whatever it took, I would pay.

"Mason, why did you do it?" Ohirra said. "Stranz loved you like a father."

"I did what I had to," I said. "You need to head to the stadium."

She regarded me for a moment. "Are you in control?" she asked.

"The game begins in ninety minutes. You don't want to miss the opening pitch," I said, hoping the alien Master wouldn't understand what I was doing... and that Ohirra would.

"Ninety minutes," she said, glancing at Stranz. "I'm not sure if we can make it."

"You have to," I said, wishing I could go over to Ohirra and give her one last hug. "It's bottom of the ninth and two outs."

"Who's at bat?"

"Thompson."

Her eyes widened slightly, then she nodded.

I wanted to go to these people. I wanted to touch them, to hug them, apologize. Instead, I walked woodenly to the nuke, disarmed it, then resealed it inside the Faraday cage container.

I watched as Ohirra got back into her suit. After a

I went to draw my pistol when Thompson stopped me.

It won't harm you.

It was on me in a flash, face poised next to mine as it tilted its head and regarded me with its multiple eyes.

Just as a video game separated the killer from the killed, I was aware that the EXO had separated me from the Cray, leveled the playing field. Standing here, merely human, even with a nuke strapped to my back, I felt insignificant next to the huge creature. Even as it brought its claws towards my face, I knew it could rip right through me. It took all my measure to keep from running.

Easy, Mason. It's just curious.

Maybe it can be curious twenty feet away.

Don't like being the bug, do you?

What the fuck does that mean?

Under the microscope, or in the hands of a child. Didn't you ever pick up a bug and look at it real close? Now you know how it feels.

If I survive this I'll never pick up a bug again.

That's the spirit.

The Cray circled me and began to fiddle with the nuke. I stepped forward, then turned. I held out my hand and waggled a finger at it. "No, no, Cray."

It tilted its head again.

"Bad doggie."

That's almost right. They have the brain capacity similar to a dog. They're task-oriented, much like an ant or a bee. Once a task is given, they perform it.

What's this one's task, to smell my butt?

Pretty much. Welcoming committee.

The Cray began to move back down the track the way it had come.

I felt the Master assert himself and felt the impulse to follow the Cray. Just a singular thought, nothing more, but it was an imperative. I tried to stop myself, pause for just a moment, but my body wouldn't allow me.

Fucking great, now I'm the video game and someone is playing me.

I'm here. It's going to work out.

You have a plan.

Of sorts.

Can you break the hold on me?

I think so.

Think?

Pretty confident, actually.

Have you tried?

Not yet.

Why not try now?

No answer.

My best bud the Cray and I came to a station. The sign read *Hollywood and Highland*, which meant above us stood the Kodak Theater. I'd never been in it, but every Oscar ceremony for the last dozen years had been hosted there. Next to the Kodak Theater was Mann's Chinese Theater, with all the hand- and footprints out front. I remember taking a girl named Suzie to see *Matrix Reloaded* at the theater. We'd joked before the film, putting our hands and feet in famous people's castings. We'd laughed at how small Shatner's feet were and come up with a game called What Would William Shatner Do?

Whatever happened to Suzie, I wondered? Then I remembered. It was a deployment to Iraq. Girls like her didn't tend to wait for grunts like me, who wanted to go to war all the time. She'd probably found a Starbucks barista or a guy who worked in the mall, trading the danger of living with me for the comfort of living with someone who wouldn't leave her to go kill something. The irony, of course, was that she'd probably died in the invasion, while I still lived. Either that or she was a fungee.

Instead of going up the stairs into the Metro, the Cray turned left and entered a gaping hole cut into the side of the wall, revealing a tunnel that ran south.

I wondered to myself now, as my feet moved of their own accord, WWWSD? Probably laugh his ass off.

Why didn't you answer my question earlier?

Because I knew you wouldn't like the answer, Thompson replied.

And what's the answer?

That we need to see what the Master looks like. We need to get near it. We need a chance to study it.

How long? How long did you and Mr. Pink know this would happen?

We suspected it shortly after the cure. We knew for sure after Salinas broke the code.

Who else knew?

Ohirra knew.

I thought back to how easily she'd seemed to take my treason. She must have known but couldn't say anything.

Why me? Why not get Ethridge to do it?

Ethridge is dead.

What about Olivares? Is he still alive?

No data. All my efforts are with you now.

What does that mean?

I've loaded my primary consciousness into a mass of fungees gathered at UCLA. I'm with you for the duration.

I hated the idea that Mr. Pink had once again used me as his pawn. *Isn't there something more important for you to be doing instead of babysitting me?*

A few seconds of silence preceded the answer.

No.

Ahead was a bright light. I knew what to expect. I'd been inside the bowels of a hive before. But this time, instead of sneaking around, I was about to be the guest of honor.

May God have mercy upon my enemies, because I won't.

General George S. Patton Jr.

CHAPTER FIFTY-ONE

A TUNNEL HAD been hewn from dirt and soil, leading south to the hive. Ten meters in we passed a group of sentry Cray. They were the wingless kind, but they looked no less menacing.

I remembered the last time I'd entered a hive, and felt a sense of déjà vu. Right now the plan was really no plan at all. I was being guided by the Master and shadowed by an HMID. I was just along for the ride.

"For a second there I actually thought you had a plan," Olivares had said, back beneath the African dirt.

"That's one of the secrets to being a hero," I'd said.

"What is?"

"Plans are for people who worry too much."

Right now I wished I knew the plan. Having nothing to do but be along for the ride was giving me too damn much time to think.

We began passing alcoves filled with the man-sized caterpillars I'd seen in the Kilimanjaro hive. They squirmed and undulated in massive piles: immature Cray, birthed by the Mother who was surely somewhere in the central hive, shoving these out.

The light was becoming painful. I wanted to squint or shade my eyes, but the Master didn't think it necessary.

Last time I'd been in a hive, I'd had thermite grenades, which hadn't just killed great numbers of the enemy, but frozen them, hypnotizing them with a light even brighter than that coming from inside their nest. Now I had no such weapons. I strode past the alcoves of immature Cray, past the Cray sentries stationed along my route, past the Cray sleeping overhead and hanging like bats, and finally into the cavernous center of the hive.

The tractor-trailer-sized Mother glowed like her own sun in the very center of the alien habitat. Around her worked other Cray, feeding her, tending her, moving newly birthed Cray to their assigned alcoves. The mother grew brighter and brighter and brighter, until it emitted an intense burst of light and subsided.

It was then I remembered what she fed on. My gaze went to the pile of human bodies and I watched as Cray retrieved them one at a time, sliding each into the Mother so she could digest them. How many of us did this creature eat a day?

Eighty-four. She eats eighty-four human bodies a day—one every seventeen minutes.

In ten days, that's eight hundred and forty bodies. I felt my anger surge. I wanted to open the nuke now and press the happy button. The very idea that a creature could come to our planet just to eat us enraged me.

The Cray I'd been following stumbled in front of me, then righted itself.

That was odd.

We turned and headed into another alcove, this one as long as a football field. The ceiling was easily thirty feet high. The space was empty except for something at the far end. We closed the distance. The Cray stumbled twice more.

And here it is, Thompson said. *You'll note that there are no Cray here. I think an EMP would destroy this.*

I began to make out the structure as we got closer. Long and tall and wide, it was a block made from a black substance like lava rock or onyx. It stood eight feet tall and was perhaps twenty feet long and half as wide.

My brain began to buzz as I approached it.

Thompson, what's going on?

No answer.

I called again, but still got no answer. Was this thing blocking the theta waves?

Suddenly the black block undulated, a ripple moving across its surface.

My brain began to itch as I felt my memories tumble. I fought to hold them, but it was like trying to hold back the ocean with my hands.

Second grade field trip to the Sea Lion Rescue.

Junior year fling with a Japanese girl in the back of her mother's SUV.

Roadside bomb in Fallujah.

Dead girl beside the road in Kabul.

My memories flipped one after the other, as if the box was looking for something.

The memory slideshow halted on the image of the black box I'd first seen in Africa. The memory languished for a time, then jumped to the same black box at Fort Irwin. The memory stayed there, as if someone were staring at it, taking in all the details. Then it flipped to Michelle, moments before I killed her.

The itching sensation intensified as every image I had of HMIDs flashed through me, as if the thing were trying to learn as much about them as possible, until everything was flickering so quickly my mind began to burn. I wanted to scream, I wanted to shout for it to stop, but the Master had me so completely under its control that I couldn't do a thing.

Then it stopped.

Cold.

The blackness swirled, lights winked on inside the block. Now I could see it wasn't a block at all, but a tank—like a giant fish tank. Lights blinked along the back wall. Wires and cables shot from somewhere into the depths of the base, running to the amorphous mass in the center. Whatever was in it was easily five feet wide and five feet tall. It pulsed slightly as if breathing. It had no eyes; it didn't seem to have a mouth. Suddenly something peeled away to scrape against the inside of the container. Then another, and another. No longer amorphous, it appeared to be some sort of octopus or squid, or at least an alien version of one.

And then it struck me. This tank was almost identical to the HMID boxes I'd seen at Fort Irwin. If the technology I was witnessing wasn't so damned advanced, I'd have thought that this was an OMBRA device.

Just how had OMBRA known to build one of these prior to the invasion?

Images began to flash in my mind again. This time they were scenes of men in black fatigues and gas masks entering a room. They fired directly at me, then all was dark for a while until I found myself in a brightly lit room surrounded by men in lab coats. One man in particular stood out. Was that a younger version of Malrimple? Then it hit me. I was reliving one of the alien's memories.

What was I seeing? I wanted to see more, but suddenly the images disappeared.

I felt something tugging at my back, then the weight of the W84 was removed.

The Cray we had been following held it in its hands, the straps cut by its claws and dangling.

Then the Cray did something that surprised me. It bent and put the W84 at the base of the tank, before ripping away the cloth from the pack I'd used to carry it. The latches were still in place on the Faraday container; at least until the Cray opened them, showing more dexterity and control than I'd ever thought it capable of.

The Cray rearmed the nuke. I watched as it reset the clock to three minutes, then straightened and turned toward me.

It grabbed me, lifted me from the ground, and ran back out the way we'd come. I felt like a doll in the hands of the monster. We entered the main chamber, where the brightness once again assaulted me. Was I to be fed to the Cray Mother? Was this to be my fate?

The Cray launched itself into the air, beating its wings faster and faster.

Was I going to have the same fate as McKenzie, dropped from a great height? Without an EXO, my death would be far more gruesome than his had been.

Up and up we flew, until we shot through the top of the hive and into the cold night air of Los Angeles.

The Cray turned north. We zoomed over the Hollywood sign. We passed above Forest Lawn

Cemetery, where many of the early movie stars had been buried, over Burbank and the studios where some of my favorite films had been made. We kept going, faster and higher, until we were thousands of feet over Bob Hope Airport. As we passed over the Hansen Dam, the sky behind us bloomed with a tremendous light.

I couldn't see behind me but knew a moment before I heard the explosion that the Master was dead. It had released its grip on me. No longer was I dangling helplessly in the Cray's arms. Now I was holding on for dear life.

I didn't know what was happening, or why the Cray had decided to save me, but I knew that to fall now meant certain death.

We flew for thirty more seconds before we reached a secluded section of Antelope Valley. The Cray brought me down and we landed on the grassy front lawn of a church. The Cray let me go and I stumbled backwards.

A figure came at me from the left.

I turned just in time to see none other than Mother, carrying a shotgun. She put it to the side of the Cray's head and pulled the trigger on both barrels. The alien's head exploded and it fell dead to the ground.

That should do the trick, said a voice in my head.

Where were you?

Carrying you to safety.

You were in the Cray?

I couldn't break the hold of the Master on you, but I found that I could control the Cray.

Suddenly a second mushroom cloud split the southern horizon. This one was farther south—Disneyland. I watched in awe as the brilliant colors of the nuke swirled in the cloud.

Mission complete, Thompson said.

Did Ohirra and the others make it?

Yes.

What about Olivares and his team?

No.

All of them?

They didn't have me to help them.

I thought about this for a moment. *You weren't there to help me. You were there for another reason. You read its mind, just as it was reading mine, didn't you? That's what you meant by needing me to hitchhike. It was the only way to get you near enough to the alien for you to get the information you needed.*

I needed the proximity. I needed you to get me in there.

Fury began to build inside me. *Did you get what you want?*

More than we ever expected.

Good, then you can do me a favor and stay the fuck out of my mind forever.

Mason—

Don't talk to me, Thompson. And stay out of my thoughts. I'm so fucking tired of being used. I don't want anything more to do with you or your kind.

Mason, do you remember when you asked if I was capable of love?

Fuck off. No, belay that. I changed my mind. I want you to tell me something. Why is it that the aliens have HMIDs too? How is it that we're using the same technology? What did OMBRA do? Sell us out?

It's nothing like that.

You grabbed one before the invasion. The Master showed me.

I saw it too. Listen, Mason. We found out that the aliens were using it to upload the reconnaissance information from the Sirens. We tracked one down and...

Reverse engineered it so you could do to human beings what was done to that alien.

I'm sure Mr. Pink will explain when you return.

You don't get it, do you? I'm not coming back. I'm out.

But you're a hero, Mason.

I'm no hero. I'm your plaything. You and Mr. Pink. You want a video game to play, you can find another sucker. I went into this mission with my own agency, running, shooting and moving my team into position. And then you and that alien took me over. There is no doubt in my mind that this was what you and Mr. Pink had planned all along.

There was a moment of silence, then:

Mason, I didn't mean to—

Of course you did. Means to an end. Am I glad we killed the Master? Yes. Am I glad we blew the hell out of the hives? Yes. Would I do it again? Maybe. I don't know. I can't really say. I'm just so tired of being used and manipulated. I'm so fucking tired of being an eternal grunt. I think I want to live for a while. Remember what it is to be human... to be normal.

You'll never be normal.

I can try.

Is that your last word?

Just go the fuck away.

> You must not lose faith in humanity. Humanity is an ocean; if a few drops of the ocean are dirty, the ocean does not become dirty.
>
> Mahatma Gandhi

CHAPTER FIFTY-TWO

MOTHER TOOK ME in as any good mother would. I've spent the last two weeks cutting wood, building fences, and teaching people how to shoot. I hear that there's been no Cray in sight over L.A. since the bombs went off. There's also rumors that GNA is working with OMBRA to use VUAA1 to kill the needlers. Without them, the vines that host the spores can't grow. It seems as if we might be holding our own against the invaders, except for the constant sea level rise and the giant creatures you can sometimes see moving off the coast.

Then of course there's the war somewhere out there in space. Our planet was to become another of many supply depots for some unknown alien race fighting another unknown alien race. Earth was destined to become a footnote in some alien ledger, as a place to get scrap metal, water, and whatever else it was we had that they wanted. I remember how infuriated Ohirra had been when she'd learned this. I'd come to accept it. We'd always thought ourselves in control of our own destiny. But just like something took control of me, something has taken control of our planet and doesn't seem to want to let go. Part of me wants to know what the war is about, who's fighting and what they're fighting for. I want to know if our sacrifice was worth it.

OMBRA has officially charged me as a traitor. Mother told me that they know I'm here, but are leaving me alone as long as I stay put. Traitor. The very idea of me being a traitor was ridiculous, unless they meant that I'm a traitor to the idea that the end justifies the means. But I can see their side as well. I was a traitor to Dewhurst who wanted me to help the fledgling government. I was a traitor to my team, attacking them. And I was a traitor to OMBRA, refusing to return.

Whatever.

I bumped into a girl I'd known the other day at a refugee camp—Suzie from WWWSD fame, of all people. She'd lost her left arm and left eye. She has PTSD really bad. She won't let anyone get close to her and shies away from even the most mundane conversation. She recognized me and it seems like I'm the only one who can get near without her screaming. I remember how alive she'd been, and I really want to help her get that way once more.

Just like I want to do for my planet.

It's funny, this whole thing started when I tried to kill myself in the same manner as the director Tony Scott. One enduring theme from all of his movies was the idea that good will conquer evil in the end. I used to think the aliens were evil, but evil has to have intent. The aliens we've gone against *had* no intent, other than to complete the tasks they'd been set. I'd known since Kilimanjaro that the Cray were nothing more than intergalactic grunts. They are an interstellar Task Force OMBRA, populated with aliens designed to best do battle with our kind. But seeing that thing in the box and how it so closely resembled an HMID made me understand that even this Master was being controlled by something else, something more powerful. Just as Michelle had been strapped and cabled to a machine, so was this creature. Did that make it evil? No, it was just doing its job.

The evil is what Mr. Pink is doing.

What Thompson has become.

If there was one thing that I'd learned at the end of the world it's that our true nature is revealed in *how* we do things. It's the doing that defines us, not the end result.

When OMBRA forced themselves on me, forced me to do things, they became the same rapists and bullies I'd fought against my entire life. I had no choice but to part ways. Still, I have no doubt that they'll eventually want me back. At this point, I don't know if I'll rejoin them. Perhaps I can find a way to be the grunt I once was without them. There's still a lot more to be done. The black hole of Texas intrigues me, as does Australia. I can't help but wonder what's really going on in those places.

As it turns out, Mother knew of my frustration all along. I remember when we'd first met and she'd said, *"Some would say that there's little chance to retain our humanity after this."*

I'd leaped in and tried to answer, but Dupree had said it best. *Humanity as a word is merely the condition of being human. Humanity as a virtue is associated with love, kindness, and social intelligence. You offering us a place to stay or sharing your tea is a sign of that virtue. So here we are at the end, and you're showing your humanity.*

I feel it's important to show my humanity for a while. Mother gave me a place and Suzie gave me a goal. I'll see her get better, or at least try. In the end, that's all we can do.

And of course ask the timeless question, *What Would William Shatner Do?* and then maybe do it.

They seem to have done it. OMBRA has once again accomplished what all the governments on the planet failed to do—*kick alien ass!* After last month's reports of two contained nuclear explosions in Los Angeles, destroying the twin hives from within, hives in Luxembourg, Naples, Shanghai, Honolulu, and Santiago have also been destroyed. We're not sure where these nukes are coming from and we're pretty sure there are more hives than nukes, but here at Conspiracy Theory Radio Headquarters, we are happy. We need to take back our planet. We need to start building again... creating, inventing, developing technologies so this will never happen to us again. Consider the invasion, or the Great Flood, or the Black Plague, or Ebola. After each disaster, we got better. Sure, we lost lives, but as they say, you have to break a few eggs to bake a cake, so it's okay, just as long as we can get back to where we were... and then some.

Conspiracy Theory Talk Radio,
Night Stalker Monologue #1693

ACKNOWLEDGEMENTS

THANKS AGAIN TO Jon Oliver for giving me the opportunity to sit in the middle of the intergalactic science fiction sandbox and toss sand gleefully into the air. Writing *Grunt Life* was cathartic and I was worried that it was too dark and full of too much real post-traumatic stress disorder stories. It did turn out dark and raw, but the outpouring of thanks from fans around the world made me feel as if I'd done something right; maybe even added something to the canon that had been lacking. So with *Grunt Traitor* I continued with my role of creating PTSD-positive characters and hope that it can help many more understand that PTSD is something we can live with and use to our benefit. Thanks also to David Moore for his brilliant editing—AGAIN! Thanks to my agent Robert Fleck for doing all of his spectacular agency things. Thanks to Brian Gross for letting me turn his brain to mush. Thanks to my own personal drill sergeant, my wife, Yvonne Navarro. And last, but certainly not least, thanks to every man or woman who ever put on a uniform (whether it be a nurse, soldier, policeman, etc) to fight for a cause greater than themselves. Each and every one of you are grunts and I'd follow you to the end of this earth and the next.

GLOSSARY

.357 Ruger Blackhawk: Large revolver.

9mm: Type of ammunition, also used to refer to a type of weapon.

AK-47: Former Soviet-era Russian-made machine gun which fires 7.62mm ammunition.

AN\PVS-7: Single-tube binocular night vision goggles.

AR-15: Former Soviet-era American-made machine gun which fires 5.56mm ammunition.

ascocarp: The fruiting body of an ascomycete phylum fungus.

belay: To stop or ignore, usually an order or command.

bounding overwatch: Also known as leapfrogging or moving overwatch, is the military tactic of alternating movement of coordinated units to allow, if necessary, suppressive fire in support of offensive forward movement or defensive disengagement.

call sign: A unique alphanumeric identifier used in communications.

Caspers: White supremacist survivalists living in Rancho Cucamonga.

New Panthers: Benign survivalist group from Corona who merely want to be left alone.

Charlie Mike: Continue Mission.

claymore mine: A directional anti-personnel mine capable of delivering 700 steel ball bearings at 1200 mps.

CO2 scrubber: A device which absorbs carbon dioxide.

Cray: Initially an overarching term for all aliens, this term really only applies to the alien creatures who reside in the hives.

Cult of Mother: A survivalist group living in Big Cieniga Spring with a leader who looks like Kathy Bates.

Devil's Thunder: Survivalist biker gang who control the I-15 corridor between Vegas and L.A.

DongHai-10: Chinese-made land-to-land cruise missile capable of delivering nuclear payloads.

DZ: Drop Zone, the location where airborne personnel and vehicles land.

ELF: Extremely Low Frequency.

EMP: Electromagnetic Pulse.

ethnobotany: The scientific study of the relationships that exist between peoples and plants.

evac: Evacuate.

exfil: Exfiltrate; get out.

EXO: Originally called the Electromagnetic Faraday Xeno-combat Suit, the EXO is an electro-mechanical exoskeleton with armor, targeting systems, and advanced weapons.

FOB: Forward Operating Base.

FUBAR: Fucked Up Beyond All Recognition.

fungee: Common term for those infected and wearing ascocarps.

Gaze technology: Advanced technology that allows a computer to track the movements of the eyes and allows selection and operations of virtual command trees in head-up displays.

GEOINT: GEOspatial INTelligence.

GNA: God's New Army. The largest survivalist group in the L.A. area, led by a charismatic former TV star.

grunt: The lowest life form in the military.

HALO: High Altitude Low Opening parachute operation.

harmonic blade: An electromagnetic Stellite-made sword mounted on the EXO which vibrates at ultrasonic frequencies, making it thousands of times more effective at slicing through armored opponents than a normal blade.

HK416: Advanced rifle system based on the AR-15, typically used by assault and special operations forces.

HMID: Human Machine Interface Device.

HUD: Head-Up Display, a transparent display that presents data without requiring users to look away from their usual viewpoints.

HUMINT: HUMan-derived INTelligence.

Hydra rocket: Adapted surface-to-air or surface-to-surface rocket fired from a pod mounted on the EXO.

Hypocrealiacs: The over-arching term for the aliens who have invaded Planet Earth.

IMINT: IMagery INTelligence.

infil: Infiltrate; get in.

JMPI: Jump Master Personnel Inspection.

Leupold Mark 4 CQ\T scope: State of the art rifle scope capable of providing night vision.

M16: Vietnam-era and most common variant of the AR-15.

M4: Modern variant of the AR-15.

M60A3: Vietnam-era main battle tank with 105mm main gun.

MAC-10: Compact submachine gun capable of firing .45 acp or 9mm.

MASH: Mobile Army Surgical Hospital.

military fatigues: Any uniform created for work or combat.

Mother: Leader of the Cult of Mother who has a striking resemblance to the actress Kathy Bates.

Mr. Pink: Recruiter for the OMBRA corporation and commander of OMBRA Special Operations Command North America. Originally a nickname given by Ben Mason because of the man's resemblance to the actor Steve Buscemi, the name has stuck and is what Mr. Wilson uses instead of his own name.

MRE: Meals, Ready-to-Eat, boxed and bagged rations used to feed troops in the field.

NAP: High-speed low altitude air travel following the contours of the Earth. Also called Nap of the Earth or NOE.

needler: Alien variant which protects and pollinates the flowers on the black alien vine.

net: A network of communication devices.

NTC: National Training Center at Fort Irwin, the location where American military forces trained brigade on brigade combat operations.

NVD or Nods: Night Vision Devices.

OMBRA: Largest world-wide defense contractor before the alien invasion.

OPFOR: OPposing FORces.

***Ophiocordycipitaceae*:** A family of parasitic fungi in the *Ascomycota*, class *Sordariomycetes*.

overwatch: Units or elements of unit supporting each other during fire and maneuver.

P226: Semi-automatic pistol which fires 9mm ammunition.

P238: Very small semi-automatic pistol which fires 9mm ammunition or .45 ACP.

prick-77: AN/PRC-77 Portable Transceiver, a man-packable, portable VHF FM combat-net radio transceiver used to provide short-range, two-way radiotelephone voice communication. Capable of communications operations up to thirty miles with booster.

PTSD: Post Traumatic Stress Disorder.

QRF: Quick Reaction Force.

recon: Reconnaissance.

RPG: A class of weapon using rocket propelled grenades.

Sirens: Alien variant which uses human brain-waves to establish alien to alien communication.

SNAFU: Situation Normal: All Fucked Up.

SOCOM: Special Operations COMmand.

spikers: Alien variant, usually in animals, with spikey ascocarps protruding from the skin.

UAV: Unmanned Aerial Vehicle.

VUAA1: Vanderbilt University Allosteric Agonist Number One, a pesticide which renders the user invisible to certain species of insects and needlers because it causes sensory overload

W54: Manufactured in the United States in 1961, these were the smallest man-packable nuclear weapons devised.

WWWSD: What Would William Shatner Do?

xenobotany: The scientific study of extraterrestrial plants.

XM214: A weapons system mounted on the EXO with a six-barreled rotating minigun fed from a backpack ammo supply through an ammo feed arm with 1500 rounds of 5.56mm ammunition.

'Weston Ochse is the new voice of action science fiction'
New York Times bestselling author Jonathan Maberry

WESTON OCHSE

GRUNT LIFE

A TASK FORCE OMBRA NOVEL

Benjamin Carter Mason died last night. Maybe he threw himself off a bridge into Los Angeles Harbor, or maybe he burned to death in a house fire in San Pedro; it doesn't really matter. Today, Mason's starting a new life. He's back in boot camp, training for the only war left that matters a damn.

For years, their spies have been coming to Earth, learning our weaknesses. Our governments knew, but they did nothing—the prospect was too awful, the costs too high—and now, the horrifying and utterly inhuman Cray are laying waste to our cities. The human race is a heartbeat away from extinction.

That is, unless Mason, and the other men and women of Task Force OMBRA, can do anything about it.

This is a time for heroes. For killers. For Grunts..